The Scribblings of J.B. Patel
By Charles Kwick

Jbpatelbooks.com

Publication, April 22, 2020

ISBN: 978-1-7347126-2-9

1

Dedicated to Moms,
the keystone of all families.
My Mom didn't dodge any bullets in
life, still she met every problem with a smile.
To rid the complications in a story, many
writers omit mothers, wherever
possible, I try to include,
Mom.

I have an amazing cadre of friends.
A special thanks to Adam, Ron, Don, and Marty.
As we traverse this thing called life,
if we are lucky, we have such
friends to lean on.

The Scribblings of J.B. Patel

And his roots as a Jack Pine Savage

By
Charles F. Kwick

The Scribblings of J.B. Patel
Contents

Samples of the 'Scribblings of J.B. Patel' along with brief introductions-explanations.

Listing of E-books by J.B. Patel

A brief introduction to the errant youth of Jack Pine Savage, J.B. Patel, AKA, Charlie Kwick.

I have been scribbling under the pseudonym, J.B. Patel ever since I was challenged to write by my friend, Don Noll, teacher at Brackett School in the Eau Claire Area School District. Under the pen name J.B. Patel, (derived from the first initials of my seven grandchildren,) I've published a dozen E books: with some trepidation I've decided it is time for me to come out of my self-imposed scribbling closet.

Regarding the Jack Pine Savage nickname, years ago at 73, the reference to my origin in northern Wisconsin as a Jack Pine Savage still arose. In this instance as I hit the golf ball over the trees cutting the dogleg to the first green at Princeton Valley Golf Course, Fred Hancock, the golf pro asked, "Where did a Jack Pine Savage learn how to hit the ball so far?" I grinned, it wasn't the first time I had been referred to as a Jack Pine Savage. Some refer to anyone raised in Northern Wisconsin as a Jack Pine Savage, since I was born twenty miles north of Antigo, raised mostly in the woods surrounded by swamps, I'd say the nickname was perhaps justified. I may add, many of those of Northern Wisconsin wear the label, 'Jack Pine Savage' with pride.

This book contains samples of my scribbling. I offer this rather lengthy introduction to give the reader insight into my childhood, hoping you will better appreciate the origin and the evolution of my stories. With an understanding of my childhood and my lack of an early education, perhaps you will forgive my trespassing on the skills of real writers.

First of all, if the reader is a troubled youth, always remember; you are the one that dictates your future. You will come in contact with teachers, friends, people who will demonstrate ideals you will want to emulate. Many times those who demonstrate those ideals will be happy to help, don't be afraid to ask. You must choose well your ideals, pursue well and stay the course. Work hard, expect hurdles, some will seem insurmountable, the pathway, your future is what's important.

  Where to start? I was born in a log cabin in Pearson, Wisconsin in 1940, but if I would choose the time of greatest impact it would have to be my eleventh birthday, October 8, 1951. All of 1951 was a very bad year, the day of my eleventh birthday became the low point. In March of 1951, my namesake, Grandpa Charles Maney, a goodly part of the glue holding the family together, passed away. Four months later, in July dad died, meanwhile mom was pregnant with her tenth child. Three months after dad died, in October on my eleventh birthday, a brother and I would face a judge after spending the night in jail. There were no constraining forces in the Antigo courtroom, later that morning there would be two less in Mom's care, with a stroke of the gavel the judge made my brother and me wards of the state until we turned twenty-one.

  In 1951 Mom's Dad died, then her husband, my brother and I were taken away, then she gave birth to her tenth child. Through all that she kept her sanity, maintained the household and a good sense of humor.

  Before Dad's death he had been sick from a blow to the head suffered while working at a sawmill. After dad died there was no social security, no welfare, no workman's compensation, there were no societal safety nets. There was just a couple bushel baskets full of Salvation Army adult coats none of us could wear and an uncomfortable meal at the neighbors where I almost choked on an apricot pit. The coats didn't fit but, in the winter if we stacked them high enough on top of us, they kept us from freezing in that uninsulated tarpaper shack we called home. It got so cold that our 'indoor accommodation,' a galvanized pail would freeze solid overnight.

With no father in the picture and ten kids in the family, we sort of raised ourselves and, at ten years old, I guess I wasn't up to the task.

As I look back on my life, I do have a small regret; perhaps I shouldn't have skipped so much school. At the time; grades two through four, when schooling was in session, I didn't find any part of it fun; besides, the swamps of northern Wisconsin were calling. Although while skipping school my education in the swamps was fairly extensive amid the peat bogs, streams, tag elders, frog ponds and even quicksand; there were no writing lessons and there wasn't a lot of reading going on.

A little later on, during the nearly six years at the Wisconsin Child Center, an institution for wayward, neglected and abused children; education was near non-existent. Few books were available in the cottages and no writing lessons. I never knew what grade I was in, I guess I 'aged out' of school at the Child Center and was sent to Sparta High School. Finally, in my sophomore year in high school I had, as part of my English class, a nine-week concentration on grammar. It was far too late; I failed grammar, the important basis of good writing, and I did so miserably.

(The following nine weeks the same English class concentrated on literature, I got the second highest score in the class. The teacher gave me a B. Her explanation; "I couldn't give you an A after giving you an F the first nine weeks." Interesting digression. Further, at the time I was incapable of putting up an argument on my own behalf.)

In way of explanation; I arrived at the Wisconsin Child Center at age 11 and spent nearly six years there. Grade school education was near nonexistent and, later on, no one at the Center checked up on our assignments from Sparta High School to assure that we established a disciplined approach to our education. No one checked to see if we were getting anything out of our time spent at the public high school. No one guided us to prepare ourselves for the future.

(With about 20 kids, aged 15 to 18 in the cottage, those in charge had all they could do to keep us fed and preventing someone from getting killed.)

So, given my Jack Pine Savage beginning, a long stint in an institution without meaningful schooling, to this day rather than writing, I facetiously refer to placing my pen to paper as; scribbling.

Regrets aside, at this attempt I'm seventy-nine years of age and, although I do try to advance my skills, I'm not going to go back to school. It isn't the idea that school is repugnant, I just don't seem to find the time; life is good, I have too many interests and too many hobbies, so, my attempts to record with pen will probably remain, scribbling. Putting pen to paper is something it seems I am compelled to do which evidently will not rise above the hobby, scribbling, level. Sometimes I do have the urge to write something of import, but, thankfully, the urge passes. (Again, I am being a bit flippant, I realize whenever one puts pen to paper; they unwittingly give insight to one's soul so to speak. Who knows, perhaps the reader will find something hidden herein they consider important.) Seriously, I try but I have too many hobbies that take up my time.

I have included a paper I wrote for the, the Monroe County Local History Room, MCLHR, 'The State has no Conscience,' the narrative is a brief description of my misspent youth and the consequential time spent at the Wisconsin Child Center. Afterward is the author bio using my pseudonym, J.B. Patel, then a brief explanation of how Don Noll got me started. What then follows is a gathering of some short story samples along with how each short story originated.

I have a wide cadre of friends, few of them know that I like to write fiction. Regarding this coming out of my scribbling closet, a good friend indicated it took guts to put my stories out, and otherwise admit the work is mine. It was through that same friend that I've come to realize that much of my writing effort has its roots in the pain, trials and tribulations of my errant youth. I've been writing for nearly twenty-five years, I thought it was about time I owned up to my effort, besides, I'm getting too old to be worried about my vanity.

Given my errant childhood and my lack of writing education and my desire to write; I have been very reticent to subject my efforts to the trained and critical eye philosophically I strongly believe the opposite. That is; in the untrained author, whether it be a child or an adult, we should look first at the content, the expression, the story… everyone has their story to tell and one should never be embarrassed by their effort to chronicle their tale.

(Reasons to write are varied, whether your story is about humor, family, illness, death, struggle, pain, or whatever; it will be helpful to lay it out in written form. Afterwards one can share, reexamine or discard. An autistic boy calmly said to his upset mother, "Mom. You have to get your anger out." Whatever the motivation to write, get it out.)

We seem surprised when we discover something entirely new about someone we've known for years. For the reader, in order to give insight into the origin of the scribbler, J.B. Patel, I'll give some early background, that is, some of the occurrences of my growing up; my Jack Pine Savage days leading up to my stay at the Wisconsin Child Center.

Born in a log cabin, I was the sixth of what would become ten children in the family. We were a very poor family, poached venison and scavenged potatoes missed by the diggers made up the bulk of our diet. In the 1940's the game warden looked the other way, sometimes they would even help. Case in point; using his flashlight and his trusty .30 .40 Krag rifle, my dad shot a deer on Pelzer hill right outside of Elcho, my dad was a very good shot. When he raised the light to look, the deer appeared to be still standing. Dad shot again. He took the deer home and was cutting it up when the game warden knocked on his door. He told my dad that he had shot a deer on Pelzer hill, if he didn't go get the deer, he

9

would fine him. Dad went and got the second deer which he thought he had missed.

To supplement our very meager diet, government surplus rice, corn meal, and rolled oats helped when surplus was available. (I'm wondering how many people would even eat rice, corn meal or rolled oats now.) While skipping school there was no hot lunch in the swamps and with a lot of skipping school I soon learned to survive off what I could find to eat in the woods, what could be stolen from gardens or picked out of the local dump.(Now, I have a finicky stomach, so I don't care to elaborate.)

Growing up in the woods, our play was diverse, we ran near naked in the rain, we tried to catch dragonflies when they hatched by the millions, we dug holes in streams to soak in and then removed bloodsuckers off from all parts of our bodies, a reward for playing in our improvised swimming hole.

By the time I was nine I was perhaps more expert with a double bit axe than most adults, now a help when it comes to my golf swing, back then a necessity if we wanted to keep warm or have fuel for the cook stove. At the time we had no electricity, an outdoor pump, an outhouse, and we dragged our wood out with Dolly, a workhorse borrowed from Grandpa.

Peat bogs over swamps tested our agility and balance, spruce trees were used as slides, birch tree groves for climbing, in streams I hunted for turtles, snakes, and frogs. During the day we would lay on our backs and imagine forms in the clouds, at night without competing light there was an unimpeded look at billions of stars in the sky; these were the elements of my playground and subjects of my exploration. Outside the family and the woods there was dearth of other kids to interact with.

I think the fact I was brought up in the woods without the benefit of a lot of social interaction, then teasing when interaction did occur; perhaps my fears created in me an introverted, day-dreaming, problem child. In my office is a print of the artist, Andrew Wyeth, named, "Faraway." Hanging next to the painting is a coonskin cap. When I saw the painting, I saw myself growing up, it was as though the artist used me as the subject. My sister Rose gave me a coonskin cap when I was about ten, recently my sister Dorothy gave me a coonskin cap to replace the one of my childhood.

Growing up my ability to make wise decisions about my safety were non-existent, to make matters worse to not accept a dare was to be labeled a chicken, something unheard of. I'll give an example of my inability to foresee potential problems, skills which would be present in most children and, accepting a dare. On both occasions I relate, I was nine or ten years old.

Many days I ran away and stayed away from home until it was dark, returning home it was so dark I couldn't see the road. All alone, I was leery of the dark, but this was an oft repeated act on my part. One would think I would have learned after the first couple of times because, other than the lights coming from the homes of a few neighbors, there were no street lamps to lead the way home. I looked up between the trees at the feint light of the open sky to point the way, if I heard a crack of a twig in the darkness my speed increased accordingly. To make matters worse, if a car came along, I would hitchhike.

On one occasion I stayed at the Post Lake, Bob-O-Link roller-skating rink until they closed the doors. Everyone else in my family had wisely left earlier. There were no street lights, I could see the sky through the treetops to show me the way down the road. This particular night when bathed in the welcome headlights of an approaching car, I hitchhiked. A young lady picked me up, she asked where I lived. I told her, "Across from "U."

She retorted, "Me? I live in Antigo." (Twenty miles away.)

I explained, "Across from highway 'U."

When we arrived at our pathway into the woods, she couldn't see any signs of the path or life. We didn't have

11

electricity and the gas lantern was shut off for the night. We had no vehicles, she saw nothing but tag elders and a swamp, she doubted my safety; she wasn't going to let me out of the car. She said she would take me home with her and bring me back in the morning. I assured her there was a pathway, there was a house, and, I knew the way. Reluctantly she let me out of the car. With no lights on in the house, I made my way up the barely visible pathway to the tarpaper shack on the knoll. Nobody greeted me at the door, everyone was asleep, if I would have gone with the driver, the family wouldn't have missed me until the next day. With ten of us in the family and no father in the picture, we had a lot of latitude and fending for yourself was necessary.

As to taking a dare. A friend, Dee Dailey, lived on a mink farm nearby. One day when I got to his place, Dee was shooting his BB gun at a skunk caught in a trap. I told Dee his gun wasn't harming the skunk. Dee said the gun had enough power to damage the skunk. To make the story shorter, I accepted a dare to prove the BB gun had no power. I put the barrel of the gun against a button on my shirt and pulled the trigger. The gun slipped off the button when I pulled the trigger, I shot myself in the belly. I plucked the BB out of my belly and gave it back so Dee could use it again on the skunk.

With no dad in the picture and all that latitude coupled with my fervent dislike for school, I elevated skipping school to an art form. On the walk down the path to meet the school bus with brothers and sisters, I would lag behind; when an opportunity presented itself, that is when nobody was looking, I hid behind a stump or bush. Then, a few minutes later I would be perched at the top of a red pine waiting for the school bus to pick up my brothers and sisters before I would head back into the swamp. In the spring, my final occasion of skipping for the rest of that school year, was because of a new math problem; I was always very good at math, but this math problem was traumatic. For peace of mind I found there was a lot going on in the swamps which needed attention and, in the swamps, there was no one with an unbreakable yardstick watching over me.

I had been out of school for some time, on my return, the teacher handed out a worksheet on long division; math problems I had never seen before. When long division was introduced, I was out in the swamp doing a study of newly hatched tadpoles. Without a clue, I turned about and got a fast lesson in how to do long division from neighbor Dee Dailey, he sat right behind me. (Dee Dailey went on to become a very good teacher.) About the time the light went on and I got the idea on how to do long division, the teacher, in stealth mode, arrived behind me with that unbreakable yardstick in hand. With what seemed like a swing akin to that of a home run swat, she belted me with that yardstick across the shoulders. She didn't say a thing, she turned and marched back to her desk. The shock was indescribable, I peed my pants on the spot. When the teacher got back to her desk and was once again totally engrossed in the letter to her aunt Gertrude, I dropped to my hands and knees and crawled out the door, I skipped school for the rest of the year. I would return briefly now and then in the fall of 1951. I had not reached the age of eleven.

After my long division lesson and crawling out the door, for the rest of that school year, I watched the school bus leave without me from the top of that red pine. Alone, and now and then with my brother, our exploring took on a whole new twist. That fall my brother and I broke into a couple of cabins, we made a mess; we were in big trouble with the law. Nearly eleven years old and raised rather isolated socially, I hadn't a clue on how drastically my life was about to change.

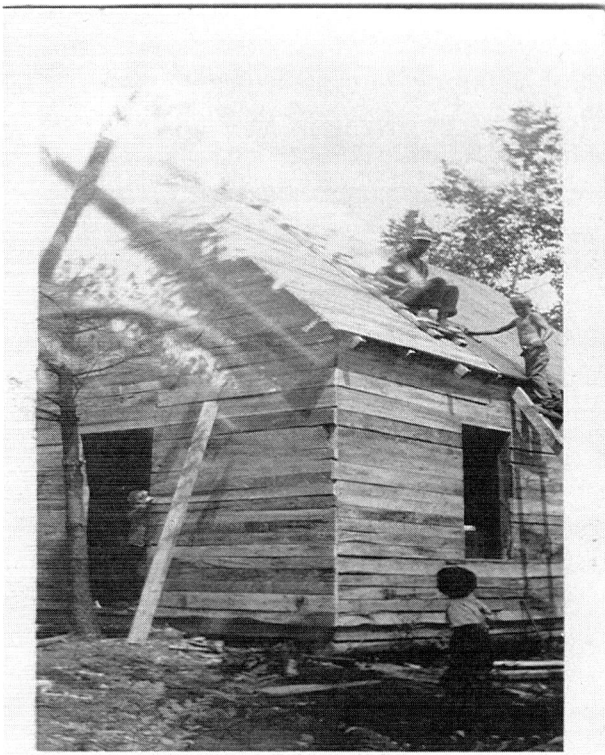

Above is the house we lived in. Consider living in forty below zero weather with a barrel stove for heat, no insulation and the house wrapped in a thin sheet of tarpaper. Within the tarpaper shack, I recall no fond memories.

I have indicated friends are surprised at the revelation I was in an institution for nearly six years. I have also indicated such revelations exists among all sorts of people when they get to better know one another. It seems we never stop learning about even our closest friends. We are social beings, I believe sharing the knowledge of our innermost self helps bond us socially. This necessary sharing is different for a child raised by an institution, for many years guilt forbade me from sharing any part of my past. (My experience tells me that a similar guilt is present in homeless children, those extremely poor, children of drug parents, the abused… such as those children separated from their parents at the border… As one of the most advanced societies in the world, we should constantly seek to remove the guilt hurdle from all children thus allowing them to become…?)

While at the Center I started teaching kids at the Sparta swimming pool; I was fourteen or fifteen, I've taught ever since. I believe that when we get into the unknown about friends, the revelations we learn of each other helps the bonding process, and as a teacher, discovering the unknown in students is very necessary to good instruction.

In the 1940's and early 50's there were no family intervention programs, no human services, no welfare, the judge had a lot of leeway and our family had nothing. My mother's treatment in the Antigo courtroom, my extended stay at the Wisconsin Child Center are the underlying basis or the fodder for some of the writing of J.B. Patel, the pseudonym of Charles Fredrick Kwick.

I thought it was important to include a copy of a paper I wrote for the Monroe County Local History Room in Sparta, Wisconsin. The Wisconsin Child Center was located there (Now closed.). The MCLHR requested written narratives about the experiences of people who were once residents of the Wisconsin Child Center. The narrative I submitted to the MCLHR describing my stay there will give the reader further insight into the origin of the scribblings of J.B. Patel.

After the description of the circumstances of my stay at the Center, I have included a variety of short stories along with a brief explanation of the origin of each. The reader will note, my scribbling started early on with Western themes. After gaining insight into the connection of the Child Center and Orphan Train through the MCLHR I then moved to recording stories of orphan train children, necessarily set in the Old West.

I have explained my regrets, I should also relate that when asked the age-old question; would you live your life over if you could? I give a resounding yes, a do-over of family, friends, favored students, even the tadpoles in the swamps and the view from the top of that red pine as the school bus drove away without me… the thought makes me smile. My regrets center on a perceived lack of ability to write with quality, my lack of an early formative education; I wistfully consider; it would be nice to be a writer instead of a scribbler.

The following narrative was submitted to the Monroe County Local History Room in Sparta, Wisconsin.

Charles F. Kwick, November, 2010

A friend indicated articles, written narratives of past residents of the Wisconsin Child Center were being collected. As a past resident of the WCC, I decided to submit my story.

To preface; I know of no format, I would suppose each of us from the Center will tell our story in a different way, from a different perspective. Now, after more than fifty years, my story will reflect in part why I was there, some events of my stay and perhaps a hint of how the experience has helped shape me as an individual. Other residents will no doubt have different ways of telling their stories with varying reasons for being there and how their stay at the WCC affected their lives.

During the summer of 2009, I visited some of the old buildings still remaining on the WCC grounds. A gentleman who was revamping the old Infirmary and changing it to a haunted house reflected that he didn't realize the Center was as large as it was. Then he asked me this question, "I've always wondered if there was a lot of abuse at the Center?"

I told him, in all the time I was at the Center from 1951 to 1957, I never saw nor heard of any abusive behavior. You see, the gentleman automatically thought the Center was a negative in the lives of those of us who stayed there and abuse would have been inevitable. I have no idea how the stay at the WCC affected others; it would only be through extensive independent studies of the outcomes of the lives of those of us that were at the Center that the psychological impact of our stay could be measured.

During a ceremony to dedicate the cemetery at the WCC, the then Governor Tommy Thompson made a speech; one of the things he said was, "We have replaced the WCC with a system of foster homes." His mentioning of the WCC was done in a manner that indicated the WCC was a bad thing. I wanted to jump up and tell him not to attempt to make political hay from the fact the WCC had closed. (The closing of the WCC occurred before his time in office.) I also wanted to tell him his attitude was insulting to those who had worked at the Center. In my estimation, the workers there did their jobs in a conscientious, professional and heartfelt way.

It is my belief the workers, the people, can only do what the State directs and funds. When the staff took on their jobs at the Center, they did so in a manner befitting one with a conscience. When the State makes a ruling to act 'in place of the parent' in my estimation, there is no conscience attached. It is people that hold the collective conscience of the State. As I tell my story, in my way, hopefully you will understand my perspective.

Everything herein is truthful insofar as I can recollect. The only 'lie' will be that of some omissions, and, I'm going to try to keep it 'light.'

The State Has No Conscience

October 7, 1951

The Post Lake, WI, constable, I believe it was Tubby Burton, stopped and asked us if we had seen anybody strange around. In an attempt to shift the blame, we told him some kids from Antigo were there the previous day. Brother Jack had the .22 rifle stolen the previous day somewhat hidden against his leg. The constable left but he soon turned his car around. When he got back to my brother Jack and me, he ordered, "Give me the gun."

18

Jack gave him the .22; then he again ordered, "Boys, get in the car."

It wasn't as though we were being invited to an ice cream social; he had us pegged and we knew it. We walked around the car under the pretense of getting in. Then, we bolted down the hill and into the woods. We ran recklessly fast down that hill. All of a sudden Jack wasn't beside me anymore, but I was too busy dodging downed logs, stumps, blackberry vines and trees. I didn't turn around to look for my brother Jack until I got to our camp. When I arrived, I looked about, my brother Jack was nowhere to be seen. It was 10 or 11 in the morning and I was all alone.

I looked around our camp; all of our loot from breaking into a couple of cabins was as we left it; the covered hammock was in place and the rest of the stuff was scattered around. Our corncob pipes with the half-smoked dried sage still lay where we left them the night before beside the black coals of yesterday's fire. I got out of there in a hurry; I figured our camp would be the first place they would look for me. Funny thing was I didn't have a clue what went on in the world four or five miles away, but somehow, I knew how to prevent getting caught. I spent the rest of the day in the deep brush dividing my time between collecting wood ticks and slapping mosquitoes. I was close enough to the road so I could hear the patrol cars go by and in a position where I could check up on camp in case my brother returned.

I waited until pitch dark to make my move to get away. Police cars had been patrolling back and forth all day long waiting for me to come out of the parcel of woods where I was hiding. Now, in the dark they had their spotlights on, searching the ditches, the trees and the brush. When the spotlights were aimed in my direction, I hid behind a tree. From where I was hiding, I could see if a police car was parked at the corner waiting for me to cross the road. Curiously the road around the other side of the woods behind me stretched a long way into the swamp. The part of the woods I was hiding in was quite small, less than ten acres

19

and they didn't even bother to get out of the car to look for me.

I waited until the second police car with his spotlight passed by my position, I didn't see any other cars, so when he rounded the corner, I bolted across the road into the woods on the other side. As I entered the brush on the opposite side of the road, I covered my face with my forearms to protect my eyes. I didn't want to get caught but I didn't want to arrive home missing an eye either. (Some think we all have a sort of sense of where we are in the dark, if a solid object looms in front of us, our 'bat' sonar kicks in. I've never collided with a big tree in the dark but running full tilt in the woods at night wouldn't be the way to test whether or not my 'bat' sonar was operational.) Anyway, I made it into the woods without hitting a tree or getting an eye poked out.

I stayed in the woods opposite the ten acres being scanned with spotlights and walked in the woods parallel to the road until I was well past the position being searched. I figured I couldn't go back to the ten acres where our camp was set up. By now the constable had probably found camp and was waiting for me to show up. All day long I had lain in hiding wondering what had happened to my brother and waiting until dark to get away. Now it was late; I was getting tired and hungry; it was pretty much time I should be getting home. Home may not have been the place to hide, but I didn't have any other place to go.

This day had been pretty much like most other days; we ran away instead of going to school, and most days stayed away from home until time for supper. Some days we would come home after dark without eating all day long, and if we didn't make it in time to eat, that was too bad as Mom wasn't about to warm something up.

When I got back onto the road, I ran as fast as I could until car lights showed up; then I headed for the woods until the car passed. I repeated this until I got home. When I opened the door, there was a very small welcoming committee waiting just inside, just my mother. Mom looked mad but mostly scared, "Where have you been?"

I thought it must have been a rhetorical question; after all, I surely didn't think she expected an honest answer. Sure enough, she didn't expect an answer at all, Mom pointed to the ladder going to the loft, "Get upstairs to bed."

Without speaking I went up the wooden ladder; in silence the eyes of brothers and sisters were upon me. I hadn't eaten since breakfast, but it wasn't the time to put in a request for a plate of scrambled eggs. That was all right; we probably didn't have any eggs in the house anyway, and the wood cook stove wasn't fired up so those eggs would have been mighty runny.

When I got into the loft, I whispered to my brother Eugene, "Where's Jack?"

Gene whispered in return, "The police have him."

I was scared, hungry, tired, dirty; in the fetal position I sulked under the covers as if they couldn't find me if I didn't see them. It didn't seem long and the constable knocked on the front door. He said, "We couldn't find him."

My mother didn't try to hide me. "He's here. He's upstairs."

The window on the story and a half house was small; jumping out of there in the dark would be dangerous not knowing what was stored on the ground below. I remember as I was climbing down the side of the log barn a year or so earlier, I had jumped the last few feet and landed on the edge of a double bit axe. That was in the daylight; besides, where would I escape to? I had already escaped to the only place in my tiny world I was familiar with, home. Now Mom, and my lack of knowledge of an escape destination put an end to my thoughts of another run as she ordered, "Charlie. Come down here."

I didn't have to bother to get dressed; I never did get undressed to go to bed in the first place. So, I tossed off the covers and made my way down the ladder. I think I was barefoot, but I can't recall for sure. The sheriff opened the door and led me to his car. Jack was waiting in the back seat. I whispered, "What happened?"

In the dimness of the dome light Jack showed me an ugly untreated gash across his knee. When we ran down the hill away from the constable, Jack drove his knee into a hidden stump; the pain was so bad he could not continue. Jack had spent the remainder of the day in the back of the police car. Mind you I wasn't starving, even after a day without eating, but I've since wondered if they fed Jack sometime during the day, I know they didn't bother to do anything to his wound. I wasn't jealous about the eating, just wondering. Usually in the north woods during our runaways we ate wild chokecherries, blackberries, bunchberries, cranberries, apples, clover blossoms, grass stems, wintergreen leaves, rhubarb, dug a potato or a carrot now and then or whatever else we could find in someone's garden, etc. For me to go without a sit-down meal all day, or most of the week for that matter, was the norm.

At the Antigo Police Station, the jailer didn't have a whale of a lot of respect for us as budding, dangerous criminals; they didn't even bother to lock the jail cell. We played tag and hide-and-go-seek in the empty jail cells. Since it was past supper time, they didn't bother to feed us. When it was time for bed, they gave us each an army blanket to keep warm. I was cold that night, but that wasn't any different from most nights at home. It was October 7, 1951; I was ten years old, still a day shy of my eleventh birthday.

On the occasion of my introduction to a jail cell there were ten of us in the family, plus Mom. Two older sisters and a brother were already out of the house. We lived in a tar paper shack in the woods north of Antigo. There was no electricity, no refrigerator, no indoor water, no indoor bathroom, no insulation, no furnace, nothing. There was just a sixteenth inch thick piece of tarpaper between us and the elements. In comparison, a teepee or an igloo would have been a far more comfortable living space.

Heat in the winter came from a stove made from a fifty-five-gallon metal barrel. During really cold times the stove would get red hot and dance around as it expanded and contracted. If one stood next to the stove you were hot on one side and cold on the other. To stay warm at night we slept beneath a stack of old Salvation Army coats donated to us right after my dad died.

Dad had been sick for a few years from a concussion he sustained while working at a sawmill. As Dad got progressively more ill, he began to lose control of his speech and movement. More and more he stayed away from the family. When Dad was home, I distanced myself from him; he scared me. Perhaps because I was so young at the time, from Dad I recall no lessons learned, no love, nothing. I suppose his absence from the picture allowed me to skip school more, run away from home more, maybe even crawl a little deeper into my own little fantasy world. Whatever; my world wasn't pretty, but I sure hadn't improved on things by breaking into those two cabins. The worst of it was, at ten years old with a complete lack of experience, I didn't really have a clue yet what was in store for me. Even in jail, life was okay; there was something familiar; my brother was with me.

It was early in the morning; the jail cell doors were still open. We were awakened, fed a breakfast and before long we were led next door to the courthouse. Mom was in the courtroom; out of necessity the rest of the kids were with her; after all, there was nobody left at home to stay with them. I figure the constable must have given the family a ride into town, we didn't have a car.

The judge asked Mom some leading questions about the family situation. In effect, purposely or otherwise, the judge scared her and she had no legal representation. You recall the picture of the scale representing the equality of justice? On this day there was a big brick on the side of the scale of the prosecution. Nothing was placed in the tray of the defense, the tray that may have provided that famous American balance of fairness.

Mom could not afford a lawyer; after dad died, we had no income. In 1951 the law didn't require we be provided a lawyer if we could not afford one. Given the judge's threats to my mother in pre-hearing questioning about not having a husband and further openly questioning her ability to control and provide for her family of ten children, Mom wasn't about to argue any ruling for fear of losing the entire family.

Jack was first on the stand. Jack was sworn in, sat in the witness chair, and cockily put his feet up on the rail and lied his socks off. Jack was about fourteen at the time. He even admitted to break-ins that happened when I was still in diapers and some property damage in a town we had never been to, had no way of getting to, and couldn't find if I we were given a map. I was a good auditory learner, that is, when I chose to listen. When it was my turn on the stand, I admitted to the same things Jack had lied about.

I think they were operating under some time constraints or maybe they wanted to set some kind of prosecutorial speed record. In diapers during the commission of some of the crimes I admitted to or not, the judge rapped his gavel and made his ruling. Jack would be sent to Waukesha School for Boys; I would be sent to the Wisconsin Child Center at Sparta, Wisconsin. Then the judge added, "as a ward of the State until he is twenty-one years old." The entire process took less than an hour. The man that had said, "The wheels of justice turn slowly," obviously never had been in the Antigo courtroom when the wheels were freshly greased.

Mom cried. I felt bad for her, but I didn't have a clue as to what was happening or why she was crying. Within minutes Jack and I went from the courtroom to the police car, without even getting a hug goodbye from Mom or a word from anyone else in the family. Late in the afternoon of October 8, 1951, about nine hours after we got out of bed in that jail cell, we arrived at the Wisconsin Child Center at Sparta. To a timid, backwoods, jack-pine savage, the Wisconsin Child

Center was a very imposing place, but I was so immature, so naïve, I did not recognize what was transpiring. I was still on familiar ground, I was with my brother.

(Perhaps twenty years later I apologized to my mother for helping to make her life a living hell when I was a kid. Mom smiled as if she had no recollection of the past. As a parent, I guess I merely smile when my children bring up things that occurred in the past. I guess I've learned that dwelling on bad memories leads nowhere.)

I've said a couple of times, as an eleven-year-old, I didn't have a clue. One indication of how clueless I was; while one of the police escorts was in the administration building at the WCC getting me registered, I was on the floor of the police car playing with the ammunition lying there. I stuffed my pockets with shotgun shells. I looked up at my brother; for reasons I couldn't understand at that time, Jack looked mighty scared. I couldn't figure out why Jack wasn't stuffing his pockets, too. I still didn't have a clue what was happening or why Jack was so afraid, but I didn't have a long wait to find out.

The officer returned to the car and we drove around the block to the infirmary where a nurse was waiting on the steps. The constable told me to get out. I stepped out of the car with my pockets stuffed with shotgun shells and the door slammed shut. It was then reality struck. I realized what the judge intended when he said I was to be a 'ward of the State until I was twenty-one-years old.' As I got out of the police car, they pulled away on their journey to the Waukesha School for Boys with my brother still inside. Not a moment was offered for a simple goodbye.

I was suddenly all alone. I stood on the steps of the infirmary watching helplessly in unimaginable and indescribable pain as the police car pulled away. Jack peeked over the back seat, his head slowly lowered as I stood, watched and bawled my head off. When that car door slammed and the police car pulled away, suddenly

25

everything and everybody familiar to me was gone. I've never again experienced anything in life since as devastating. Coming from a twenty-foot by twenty-foot tarpaper shack in the woods and a family of ten, I was now totally alone and lost in the massive Wisconsin Child Center. No brother Jack, no family, no grandparents, aunts or uncles, no friends, not one thing familiar.

I wasn't given long to consider my condition. The nurse took my hand and led me inside the infirmary to the left and down the hallway; still crying, I was shown to a room. The nurse told me to take a bath as she handed me clean clothes. Then the survivor in me kicked in; as deep as I was in trouble, I knew if I was caught with the shot-gun shells I would be deeper. Once in the room I crawled under the bed and emptied the shotgun shells onto the floor in the corner; then I took a bath and put on the clean clothes.

The plan was for me to stay at the infirmary for a few days to isolate me from the rest of the population in case I was carrying some dreaded disease. Contrary to the idea of isolation, that evening the nurse took me to a movie. When she looked at my record, she had discovered it was my birthday. I was eleven years old. Some birthday, at eleven-years-old I woke up in a jail cell, spent part of the morning in court, most of the day in a police car, then was plopped on the steps of a very imposing institution late in the afternoon.

If it wouldn't have been for that nurse telling me it was my birthday, I never would have known it. That was the way it was for the next five birthdays; most times my birthday would go by without me knowing until the day passed. What that nurse did was a simple act of kindness that I've thought about many times in my life. I was a 'ward of the State until I'm twenty-one-years-old,' but evidently that did not include helping me recognize or celebrate my birthdays. Putting my situation into perspective: here I was, a hardened criminal, who had broken into two cottages at eleven years old. I'm a big danger to society, so what do I really deserve in way of consideration? Unlike the State, the nurse supplied the conscience; she figured my birthday needed some kind of recognition or celebration.

I hung out at the infirmary for about three days; then, Jimmy Allen Daniel Befort came to escort me to my new home Cottage C. On the way across the field to the cottage, Jimmy filled me in on everything I needed to know about my upcoming life in an institution. He told me who was the toughest kid in Cottage C and who was the oldest and toughest kid in the entire place. He told me who the adults in charge of the cottage were and what I could and could not do.

I arrived at Cottage C during full military preparations for going to Boy Scout Camp Decorah at Holmen, Wisconsin. Bedrolls and backpacks were everywhere. Nearly everyone in the cottage was going, but I would stay since I had not been at the Center and had not been active in the Boy Scout program. That was the only time I would miss taking the trip to Camp Decorah.

A couple of days into my stay at Cottage C Mrs. Kunes came to me and asked me if I knew anything about a pile of shotgun shells in the infirmary room I had used. It was one of the few times at the center where I felt it necessary to lie. I lied my socks off. Self-preservation.

A question most would ask, "Why didn't you just run away?" If I were in a tunnel, I'd have to see a little light up ahead to run to. Remember, I'd just turned eleven, I was raised in a near virtual vacuum socially, the most distant spot of my travels until now had been fifteen miles away from my home to the town of Antigo where I saw the movie, 'The Yearling.' On my own I don't think I could have found my way to Antigo. I think to be confident enough to run away, you have to have some idea of where you are and where you intend running to. Where would I have run to? Home was a couple hundred miles away and I had no idea how to get there, and I admit at that stage of my life, I had doubts I would be welcomed back. You can understand why my mother under duress couldn't fight to keep me with her, but her lack of fight did give me some doubts about where I stood.

 Getting into the rhythm of life in a cottage with about twenty other boys my age was pretty simple for an eleven-year old. I had kids to play with and someone to make sure I stayed within given limits. Harley Kunes, his wife and their son Gene were in charge of Cottage C. They were great at directing traffic and making sure we had something to do. They were outdoors people, so trips to the woods, skiing, swimming, boy scouting, ice skating, were all activities they provided. We played hard all day and went to bed tired. I had no time for thought about my plight, whether justice had prevailed or whether a gang of like-minded clowns had acted in haste and my present confinement was a harsh result.

 (Earlier I gave a clue as to how I feel now about my Mother's treatment in the courtroom? My mother at least deserved better, she didn't deserve to be intimidated to the point of not being able to defend her children. She deserved a sympathetic look at her situation. My father, her husband and provider for the family had recently died. She had nothing; she needed assistance instead of a small group of men putting their heads together and deciding to scare her into submission, deciding a family, more manageable in size would solve the problem.)

 But, this was 1951 at the WCC; I had just turned eleven, and I played all day now with distinct established limits. Under these conditions I was a model child, but one of the things I didn't care for was the weekly trips to the psychologist. I would be told to report to his office. He would take me down to a room filled with toys and ask questions while I fixed this crane with about two hundred strings running through a maze of pulleys. Each time I visited the strings would be all tangled, I would untangle the strings and put the crane into working condition again. I had no idea what he got out of our visits, but the meetings were cutting into my playtime with the other kids.

One day while I was playing in the yard, we were about to go to the woods, one of my favorite play spots, a place where I felt temporarily free. I told the kid I was playing with that I couldn't go along to the woods, because I had to go see the psychologist. His response was matter of fact, "Oh! Haven't you cried yet?"

I asked what he meant and he replied, "He'll keep having you come to his office until you cry."

When I asked what I would find to cry about, he responded, "Tell him your father beat you."

I told him that would be a lie. My father wasn't the friendliest man around, but he didn't beat me. The boy shrugged indifferently; family abuse was fairly common among those at the WCC. "You'll have to find something to cry about or he'll keep seeing you."

I went to the psychologist. Within a few minutes, he asked me about home; I told him I was afraid of my father. He asked if my father hit me. I told him he did. I cried with my head down so he couldn't see how insincere the cry was. Bingo, end of session. He let me go without even having to go down to the playroom to untangle all the lines on that crane.

I wasn't totally lying. My father had had this game where he was sitting on the daybed next to the door. We would try to dart out the door before he could pull his belt out of his pants and crack us on the backside before we got out the door. I can't recall getting out the door without getting cracked with his belt, but I also can't recall the game being painful or negative. It was us boys who had begged for the game.

So much for the man with the long name and the bigger paycheck, the psychologist. He wasn't around when we needed him anyway. Like the time a new boy Floyd came to Cottage C. Floyd was a nice gentle kid. It was winter, but there was unseasonable warmth. It rained, then toward morning everything was frozen solid. There was ice all over the place. Floyd couldn't ice skate yet, but he was on skates

29

and trying to learn. He came over to the bolt swing where I and about four others were swinging. (Bolt swings were something like a fourteen-foot battering ram. Sometime after this incident bolt swings were outlawed.) Floyd held onto the braces on one side of the bolt swing because he was unsteady on his skates. He asked to get on the bolt swing with us. Whoever was standing and driving the bolt swing told him he'd have to wait. Once the bolt swing was in motion it took some time to slow it down and stop it. When Floyd asked to join us, the bolt swing was going about as high as it could go.

Floyd timed his movement when the bolt swing was going in the opposite direction, for some reason attempting to skate to the opposite brace. The end of the bolt swing struck him in the left side of the head right near his ear. Floyd got up and went into the cottage. That was the last we ever saw of him. Floyd died later in the day as a result of the blow to the head. That evening in bed, the head of our cottage announced to everyone in the dormitory that Floyd had died. That was it. No assurance that it was merely an accident; no admonishment for safe play, nothing. I was perhaps five months past my eleventh birthday; I needed a lot more. I could have benefited from some comforting words, some sage advice from the guy with the long name that somehow made everyone cry so he could make final and conclusive entries into his documents.

With too much guilt to begin with, after the explanation of the death and after the lights were out, I pulled my head under the covers. You know the hiding drill, like when nightmares visit, like when the sheriff comes… same thing; I thought maybe my guilt couldn't find me if I couldn't see out. In my hiding place beneath the covers of my bed I drew myself into that fetal position. I hid my response from everyone, had my cry during which I said a bunch of prayers begging for forgiveness and finally fell asleep. I had been a participant in the death of a friend. One would think a 'ward of the State' would be looked after pretty good, given some counseling or at least a hug in a situation like that; that is, if the State had a conscience.

This prayer business. I would guess that prayer was not a typical release during stress or need among very many children at the WCC, but as a child I had gone to a neighborhood church where my grandmother played the piano, and we learned a lot of traditional songs, and of course we learned to pray. In our home we had nothing and we soon learned that praying for things got us more of the same, along with a healthy dose of ridicule, but somehow, I did learn to pray. In this case my prayers were for forgiveness and the peace of sleep.

A day or so later two black cars came into the Center; we watched as they made their way to the WCC cemetery. Some forty years later I met Floyd's brother at the dedication of the WCC cemetery. He indicated they had no record of where his brother Floyd was buried. I told him I recalled the hearse going to the cemetery at the Center. There is a grave marked UNKNOWN at the cemetery. If the 'State had a conscience,' that grave would have been marked.

I no longer had the psychologist interfere with my play, and I gained a good friend in a new boy, an Indian my age. Benny loved to laugh. He could speak Indian better than he could English; when he spoke, he would butcher some of our slang pretty good. Instead of 'wait up,' he would say, "quay yup." At first, he had to repeat it several times in context before I got to understanding what he meant by 'quay yup.' The language idiosyncrasies didn't matter though because Benny loved to laugh so we got along great.

Before Benny and I nicked ourselves and became blood brothers, we did have a small falling out. Seems I came up short a couple of belts I had made from kits. I discovered Benny had both of them in his locker. I was stunned that one would steal from a friend. On the way back from a trip to the woods I walked up beside the head of the cottage and spoke loud enough for Benny to hear. "Mr. Kunes, what do you think of a guy that would steal from a friend?"

31

I think Mr. Kunes knew what was going on because he quietly responded, "I don't like anyone that steals."

Then, to make matters worse, I broke into a little chant, an impromptu verse sort of to the tune of the Ten Little Indians, "I once had an Indian friend who stole my belts from me...."

I went on singing with a couple of Indian words Benny taught me tossed in. Just before we got back to the cottage, Benny ran ahead, his head was down and he was mad. The moment I entered the door going down into the basement, Benny jumped me. Down the steps we fell. When we got to the bottom I somehow ended up on top and flailing. Before either of us did any damage, Mr. Kunes separated us. Mr. Kunes had come in the door right behind me. In the resolution, I got my belts back and Benny and I were the best of friends again.

On the way to movies, Benny and I would bring up the rear of the line. He would tell me about Indian dances and sing some Indian songs to me. A couple of the other Indians didn't like the fact that Benny still knew his native tongue. Some of the Indians there only knew English.

On Sundays we went downtown to church and we were given a nickel in an envelope to put into the offering. After a couple of months, I was shown how simple it was to make a little slit in the edge of the envelope and remove the nickel. There was a little shop across from the church where we spent the nickel, mine was spent on Bit-o-honey. I still like that candy, and I have a daughter that I somehow corrupted. Bit-o-honey is her favorite, also.

Going to church on Sunday led to another pastime. There were pigeons nesting all over the church, I got up on the roof of the porch and took a couple of babies out of their nest. I took them back to the WCC. Duane Kunes had built a pigeon house for us, a few of us purchased pigeons; the coop was about fifty feet from the cottage, some of us spent a lot of time with them. We bought quite a few pair of pigeons and Duane got someone to come to the center to teach us how to care for them. I asked him how to raise the two little ones I

32

took out of the nest; he told me they would die if I didn't chew up corn and feed it to them. So, I chewed the corn and they would eat it right out of my lips. They lived and were very friendly birds.

I also had a blue check racing homer which I had people take when they went on trips. They would release him and I would check to see how fast he got back to the coop. One time someone took him on a trip in the winter when the temperature dropped way below zero. It took that bird three days to return. I figure he held up in a barn somewhere until it got warmer.

We went to the downtown churches of our choice; school on the other hand was at WCC and sporadic at best. We had a little library which I recall visiting once. Our classrooms for the most part segregated boys and girls when they were held. I do not recall ever having any homework or even carrying a book home. My final year in school at the Center we went through at least three teachers. The last teacher saw in me enough ability that he passed me into the ninth grade which meant I would go to Sparta High School the following year.

I had to make a few trips to the infirmary; my visits to the dentist office were not to my liking. When I had lived up in the Pearson area, I'd never owned a toothbrush. I had quite a few cavities and it seemed the dentist loved to drill. I feared and dreaded my visits to the man. One time he told me I had a baby tooth that would need to be pulled if it didn't fall out by itself. I opted to take care of the tooth myself; before I got out of the infirmary, out of fear of the dentist, I jerked it out. Bleeding, I took the tooth back in and showed it to him. It was the first time and only time I ever saw him smile.

As you entered the infirmary, the dentist office was on the right; there was also an exam area in that same room for eyes. The eye doctor told me I may need glasses. I talked to one of the other kids, Dick Kramer. Dick told me to memorize the eye chart and he told me what lines to memorize. The top row was A-P-E, the next row was O-R-F-D-Z. Memorizing that chart took care of my need for glasses.

On another visit to the infirmary I was there for a couple of days. I had a boil removed from my hand. On yet another visit I had my tonsils removed. The room where the operation took place was inside the infirmary to the left. Once I was sick, I'm not sure of the ailment but I spent about three days in the infirmary. I recall receiving very good care. I also recall that during the operation on my tonsils, my life passed in review, quite an experience.

Once during a polio epidemic, I was playing on a rope swing with a friend. He would wind me up then turn me loose. I would spin like a helicopter while I unwound. We did this so many times that when I went back to the cottage, I proceeded to get sick. It was something like I was drunk, unable to stand, lethargic, very little physical control, couldn't hold my head up, nearly unconscious, all possible symptoms of polio. I was somehow transported to the infirmary where I was given a spinal tap to check for polio. I recall lying on my side while they stuck a needle into my spine. I woke up the next day back to normal. When asked what happened, I related the rope swing incident.

In that case, I was so sick I really thought I had polio. It was a mighty lonesome thought that I would spend my life as an invalid, but I was so sick I didn't much care. The next day when I walked across the field back to Cottage C, I really thought the Lord had spared me for something.

Many of us have the idea that the Lord has something in mind for us and our existence. I've had a few occasions to have this reinforced. Once when I was playing in the WCC cemetery with a few others, we tied an old garden hose up to branch of a big oak tree and took turns climbing the tree and swinging down on the hose. After a couple of trips up the tree and down the hose, it was my turn again. For some reason, before climbing the tree I took a hold of the hose and gave it a gentle tug from below. The hose was evidently fatigued to the point it could take no more and broke at the branch and tumbled down to the gravestone below. Maybe there is something to that business, but in my case if the Lord has something more in mind, he'd better hurry; it's getting late in the game.

(I visited the cemetery during the summer of 2009, the branch from that old oak tree overhanging those grave stones still exists.)

Cottage C was a large, well-built brick structure complete with a wide winding staircase, large dorm rooms up, spacious living space with a pool table on the main floor and in the basement were our lockers, showers and a room with benches where we assembled now and then. Each week we would have a contest to see which cottage could earn an extra movie. Everyone had a task. We cleaned everything, even polished the woodwork. Most weeks Cottage C won the extra movie.

In all the cottages there was seldom a problem with discipline. I recall only one during my time in Cottage C, where some kid had himself a tantrum and someone warned Mr. Kunes. The kid came running in an attempt to get past Mr. Kunes. Mr. Kunes put the kid on his back so fast I didn't see how it happened. Mr. Kunes had only a few fingers on one hand but those three fingers were at the kid's throat. Mr. Kunes quietly said to the lad, "Are you going to behave yourself so I can let you get up?"

The boy nodded, his eyes open wide; the problem was concluded in seconds. Whereas that guy with the long name whose goal it was to make kids cry would have filled out a dossier on the boy, would have felt the problem was solved when the boy chose to finally donate a few tears during the forty-second session.

One may think Mr. Kunes' actions were harsh, but I thought appropriate. The kid had already insulted another of the workers, no telling the damage he might have done to himself or others if allowed to continue.

The only other problem dealt with harshly in the five years I was at the WCC was at Cottage L when a kid blew up, then

35

ran away. He was brought back, placed in a locked room with a screen that wouldn't allow him to get out. He stayed overnight there until he calmed down. I believe he was transferred to Waukesha School for Boys, a more secure facility to handle the unruly ones.

As I have indicated earlier, due to the Kunes family's efforts, we were involved in many outdoor activities. A favorite activity, swimming in the municipal pool just outside the center, was something we were given if we behaved. Most all of us learned how to ice skate, too. Harley Kunes would flood an ice rink for us, and he had built a four-foot-wide shovel that we pushed about the rink to keep it snow free. On extremely cold mornings Harley would take a hose and layer on more ice.

As for activities, trips to the woods were my favorite. I could run and think of myself being free. Also, Duane Kunes took us skiing many times. We'd ride up to the hills of Cataract in the back of a dump truck covered with a canvas to keep out the wind. Duane also had us garden during one summer. I still like to garden. We played soccer, football, softball, basketball, had dances, we learned to play pool, had a boxing ring in the basement of Cottage L and spent a lot of time playing cards at night before bedtime. Canasta was a favorite.

Duane Kunes talked me into taking on a paper route. I did that for a few years before losing interest. I was able to buy a Zenith radio and a black Schwinn bike because I had too much money in my account. The rules were that we could only have so much money on hand. Duane also had me run the irrigation system for the corn planted in the fields where the Sparta Golf Course is now located.

Another job I had now and then was waiting on tables in the central dining facility. I don't know who was in charge, but she was the boss and demanded tables be set properly, silverware be handled within the drying towel by the handles, etc. I recall once when I was serving coffee, I stepped up behind Mrs. Kunes to fill her cup. As I reached for her cup, she also reached and nearly knocked the cup from my hand. I said I was sorry, but what was surprising about the incident was Mrs. Kunes apologized to me and readily admitted the mistake was hers. I got a boost in confidence when, if she had shown any disappointment at all, I would have been made to feel pretty small. Mrs. Kunes was a super lady.

During the WCC cemetery dedication I met Charlie Burch, (Not sure of the spelling.) Charlie was the activities man at the center. Charlie told me Duane Kunes had a place in Hatfield. Every summer since my son was two years old, (Scott was born in 1972) we have camped at Hatfield. So, I went to visit with Duane. Duane greeted me warmly, talked about old times, and then he asked a very insightful question. He said, "I've always wondered how in the world you kids survived?"

Duane Kunes came from a strong family background. He worked diligently in scouting and a ton of other activities designed to keep us busy. The basis for the question of our 'survival' was our lack of an anchor, we had no family. Most kids get the strength to explore and move forward knowing full well they have a supportive family foundation they can fall back on. WCC children did not have family. In times of emotional stress, like the death of a friend, we had to, in terms of current slang, 'suck it up.' Deal with it! We had to somehow cope with the stress and move on. In my case, early on, my coping was in darkness beneath the covers in that fetal position repeating memorized prayers.

I am sidetracking and rambling here. To give you a sample of coping, I think you first have to understand the guilt mechanism of residents of an institution such as the WCC. During our stay in those slack times, we did consider our condition and we idealized; we idealized family and behavior. The ideal was what we sought, and one way we sought the ideal was by observing people we came in contact with. The Kunes family provided things for us to do, but the Kunes family, the Kittlesons, and others unwittingly taught us something about living, and being a father or even a grandfather. The workers taught us by example to go a step farther, deliver our best shot to a job rather than sit back and take an easier route.

Duane Kunes worked hard at keeping us busy, but he also showed us something about how to be a parent by his response to his wife and son. That simple act of tearing an old bike apart, spray painting it, putting it back together, then building a seat for his son, was a valuable lesson on family and parenting. The time Harley Kunes had success deer hunting and shared a tub of venison barbeque with all of us when he was off duty, sharing a joking, friendly, relaxed, 'real' side of himself.

One evening when I first came to Cottage C, Marlene Kittelson walked over to our cottage and we played hide-and-go-seek. Marlene was about seventeen years old, a daughter of one of the workers in the next cottage. When it was time to hide, Marlene took my hand and another boy's hand and ran to a hiding spot. My feet touched the ground once about every six of her paces. I believe it was the first time I flew. Marlene treated us like people... people untainted even though our lot in life included a stint in the WCC.

One day Marlene's sister Joyce was walking a child confined to a stroller. I believe the child had spina bifida. Joyce always interacted with us and with some of the special populations without prejudice. We learned on those occasions that we did not have leprosy. We learned maybe we weren't as dirtied by our stay at the WCC as we thought. Because the Kunes family, the Kittlesons and many others interacted with us without showing prejudice, we learned about acceptance and tolerance. Again, the Kittelson family, like the Kunes family and many other workers demonstrated what a family should be. Sadly, as residents of the WCC we never gave those workers, or in this case the children of workers, any kind of thanks for those lessons.

So, to the point, "How did we survive?" We took the lessons usually gained in a family setting from the workers and worker's families at the WCC and used them as a model of what life as a family should be. But without family to lean on, with no freedom, all kinds of unwarranted fears and stress; on many occasions to survive we had to, in terms of today's vernacular, 'suck it up.' Deal with it. I had to suck it up when I was dropped off at the infirmary, when I thought I may have polio, when my tonsils were removed and my life passed in review, and when I was participant in Floyd's death. I had to 'suck it up' every night when I lay my head on a pillow before I went to sleep and had time to think about my condition. I had to 'suck it up' when I considered that family and real freedom to explore and grow with normalcy was beyond the fence surrounding us.

Times of extreme stress and fear were intensified because there was no family to lean on. Take one of the polio scares. One year we were quarantined at the center while news on TV showed pictures of iron lungs doing the breathing for victims of polio. I was in great fear of contracting polio, not so much fearing polio but the horrible isolation of the disease without the benefit of family to lean on.

During the polio scare one of the residents of cottage L had a seizure. I was awakened and asked to come out into the great room; Mr. Hoffman asked if I would help him get the boy over to the infirmary. I saw the fear in Mr. Hoffman. I too was so afraid of contracting polio that I refused to help. I wouldn't go near the lad and I returned to my room. Remember that one of the things about our stay in the institution was that our guilt mechanism simply gets overdeveloped. I was so guilt-ridden for not helping with the lad I could not sleep that night. Beneath the covers in that fetal position I prayed all night, there was no family member to lean on, no way to put the incident into perspective. It was one of the worst nights I had at the center. I had to 'deal with it!'

My thoughts of my family were with me nearly every night before I fell asleep when I had time to consider my situation. During my stay at the WCC at one point I thought I should go back home. One day I conveyed this idea to my social worker, Miss Eleanor Hartleb. She asked what I would do at home. I told her that I wanted to help out. Her response was simple, "Charles, your contribution to the family should be one of example. You are responsible for yourself only. You live your life in a way that your family will look up to you." I don't think I had a choice in the matter, but I ended up staying at the WCC. I was at the Center from October 8, 1951, to June of 1957.

(Later on I went to college, gained a master's degree. I am the only one of the ten of us to end up with a degree. I retain about the same goal given to me by Miss Hartleb; to live my life in a manner whereby my family can have pride.)

On trips to the Sparta community swimming pool I got to be a good swimmer and diver; on trips to Camp Decorah I gained a lot of background in lifesaving, boating and canoeing. After my sophomore year at Sparta High School, during the summer I took a job at Camp Decorah as assistant waterfront director with Fritz Hagerman, a recent graduate of La Crosse State University. The director of the camp, Fritz's father Sam Hagerman, asked me to stay with him in the fall as a foster son.

I had gone out for football during my sophomore year at Sparta High School. I loved the sport. I loved to hit people. By the end of the season I played varsity football. When I left Sparta to go to a foster home in Holmen, Emil Hoeft, Sparta's football coach wasn't too happy. Mr. Hoeft told Sam Hagerman I was a good football player. Sam Hagerman took that to heart. He and a few others went to a school board meeting at Holmen and pushed through the start of football at Holmen High School during my senior year, the 1958-59 school year.

I'll give the reader an indication of where we, WCC children, were in terms of our thinking of being a foster child

40

in 1957. First, among us we discussed being a foster child and, of course, we talked in terms of the ideal. The ideal was being a part of the family, but in my case, I had a mother, so to go to a foster home held some trepidation. My allegiance was with my family. To go to a foster home and call another person Mom, would hold considerable guilt. I would suppose to the reader this all seems so simplistic? Yes, very simplistic, but remember we were children in a closed community. At no time were any of us talked to about the philosophy of the fostering process. On our side of the thought process, if we went to a foster home, we wanted to be treated just like any other child in the family. As a child at the WCC, our ideals for a foster home set the bar so high that perfection was unattainable. The foster parent could not possibly fulfill their end because as a child we were expecting too much to be accepted unequivocally as family.

When I walked out of the child center, I took my Sparta High School freshman annual with me. The other items of value, like my bicycle, I gave away; I didn't even go to my room to check for any other items important to me. The day we checked out, I spent some time with my social worker, Eleanor Hartleb. She reassured me. She indicated I was a good person and that I would do well. Miss Hartleb indicated she had considered taking me in as a foster child. What a boost in confidence she gave me. At this point I was still a very shy person, incapable of uttering a word, even a simple thank you.

Miss Hartleb had actually indicated I was a good person. This was something that I needed to hear. When one spends a lot of time at an institution such as the WCC, one feels 'dirtied.' This affects us all of our lives. Even at this time, some fifty-two years after the fact, only very close friends know of my stay at Sparta.

I still feel the State made a mistake by taking me away from my family for those very crucial six years and then two more years as a foster son. Since I was absent during those defining years, missing shared experiences with family,

41

relatives and family friends, there now is very little we have in common. In many respects my brothers and sisters cannot understand why I had to spend so much time at the WCC: indeed, they were more disturbed by my being taken away than I, especially since my brother Jack was sent home in about six months while I was left at the WCC for nearly six years. (That has always been difficult for me to think about.)

Without immediate family, I looked at examples in others and, in this way gained experiences otherwise learned in the family setting. Because of the examples I chose, I created goals and direction for myself that in many ways surpassed my brothers and sisters. So, in a way, the Antigo judge and his underlings could argue their methods were justified. If I were asked my opinion, I would say that families in trouble should be given assistance rather than being torn apart.

Since 1957

After leaving the WCC, I was in a foster home with the Hagerman family at Camp Decorah, the boy-scout camp. I completed high school at Holmen in 1959, after which I spent three years in the US Army as a Military Policeman and self-trained as a Sentry Dog Handler. After serving my term in the Army I completed a degree in physical education at La Crosse, Wisconsin. I taught school in Eau Claire, Wisconsin for twenty-nine years. I taught at North High School for ten years and then worked as district coordinator of physical education for the remainder of my career. I am now retired and living in Eau Claire, Wisconsin. My wife, Carol and I met at Holmen High School. We have been married since 1961; Carol and I have three children and seven grandchildren.

To fellow occupants of the WCC reading this, regarding the constant feeling of being 'dirtied' and less of a person because of our stay at Sparta; we should always consider that we were but children. We were placed at the Child Center by adults thinking our best interests were foremost in their thinking. The fallacy in their thinking: the WCC, acting in place of our families, was an end-all answer to our problems. To compound the fallacy, those same well-meaning adults soon forgot about us and failed to follow up to measure the worth of their decision. The confusion will remain ours, but we should harbor no guilt; as I indicated, we were but children.

To the question: Did the stay at the WCC had any deleterious effects on me? I don't think so. As I indicated, I do not dwell on the circumstances. I do wish things could have been different, but if things had been different, I wouldn't have met my wife, I wouldn't have three phenomenal children and seven fantastic grandchildren. I've come to that time in my life when I am a sentimental, crusty old bugger and happy with my lot in life. When in church, now and then, I cry a bit, but usually tears considering the many joys of my life.

Finally, I respect the staff of the Wisconsin Child Center, but still harbor my contention: The State Has No Conscience. It was the staff that provided as best they could a conscientious and, in many cases, a great substitute for family. To date, I harbor no great anger toward the State although some of my statements concerning 'lack of the State's conscience' would suggest otherwise. Always I will feel tremendous gratitude for any and all of those workers and families connected with the WCC. For the time, effort, and concern of all past workers and families at the WCC, now, over fifty years late, I very warmly thank you for providing the conscience.

Charles F. Kwick

Footnote to 'The State has no Conscience,' 2018.

People have indicated that there are a few 'holes' in the above submission. The most often asked question is in regard to my biological mother, I did reconnect with her, I was able to give her assistance in way of a couple mobile homes, land, sewer, water, foundation, most important, many laughs. Of importance to me, I apologized for my misspent youth, she merely smiled; it was 'water over the dam.' I think her response is typical of most parents, she tried her best under horrific circumstances, reliving the bad occurrences made no sense.

I also reconnected with the rest of the family, I still enjoy talking to biological family along with a favored foster brother. I enjoyed many years of hunting, fishing, and visiting with brothers and sisters. A nephew does some of the book covers for my E-books,. (A friend, John D. Beck, did the artwork on a few of my first E-books.)

After retirement I spent many years working with Amish friends doing woodworking, I also did a lot of traveling, golfing and camping. I've now moved to Eau Claire; for hobbies, I golf, I make jams and jellies, scribble, and I cross-breed hostas. (At this time, six of my hosta creations have been selected for tissue culturing with the potential for international sales.)

Regarding this scribbling thing; I like to put pen to paper, I think everyone should take time to do so, if you have a little more grammar background, you can call it writing. Write about yourself, your family, your hobbies, things you love, and things that cause you problems. Putting pen to paper can be cathartic, a great release and maybe a gift to your future generations.

To my educator friends; teach grammar, but, never during a student's writing when it is about them, their family, their problems or joys. Grammar should never be a cudgel that prevents the student from expressing themselves, learning grammar should never turn a student off from the writing process. By writing or whatever method, the more the teacher understands about the student, the better teacher we become. That's enough of injecting my teacher thoughts.

(I'm including the author bio at this time as a part of my introduction as a scribbler.)

As I will indicate in the following author bio, while at the Child Center I put myself to sleep at night daydreaming, trying to escape from thinking about my condition. In my day-dreaming, I placed myself far away from the Center, mostly out West. In 1990, when I started putting stories to paper, I guess I reverted back to what helped me to find peace and put me to sleep at night when I was in the institution at Sparta.

The first E-book I assembled and marketed was, "Five Star Ranch" a collection of a dozen short stories that I had written some time earlier. Then came E-books, "The Hangman" and "Lonesome Valley," both collections of short frontier stories. The title short stories of the second and third books of short stories follow the author bio. Most of my early writing was focused on western frontier until later on when I learned about the orphan train and the Wisconsin Child Center being located at Sparta to allow for Wisconsin to place children on the orphan train.

Wishing Western; a brief biography of J.B. Patel

Here I am a Jack Pine Savage, born in a little town in northern Wisconsin, yet with the exception of "Two World's Ridge" and a few other short stories, most of the stories I write are Western romance. It seems from the time I was born I wished Western. Early on I wished for a pair of six guns strapped to my hips, cowboy boots, cowboy hat, and of course horses. I'm in my seventies now, at this time of my life I've moved to town and left the horses behind but I still have the boots and the hat. A city dweller now, I'm still writing stories; stories born mostly out of a misspent youth and a dysfunctional beginning.

The compliments on my writing have centered on my sincerity, passion, and maybe even a little anger, never on my grammar. When it comes to grammar, if you are critical, you will have a good time reading my stories.

Where do the stories come from? I was born in a log cabin in Northern Wisconsin, there were ten in the family. Dad died on the operating table just before his tenth child was born. I was ten when Dad died, I got into real estate and exploring, the trouble was; I explored other people's real estate. A brother and I broke into a couple cabins and made a mess. On my eleventh birthday I woke up in a jail cell, shortly afterward I stood before a judge. In 1951 the judge didn't have to wait for any input from a defense lawyer, there was none. By four o'clock in the afternoon, eighteen hours after I was caught, I was dropped off at the Wisconsin Child Center at Sparta Wisconsin, 'a ward of the State until I turned twenty-one.'

Because of its proximity to the railroad, the Wisconsin Child Center was built as a dropping off spot for orphans in the late 1800's. From about 1880 to 1933, every Tuesday excess orphans at the Center were placed on the train and shipped

46

out West to be adopted or indentured. Thankfully my time at Sparta missed the Orphan Train era. The Center was enlarged and became the temporary home to children of troubled families. I was a poster child for troubled.

At the Center, the nights were the hardest. For the nearly six years at Sparta I put myself to sleep with my head on the windowsill daydreaming. My experiences at the Center, my daydreaming and imagination are the subjects for many of my stories. Some of my stories include orphans, runaways, the abandoned or the disenfranchised.

After my stay at the child center, I won the lottery. I was able to spend two years at a foster home with a super family and I met a great gal who I married, she even had horses.

Here in the autumn, or is it the winter of my life; ideas for stories still pop into my head, I still enjoy scribbling them down. I characterize most of my writing as Western romantic fiction. I've been trying for some time to figure out why my stories have to finish with happy endings. As I think back, during the daydreaming while I was cooped up at the Wisconsin Child Center, I had to have happy endings. One of the supervisors at the Wisconsin Child Center once asked me some years later, "I've often wondered; how did you survive?" I'm guessing those happy endings to my daydreaming helped.

The pseudonym, J. B. Patel, is made up from the random scrambling of the first initials of my seven grandchildren. (After I arrived at the J.B. Patel pseudonym, I found out that the name, Patel is a very prominent name in India. I bet people wonder, what is a guy from India doing writing American westerns? jbpatelbooks.com)

How did I get started writing? The first book that I
wrote has yet to be published. When it does get to press, the
book will be dedicated to Don Noll. What follows is an
explanation, of sorts, of how I started writing, which I refer
to as scribbling. I was working as a physical education
coordinator; my job was to teach classroom teachers how to
teach their students physical education. In the case of Don
Noll, and many more dedicated teachers, my task was fairly
simple. Don Noll, fifth and sixth grade teacher, went above
and beyond what was expected of him in every subject he
taught; at his funeral, I indicated that Don was the
penultimate educator.

On one of my many visits to Don while he was dying of
leukemia, we were discussing recreational reading. I had
been interested in anything Western ever since I was a kid.
We spoke of Western writers; in a casual offhanded attempt
to make small talk, I mentioned that some Western books
were fairly simple in plot. I told him I thought I could write a
Western. Don looked at me over the top of his glasses,
nodded, and then said, "I think you can too. Why don't you?"

For about twenty years I worked with teachers as a
specialist. In my years of communicating with staff it was
necessary that I write curriculum, instructions and memos.
My memos were written without confidence; in short, when
starting this book, I didn't like to write. Don had an uncanny
ability to challenge, whether it be fellow staff or students. In
this case I made an offhand statement. I had no intention of
writing a book, but Don's look, then his challenge, and
suddenly I felt I had no choice.

I began to outline the book a few days before Don died.
(May 4, 1990) I laughed and told Don that if I finished, I
would dedicate the story to him. He smiled, again he peered
over his glasses and said, "You'll finish the book." Suddenly,
when I had hardly begun; how could I do anything but finish
the book. I have set the work aside many times in the past; I

have completed Don's challenge, now I have to get it to press.

Don Noll was a teacher's teacher. When he taught, others tried hard to emulate him, to get their students to achieve at the level of Don's students. In the forthcoming book, 'Son of Two Bears,' I've tried to portray "Mikasa," as an unbending teacher, a teacher who will allow nothing to get in the way of his student's education. Don Noll and the fictional character, Mikasa, both had the philosophy that for optimal learning to take place, good physical fitness was necessary. Don was convinced the reason his students scored so high in math, science, reading, and writing was because of his concentration on their physical fitness.

Don Noll dedicated himself to his students. Don was written into the character, "Mikasa," a great teacher every student deserves to be exposed to in his or her life.

To Don. If from beyond the Pearly Gates you happen to read the "Son of Two Bears", or this introductory book, please forgive the grammar, I figure it isn't up to your standards. This book and, "Son of Two Bears," have been a labor of love, but as a grammarian and author, I still have work to do.

The next four stories are "Westerns." In the evolution of my scribbling, they represent some of the first of my attempts at putting stories to paper.

Introduction to, 'The Hangman.'

I included my second E-book's title short story, "The Hangman." The story will give an indication of one of my early attempts at story telling which I think was more typical of 'westerns' in terms of violence. Also, the story got its start in a casual conversation with a North High teacher-friend that loves to read westerns. We were talking about a good first sentence. Since we were sipping a beer at the time, we therefore laughingly decided upon, "Give me a beer," as a first sentence. Although the hero really isn't a drinker, the sentence was worked into the story to set the stage. The story is about a man that decides to stop pursuing outlaws and settle down well away from people. He soon discovers he has to clean up another bunch of cattle rustlers in order to achieve a better and somewhat different kind of peace and quiet than he originally began searching for.

"The Hangman"

"Give me a beer."

The bartender poured the beer and blew off a little of the froth and topped off the glass, "On the house Grant. Been a long time since you've been in our little town."

Grant took a sip of his beer, smiled and quietly replied, "Trying to keep a low profile. Figured fewer people know me in these parts."

The bartender chuckled, "Low profile? Difficult thing for a man in your line of work isn't it?"

Grant nodded, "Be easier now, decided on retiring."

The bartender laughed, "Grant. This is the first time I ever see you drink a beer, you celebrating your retirement?"

Grant smiled then sipped his beer, "Yup. I did have a beer a couple years ago in Helena. Year or two from now if it's a hot day, I may come in and buy another."

The bartender wiped off some glasses he had been washing, "You looking for something to do?"

"Maybe. Mostly I'm looking to buy a place. Some place out of town where I can raise a few cattle. Away from people. Anything like that available?"

"Could be the S bar J."

"The Sweet Jenny?"

"Heard of it?"

"Just the story. Named after his wife Jenny?"

"That's it. The old man, Ralph Armstrong got himself killed a couple of years ago just outside the front door in a stupid bar fight he could have avoided. He spent a little too much time in here drinking beer."

"Some of those bar fights are hard to avoid."

"Walking away from this one would have been easy. Armstrong's problem was, he liked a good fight. The guy Armstrong whipped didn't like taking a whipping, he pulled a knife. We had to hang the guy, but Armstrong is still dead. Anyway, the Sweet Jenny is losing cattle like pouring sand out of a boot. Every two-bit rustler in the area is walking off with her cattle. Worse than that, seems like the rustlers are organized, the Sweet Jenny takes the most of the losses. I figured when I saw you that was what you were here for. Jenny, she's lost all of her hands, no money to pay them, no marketable cattle left to make any money, she gets no help out of the kids, the oldest one is only fifteen. If she was smart, she may want to sell. You could give her an offer."

Grant shrugged, "Where is her place?"

"Ten miles due east."

Grant nodded, "That'd be far enough away from people. How do I get there?"

"Due East. There's a well beaten trail that goes right to the place. Like I said, the old man used to make a lot of trips in here."

"Didn't bring Sweet Jenny in here with him?"

"Nope."

"How many kids did you say she had?"
"Eight kids. Fifteen, fourteen, twelve, ten, eight, six, four, two. Every two years just like clockwork. She had the last one a week after her husband was killed. Shortly after that the rustling started."

Grant shook his head, "A mother of eight with no husband and rustlers are stealing from her?"

The bartender merely nodded.

Just then three cowboys entered the saloon, the bartender gave a warning; "These three could cause grief. I figure they don't have a job, local boys, they like to scrap in their spare time and they have a lot of spare time. Want me to haul out the war club?"

Grant Baker turned enough to glance at the loud threesome, "Naw. Just kids."

One of the three spoke loudly, "Rooster. We got us a paying customer. Let's see if he'll buy us a beer."

Rooster moved to one side of Grant, the other two moved to the other side, "Mister. How would you like to be neighborly and buy us a beer?"

Grant smiled and shook his head, "Naw. I'm not your neighbor. Get you boys a glass of milk, you are a little too young to be in here, aren't you?"

Rooster shook his head, "Man. Do you know who I am?"

Grant shrugged his shoulders, smiled, then shook his head, "This little guy here called you Rooster. Is that you?"

"Bet your boots. That little guy next to you is called Banty; he loves to whittle down bigger boys like yourself. Ever heard of us?"

"Sorry. No. Who is the other one?"

"Johnny."

Grant lifted his beer, "Nice to meet you, Rooster, Banty, and Johnny. I'm Grant."

"You never heard of us?"

"Sorry. I don't get around much."

Banty didn't like the remark about the milk, "You suggesting that we are still in need of milk?"

Grant smiled, "Well yes, I didn't mean to be insulting, drinking out of a glass not suckling. Grant laughed then apologetically added, "I'm sorry boys. Since you were begging for a beer, I couldn't resist."

Banty was a head shorter than Grant; he gave Grant a push on his arm, "We weren't begging. How'd you like it if I broke your nose?"

Grant looked down at Banty, he continued to grin, "Boys. I really don't want to play and I'm not going to pay for your beer. I don't even know you. One more thing. Until we do get to know each other a little better, don't touch me again."

Banty's ire raised quickly, "Let's you and I step into the middle of the floor so I can thump some knobs on your head."

Grant chuckled, "You going to do this thumping by your lonesome or are your friends going to lend a hand?"

"I don't need any help with the likes of you."

Grant nodded, "Well Banty, if you insist. Let me finish my beer."

Grant slipped on a pair of gloves, finished his beer and motioned for Banty to step onto the floor, the bartender calmly spoke, "Banty. Can I talk you out of this before you get your nose broke?"

Banty was hot under the collar and couldn't wait; he took two steps away from the bar, turned about and swung a roundhouse right hand that came down from above. Grant moved to the right and lifted his left hand from his hip, his fist connected with Banty's mouth and nose. Banty walked backward until he fell over a chair onto the floor. He sat there in a daze; his lap was quickly sprinkled with blood.

Rooster was mad because his partner took such a walloping; he grabbed Grant's shoulder to turn him around. Grant backhanded Rooster across the face, and then sent a quick right fist to Rooster's nose. Grant looked to Johnny who was still standing calmly with his elbow on the bar.

Grant took a half dollar out of his pocket and tossed it to the bartender, "Give Johnny a beer for having good sense. Thanks for the tip Al. I think I'll be around for a while. Seems like a friendly place, I'll drop in to see you now and then."

"Welcome. Come on in any time Grant."

After Grant left, Al poured Johnny a beer while Rooster and Banty made their way to the bar, "Boys. I tried to warn you."

Banty wiped the blood from his nose and mouth, "Christ. I didn't even know what hit me. Did he hit me with a shovel?"

Rooster was looking into the mirror behind the bar, "Look at my damn nose."

Bartender nodded, "It's broken. Want me to straighten it out or do you want to go around the rest of your life with a crooked beak?"

Rooster leaned over the bar and closed his eyes, the bartender pinched Rooster's nose and pulled it back into place, "I tried to warn you boys."

Johnny asked, "Who the hell was he?"

"You ever heard of Grant Baker?"

"No."

"You ever heard of the man they call, The Hangman?"

"God all mighty. He's the one that helped hang Jake Plummer and the Plummer gang, just lately he worked up at Helena cleaning out rustlers?"

Al filled in the gaps in the background of Grant, "From that Plummer gang hanging, that's how he got his name. After that he spent a few years at Butte during the gold rush days, he was a deputy there. Largest gold camp in the world, he had to hang a few more men there. Most figure he was in on close to thirty hangings by the time he was eighteen years old. There are more stories connected with him than anyone I know. He helped chase Chief Joseph until the chief called it quits. Before that he was with Baker at Billings and fought the Sioux. Heard he even spent the winter with Nelson Story in '66' when Story brought up the first herd of cattle from Texas. Last few years he's been up to the capitol working with the Stock Growers Association cutting into the rustling problem."

The bartender poured two more drinks for Banty and Rooster, "Grant left enough here to pay for you two boys. I'm glad Grant is here; a few of those rustlers made their way onto our range, now we are having the same problem. Grant is a good man. I sent him out to the S bar J to help her out."

Rooster continued to wipe the blood still dripping from his nose, "If he can cut down the number of rustlers around here, he'll make a believer out of me."

Johnny finished his beer, "Come on you two. Let's get back to the ranch and do something we can handle without getting hurt bad."

Grant Baker took a wide circle around the S bar J, ranch to get the lay of the property and make a count of the cattle. It was getting late in the afternoon, he was moving toward the ranch buildings, he was only a mile or so away. He came over a rise in the land, below him two men had started a fire and were about to put a running brand on three head of cattle. Grant slipped the thong on his pistol and rode nearly up to the fire before the two men noticed he was there.

Grant slipped his pistol out and aimed their direction; he continued moving forward, "Boys. Looks to me like you are about to commit a crime. The crime is cattle rustling and I do believe that is a hanging offense."

One started to reach for his sidearm but decided against doing so after looking down the barrel of Grant's .45. "None of your damn business. We are branding loose cattle."

Grant slipped out of the saddle; his pistol was still pointing their direction, "The cattle belong to the S bar J. What brand were you about to put on?"

The one holding the iron put it in the fire, it was just a rod with a small bend in the end, the rustler could use it to put any brand on he wanted. Grant delivered the next order, "Take your partner's gun out real slow and toss it to me. Then tie him up. Hog tie him good and tight."

With a considerable amount of cussing the man did as he was told, afterward Grant took the rustler's gun and hog tied him alongside his friend. Grant went to the fire, took a wire from his saddle bags and toyed with it while he spoke to the twosome, "Boys. What are your names?"

After a while one spoke, "I'm Pete. My partner is Jimmy."

"When we get out of this, we'll get your hide and nail it to a tree."

Grant continued to work with the wire, "What brand were you boys going to run?"

"None of your damn business."

Grant smiled, he continued in a soft-spoken relaxed tone, "Tell you what, Pete, Jimmy. When I get done with you two boys. I want you to help me spread the word. I'm sort of an ornery cuss and I don't want any more rustling in the area. Go someplace else to do your rustling, or better yet. Go someplace else and get a job. Make your mother's proud of you boys."

"We aren't spreading any damn word anyplace."

"Like it or not. You'll be helping to spread the word."

Pete was belligerent, "Like hell I will."

Satisfied that the wire was bent to his liking, Grant put it in the fire, and then he went to stand beside one of the men, "Jimmy. You be sure to tell everyone, this range is owned, there will be no more rustling. You do that and I'll be a little kinder to you the next time we meet."

Hogtied, Jimmy couldn't move without choking himself, "Next time we meet you'll be a dead man."

Grant chuckled, went to the fire, took a pair of pliers and picked up the red-hot wire from the fire. Grant moved to Jimmy, put his foot on the side of Jimmy's head, he dug his heel into his jaw to hold his head steady, then he pressed the red-hot brand into Jimmy's forehead to the tune of a lot of screaming.

Grant walked back to the fire and put the wire brand back into the hot coals; he moved to Jimmy and cut the rope from his neck, then took the rifles and side guns from both men and packed them into his outfit. Jimmy was still screaming and cussing and crying at the same time.

The wire was retrieved for Pete, Grant could see the hate in his eyes, Grant stepped on Pete's head the same way, he waited for him to attempt to struggle, the attempt choked Pete, he quieted and Grant pressed the wire into his forehead. Grant cut the rope around Pete's neck so he wouldn't choke himself to death then waited for him to settle down.

Grant took one of their canteens and poured water on his little wire brand, then got into the saddle and spoke quietly to both men, "Pete. Jimmy. You made your brag, I'll make mine now. Leave the country, if I see you again on this range, I'll give you the same treatment as I did with the Plummer gang. The same treatment a few men up at Butte got, then a few more at Helena and in between wherever there was a need. I figure I treated you boys pretty easy considering I should have hung you. Take my advice and get out of the country and pass the word. Your treatment was harsh but it will get worse if we meet like this again."

This time Grant was met by silence, "Pete. I'm going to turn your feet loose, hold still."

As Pete looked up at Grant, Grant drew and shot the rope between Pete's ankles, then rode off toward the ranch without looking back.

Early evening Grant rode up to the steps of the S bar J, a tall blond woman came out to meet him; "You would be Jenny?"

"Yes."

"My name is Grant Baker. I spoke with Al in town, he sent me out here to talk to you. I'd like to make you an offer on your ranch."

Jenny didn't smile, "I'm not interested in selling."

"I'd promise you a good offer?"

Grant knew the ranch would fail, the cattle numbers were down below that necessary to produce an income, and the rustlers were continuing to take what was left. Jenny also knew the only way the ranch could continue to exist was for her to sell or take on a partner. If she took on a partner, she would have to get more money than the ranch was currently worth, "Come on in. We can talk. We've eaten. How about you?"

"Had a meal in town this morning, had a little hardtack a few hours ago."

Jenny turned and spoke to one of her daughters, "Susan. Make Mr. Baker a sandwich of some of that beef we had for supper. Mr. Baker. Do you have an idea what the ranch is worth?"

"Yes Jenny, a very good idea. I made a little check of the cattle count. I heard there has been a lot of rustling. Matter of fact I had to persuade a couple of men on the way here that rustling would no longer be tolerated on this range."

Jenny pointed off the direction he had come, "I heard a shot."

Grant nodded to indicate the shot was fired by him, "I don't know if you have a mortgage. With the cattle on the range, the ranch is worth about three thousand."

Jenny hung her head; it would take nearly four thousand to pay her mortgage off. If she got half of the four thousand in a partnership, she wouldn't be able to hold up her end of the bargain, "You are generous. The cattle remaining won't be marketable for at least one year. Truthfully, my mortgage is four, I want to stay but I don't see how it will be possible. To be honest, if you purchased the ranch for what it is worth, I couldn't pay off the loan."

Susan placed a sandwich in front of Grant then asked, "Can I get you something to drink? I can make coffee."

Grant had very little contact with children for many years, it interested him to see all the eyes on him and how competent Susan seemed at such a young age, "How old are you Susan?"

"I'll be thirteen in a week."

"I would love a cup of coffee Susan. Thank you."

Grant looked at Jenny; the poor girl was literally whipped, beaten, there was no hope for her. Grant took a bite out of the sandwich, then looked to Susan the sandwich maker, she was looking his way, he raised his thumb in approval, when he quit chewing, he nodded, "Very good Susan."

Since he was fourteen years old, he had made his way around Montana as a vigilante, then a lawman, a bounty hunter, a scout, then back to bounty hunter. He wanted a ranch all to himself where he could work with cattle without any other responsibility, without having to even think about people. Suddenly parked with his feet under a table and looking back at all the wide eyes in the room looking his way, it all reminded him what he had missed for the past twenty years.

He ate the sandwich slowly, as he sat there, he considered it a privilege to be sitting in the midst of this family. Grant Baker, The Hangman, smiled and shook his head at what he was considering. He had been meting out justice all his life, how just would it be to throw this family off their ranch? What would a family of nine do out here with nothing, the ranch was their home?

Grant shook his head, silently cussing himself and feeling good all at the same time. He looked down at the two-year-old who was brave enough to approach him, he smiled, "Jenny. Here's my offer. I'll pay off the mortgage, for?"

"Four thousand dollars."

"I pay the mortgage for four thousand. If I put livestock on the ranch, we'll keep track of the numbers. We will be full partners. If you decide to dissolve the partnership, you pay off whatever I invest and the ranch is all yours again."

Jenny smiled, "The ranch is mortgaged to the hilt. Above the paid mortgage, I get to profit from the cattle you place on the ranch, yet I can dump you as a partner by paying you off at the price of your initial investment with the profits from your cattle?"

Grant nodded, "Mr. Baker. You are not a very good businessman. For me and my family, this is more than we could possibly expect."

"Sounds like a good deal to you Jenny?"

"Very good. Too good to be true."

"I am a man of my word. But there is something I must tell you."

Susan delivered the cup of coffee, Grant cradled the hot cup in his hands, he smiled, it was a habit his mother had; the memory was more than twenty years old. For the moment he recalled a statement his father made, 'Son. The world of our family rotates around your mother.'

Grant figured that besides being a pretty smart person, Jenny proved to have a sense of humor, "Now is when you tell me there is a price on your head for being a long-lost member of the Plummer gang?"

"No Ma'am.

"What I have to tell you is this. When I was fourteen, I helped out with the hanging of Jake Plummer, then the rest of his gang. I've been lawman and bounty hunter for more than twenty years."

Grant hesitated, "I've presided over so many hangings, people refer to me as; The Hangman."

Jenny cringed recalling some of the stories, and then she shrugged, shook her head and finally responded with disdain, "And I don't even spank my children."

Grant laughed, Jenny stood, "Mr. Baker. I don't have any choice. I agree to your deal. I know I won't find another offer like it. From here on out. We will be partners."

Jenny reached over to shake his hand, "You can sleep in the bunkhouse. Breakfast is at daybreak. The two boys will bunk with you out there if it is all right with you?"

"Fine. The names of the two boys?"

"Frank and Billy."

"Have your boys learned to shoot a gun?"

"They have hunted. They are good shots with a rifle. We only have one."

"Now you have three rifles and a couple of handguns. I'll teach your boys how to defend the ranch. While I'm here, any other use of guns I'll take care of myself."

"What do you mean?"

"They can defend the ranch only, no hunting or defending away from the buildings."

"No hunting?"

"Nothing away from the ranch. Not until it is safe."

Jenny thought the request strange coming from a man reputed to be without conscience when it came to meting out justice. It would be a good rule; she didn't want her boys ever to have to shoot at someone, "Sounds like a good rule."

"You and the girls? Can you handle a rifle?"

"I can. We've never taken time to teach the girls."

"In due time, I'll teach them enough to get by. Can you shoot a hand gun?"

"Yes."

"I'll get two loaded handguns; you put them where you can get to them in a hurry. Someplace where the little ones can't get at them."

"You expecting trouble?"

"Yes Ma'am. The rustlers been having their way around these parts. Some of them are smart; they will pack up and get out. Some will no doubt try to keep things going in their favor. They have the feeling your cattle are there for their gain. I mean to put a stop to that."

"All by yourself?"

Grant nodded, "That's the way of it. The boys will defend the ranch only and I hope the need will not arise. Early in the morning I'll make a swing around the ranch and head to town to send a wire and pay off your mortgage. If you hear any shooting away from the ranch, stay put. The boys will be told what to do. I want to try to be back by noon tomorrow."

With that Grant got his hat, "Frank. Billy. Come along I have some things I want to talk to you about before it's too dark."

Grant stowed his gear in the bunkhouse, the two boys entered the bunkhouse very quietly; "Your mother has taught you boys how to be polite. Always remember, what she teaches you will have far more importance in your life than what you'll learn from me about defending your home."

Grant let the statement sink in before he continued, "If you hear shooting out on the prairie in the morning? Your job is to take both of these rifles and head to the house. If you see a rider coming, go to the house with the rifles."

For the next ten minutes Grant told the boys how to respond if someone came into the ranch yard, then he asked questions to make sure they understood, "Billy. You first, you hear shooting; what do you do?"

"Get the rifle and set up to watch the yard in the front of the house. Make sure all the kids are laying down on the floor. Mom will have them in the bedroom with the two pistols. I'll have Susan check the other side of the house and let me know if anybody comes from that direction."

"Frank. What is your job?"

"Cover the back of the house and go to Susan's position if she yells."

"I don't think you'll have any visitors yet tomorrow, but, just in case, you'll know what to do. Here is the hard part. If someone comes to do you or your family harm. Shoot them. Don't let them in your house. You protect your house and your mother. Remember this; the center of your world is your mother. She is the one that all eight of you children cannot do without. Stay in the house and protect her."

The two boys absorbed the information with eyes wide open, there were no tears or questions, Grant grinned, his small show of appreciation, "I should be back here by noon.

"Billy. Before you go to bed. Run to the house and ask your mother to make a list of supplies she needs. If I'm sleeping when you get back out here, put the note in my boot."

In an early morning circle of the ranch Grant found no tracks, no sign of fires, at eight in the morning he was in town sending a wire. Afterward he headed to the mercantile and picked up the supplies needed at the ranch along with several boxes of shells. The café was busy when he arrived, Johnny, Rooster and Banty were sitting at the counter, and the waitress was soon in front of him, "Coffee, whatever else is really fast. I'm in a hurry."

She turned and placed an order then returned with a cup of coffee, "I'm thinking you are in a hurry so you can get out of town before Rooster and his friends jump you again?"

She had a grin on her face, Grant smiled, "News gets around fast."

"Johnny is my brother. He can't seem to find a job. Same with Rooster and his friend Banty. Rooster and Banty like to fight, but they evidently aren't as good at it as they thought."

"Tell Johnny I would like to talk to him."

The waitress sent Johnny to Grant's table, Grant offered him a seat, "Hear you three don't have a job. I have a job for the three of you guarding a ranch. Any drinking fighting or cussing, you will be fired without pay. Job pays room and board, twenty a month. Talk it over with your friends. I'll be leaving in fifteen minutes. That's all the time you have to decide. The job is honest work."

Johnny pushed back his chair, "If my friends don't accept, I will."

Shortly Johnny and his friends stepped to his table, "We'd like the job sir."

"Had breakfast yet?"

"Yes sir."

"Get your gear; I'll be leaving in a few minutes. If you don't make it back to go with me, go to the S bar J, your job will be to make sure the family stays safe. Until I see you at the ranch, any questions?"

There were no questions, the threesome walked out the door, and soon the waitress was by his side with a plateful of food, "Like I said. They are good boys. I figure they need some direction and something to do."

"I hired them to do honest work."

Grant smiled and added, "I figure they will be well directed."

Grant visited the bank, he was back at the ranch well before noon, he took the supplies to the house, he was met by Billy and Frank, "Nobody showed up, when we saw you coming, we were prepared."

"Good. Take the supplies inside. I need to talk to your mother."

Jenny stepped out onto the porch, Grant tipped his hat, and Billy pointed behind him, "Three riders coming."

"Billy, Jenny, Frank. Those three men I have hired to guard the ranch. I'll give them instructions before I head out. They are here to guard only for a while. Hopefully in a couple months there will be no need for guards. I got a bunch of extra supplies; room and board are part of their pay."

"You said you are heading out?"

"Yes Ma'am. I'm checking the lay of the land and looking for rustlers."

After introducing the threesome, Grant led them to the bunkhouse and gave them instructions, "Boys. There is a woman in the house. She is the center of the world for all eight of those kids. Your job is to protect her and her children. From the loft in the barn you can see a long way, someone should be there checking both ends of the barn all during the daylight. One should be sleeping so you can be alert at night, the other can take short rides out to the hill and back and check for anyone that shouldn't be here. Your job

64

is not to try to chase them down. Mark the time and the place where you see them, let me know when I return."
Grant hesitated before asking, "Any questions?"

Jenny watched as Grant directed her boys and the three men, he was a leader there was no doubt, her boys and the three men were careful to follow his direction to the letter. It didn't seem like there was much ranching being done but there was a lot of activity, "Billy. What did Mr. Grant say to those three?"

"Told them the same thing he told us. Just said they were here to guard you and the rest of us kids. I never thought about it before."

"Thought about what?"

"Mr. Baker, said you were the center of us kid's world. Without you, we won't have much for a family."

For a moment Jenny considered The Hangman's statement, "What else did he tell you?"

"He said we were being brought up proper. Respectful. He said to remember whatever you teach us is more important then what he will have us do."

Jenny gave her son a hug, for some reason this time he didn't pull away to demonstrate he was too old for such things. The lad's thinking was being broadened, he had been forced to see the world from a different perspective and in the process, he had matured and was beginning to see that he played a part.

Grant had a couple of fistfuls of jerky and some hardtack; he was used to a spare diet, he could be out on the range for a month if he chose. Moving a lot and with a telescope he checked out the range for a day and a half before he spied a tendril of dust coming from the place where he saw a group of fifty head of cows the previous day. He checked the lay of the land, the direction of travel of the rustlers and determined where he could cut them off.

Grant was hiding on the top of a small hill as the herd was pushed through the draw below; Grant backed down and mounted his horse. He waited until he heard the sounds of the cattle moving slightly in front of him; he wanted to approach from the rear, maybe save a life or two.

Grant rode over the hill behind the cattle drive, as he rode down the hill behind one of the rustlers, the man turned around in time to gaze into the barrel of Grant's .45. Grant motioned for him to get his hands up, the rustler quickly complied. Grant moved forward and lifted his rifle and pistol and put the man's side gun in his saddle bags, he tied a thong around the rifle and hung it from his saddle horn, "What's your friend's names?"

"Erv, the other one's Able."

"Put your hands up high. Call out to them. Tell them to behave themselves, put their hands up or I'll kill them."

He did as he was told, the closest one raised his hands, the other swung his rifle around, Grant shot him out of the saddle, "Ride up next to Erv."

Grant picked up Erv's guns, and then picked up the guns from Able, "Boys. First of all, let's bury your friend Abel."

A half hour later Grant ordered them back into the saddle. "Now, let's push the cattle back to where they were."

In silence the twosome drove the herd back to where they were grazing; Grant ordered them off their horses, "Start a fire, boys."

"What do we need of a fire?"

"I see you two didn't bring a branding iron. Do you sell them without a brand and let the new owner brand them?"

He was met with silence, "You boys have anything good to eat in your bags?"

Grant looked through their saddle bags, one had a small package of freshly baked biscuits; the same type he saw at the café in town, "You boys eat pretty well. The boss takes pretty good care of you."

Erv growled back, "That same boss will take care of you when he hears about this deal?"

The fire was started, Grant tossed a rope to the feet of one of the men. He figured they weren't too bright because they let him know they were part of some kind of organized rustling group, "Tie up your partner. Hog tie him."

"I ain't gonna hog tie him."

Grant smiled and pointed his .45 at the man's arm, "Do it. It will be easier with two arms than one."

Soon Erv was hog tied, Grant hog tied the other one; "I can't recall your name?"

"Go plumb to."

"All right Mr. Go Plumb To. You'll go first."

"Go where? I'm hogtied, I can't move."

Grant put his wire brand into the fire and waited for a few minutes, "Before I get started here. You boys want to tell me who you are selling the cattle to?"

Again, he was greeted by silence; Grant removed the wire brand with a pair of pliers, stepped on the second rustler's head and branded him, "There you have it Mr. Go Plumb To. You've just been branded with the S bar J."

Slowly Grant made his way to the fire with the brand; he left the wire in the fire to heat as he removed the hoop from about the second rustler's neck, "Mr. Go Plumb To. You handled that pretty good. It's a hard thing to do with that rope around your neck. How do you think your friend Erv will do? Is he a screamer?"

Grant removed the wire from the fire and stepped to Erv, "Erv. You have three seconds to tell me who your boss is? And, who is buying the cattle from your boss?"

Grant stepped on Erv's head, "Hurry up. The branding iron is cooling down."

After a few seconds Grant shrugged, "Time is up. Too late Erv."

After branding Erv, Grant cooled the wire with water from one of their canteens, after he cut the noose from around Erv's neck, Grant squatted in front of Erv, "Mr. Go Plumb to, and Erv. It is said I have a somewhat mean disposition. Me, I figure I'm nothing but a pussycat. Tell you what boys. This time of the year it's branding time. You boys look a little like cowmen, you know the cattle business. Branding comes now, soon it will be time to be castrating. Consider yourselves lucky you made it here during the branding season, and not the other. You boys will carry the brand I gave you around these parts and let everyone know that you were stealing from the S bar J. If I see you back here, I'll hang you; unless it's castrating season. I've had a lot of experience with the hanging part, but I'm willing to bet I can do a fair job of castrating on you boys as well. So, choose your rustling season well or better yet, stay off this range. And don't forget to say hello to your boss."

Erv gritted his teeth, "We'll tell the boss to say hello. What's your name?"

"Name is Grant Baker. Some call me, The Hangman."

After collecting all the guns Grant mounted his horse, drew and shot the rope from between the legs of Erv, "Now you boys should be able to get untied. Be off this range in an hour or I'll make good on my promise to hang you."

As Grant rode away, he noted they scurried to get together to untie each other's ropes, Grant left with a fistful of the biscuits, just like the one he had for breakfast. Again, Grant made a circle around the ranch to make sure they had no visitors; then made his way to the bunkhouse to talk to the guards.

Back at the ranch that evening it was past time for the evening meal, Grant went to the house and knocked, Susan answered, "Susan. I'm hungry as a bear. Would it be possible for you to make one of those sandwiches you put together so well?"

Susan smiled politely, "Come in. Do you want a cup of coffee?"

"Please."

Jenny came from her bedroom; she was looking refreshed and somewhat relaxed, "Jenny. How are things around the ranch?"

"No visitors yet."

"I'm thinking that is good right now."

"How are things out on the range?"

"Good. I spoke to some rustlers today. Don't know quite yet if my speech will do any good. It shouldn't be long before we know."

Jenny knew she was being kept out of the loop, she smiled and asked, "Do I want to know what kind of speech you gave them?"

Susan placed the coffee and a sandwich before him, "Susan. What do you put on there to make it taste so good?"

"Mom makes mustard."

"Mmmm. Good."

Jenny smiled at the attention given Susan and asked, "The speech?"

"We talking about the different seasons on the range. We got into a little branding session. I told them they were lucky it wasn't time for cutting."

Jenny whispered, "You branded them?"

Grant nodded, "On the forehead."

"What?"

"The S bar J."

"You didn't?"

"I did. I told them if they came back, I'd have to live up to my name."

"What will they do?"

"Either get out of the country or try to do me in."

"Will we survive this?"

"That's the important part. I just sent for a thousand head of cattle. They should be here in two weeks. Either we'll have plenty for the rustlers to steal, or we'll put them out of business."

Grant got up to leave, and then stopped, "I may be taking a ride to town early tomorrow morning."

"Don't like my breakfast?"

Grant grinned, "Jenny. I would much prefer the company of you and your family. But there may be something happening in town early in the morning."

After Grant left for the bunkhouse Jenny shook her head. She had heard all sorts of stories about how brutal the man could be, but around her and her children, he was a gentleman. She felt he honestly did indeed enjoy the company of her family.

Grant made his way to town before daybreak; the early crowd was just entering the café. Grant sat down on a bench across the street and watched. The blacksmith and the owner of the mercantile were the only ones to pick up sacks of food from the café. Grant entered the café and ordered, the same waitress greeted him; "How's my big brother doing?"

"I like Johnny. He's pretty smart and he's polite. What does he have to say about his partners?"

"Same thing I told you. Fun loving, like to fight, or think they fight. But once you get to know them, they're pretty good. What do you want today?"

"Same thing as yesterday."

In five minutes, she returned, he asked, "What's your name?"

"Sharon."

Grant moved a silver dollar out onto the table, "This is for breakfast; the rest is yours whether or not you can answer this next question."

Sharon smiled, "And the question is?"

"Yesterday. Fairly early in the morning. Who all picked up a sack of your biscuits?"

Sharon pointed to the biscuit on his plate, "Those?"

"Yes."

"Our biggest customer is the blacksmith, I don't see how one man can eat so many biscuits. But, yesterday, if memory serves me correctly, the owner of the mercantile also picked up a big bag."

"He picks them up every day?"

"Yes. But yesterday, he got more than usual."

Grant slid the dollar across the counter, "Thanks. Please don't mention the question to anyone."

Grant finished his meal, left the cafe and led his horse to the blacksmith shop, "Howdy. How are chances of you looking over my horse's shoes, he's been covering quite a few miles."

The blacksmith checked the four shoes, Grant sniffed the air. What smells so good?"

"Biscuits. Have one."

"Neighborly of you."

"I eat them, the kids eat them, and I give them to my customers. I figure if I don't give them away, I'll end up eating the whole sack.

"Shoes are in good shape. We'll let it go this time."

"Again. Very neighborly of you."

"You from around here?"

"Grant Baker. Partner at the S bar J."

The blacksmith smiled, "Heard of you. That's good. Jenny could sure use a man out there to help her out."

"You've met Jenny?"

"Sure. She's a mighty bright lady."

"That she is."

"You have any interest in cattle?"

"None other than for eating. Why? You interested in selling one?"

Grant smiled, this man wasn't stealing cattle, he just happened to like those biscuits, "If I find one out there ready to butcher that the rustlers haven't walked off with, I'll be glad to sell it to you."

The blacksmith's face got serious, "How can anyone pick on such a fine family?"

The blacksmith bounced his hammer off the anvil, "I'd like to work on them a bit."

Grant smiled, nodded, then agreed, "I've had to do in a couple, and I branded a few, but I don't know if I've made much of a dent in the population. Looking for a few items. Do you do much shopping at the mercantile?"

"When I have to."

"Owner, good sort, is he?"

The blacksmith's head tottered back and forth as if he didn't want to commit himself, "He's quiet. Doesn't seem to

71

go out of his way to learn your name or be really friendly. He's all right I guess."

Grant tipped his hat, "I'll be back again. Thanks."

Grant made a circle of the ranch then made his way back; he figured it was time to give the girls a lesson in self-defense. He took them to a grove of trees so the sound would be muffled in case the enemy was about. For an hour he gave them lessons in loading and firing, satisfied they could send the lead in the right direction if the need arose and use the gun to effect without hurting themselves or family, they returned to the house. Grant took them inside and told them how to protect themselves while firing. He figured a couple more rifles shooting out of the house would give the appearance of greater numbers.

Jenny met him on the porch, "You missed the noon meal. I'm beginning to think you don't like my cooking."

"Been busy. Any leftovers?"

"Come on in."

Grant sat down while Jenny fixed a plate, Jenny turned, Grant was watching her, when the two-year-old boy grabbed onto Grant's pistol in an attempt to pull himself up onto the bench. Grant's hand shot down rapidly to the grip of his pistol, then as suddenly as he moved, he quieted, then helped the two-year-old onto the bench. The two-year-old giggled at the rapid movement then moved to a seat on Grant's leg so he could see on top of the table, "You hungry again lad?"

He shook his head no; Grant shifted him over to the other side so he could eat right handed, "Jenny. Has the owner of the mercantile been around long?"

"Two years. The other owner suddenly died."

"What of?"

"Never did hear. Why do you ask?"

"I've a suspicion he's the one behind all the rustling. If he is, one of these days his boys will be visiting us, if he can keep them together."

"How did you find that out?"

"By tracking the biscuits."

72

"Biscuits?"

Grant told her about the biscuits and his trip to town.

"You going to be here for breakfast tomorrow?"

"Yup. I'm going to send Johnny in tonight to do my biscuit spying."

Jenny smiled, "Then maybe I'll have to make biscuits in the morning."

"You don't have to do that."

"They are easy and fast."

"I'm mighty glad I got into this partnership."

Jenny smiled, "Only cost you seventeen thousand dollars for those biscuits. Pretty costly biscuits if you ask me."

Grant nodded his head, with his left arm around the two-year-old he looked down at the boy smiling up at him, "I figure I got the best end of the deal. I think I bought into a gold mine."

Grant left right after lunch and didn't make it back until near midnight when he nearly got himself shot by Rooster who was on duty. Grant was up early in the morning, washed and was sitting on the porch when he was joined by Sharon and Susan, "How are you two sharpshooters today?"

Susan answered, "We are good. We are glad you came to the ranch."

"You are? Why?"

"Mom is happier."

"Why is that?"

"I don't know. She feels better for some reason."

"I'm glad she feels better. I'm glad I came. I like your ranch. I like your family."

Sharon took his arm, gave it a hug then pulled it around her. Grant Baker could not speak. In all his years of chasing bad men about the country, he had never experienced the simple act of a child showing their affection. He gave Sharon a gentle hug, soon Susan was under the other arm. Children were something he had almost no experience with, he figured he could sit on the porch all day.

Jenny finished feeding the four little ones; she stepped to the door to ring the bell and waited a minute to watch her two girls as they were showing and in turn shown affection by none other than, the Hangman. Jenny marveled at the fact that her own husband would never have been content to just sit on the porch and hold his children. After a moment Jenny spoke up, "Hey. Are you three going to eat or do I throw it out?"

Johnny's orders were simple, he was to find out from his sister how many biscuits the owner of the mercantile picked up. If he picked up a large bag, he was to get the information back as soon as possible; under no circumstance was he to speak to anyone other than his sister. With the news gathered for Grant, Johnny made his way back to the S bar J; Grant was there to meet him.

"The owner of the mercantile got a big bag of biscuits this morning; Sis says the biggest bag he ever picked up."

"All right. Frank and Billy. You are going to water all the horses, feed all the animals, and then I want you to stay close to the house for the rest of the day. Listen carefully. Your jobs are to protect the house only. Rooster and Banty will be up in the barn; Johnny will be in the bunkhouse. Our jobs will be to make sure they don't get to the house. Go get your chores finished then get to the house."

Grant turned his attention to the three hired men, "Boys, you know what you have to do. I'm starting out on that hill up there; I'll have a telescope and a mirror. If they come, I'll shine the mirror. I'm going to try to make them come to me. My back will be facing the ranch, if they get someone around behind me, you boys can pick them off. Get all the shells you need and get set, I'm going up to the hill."

Johnny asked, "What if they go out and rustle cattle instead of coming after us?"

Grant smiled, "Could happen, but I think I scared them enough so they will come after me first then look for any beef left on the ranch."

It was a little before noon when they arrived, Grant chuckled; he figured they timed their arrival for lunch time. Sure enough, behind him at the ranch, the dinner bell sounded. The group of seven riders approached with confidence in their numbers and they were betting the family would be sitting down to the table. Grant turned and signaled the farm with his mirror.

Grant put his telescope on the band of riders, Pete was up front, his partner Jimmy was nowhere to be seen in the group. Erv and his partner Abel, the man he dubbed, Go Plumb To, were riding with the group. Grant put his sights on Erv, he figured Pete would be next, then whoever fell into his sights.

At less than one hundred yards Grant opened up, three men were knocked out of the saddle, the rest turned about. Grant took careful aim on another, the bobbing of the horse and rider caused him to shoot low, the horse went down, the rider had a hole in his leg. One of the men turned about to pick up his friend, Grant emptied the saddle with a well-placed shot. The last two were out of range.

Grant went down to the one he shot in the leg; by the time he got there the man was dead. The shot broke a main artery; he bled to death within minutes. Grant went to the one that returned for his friend, the bullet had entered his chest; he too would be dead before long, "Well if it isn't, Go Plumb To. You had some good in you, came back for your friend."

"He's my brother."

"Why did you get into this line of work?"

"Easy money."

"Heard that a lot. Anybody you want me to contact?"

"I'm Abel Henry, my brother is John. Mom's still alive in St. Louis."

"Want me to contact her?"

"You can. Tell her she was right all along."

"She warned you, did she?"

"Yep."

"If it's any consolation, my mother warned me my life would be pretty hollow doing nothing but chasing rustlers. She was right also."

Abel winced from the pain as he spoke, "Maybe you can change. Got time and no holes in your chest."

"Abel. Maybe you are right. I'll contact your mother. You came back for your brother that should account for something."

Abel's head bobbed, then he tried to say something, "Two groups,,,,,, other side of the ranch…, attack…" then he was gone. Grant moved to the others, they were all dead. Suddenly gunfire broke out back at the ranch; he understood what Abel was trying to tell him.

Grant dug his spurs into his horse, he was back to the ranch within a minute, the shooting was already dying down. Grant raced into the yard and up to the front of the house, "Billy. It's me."

Grant ran to the house; the door was tossed open just before he entered. He stopped just inside the door, his eyes tore around the room and rested on Jenny, "Is everybody all right?"

Billy nodded, "Yes sir."

Jenny stood in the doorway to the bedroom with a smile on her face, happy with Grant's concern, "We are doing fine. I can't say the same for the five men that charged the house."

Grant stood, he had never felt so helpless in all his life, he stepped to Susan who was standing by the east window with a rifle in hand, he put his hand on her shoulder as if to touch her to make sure she was all right. She smiled and wrapped her arms around him, he thought; here this little girl is helping him to cope. He whispered to Susan, "I was afraid one of you may be hurt."

She smiled and whispered, "We did fine. Everyone is all right."

Again, Grant looked at the faces of everyone, Billy looked a little pained, Grant went to him and spoke softly, he recalled the hanging of Jake Plummer and his pretended

76

aloofness. Grant recalled the pain of living with the memory of his involvement, "What is it Billy?"

Billy's voice was a whisper, "I think I shot one of them."

Grant put his arm around Billy, "Billy. This is something that will stay with you for some time. Always remember this; you did your part well, you had to protect your family. The memory of what you did is a bad memory that will go away. It is something you had to do, remember, it is something you only do when you can't possibly do anything else. Remember the real important things we talked about out in the bunkhouse. Those men were here to ruin your world. You did your job and your family is safe because of what you had to do."

Grant motioned to Jenny, she too could soften the impact of what occurred there that day. Grant excused himself and went out to check up on the guards. Five men lay in the yard and two horses; one of those attacking was still alive, Grant went to the man, "You caught one in the stomach. You are going to have a bad go of it."

The man grimaced in pain, "Burns something fierce."

Grant nodded, "It will get worse. What did you men hope to get done here?"

"Wanted you dead and out of the way."

"You didn't care about the family?"

He shook his head, Grant asked, "The mercantile man. What is his name? Where did he come from?"

"We were up in Helena when you came up there and started cleaning house. We got out and come down here, this time the boss said we weren't leaving. Where the hell did you get all the firepower?"

"Three friends, a gal and her kids."

"Christ."

"Might be a good idea if you spoke to him for a while. I don't figure you have too long."

Grant turned to Johnny, "I'm going to town to finish this. I figure there are at least three left."

"Do you want me to go along?"

77

"You'd violate the rule. Don't go hunting. Just stay here and guard the home front."

Johnny shook his head, "When you get back you are going to have to explain this no hunting rule to me."

Grant nodded, "When I get back."

Grant kicked his horse into a ground eating canter; he would come into town from a grove of trees behind the café. Grant entered the back door of the café through the kitchen, he asked for Sharon, Sharon came into the kitchen, she was worried, "Is Johnny all right?"

"Yes. We were attacked by a dozen men. Rustlers working with the owner of the mercantile. Two of them got away, have you seen any activity at the mercantile lately?"

"Nothing unusual."

"I'm going to have to go in there. I hate to beard the lion in his den but I guess I'm going to have to."

"Be careful."

Grant chuckled; he figured that was a part of him that was in need of a big change, "Yes, I know, I'm not as young as I used to be."

"You mean, now you do think about the future?"

Grant checked his guns and headed out the back door, "You women, I figure you have eyes that see right through a man. Starts about the time you are about six years old?"

Sharon nodded, "Sometimes before that even. We look into a man's eyes and we sometimes see what he sees."

Grant nodded, "Sometimes, it is downright scary."

Sharon didn't have time to answer, Grant stepped out the door and made his way around the side of the café. He decided he would cross the street quickly and enter by the front door of the mercantile hoping they would expect him to come in the back. Grant knew the situation was charged with danger; he was at a great disadvantage entering the mercantile. Grant figured he would move quickly into the front door and step away from the opening once inside. He was hoping they would expect him to come in the back.

Grant moved quickly across the street, quickly he stepped into the doorway then jumped to his right. As he jumped right, he felt a fire explode beneath his left arm, someone shot from behind the counter. Grant returned the fire, while he kept moving to the right. Someone, who evidently was waiting for him to come in the back door, stepped into the room from the rear, he looked to the door, by the time he saw Grant; Grant slammed two bullets into his chest.

Grant made his way to the counter, he picked up a blanket off the shelf and moved it around the counter, the moment the blanket was exposed a bullet passed through it. Grant put his pistol over the counter and emptied it, then quickly changed guns. Grant opened the blanket and tossed it behind the counter then followed with pistol ready. There was no need, a bullet caught the one behind the counter in the throat.

He took a big belt and cinched it around the towel to stop the blood flow, then he figured he had to get the leader before he got so weak he couldn't hold up his gun. He thought he was thinking strange but he hurried to the back door, a shot broke the stillness, he looked numbly down at his gun to see if it went off, then took a couple more steps and fell through the back door.

Johnny rushed to his side, "Where are you hit?"

"Under the arm. Why are you here?"

"I caught the boss as he came out of the mercantile, he's got a bullet hole in him, but he'll live so he can hang."

A buckboard pulled up around the corner of the mercantile, Jenny was driving. Jenny ran to his side, looked under the towel, put pressure on the wound and snapped orders to Johnny, "Go in the store and get me some bandages and some iodine."

Grant looked up at Jenny, he smiled and mumbled, "What are you doing here?"

"I figured I got me a good partner, I didn't want to lose him."

Jenny put pressure on the wound to stop the bleeding, Grant looked up and felt good at the concern shown on her face, "Will I live?"

"The bullet went right through. You lost a lot of blood, but you'll live."

"Why did you come?"

"I watched my children with you. I figure they can use you. I saw when you charged into the house, your fear one of us was hurt was evident, I saw your pain and your relief. I see a lot, Grant Baker."

"When I came to buy your ranch, I wanted a place to hide for the rest of my life. Then I met you and your family. One minute with you, I knew I didn't want to hide and I didn't want to be alone."

The wound was bandaged, Jenny asked Johnny to help her get Grant into the buckboard. Grant looked to Johnny, "You left the ranch."

"Yes. Jenny didn't give me any choice."

"Well, you are forgiven just this once."

Johnny grinned, "I appreciate that. You were going to tell me why I couldn't leave the ranch?"

"Didn't want you kids to get to chasing crooked people, it's not a good life."

Johnny nodded, "Don't worry. From now on I'll stick to raising cattle."

Jenny gave orders, "Johnny. You drive the buckboard. I'll ride back here with my partner. Take your time. We are in no hurry."

Introduction to, "Lonesome Valley"

Cassandra, the brave young lady in "Lonesome Valley" was inspired by a documentary on Annie Oakley. Annie Oakley was placed in an orphanage when her father died, she was released into a home that abused her, she returned to the orphanage. By the time she was fifteen, by hunting with her father's rifle she supplied the family with meat and made money selling game sufficient for the family to live on.

She was such a good shot she beat a renowned skeet shooter, he was so taken with her he married her. Even after coming from a horrid beginning she became known the world over for her shooting and also her very Victorian demeanor. Throughout her life she set and maintained high standards for herself.

Annie Oakley was from the Southeast, I took Annie's Victorian demeanor and unequalled shooting ability and put her in the foothills of the mountains of Montana.

"Lonesome Valley"

Cassandra Blakely was dead tired, she watched from her vantage point at the kitchen table as an unknown rider approached boldly down the lane. She felt literally crushed. She didn't have the energy to get up to use the buffalo gun to scare him off. Her brother's .44 lay cocked in her lap, its muzzle pointed at the doorway. All she would have to do is point and pull the trigger if the stranger entered the doorway. In an exhausted daze her eyes trailed slowly to her right, her brother's body lay on the floor, painfully she closed her eyes. No tears came; she no longer had the energy to cry. She gazed to her left, on the day bed lay her sister's body, in the bedroom were the bodies of her mother and father. For the past three days and nights of the siege she had not slept, she kept up the vigil now in a dreamlike state somewhere between reality and an awakened nightmare.

As Markus Redmond rode down the lane he sat bolt upright in the saddle, his military life had disciplined him so. He had just crossed the open plain on his way to this ranch, he noted riders barely visible heading off to the southeast. Markus Redmond continued down the lane, he heard in town this lonesome out-of-the-way ranch may be for sale; lonesome was exactly what he wanted. Ever since his wife and baby died during childbirth, he wanted nothing but lonesome. After the war he spent a few more years training young men to kill, then for too short a time he found love and happiness, now with luck he would hide on this lonesome ranch.

As Mark entered the gate, he looked at the drift fence blocking cattle from entering or leaving the valley beyond the ranch buildings. The drift fence was cut in several places, there were four dead saddled and shod horses scattered about the space between the drift fence and the buildings. There were three bodies in cowboy apparel among the dead horses.

He pulled the Winchester out of the sheath and continued toward the buildings, the door to the ranch house was open. He held the rifle by the barrel, not at a ready position, a sign he was no threat. Other than a horse stomping in the barn and chickens clucking, no signs of a living human were evident. Windows on the ranch house were open, no doubt for shooting out of during the attack. From the looks of the bloated bodies the battle extended over at least three days, he tied his horse to the rail in front of the house and walked up the steps.

Mark had few illusions, he felt he could be shot at any time, he had been in many battles; some of those battles the ground was so strewn with bodies it was necessary to walk on them to advance. Now he was ambivalent, he wasn't involved, nor did he want to be, he could be shot, he just didn't care.

Mark stood in the doorway, inside he noted a young lady sitting at the table looking at him in a near trancelike state. On the floor to her right was the body of a young man, to Mark's right lay the body of a younger girl on a cot. The house had acquired the smell of death, another sign the battle had been going on for days, Mark put his Winchester against the wall and spoke, "Looks like there are some people here need burying." the young lady looked off to the bedroom without speaking.

Mark followed her gaze and stepped into the bedroom, he saw two bodies on the bed; the bedroom had a more intense smell of death, the bodies were evidently there for a longer period of time. He turned around and noted the girl had the muzzle of the .44 pointed at him, "If you tell me where the shovel is and where to dig, I'll start with the graves."

She remained seated at the table. She merely pointed at the wall behind the door, Mark retrieved the shovel and his Winchester and walked out the door. He looked about the yard for some time before he noted a lonely grave marker toward the east of the house a few hundred feet away on a little bench. It was past noon when the bodies were placed in the ground and covered. The three bodies of the attackers out in front of the house would have to wait. Mark sat above the graves in the rocks resting and watching the open prairie beyond the ranch as he was approached by the young lady.

Cassandra stood looking stonily at the graves, finally she murmured, "Thanks for your help."
She wavered as she spoke, "I want to leave this place."

Mark nodded, "I was sent out here by the barber in town, he said the place may be for sale. I'd be interested in buying. What is your name?"

Cassandra stood as in a daze, still with pride and dignity she answered, "Cassandra Blakely. I'll make out a paper. I'd like to take a few things with me."

Cassandra barely heard the stranger's reply, "Cassandra. You can take whatever you want, if there is anything you'd like or want later on; let me know where to send it. I'll pay whatever the going price and I'll pay for whatever stock you decide to leave."

Cassandra turned, as if the price had no bearing, and headed to the house.

Mark was tired from digging the graves, he continued to sit against a rock looking out over the flats to see if the attacking force would return. From his vantage point he could see the entire drift fence, the entrance to the valley, the ranch buildings and the slope on the other side of the opening to the valley. He watched sadly as Cassandra stumbled back up the slope toward him, cradled in her arm was a buffalo gun, she was carrying two small flour sacks of belongings with her.

Cassandra Blakely stood before him; he noted she was not much over five feet tall, a very petite girl and beautiful girl who now looked totally beaten. She handed him a signed bill of sale and the title to the ranch. She swayed back and forth. Mark was about to get up to give her aide, Cassandra's shoulders drooped and it appeared she attempted to turn to sit on the rock at his feet. Suddenly she collapsed, the buffalo gun dropped into the grass, Cassandra ended up sitting down on his lap, passed out. The two bags she was carrying lay on the ground beside him, Cassandra was suddenly fast asleep, exhausted in his arms.

Markus Redmond sat with Cassandra on his lap not sure what to do. Her head was on his chest beneath his chin, she was light, he decided not to disturb her. Based on the condition of the bodies in the house and in the yard, he figured one had been dead for at least two days, most likely three or more. The girl on his lap had gone through a lot in the past few days; from experience he figured the best thing for her was sleep. By disturbing her now there was no telling what her mental condition would be.

Mark continued to watch the prairie. He reached over, picked up the buffalo gun, checked the load then leaned it within reach against the rock. One of the bags was open; it contained a .44 pistol, a gold watch, a mirror and a teacup. He assumed somehow the items were individual memories of her brother, her sister and her parents, memories she wanted to preserve. The other bag contained some personal belongings.

Cassandra remained in his lap for nearly five hours. She began to stir as though she were having a bad dream, he patted her gently on the back. He realized when she woke up, she could literally be shocked out of her mind; he had no way to wake her comfortable with a totally new reality. He recalled seasoned military men who had gone through much less losing their minds; as a precaution he moved the pistol out of her reach.

Cassandra's eyes slowly opened, she noted her position in the stranger's lap, her head on his chest, she recalled coming back up to him with the title to the ranch; she felt the soothing patting on her back. She sensed she was unharmed, she noted her father's buffalo gun against the rock and her two bags of belongings at her feet. The stranger's voice softly asked, "Cassandra, how are you doing?"

Too weak to move, Cassandra dizzily replied, "How did I get here?"

The stranger's voice softly answered, "You came back up to see me after collecting items you wanted to take with you. You collapsed onto my lap. You've been sleeping for nearly five hours now. You've been through a lot."

Cassandra looked below them at the four grave markers, she wanted badly to get away and cry, the stranger's voice again was soft and seemed to read her mind, "You are a mighty brave girl Cassandra. You have been through way too much; you've lost a lot of your world. I want you to know you are crying inside, it's alright to cry."

Markus Redmond observed many a soldier that remained stoic in the face of great personal loss. Instead of a simple cry, a simple show of emotion, they kept their grief inside until drink, anger or even humor provided a release. He smiled at his own grief, the trail of lonesomeness became his outlet. He figured maybe he would have been better off taking his own advice.

Cassandra buried her face in the stranger's chest and cried while he gently patted her back and waited. After some time, Cassandra rose, "I am so weak. I'll have to get something to eat. I'm afraid I haven't eaten or slept for two or three days. We have something at the house."

Mark didn't know if he was invited or not, "Maybe I should keep watch?"

Cassandra picked up the buffalo gun, "I can see a long way from the house. I'll fix something for us."

Cassandra stood, she was dizzy, she reached for his hand, Mark picked up the two flour sacks and his Winchester then he put his arm about her waist to hold her up. They made their way to the house, between the two of them they fixed something to eat. After eating Cassandra began to talk about the ranch, "I know Dad always talked to the barber when he went to town about selling the place, but I don't know if he really wanted to leave. He never spoke seriously to us about selling.

"The real value to the ranch is in the valley behind us. Father built here so he could easily fence off this quarter mile entrance to the valley. The valley itself opens up into three small valleys. There are no outlets out of the valley, so we haven't been bothered by rustlers or Indians.

"In seventy, when R.S. Ford trailed in a herd of cattle above the Missouri River, father bought a hundred head from him. They have been in the valley for seven years now. He had two Hereford bulls brought up the Missouri, a year later.

Other than two-year-old steers, Dad hasn't marketed any of the cows."

Markus Redmond watched the prairie as he asked, "You've grown up here?"

Mark picked up empty shell casings as Cassandra continued to work cleaning the dishes as she spoke, "My brother and sister and I played on the slope behind the house so much I know every rock and pebble. From above the graves I can see clearly over a mile. Dad always said I had eagle eyes because of the details I could make out."

Cassandra spoke for some time about childhood memories, then spoke of the battle, "I don't know who was trying to do us in. We didn't recognize any of the men we shot out front."

Markus Redmond offered, "When I came, I saw horses riding off to the southeast."

Cassandra stopped what she was doing, "Southeast? That would be the Card ranch. I thought it may be the Larkin ranch to the southwest."

Sometime after they ate Mark had picked up shell casings and separated them for reloading. Cassandra stepped to the doorway, "Four riders are coming."

Cassandra picked up the buffalo gun, tucked the .44 in her apron and spoke, "I just want to tell them I'm leaving."

Mark looked across the prairie, he couldn't see anything, he thought for a short time, "Cassandra. Let's go up above the graves where we have good command of the entire ranch."

Cassandra nodded, "Alright, that's a good idea. Let's go out the back way and make our way up through the rocks so they can't see us."

Cassandra led Markus Redmond out the back way through the rocks back to the spot above the graves, "Cassandra. Those men may be coming to kill you. If the law finds out they've killed the rest of your family, they will get the hangman's noose. Even though you've sold the ranch, I'm afraid they may not let you go."

Cassandra nodded, one could see she was regaining her strength and her ability to think clearly, "I see. I still want to talk to them. I'm tired of the killing. If they will let me go, I'm leaving."

From his vantage point Markus Redmond could finally see what Cassandra saw earlier, four men were approaching from the southeast, "Cassandra, I'm going to stay hidden in the rocks, when they get close enough, allow only one of them to come up to talk to you. If you can find out what their intentions are, then maybe it will be safe for you to leave. We won't learn their intentions if they know I'm here. If they do allow you to leave, then if there is to be a battle, they'll have to fight with me."

Cassandra seemed to understand, when the foursome were about three hundred yards away, she shot in front of them, then yelled, "Only one of you, come up to talk."

For a short time, the foursome talked, then one rider came forward, Cassandra slipped another shell into the buffalo gun and spoke so Mark could hear her, "I recognize the man they are sending up to talk. He's called, Case. He's a hired gunman. He's killed men. I think you may be right. He may want to kill me."

Markus Redmond gave directions, "Stand so you are behind the rock, make him stop near the graves, point your gun at his chest. I'll have him covered also. You talk to him and see what he intends. If he makes a move to harm you, I'll take care of him."

Cassandra waited until Case was nearly up to the graves, he was seventy feet below her, a difficult shot with Case's handgun. She spoke, "Stay right there, Case. What do you want?"

Cassandra had the buffalo gun pointed at his chest as he spoke, "Missy, I see you've had a little grave digging to do, thought you'd be fast asleep by now."

Cassandra's voice was sharp and to the point, "What did you come for?"

Case smiled, "Missy. In your hands that gun doesn't scare me none. I came up here to finish the job, but I'd just as soon keep you in one piece for a while."

Cassandra's voice was calm, "If you get off your horse or touch your gun you are a dead man. All I want to do is leave this place. Are you going to allow me to leave or not?"

Case swung his right leg over the cantle, "Can't do that Missy. I'm afraid you'd bring in the law."

Case took his left foot out of the stirrup, as he slid out of the saddle, he drew his .45, Markus Redmond shot him through the chest. Cassandra looked below her at the body of Case. Her statement was calm, "I guess you were right. I should have known better, what do you think we should do now?"

Mark was used to making judgments, "Take your buffalo gun and put a bullet among the three that are left. That way they'll know to keep their distance and they'll know you can still shoot."

Cassandra leaned the buffalo gun on the rock, took aim and shot, one of the men was knocked from the saddle. They watched as the other two men picked up the wounded man then rode off. Markus Redmond came out from behind the rocks and spoke, "Looks like I'll have to dig some more graves."

Cassandra's voice came back sharp, decisive, "No. Not on this ground with my family. On the other side of the fence anyplace you like. Perhaps outside the gate."

Mark took Case's rope, snared his foot and dragged him out onto the land owned by the Card ranch. After burying Case and the other men that were laying in the yard, he put up a marker simply stating, 'Gunmen of Card, all shot trying to kill a girl.' Next Mark hitched a team and dragged the horses killed in battle well out onto the land owned by Card, he stowed the saddles in the barn and the extra firearms in the hay. By that time darkness was approaching, Mark turned to the house, Cassandra had a meal ready.

Mark put four hundred dollars on the table, Cassandra asked, "What is that?"

Mark explained, "I think it is blood money. Money Card paid the men I buried to wipe out your family."

It was quiet for a while, then for some time that evening Cassandra spoke of the ranch and childhood memories, then, she was quiet for some time while Mark kept a watch for Card's men. To break the silence Mark spoke, "That was a pretty lucky shot you made today. From that distance it would be pretty easy to miss entirely."

It was then Cassandra surprised him, "I had to aim at his left shoulder, if I would have hit him in the right shoulder, I may have killed another hand behind him."

The information was given factually, without emotion. Incredulous, Mark asked, "You aimed at his shoulder?"

Cassandra nodded, she turned down the lamp so there would be less of a target if someone did approach the buildings at night, "His left shoulder."

Mark was amazed, he had taught marksmanship for years, never had he encountered a man that could shoot a three-hundred-yard shot with the accuracy Cassandra spoke of, "In all my years, I've never seen such a shot."

Cassandra had been talking of herself and the ranch. She wondered about this stranger who treated her with such kindness and consideration. She asked, "In all your years? Tell me something about yourself and all your years."

Mark nodded, he smiled as he recognized some of her personality was returning, "My name is Markus Redmond, I'm twenty-eight. I hail from western Iowa. Our family members were farmers, teachers and businessmen; then, the war happened. I went through the ranks; my job was to lead men into battle."

Mark hesitated, it was then he recognized the intelligence of the young lady as she asked, "You don't want to offer a lot of detail about the war?"

Mark nodded, "You are very perceptive… It was a most brutal war…" Mark didn't want to start with any description, there would be no end, he continued, "After the war, my job was to teach men to kill. I left the army a captain and, I married... I,"

Markus Redmond tried to start again, "I was married..."

In the dim light Cassandra divined, "Markus Redmond. You told me it was alright to cry. You've never taken your own advice, have you?"

Mark was silenced by her question for a time. Her intuitiveness was astounding, "How did you know?"

Cassandra continued to rock in her mother's favorite chair, "I could sense it in your voice. I could feel your pain still is with you."

Mark tilted back his head, "Cassandra. How old are you?"

Cassandra smiled, "In a couple of weeks I'll be seventeen," she chuckled as she added, "and the reason I haven't run off and gotten married was because I've always been so happy here. And, I haven't found anyone I thought could take me away to a better place, someone I wanted to spend my life with."

Cassandra asked, "Why do you ask?"

Mark answered honestly, "I guess I didn't expect one so skilled to be so young."

She asked, "Skilled?"

Mark explained, "Cooking, shooting, coping, reasoning, your ability to read people, to name a few."

Cassandra nodded, the stranger did a good job of describing who she thought she was, "Out here age is something difficult to put numbers to. I've seen grown men in their thirties and forties act like children. I've seen children forced to become adult's way too fast. To be honest, I'd still love to run and play in the rocks above the house with my brothers and sister, but we outgrew the playtime.

"My sister was two years younger; she was talking about comparing eligible men, marriage and having children already," Cassandra hesitated, then asked, "Your marriage ended sadly. What happened in your marriage?"

91

Mark closed his eyes, here was a young lady who recently went through absolute hell, and she was trying pull the pain out of him. Since she had gone through so much, he found it easier to tell the simple tale he found so difficult to accept, "I left the army because I found a woman I loved dearly. We were married a little more than a year, she and the baby died in childbirth."

In the near darkness Cassandra could be seen wiping her eyes as she sensed his pain. She finally stated, "In time you will be able to start over."

Mark slowly shook his head wondering if it were true, "I found your ranch because the barber said it was a lonesome valley, I figured that was just how I felt. Terribly lonesome."

Cassandra stood, "I'm very tired. I'm going to bed."

As she walked by his chair, she patted him on the shoulder, "Markus Redmond, remember this; you are too good a person to spend the rest of your life lonesome. As for this ranch, life was never lonesome here. Now, even when I am truly alone in the valley, I feel a part. I feel the presence of the familiar, I still feel at home.

"Now Markus Redmond, would you please sleep in the barn tonight, I wouldn't want to give people the idea there was any impropriety."

Mark nodded, "I have a bedroll. I'll sleep outside."

Cassandra, strode off to her bedroom, "I get up early for breakfast. I like to eat breakfast as the sun rises. I have some horses penned up outside the barn, if the Card men come in the night the horses will alert us. If they come, don't try to come to the house, I can see well in the dark, but I won't know who I am shooting."

Mark slept on the hillside above the graves where he would be able to see the ranch and its surroundings. In the morning as he rose, he could hear the sound of a fire being stoked in the cook-stove. He looked the prairie over, finding no dust or sign of company he headed for the house, eggs were frying when he got there.

Mark rapped gently on the door; Cassandra looked his way and said without smiling, "Do you always get up so late in the morning?"

Mark recognized the joke, "Sun's coming up in the east. Did you fry enough for company?"

Again, Cassandra surprised him with her acceptance of his presence and her humor. She responded, "I looked the prairie over, I don't think we'll get any company for breakfast. Would you like to eat out on the porch?"

Mark smiled, "I love to watch the sun rise in the morning."

While they were eating breakfast Cassandra asked, "What do you think we should do today? We can't leave or they'll burn the place down. I don't know if they have someone waiting for me if I head to town, so I think I'll have to stay close to the ranch."

Mark was surprised he felt very happy to hear she wasn't anxious to go to town. He felt if she asked, he would escort her, but he liked the idea of her being there. He mentioned some things that could be done to prepare them for another attack, "I'll try fixing the fence, that will slow them down a bit and prevent the cattle from leaving the valley."

Cassandra, nodded, "I'll keep watch and reload some shells. If I see anybody coming, I'll ring the dinner bell."

Mark smiled, "We know they are trying to kill you. The next time you get one of them in your sights, maybe you should try to do them in."

Cassandra's table manners were as polished as anyone Mark had ever dined with; in all respects she was a lady. She answered with conviction, "No. I've decided, from now on, I'm going to wound them in the left shoulder."

Mark smiled as if it were a joke, "In the left shoulder?"

Cassandra nodded, "Yes. Just think of it. If one or two more of them are sent back to the Card ranch with a busted left shoulder, what will the others begin to think?"

Mark could see the logic; he smiled as he added, "After a few come back with bullets in their left arm the rest will get pretty nervous. They will know you have the ability to hit them any way you choose."

Cassandra smiled, "That's what I thought, and, in the future, people walking around with holes in their left arm will be marked forever as a murderer of the family at Lonesome Valley."

Mark smiled at her reference to the ranch as 'Lonesome Valley,' she somehow had begun to cause him to think differently about the business of being lonesome.

For the next two hours Mark restrung and nailed up broken down and cut fencing before he heard the dinner bell. He mounted his horse and rode back to the ranch, Cassandra met him at the door with the buffalo gun in her hand, "Coffee is hot."

Mark looked out over the prairie, he could just barely make out four riders coming their way. Cassandra placed the buffalo gun on the window frame and waited, the drift fence was over two hundred yards away, Mark watched in awe. She was going to try to repeat a hit to the left shoulder from such a distance? From a kneeling position inside the window she adjusted the sight, she looked at him, smiled and asked, "Did you try the coffee or are you waiting for me to pour?"

Mark grinned. He went to the cupboard and got himself a cup, he poured the coffee then stood behind her as she took aim. When the gun finally erupted, he noted one of the men dropped out of the saddle. Soon the men were helping to put him back on his horse as Cassandra reloaded. Another of the foursome stood still a moment, Cassandra took aim, then fired, this time the one watching fell forward in the saddle.

Cassandra watched as they rode away, "So, how do you like the coffee?"

Mark watched as the foursome made their way back to the Card ranch. He exclaimed, "The coffee is very good, and you are an amazing shot. The best I've ever seen; and I have taught the best. Where did you learn to shoot so well?"

Cassandra retrieved a cup and a small plate of biscuits, "I think I learned out of necessity and I'm blessed with good vision. When we first moved in here, I had to do a lot of hunting with my brother, we had to do away with packs of wolves, a few grizzly bears, and mountain lions. My brother took me along to help skin out animals and watch his back. Mountain lions like to get behind you, you become the hunted. Anyway, soon I was doing the shooting, he was doing the skinning. We were hunting one day, I told him to shoot a mountain lion up on a ledge. He couldn't see it. I took the gun and killed the mountain lion. He said it was over three hundred yards."

Cassandra closed her eyes to allow the memories to pass, then she smiled and continued, "He was a lousy shot, but a good brother."

Mark recalled the first grave, "You had another brother?"

Cassandra nodded, "Ben. We found him shot down by the stream a week ago, couldn't find any tracks. He was a year older than Dan. Dad said the bullet hit him under the left arm, he figured he didn't even know what killed him. Card has some cowards working for him."

Nearly an hour passed, there was little chance of Card's men returning, Cassandra took his cup, "You better get back to work, the boss will fire you for loafing."

Late in the afternoon the fence was repaired and the gate was shut, Mark rode back to the ranch house, he again rapped on the door, there was no answer. The two flour bags with Cassandra's possessions still lay on the table. He knocked a little louder, still there was no answer. He tied his horse and went to the barn, as he stepped into the aisle of the barn, he saw Cassandra in a stall with a small pinto, she was crying. He walked down the aisle not trying to hide the sound of his movement, when he got close, he spoke, "I would guess that may be your sister's horse?"

Cassandra dried her eyes, nodded and replied, "I had the greatest family one could hope for."

Mark was reminded that he had the beginnings of a family he felt the same about, upon losing his family he wanted to be far away. Cassandra spoke about her loss without anger.

He marveled at the adjustments she was making to a hellish change in her life and showing tremendous maturity in one so young. Mark didn't know what to do or say, "Can I help in any way?"

Cassandra looked up at Mark, he was twenty-eight years old, he was a handsome man, tall and straight; that he respected her in every way during this battle she was thankful. Her mind was a whorl of consideration of her future, just how kind was he? She looked up at him and asked with some trepidation, "At a time like this a hug from my father or brother would go a long way toward helping me to heal."

Mark put his arms about her and gently stroked her back, "Cassandra, you've lost most of your world. If there is anything I can do to help, I'll try my best."

For some time, Cassandra stayed in his arms, he held her warmly and made no attempt to take advantage of the situation, after some time she gave him a gentle squeeze, "Thank you Markus, I think I'll turn Susan's horse loose. Otherwise I'll be out here bawling every day."

When they got back to the house, Cassandra started to work in the kitchen, she poured Mark a cup of coffee then sat down across the table from him and spoke, "You said you'd do whatever was needed to help me out of this situation?"

Mark didn't hesitate, "Yes. Just let me know what you'd like."

Cassandra looked carefully into his eyes, "Even if I told you to rip up the bill of saleI gave you, and give me the title back?"

Mark took the title and the bill of sale and put it into her flour sack. He then reached across the table and took her hand, "Cassandra, you signed the note when you were exhausted and emotionally distraught. I couldn't hold you to that. If you choose to back out, we'll rip the bill of sale up and you can have the title back."

Mark continued to hold her hands, "Cassandra. I told you before; you are a very thoughtful, wise, caring person. You deserve whatever life you choose. I'll not be a part of forcing something upon you. You make a decision; you let me know what you desire. And, you've been through a lot, so, don't be in a rush; take your time."

Cassandra got the coffee pot, "So you don't mind if I hang around long enough to make up my mind?"

Mark nodded, Cassandra smiled, "Even if it means you'll have to sleep outside until I figure out what it is, I want?"

Mark nodded, "I like it here. I like your company. I can wait as long as it takes."

Cassandra wanted to know if in the back of his mind he may go back home, she questioned, "If it doesn't work out here? Would you end up back in Iowa?"

Mark shrugged, "If it doesn't work out here? I'll try to find another ranch; this time however, maybe I won't be looking for the lonesome part. Iowa and the family there? That is not something I have to avoid, but, like I said, I like it here. Breakfast watching the sun come up from your porch was one of the most peaceful interludes I've had for many years. Iowa? I suppose if I had the right company, and if she insisted on going to Iowa? Maybe I could be pulled away."

Cassandra asked, "What? Do you mean these hills are starting to grow on you?"

Mark nodded as he got up and retrieved his hat; he looked at her and smiled warmly, "Yes Cassandra. The hills are growing on me too."

That night Cassandra lay awake thinking of her future; rested, she no longer wanted to be gone, this was her home and every part of her being told her to remain. Who would she get to share the ranch with? There wasn't a cowboy within fifty miles she was as excited about as… Markus Redmond. His reply to her question whether the hills were growing on him, 'the hills too.' She smiled, she was growing on him…, but he was eleven years older than she, but her

Mom was twelve years younger than her Dad. He would go back to Iowa, only if he had the right company and if 'she' insisted on going to Iowa. The way he looked at her; Markus was talking about her. Like her sister, she had been thinking of marriage for nearly two years now, during that time not one person in the area did she consider. She tossed about in the bed for some time before falling asleep.

Mark was awake early, as he started to the house, he noted a shadow dart from the brush toward the barn. Mark ran into the front of the barn and quickly stepped inside the front door then moved behind a pen so he wasn't outlined in the dim morning light of the doorway. Soon, entering the back of the barn the man was outlined with some kind of unlit torch in his hand, Mark commanded, "Drop the torch or you are a dead man."

The man froze, he held the torch in his left hand. He continued to hold the torch in his left hand and gun in the other as he looked for Mark. Mark smiled as he pulled the trigger. The unlit torch was dropped, the intruder dropped to his knees. Mark ordered, put your hands in the air or this time it's dead center."

He raised his right hand, "My arm is hit. I can't lift it."

Mark moved to his side and picked up the pistol from the ground, "That is where I aimed. Now, when you go back to the Card ranch, I want you to tell your boss this. I'm tired of fooling around. After this, there will be no more wounds to the left shoulder. From now on it will be dead center.

"Do you have any questions?"

He was holding his left shoulder to keep it from bleeding, "You've been hitting us there on purpose?"

Mark nodded, "On purpose. From now on it will be center of the chest. Tell your boss he better get out of the country or be prepared to hang."

As he walked away, he advised, "He won't quit. He wants the water from that valley."

Mark smiled, "Before you go, give me the one hundred dollars he gave you."

He reached in his pocket, "How'd you know he gave us one hundred?"

Mark shrugged, "That's what the others had on them."

Mark asked, "Where does Card have men posted?"

As he stumbled away in the predawn light he replied, "Just at the ranch. He's been sending us out mostly in fours to do damage. Who are you?"

Mark shrugged, "I'm maybe the new owner."

When Mark got to the house Cassandra had the buffalo gun in hand, she seemed relieved, "Heard a shot. You bleeding?"

Mark smiled, he thought he sensed some relief, it made him feel good, "Bet you wanted to have all the fun. I thought of you. I wounded him in the left shoulder. I also told him from now on it would be in the center of the chest. I told him to tell Card to get out of the country or I'd have to take the battle to him. He said Card wouldn't quit, he wants the valley because of the water. He begrudgingly gave up his hundred dollar pay."

While they ate breakfast Cassandra related, "The stream used to go through Card's spread a few hundred years ago, but it cut a new pathway south through Larkin's place. I suppose if Card dammed up the stream and diverted all the water back to the old bed, he would eventually be able to control Larkin's place also. Larkin gets some runoff from the mountains, but most of his water comes from the stream coming out of "Lonesome Valley.""

Mark smiled, "You don't have to call it Lonesome Valley any more. We have had too much company to call it Lonesome."

Cassandra seemed in a good mood, Mark asked, "So boss. What do you suggest for the day?"

Cassandra smiled, "I think I'd like to take a trip to town. Do you think it is safe?"

99

Mark shrugged, "I don't want to encourage you in any way to leave, if I give encouragement it will be for you to stay. But, when I spoke to the gentleman this morning, he said Card's men are all at the ranch. With your eyesight, if you stay out in the open and take that buffalo gun with you, you should be safe.

"If you do leave, will you be coming back to the ranch?"

Cassandra shrugged, she watched his every expression trying to read his feelings, "If I don't return the ranch will be yours."

It was obvious the news of ownership didn't make Mark happier, "If you don't come back, I'll surely have to call it Lonesome Valley."

Cassandra smiled, "And if I do make it back?"

Mark smiled and shrugged, "We'll figure out a more appropriate name."

When Cassandra left, she didn't take the two flour sacks with her, she went above the graves to view the surroundings before returning to her horse. As she mounted, she again looked into Mark's eyes for a few moments, then smiled and said, "Sleep in the rocks above the house, that way they won't catch you napping."

Mark nodded, "Good advice." Mark handed her the five hundred dollars, "Put this in the bank in your name."

Cassandra put the money into her pocket and took one longer and searching look into the eyes of Mark before she left the ranch at a ground eating canter.

Mark watched until she was out of sight, then said to himself, "Well, what are you waiting for you fool, do you think she'll turn around and come racing back?"

The next day Mark fended off two attacks with no bloodshed, late in the second day the third attack came from the ridge across the valley. Two men made their way through the ridgeline and came down in the valley some distance behind the house. Mark had been watching them for some time, he looked the area over near the drift fence and down by the stream, the twosome was all he could see. He was about to fire when he heard shots coming from far downstream, the bullets were hitting the house; he thought the gunfire was a diversion for the twosome coming up behind the house.

Mark checked one more time, there was nobody coming by way of the stream, just the twosome below him behind the house could be seen. He moved through the rocks to get closer and above the house, he found a good hidden spot in the rocks, then took careful aim and shot. The first man went down, the second was in the open looking about to try to find where the shot came from, Mark shot the second man in the shoulder. When he stood Mark spoke, "Leave your guns on the ground walk toward the side of the house."

After tossing his rifle and handgun on the ground the man grasped his wounded shoulder and protested, "They are shooting at the house."

Mark laughed, "Get going. Maybe they will recognize you."

Mark walked out of the rocks and met the wounded man. Mark stayed behind the house, "You've spent quite a bit of time sliding around that rock surface getting around behind the house. Card pays you boys well. Is the hundred in your pocket?"

He touched his pocket, Mark smiled, "Tell you what, take your pants off."

The man did as he was told, "Now get going, if you don't get shot by your men you are going to hang anyway unless you get out of the country."

Mark walked him around the side of house, "You better tell all the rest of your friends that have left shoulder wounds to get out of the country, you are all pretty well marked for the noose. For now, the way I figure it, the rest of Card's men are down by the stream somewhere providing a diversion for you two. You can walk down there and climb through the fence, if they don't shoot you, they should take care of you."

After some time, Mark put the captured guns in the hay in the barn, saddled his horse and went to drag the body outside the gate where Case's grave and the rest of Card's men's graves were. He roped the foot of the man and with shovel in hand towed him out beside the other graves.

That evening Mark thought about Card, he had been sending men over at the rate of four a day for five or six days, he thought, Card knows he is dealing with someone outside the family. Either tonight or early in the morning they would attack in force. He prepared a defense in the rocks above the house with guns and ammunition in three places giving him vantage points for attacks from three directions. The most likely form of attack would come simultaneously from below the barn and through the front gate, his firing positions took into account protection from both directions while shooting. He doubted if there would be any more men working their way behind the house into the back of the valley.

When it was fully dark, he made a trip out to the gate with empty tin cans and rigged an alarm, then he made his way into the rocks above the graves and prepared his bedroll. The next day would make it the third day of waiting for Cassandra's return. It only took a half day to get to town, Mark figured perhaps she would not return. He had been thinking he had to stay and protect her home... he thought, wishful thinking... Perhaps, if Card didn't attack in force tomorrow, maybe he would take the battle to him...

Mark forced himself to sleep, it was just breaking day when the cans on the gate clattered to the ground. Mark leveled his Winchester at the gate. He was about to fire, then thought, maybe it was Cassandra returning, he waited. A force of at least ten men galloped down the lane, Mark opened fire. He emptied his rifle, then ducked into another position while the bullets whined about him.

Again, he emptied another Winchester into the riders, again he ducked back into another firing position. Now the bullets were striking the rocks all around him as he went to the third position and snatched up another rifle. This time he waited for better light and a good target. With full light there would be no sign of flare from his barrel to give away his location as he shot. He waited and listened for activity. Someone was now in the house, he could hear noise as if they were looking for something, then he recalled the title to the ranch.

It was full light, someone was inside the barn and probably looking for his position. Mark could see his boot, Mark aimed at the board wall he was hiding behind, chest high and squeezed off a shot. A hail of bullets rained through the rocks, this time they were just shooting, not at his position. Mark slid over so he could see the house and the barn, someone in the house walked by the door, Mark aimed at the next window, when he saw movement, he pulled the trigger.

Mark moved back up so he could see the graves, it was a likely spot they may attempt their assault from. He reloaded one of the rifles and waited. There were two bodies in the lane, two horses were down and closer to the house another body lay in the pathway. He heard the sound of a shoe on a rock and lifted his rifle; suddenly someone darted across the opening behind a rock below him. Mark aimed and waited, a few seconds later another tried the same, Mark shot him as he dove for the cover of the rock. Immediately Mark swung his aim to the rock, the one behind the rock rose, Mark shot, a bit too low, his bullet hit the rock and sprayed lead and rock fragments into the screaming face of the attacker.

Mark quickly went back down to the firing position overlooking the house in time to see three men dart into the rocks below him. He fired three shots, glancing shots off the rocks beside the three men. One of the men ran back toward the house, Mark was able to get a bullet into him then he quickly made his way back further into the rocks carting two rifles with him. He figured his cause was nearly lost now, once they got into the rocks, they would be able to surround him. He moved higher and a little farther away from the house.

Mark checked the loads of the two rifles, his two handguns were still full and ready. He leaned back against a rock and smiled; about now he would like to be eating breakfast with Cassandra and watching the sun rise. He decided if at all possible, he would try to make sure the ranch was safe in case she wanted to return. Mark knew he didn't stand much of a chance attacking, but that was the way it was going to be.

He crawled on top of a rock, he knew nobody was above him, he lifted his head high enough to watch the barn, from the barn they may be able to hit him. There was nobody keeping watch from the barn, they were all coming up through the rocks to get him. He inched a little higher so he could see the house and down into the rocks below him. There was a half-dozen men sneaking up through the rocks toward where he had been shooting from.

One of the men below him rose and pitched backward, then came the sound of a buffalo gun fired from somewhere out on the prairie. Then another man yelled followed by the report of the buffalo gun. The attackers turned to see who was shooting, another man screamed in pain, another report came from the buffalo gun. While their attention was diverted Mark shot into the arm of one of the men hiding below him, another had nowhere to turn. He dropped his rifle and held his hands in the air.

Mark spoke to those remaining, "Throw your guns out onto the ground, raise your hands in the air. You are covered from both directions."

Mark slid off the rock, "I'm coming down there. Keep your hands high in the air and I think you'll be safe."

Mark made his way down through the rocks, "You are all going to walk down toward the graves, keep your hands in the air and you may not get shot."

Mark had four men in front of him they walked slowly thinking they may still be shot any moment, "Where is Card? I expected him to be here today."

104

One of the men glanced to his right, Mark looked off in that direction, suddenly the buffalo gun sounded again and one lying in wait for him pitched out into the opening. He lay on the ground clutching his left shoulder. Mark decided to make the entire group a little more skittish, "You boys tell me about the next one or I'll start firing from behind. Normally I wouldn't back shoot a man, but in you men's cases I'll make an exception. Anyone who would murder an entire family doesn't deserve fair play."

Mark had been keeping low behind the rocks as he descended, now he decided to stay put for the time being, "Boys. Is Card in the house?"

They weren't going to give an answer, "Boys, one by one I want you to take your hundred out of your pockets and give it to the tall skinny one. One at a time, better do it slow."

When he finished Mark directed, "Tall and skinny, you put the money on the ground, then go to the house and invite Card out here and anybody else that's in the house. You stay out by the hitch-rail in case I decide to shoot your sorry carcass."

Bootless, the tall one tip toed out through the pebbles toward the hitch-rail, when the rest were all without boots, Mark ordered, "Now, all of you, go stand in the lane next to that downed horse."

Mark knew if he walked out into the opening, he would get shot by whoever was in the house, the tall and skinny emissary was having no luck talking them out of the house. Mark looked off onto the prairie, he couldn't see where Cassandra was shooting from. Off to his left he could see a cloud of dust. Soon he could make out a large group of men headed toward the gate, he saw Cassandra on her horse with the buffalo gun across her lap.

The one leading the group had a shiny star on his chest, Mark waited, for his part the siege was over. The Marshall introduced himself, "I'm Marshall Jase Woodman. Looks like you boys with the dirty feet aren't going too far. Where's Card?"

One of the men answered, "In the house."

As the Marshall turned his horse toward the house a shot was heard inside, Card evidently knew he was done.

Cassandra looked up toward Mark sitting behind a rock grinning broadly, obviously happy to see her return. With her hands on her hips she spoke, "Markus Redmond. I'm glad to see you are in one piece. I brought the Marshall and some men for burial detail. And, I asked William Thorton to come along. Reverend William Thorton. We'll have some graveside prayers to take care of. And, I thought…, while we were at it, I was hoping you and I, maybe we could have another use for the reverend."

As a smiling Markus Redmond quickly made his way down from his position, Mark looked into the smiling and anxious eyes of Cassandra. Mark took her hands and whispered, "Does this mean I'll be able to sleep inside the house?"

Cassandra smiled happily, she whispered in response, "Just as soon as the preacher takes care of the wedding details and the company leaves."

They walked to the house, Card was being carried out. Inside the place was littered with items moved about during the search for the title. Cassandra gasped, "What in the world were they looking for?"

One of the prisoners answered, "He was looking for the title."

Cassandra stepped to the kitchen table and removed the title from one of the flour sacks, "Wonder why he wanted the title, it's no good without a signature and a bill of sale."

The same prisoner offered, "He said the entire family was dead and someone else had taken over. He was going to tell the law he was just protecting the property. He wanted that water pretty bad."

Cassandra shook her head, "If he would have come to Dad and talked, Dad may have diverted half the stream onto his land."

It was early evening, the new graves were dug and filled and everyone had left for town. Cassandra led Mark up above the graves and had him sit down in the same position he was in when she collapsed into his lap. She sat in his lap and put her head on his chest, "This is my first memory of you. We'll build a lifetime of wonderful memories here in Lonesome Valley."

Mark smiled, held her close, she lifted her chin to kiss him as he smiled and replied; "We don't have to call it Lonesome anymore."

Cassandra wrapped her arms about his neck and replied, "Lonesome is what brought you here. So Lonesome Valley is what we'll call it."

Mark kissed her, she returned the kiss eagerly, as he held her, he whispered, "Lonesome Valley it is, Mrs. Redmond. Somehow I doubt that any of our future memories will be lonesome."

re they looking for?"

One of the prisoners answered, "He was looking for the title."

Cassandra stepped to the kitchen table and removed the title from one of the flour sacks, "Wonder why he wanted the title, it's no good without a signature and a bill of sale."

The same prisoner offered, "He said the entire family was dead and someone else had taken over. He was going to tell the law he was just protecting the property. He wanted that water pretty bad."

Cassandra shook her head, "If he would have come to Dad and talked, Dad may have diverted half the stream onto his land."

It was early evening, the new graves were dug and filled and everyone had left for town. Cassandra led Mark up above the graves and had him sit down in the same position he was in when she collapsed into his lap. She sat in his lap and put her head on his chest, "This is my first memory of you. We'll build a lifetime of wonderful memories here in Lonesome Valley."

Mark smiled, held her close, she lifted her chin to kiss him as he smiled and replied; "We don't have to call it Lonesome anymore."

Cassandra wrapped her arms about his neck and replied, "Lonesome is what brought you here. So Lonesome Valley is what we'll call it."

Mark kissed her, she returned the kiss eagerly, as he held her, he whispered, "Lonesome Valley it is, Mrs. Redmond. Somehow I doubt that any of our future memories will be lonesome."

Introduction; "The Hash Knife Rustlers"

When I was trying to select samples of my stories, I came upon the following short story. The Hash Knife Rustlers had remained hidden in the bowels of my computer for quite a few years. While looking for something unrelated, I found the following story, modified it a bit and decided to include it. It is fairly typical of what I've written in terms of the earlier western romance stories. The hero, Blaine, sets out on the trail of three men, after a shootout, he thinks he is done but returning the horses to their rightful owner draws him to a ranch, rustling, saving a family and finding love.

The Hash Knife Rustlers

Blaine followed three sets of hoof prints ever since he left Billings, Montana. Now he figured that the three men he was following were trailing behind a single rider, he knew the fourth rider was always out front, his horse's hoof prints were never seen to cover the trailing threesome's hoof prints. Blaine had put on a lot of miles since the shooting in Billings and he didn't have a clue how far or where the threesome would lead him.

He suddenly noted that all four tracks ended. Traces of brush marks indicated the tracks were purposely rubbed out. He slowed his horse and looked the trail over and noted some of the deeper prints were still barely visible. The steel dust had a mind of his own, a short way ahead suddenly the horse walked off the path and stopped on the edge of a dry wash. Blaine heard moaning, he quickly dismounted and discovered the body of a man mostly covered by a caved in wall of the dry wash.

Blaine knew instantly the guy didn't crawl under the bank and cave the wall in on top of himself on purpose or by accident. He now understood the reason why the trail was covered. The threesome had caught up with the one they were following.

Blaine quick slid down into the dry wash and gave the guy a sip out of his canteen. After he took a sip of water he pushed the canteen away and told Blaine it was a waste of water. In a short five minutes Blaine found out his name was Roland Williams he owned the MJ ranch about one-hundred miles west of where they were just shy of Livingston. He said three men stole his money and his horse. He said one of the men was named Rupert, he heard one of the others call Rupert by name.

Blaine took him out of the dry wash and buried him, the grave was shallow so he covered it with rocks. Then he looked for tracks. The threesome he was following covered almost every trace of their tracks close to where they waylaid Williams but not far up the road he picked up two sets of tracks heading west. Judging from the tracks it looked to Blaine like one horse was being led. Another mile down the road and the other two rejoined the one leading Roland Williams horse. Not much later in the afternoon Blaine could see a little town up ahead.

Blaine thought the threesome he was following didn't have much more than a half day's start. He thought they would feel pretty confident that Roland Williams was dead and his body would never be found. Blaine was pretty sure of what he was up against. He would be going against three men that would rob, murder a man in cold blood and throw him in a ditch. Blaine wanted all the edge he could get.

There was only one saloon in little town of Columbus, it was late in the afternoon and it was busy. Blaine tied his horse to the hitch rail and looked at the hoof prints. He picked out the four horses he had been trailing. He walked across the street to a café, he had a way to go yet. With a belly full he walked across the street, checked his war piece and entered the saloon.

Blaine got a beer, he sat in the corner and waited for someone to mention Rupert. Within five minutes Blaine figured he had Rupert picked out. Another few minutes and he was sure.

A tall mean face gent got up from a card table and said, "Lost my money, but I got a horse and saddle outside I'll sell. Twenty bucks. Look him over, it's the tall black horse." The one that appeared to have won most of the money tossed a twenty dollar gold Eagle on the table and said, "I'll take the horse Rufus, sounds like a fair price."

Rufus moved to the bar, he was now standing between two other men. Blaine could see they knew each other. He thought if he made his play right then he may be able to get some help from the rest of the crowd. Blaine figured Roland Williams got Rufus mixed up with Rupert. Blaine came right out and asked him, "Rufus! Roland Williams figured your name was Rupert."

Blaine had raised his voice, the saloon was suddenly silent. Rufus growled, "I don't know any Roland."

Rufus gave Blaine a mighty mean look, Blaine could see guilt written all over him. Blaine got up and faced Rufus and said, "Roland is the guy you left in that dry wash to die half buried with a bullet in his back. Roland lived just long enough to name you. You three stole all his money and his horse, that big black out front."

Rufus didn't even bother to try to lie his way out, he just grabbed for his side gun. One reason Blaine put a lot of miles between him and Billings was because the Billings sheriff spread the word that he was getting too good at jerking that hog-leg of his. There were two men buried in Billings with lead from his .44 in them. Rufus wasn't the fastest, Blaine planted two chunks of lead in Rufus's chest before the gent to Rufus's right got into the fracas. Blaine hit the second one hard under the right armpit, the bullet went through him and hit the third man dead center.

Rufus and the unlucky one were dead and the one with the bullet through his armpit was on his knees in a fast-growing

111

puddle of blood. Blaine stepped to the bar and picked up the twenty dollar gold Eagle. Blaine asked the wounded one, "Do you have any of the money left?"

The wounded man shook his head, "Rufus lost it all."

Blaine turned to the men at the card table, "The horse wasn't his to sell. The money he gambled with wasn't his."

The threesome at the table said nothing. Blaine asked, "How much did you win from him?"

Still there was no response. Blaine said, "I've gambled a bit. I know just what I won or lost. Rufus and those two killed Roland Williams. Roland said he left a wife and kids behind. Are you boys going to steal from a widow and her family?"

Still there was no response, Blaine shook his head in in disgust. As he shook his head and said, "You, are three sick thieving bastards."

Blaine turned to the wounded one, he was laying on his side, one of the men that attended to him said, "He's gone."

Blaine glanced about at the crowd, "What about the widow and her children of the man they ambushed?"

The crowd didn't seem to care about the plight of the widow as long as she wasn't from their town. Before Blaine stepped out the door, he told the crowd, "None of the rest of you people are far behind those three thieves."

Blaine gathered the reins on all four horses and led them out of town. When he got to the west end of town, there was a breeze out of the west. He considered lighting a fire, he figured the whole town would go up in smoke. Blaine shook his head, he figured there wouldn't be much of a loss.

Three days later he arrived at the MJ ranch. In a brief talk at the water tank he learned from Mary Jane Williams that her husband Roland had over six-hundred dollars stolen from him. Blaine thought he should go back and burn the town. One look at the MJ and he could see that the money would've done a whole lot of good. Mary Jane was a tough woman, she took Roland's death in stride. Blaine thought she knew when she saw him come into the ranch leading Roland's horse and the others with empty saddles.

Mary Jane motioned for the rest of the family to put the guns down. That made Blaine feel a little bit better, that rifle aimed at him from the window didn't make him feel any too welcome. Blaine thought he was going to unload the four horses and get on the road but Mary Jane invited him to supper.

Blaine took care of the horses, when he got into the house he didn't notice any tears. There were seven kids in all, Mary Jane introduced them from the oldest to the youngest. Blaine didn't think he'd be around long enough for the names to matter but he politely listened. Rose was eighteen, she was a slight gal and looked like she spent most of her time inside. The next was sixteen year-old Molly. Molly appeared to be a little more solidly built, Blaine would guess that she shared pretty much the harder outside work. The next was Pete, he had a slight smile. Blaine guessed Pete would be pretty easy to get along with. Twelve year-old Robert was all business. He was standing next to that sharps .50 caliber rifle that Blaine saw sticking out the window earlier. Blaine decided right away Robert would be a steady one.

The next one in line was Faye. Blaine figured if good humor was doled out to the family, Faye ended up with most of it. She stepped forward and offered her hand with a playful smile. The next in line was six-year-old Catherine, Catherine stayed pretty close to her mother's dress. The last one was John at two years old. Blaine figured whatever humor was left over after Faye took the lion's share, John ended up with. John wasn't hiding, he wanted to shake hands like Sister Faye.

They all sat down to a very good meal, Blaine discovered Mary Jane and Rose were great cooks. He was getting ready to head down the road, he didn't know how far town was when Mary Jane asked, "I don't suppose you would be interested in staying on and helping us for a while as foreman."

Blaine had looked the MJ over as he rode in, as far as Blaine could figure, he would be the only hand. He smiled and asked, "How big of a crew do you have?"

Mary Jane smiled as she answered, "Molly the two boys and you. Now and then Faye will go along mostly to get in your hair."

Blaine grinned at her honesty, he had noted with interest two strange brands on the horses he brought along that were owned by the men that killed Roland. He noted a brand on a cow not far away from the MJ buildings, the cow brands looked like they were blotted over. He made a quick decision, "I'll stay for a while and get the way of things. In a week or two we can come to some sort of an agreement if I decide to stay."

By the time Blaine got the saddles and the horses taken care of it was getting dark. He made a place to sleep in the barn in the back seat of the buggy.

In the morning Mary Jane rang the dinner bell, Blaine headed to the house to eat. He would spend the day getting the lay of the land. It was decided Molly and the two boys would show him the northeastern border to the ranch. Faye decided she was going to tag along. With a generous smile Faye said, "It may take all five of us to move Colonel Bradbury's Box B cattle off from our land."

Blaine looked to Mary Jane who explained, "The Colonel doesn't seem to recognize our boundary."

Blaine now knew where the brands on the horse came from which raised more questions. Were the horses stolen or was the Box B in some way connected to the Hash Knife rustling. He asked, "Do you have a title that shows your boundary?"

Mary Jane nodded, "Yes."

Blaine asked, "Will your kids be able to show me where the boundaries are?"

Mary Jane nodded, "Yes. We all know the boundaries."

That was all Blaine needed to know, an hour later they were driving Box B cattle north. They fanned out and on the return trip collected another small group of cattle. Blaine

114

noted with interest a few of the Box B brands were blotted over other brands. It was early evening when the five riders got back to the ranch. Blaine figured they would they would take one more trip north the next day removing Box B cattle. The only thing Blaine didn't enjoy during the day was a constant squabbling that went on within the family. Even as he was washing up he heard the same kind of thing going on inside the house. When he stepped inside they seemed to stop.

Blaine smiled to himself, he considered his mother who always said he was too outspoken. Blaine decided there was too much tension in this family, he didn't understand it and he surely didn't like it.

They sat down at the table and Mary Jane said a prayer. When she said amen, Blaine spoke his piece. He cleared his throat and spoke, "When we worked today the only thing I didn't like was the disrespect you showed each other. Tomorrow we will complete the job of moving the Box B cattle off your ranch. You are all good workers. You are also a family. You will treat each other with respect. There will be no more snapping at one another. If you can't talk agreeably to one another, then remain silent or find a way." Blaine looked around the table at a lot of wide open eyes, then he looked down at Johnny by his side and winked. Blaine smiled as he said, "Now would you please pass the potatoes. Johnny is hungry."

The next day went much better, there was a lot of respect shown, no more snapping. It was late in the afternoon when Blaine rode up beside Molly. Molly had been too quiet. She had thought she was the boss the day before and she barked orders in a pretty severe manner. As Blaine rode beside her he said, "Molly. I want you to know, your brothers and Faye, they look up to you. You are a hard-working leader for them to pattern after. My mother always told me, you can make more headway with a smile."

Molly was quiet for a bit then she said, "Dad always left a lot of the jobs in my hands. I had to give orders."

Blaine was a bit saddened by her statement, her father set her up for failure when it came to her brothers and sisters. He nodded and chuckled, "I won't take your job as leader away. I just want you to understand, how you get along with each other is even more important than the job you have to do."

"What do you mean?"

"Molly, I mean that your family is everything."

Molly seemed to soften a bit, "So. What do I do?"

Blaine shrugged, "As you work, work with them, and mostly just enjoy them when you can. Won't be too many years and you'll have a family of your own. Then, believe it or not, you'll miss your brothers and sisters. So, enjoy them now."

They had twenty Box B cattle in a bunch a quarter of a mile from the line when two Box B boys came galloping toward them. Blaine didn't like the implied threat. He told Molly, "They don't look any too friendly. Take the others and head back to the ranch, right now."

Molly clearly didn't want to leave. She said, "You will need help."

Blaine smiled, "Thanks Molly. Go. Now."

Molly gathered the other three quickly and rode back toward the ranch. Blaine kept the cattle going toward the approaching twosome. He glanced over his shoulder, Molly and her charges were about out of gunshot range. He hurried the cattle along.

When the galloping twosome approached he was still a short distance from the boundary. Blaine knew the cattle would disperse when the twosome arrived. While they were dodging cattle Blaine pulled his .44.

One of them yelled, "What the hell are you doing?"

Blaine smiled and calmly answered, "Since I have the .44 and you are on the MJ spread, I'll ask the questions. What the hell are you doing intimidating the Williams children on their own land?"

The same one snapped back, "Those are Box B cattle."

Blaine's tone got a bit colder, "What's your name? Just in case I have to bury you here on the MJ."

116

"Jace Hardgrave."

Blaine chuckled at the name and the reference to his burial. Blaine then said, "Hard-grave. You two take your guns out real slow and throw them on the ground."

Hardgrave tossed his gun on the ground, the other followed suit. Hardgrave snapped, "What are you going to do?"

Blaine got down and retrieved their guns. He then told them, "I'm going to watch you two gather those cattle and drive them onto Box B. Get started; I don't want to miss supper."

Hardgrave stood his ground, "You feel pretty good when you got the drop."

Blaine thought he had it with Jess Hardgrave. He dropped his reins and slid out of the saddle. Blaine snapped, "Hardgrave! Get down!"

Hardgrave was a little wary now, he slid out of the saddle. Blaine stepped up to him and slipped a gun into Jace Hardgrave's holster. As Blaine walked backwards he spoke, "Any time you are ready to do something more than talk. Your friend can take your carcass back to the ranch after he gets the cattle off this range."

Blaine stopped less than four paces away. At that range a .44 would almost cut a man in half. Somehow Hardgrave suddenly wasn't so tough.

Hardgrave was silent, Blaine walked forward and took his gun away, he commanded, "Hurry up and move the cattle!"

Hardgrave didn't speak this time, he did as he was told. Blaine got back to the ranch house as everyone was ready to sit down for the evening meal. It was pretty quiet when he entered the dining room. He grinned as he entered, "Did I get back in time for supper?"

As Blaine stepped to the table he put his arm around Molly and said, "Thank you Molly. That was mighty fine of you."

Blaine figured Molly needed to have that bridge rebuilt between them, besides her thought of staying to help him out in a time of need impressed him and needed mentioning. He didn't know what Molly or her mother would think about him putting his arm around her. He went to the wash stand and cleaned up.

With Johnny practically on his lap Blaine gave orders for the next couple of days. There were fence posts and Barb wire in the barn. They would build the drift fence too long ignored on the northeastern part of the ranch that would keep the Box B cattle from entering the MJ.

The drift fence was in and the barbed wire fence stretched, they had put in a hard two weeks of work, it was Saturday about noon, they were walking toward the house when Faye took his hand. Blaine looked down at the mischievous smile he had grown to like and asked, "And, what is on your mind, Faye?"

Sue shrugged and said, "There's a dance in town tonight. Church in the morning. We missed last week."

It was easy for Faye to make a person smile. Blaine asked, "Have you ever been to the dances?"

Sue was excited, she fairly skipped along, "Usually the whole family goes. We stay at a friend's house. Mr. Tollifson's home. We go to church in the morning, then come home."

Blaine shrugged, "I'm game."

Faye sprinted the rest of the way to the house to talk to her mother.

Two hours later the entire family was in the Surrey heading to town. Blaine rode along beside the surrey on his steel dust. Blaine enjoyed the dance and church much more than he thought he would. A lot of people attended the dance and the church service the next day.

Evidently there were a lot of stories about Roland's death and Blaine killing the threesome responsible. Blaine danced with all the girls in the family. Pete and Robert took his lead and danced for the first time. Little Johnny had to get into the act and danced or was carried about the floor most of the night by someone.

While dancing with Molly Blaine related, "Molly, are you having a good time?"

118

Molly was enthusiastic, "I love these dances. I've danced with Robert and Pete for the first time. They even danced with Johnny and Catherine, and even Rose."

Blaine felt good also, he related, "Molly, at times like this; this is what family is all about."

Molly nodded agreement, "Yes. Thank you Blaine."

As the dance ended Blaine related, "You have a great family Molly, and you play a strong part."

After church on Sunday there was a social gathering that the family had not participated in the past. Blaine was hungry, he shrugged and had the family stay. Mary Jane protested for a moment. She explained, "We have never stayed for the social before."

Blaine asked, "Why not?"

Mary Jane smiled as she briefly outlined the problem, "It seems there has always been some friction. I think Colonel Bradbury wants our land, so we've never so much as said hello. I don't know about Alton Langford. He always seemed standoffish. Roland thought we were treated like we didn't measure up."

Blaine smiled, "They are about to eat. I'm hungry. I'd say you measure up just fine. Don't ever allow anyone to look down their nose at you. Besides, I think they are talking mainly about my run-in with the men that killed your husband. Can you tell me who the Colonel is and the Langford's so I don't open my mouth at the wrong time?"

Mary Jane took Blaine's offered arm and walked to the serving table, the rest of the family fell in line. Mary Jane quietly informed, "The Colonel isn't here. Helen Langford is the tall well-dressed woman serving. I don't see Alton or his daughter. It seems his daughter Charlemagne pretty much follows her father's lead. Neither of them were at the dance last night either or any of their hands. Usually they come, they perhaps were building a drift fence."

Blaine smiled at her joke, by the time they got through the line Blaine was carrying Johnny while Mary Jane filled a plate for the two-year-old and was helping Catherine. Blaine looked into the eyes of Helen Langford and sensed a very peaceful, pleasant, kindly and motherly woman seemingly without pretense.

The social was over, there wasn't much interaction on the part of the Williams family except with Wilmer Tollifson, the gentleman that they stayed with the previous night. Blaine thought the same was true at the dance, the family stuck pretty close together. There was little interaction with the rest of the crowd. Blaine didn't know if the town was responsible or if the Williams family was a bit standoffish. The following week they concentrated on the southern part of the ranch. They moved a few of the Langford cattle back across the creek separating the two ranches. They found quite a few marketable MJ stock missed in the previous year's Roundup which they drifted closer to the ranch buildings. Now and then they observed riders from the Langford ranch from some distance. On one occasion Blaine was showing Molly how to maintain taught rope so he could check up on a wound on the thrown steer's flank. When they finished Blaine thought he saw someone looking at them through a telescope from some distance off. At first Blaine smiled, he figured they could look all they wanted as long as the telescope wasn't mounted on a rifle.

After he considered the use of the telescope he changed his mind. He told Molly, "Molly, I'm going to take a little ride over to the hilltop and visit with the neighbors. If there is a problem you take the kids and go home."

Blaine cantered his horse directly up the hill to the one with the telescope. When he got there he introduced himself, "Howdy. I'm Blaine, I work for the Williams family. I understand you are one of the Langford men. When I first saw the telescope, I thought as long as the scope wasn't mounted on a rifle it was all right. Then I got to thinking, since we are neighbors, it isn't the neighborly thing to do. From now on you are welcome to come and talk, but don't be spying."

Getting no response, Blaine touched his hat, turned and rode away.

Sue didn't wait until Saturday at noon to ask about the dance. On Friday at quitting time she took Blaine's hand on the way to the house. With her generous smile in place she asked, "Are we going dancing tomorrow night?"

Blaine shrugged, he smiled and said, "It's up to you Faye." Faye laughed and ran to the house to make the announcement.

Helen Langford was a very observant woman. She remained in the background of family, nevertheless her contributions were great, but given only when she figured they were needed. Most of the time she allowed things to take their course, unless she thought a gentle nudge was necessary to maintain what she considered good family ethic.

Helen watched and listened to the talk about the Williams' new man. She wasn't satisfied with the lack of charity shown by the town when the Williams' father was killed. She didn't like the fact that her husband joined in on the talk. She didn't like the fact that her daughter followed without question her father's lead. She heard the story regarding Blaine killing Roland Williams' murderers, she knew much of what happened at that time in the way of justice was brutal. Helen figured the latest talk that she overheard may get somebody killed. The subject of the talk was the new man Blaine, and the women on the Williams', MJ ranch. Helen had watched Blaine for much of the time at the last dance. Blaine was attentive to all the Williams children including the two-year-old boy and the six and ten-year-old girls. He seemed to respect Mary Jane Williams and of greatest interest was the demeanor of the Williams family shortly after his arrival. The entire family seemed more respectful and caring of one another. The two older boys now danced with their sisters, everyone took time to attend to the younger ones. In all, the Williams family seemed happier and more outgoing.

At this week's dance Helen watched with great interest as Blaine went to the food table and met her daughter Charlemagne for the first time. Blaine had just picked up a piece of pie when he looked up into Charlemagne's eyes. As Charlemagne handed him a hot cider drink both of them seemed transfixed. Helen smiled, Blaine was usually outgoing, now he seemed riveted in place. Finally Helen heard him weakly ask, "If there is space on your dance card, I would be honored to dance with you."

Helen smiled at the genuine nervousness of the usually confident young man. Then her daughter disappointed her with her answer. Charlemagne slowly shook her head as if in a quandary. Finally Charlemagne said, "I… I don't know. I'll be busy."

Helen could see Blaine was confused by her answer, but he politely thanked her no less. When Blaine left to nibble on his pie, she could sense his confusion. Helen scowled at her daughter then walked off to speak to the fiddler.

Helen watched as Blaine finished his pie then decided he wanted to step outside for a breath of fresh air. Sooner or later everybody had to venture outside to visit the outhouses or just to talk or cool down. As Blaine walked down the steps he was met by four men from the Box B.

A tall Box B hand stopped him and said, "You're the new man on the MJ spread."

Blaine stopped, smiled and replied, "Yes, and you are?"

The Box B hand sneered and said, "I'm Barney. I hear on the MJ you've got them all ages."

Blaine swung from the hip, a second later Barney was on the ground with his jaw askew. Blaine turned and went back into the dance hall to get his things.

Helen Langford watched the entire thing, she figured Blaine intended on leaving. She motioned to the fiddler who started playing a waltz. Helen Langford walked up to Blaine, "Young man. The fiddler is playing my favorite waltz. I'd like to dance with you if you would be so kind?"

Blaine smiled, it would be impolite to turn a person down. Blaine answered, "It would be my pleasure Ma'am."

It took Blaine only a moment to recognize he was dancing with a graceful well-schooled lady. He smiled and said, you are Helen Langford. You live just south of the Williams ranch."

Helen nodded, Blaine added, "You are a very graceful dancer."

Helen Langford thought she already knew a lot about Blaine from mere observation. Now she realized he was brought up well, in a very good home, she would be willing to bet he would be complementary about his mother and perhaps his father. Blaine reinforced her opinion when he spoke to her daughter and mentioned her dance card. The dance card was not used in the West, only in the East at dances of the upper classes.

Helen answered, "You were well schooled also. Is that complements of your mother?"

Blaine smiled and nodded, "Yes. You have good insight. My Mom is particular about pomp and circumstance. May I call you Helen?"

Helen smiled, "I would like that. I must ask. What did you think of my daughter?"

Blaine didn't know the beautiful creature serving food was her daughter. He asked, "Did I meet your daughter?"

Helen nodded, "She was at the serving table."

Blaine was honest, "Serving the hot apple cider! My Helen. She is the most beautiful gal I've ever seen."

Helen smiled at his honest answer. She said, "Charlemagne won't be impressed if you tell her she is beautiful. She's looking for somebody that sees her inner person."

Blaine smiled and said, "Thanks for the warning."

As the dance ended Blaine thanked her and said, "I think I'll probably be leaving for the night."

Helen shook her head, "No. Absolutely not. You stay."

123

Blaine admitted, "But Helen. Just before this dance, I think I broke a Box B rider's jaw outside. I'll have the town on my back if I stick around."

Helen reassured, "Not the whole town. I saw it. As far as I'm concerned, he got what he deserved. Besides, the Williams kids need you right now. Rose in particular is looking pretty scared."

Blaine looked to the Williams family, they did look a little scared. Blaine bowed and said, "Rose is a soft-hearted gal. Thank you Helen. My Mom is a long way from here. If I need advice or guidance, I'll be at your doorstep."

Helen laughed as Blaine walked back to the Williams family. Rose did look scared as he said, "I decided to stay. Rose. Would you like to dance?"

Blaine took her hand and led her onto the dance floor. He said, "Rose. Smile. You are prettier when you smile. When you smile it shows who you really are."

Rose replied, "I don't care."

Blaine gently answered, "Of course you care. You are a great person with Johnny and Catherine and Faye. You are a great cook, a super lady. One of the Cowboys or young men here should recognize that and also see that you are a pleasant person to be with."

Rose soberly said, "Dad was all business. Seems he was always snapping at us." For some time Rose was quiet, then she chuckled and replied, "You want me to seem to be a more pleasant person? You want me to take your advice when you just broke someone's jaw?"

Blaine laughed and nodded at her smile, "That's the spirit rose! Keep it up. Think about what all is great about Rose and keep smiling."

Soon a cowboy tapped Blaine on the shoulder, Blaine was ready to fight. The cowboy politely asked, "May I cut in?"

Blaine smiled at Rose and said, "You may. Thank you kindly Rose."

As Blaine stepped back to the Williams family he noted a smile on Helen Langford's face.

Helen Langford moved to her husband's side as Alton Langford spoke to the foreman of the ranch. He was asking, "What did the Box hand say?"

The foreman shrugged, "Don't know. Guess he didn't have time to say too much. He hit him once and broke his jaw. The Box boy, Barney will be eating meals of soup for the next month or so. Another Box B rider, Jace Hardgrave, said Blaine pulled a gun on him a couple weeks ago out on the Prairie. Jace figured he was a dead man. He said he didn't know how much more the Box boys were going to take before they drove him out of the country. I figured if the Box foreman was here there might have been some shooting."

The Langford foreman added, "The Box boys said they didn't know he killed those men over east of here. Two days ago he rode up and told me not to be using the telescope on them."

Alton Langford shook his head, "Bart, tell the boys to avoid him for right now. If he steps on our toes we will show him how we handle his kind."

Bart started to walk off to talk to the other hands. Helen spoke, "Bart. One moment please."

Bart stopped and looked to Helen. Bart understood her to be a very quiet person that every once in a while made the decisions. Helen smiled, "Bart. Explain that business with the telescope."

"They were working around the stream between our ranches, I was on the hill. I was watching them with the telescope. He rode up and told me he didn't want me spying?"

"Is that all that was said?"

"No Ma'am. He said it wasn't neighborly. If I wanted I could come down and talk but I shouldn't be spying."

"How long did you use the scope?"

"It was quite some time."

"Then I agree with him. There are boys and girls working, you overstepped. He was right to admonish you, and you should have thanked him for being neighborly. Don't you agree?"

"I think you are right Ma'am."

"Now Bart. You will tell the crew that the Williams family are our neighbors. We'll treat them like neighbors. No intimidations, no threats, implied or otherwise. For some reason tales are being told. We will not be a part of spreading gossip. Just a few weeks ago the Williams family lost their father. If you look carefully at the family, they are doing well in spite of our distrust; in spite of our complete lack of charity. And, the next time you are working and you see the neighbors, go and say hello. I don't think that any of them will bite. That will be all Bart."

Bart grinned, "Yes ma'am."

After Bart stepped away Helen Langford smiled warmly at her daughter, "Dear. You have been listening to gossip and I think you've created notions in your head that need to be reinforced by facts or gotten rid of. The young man asked you to dance and I think at a minimum you either owe him an explanation or a dance."

Charlemagne smiled at her mother. She knew her mother handed out lessons judiciously, and, she understood her to be right most of the time. She understood that there was a lot of chat about the Williams family and Blaine that were false in her mother's eyes. Charlemagne nodded, "I think you are right. I didn't give him the benefit of any doubt did I?"

Helen smiled, gave Charlemagne a hug and whispered to her, "I can't be too critical. I saw the awestruck look on both of your faces. He said something about your dance card. There aren't too many men out here that even know of the dance card. The boy has had a good upbringing. Just be patient and observe for yourself."

Charlemagne watched as her mother and father danced about the floor. She realized her mother would move mountains for her but her mother would never cease to give advice when it was needed. It was clear that her mother was disappointed in everyone's response to the Williams family.

Charlemagne turned her attention to Blaine, she watched as Blaine danced with the six-year-old Catherine Williams and the little boy, Johnny. Here was a man that killed men on his way to the Williams ranch then soon after threatened a Box B rider. It was said he had little or no reason to break the jaw of the Box B man, she would ask her mother about that. Charlemagne figured the man called Blaine was an enigma. Albeit a very good-looking enigma. She didn't want her looks to be a reason for young men to pursue her, but here she was giving a lot of thought to his looks, and those beautiful blue eyes.

Charlemagne was shocked she was admiring qualities in him as he danced playfully with the young Williams children. Very few of the young men in town would spend time with younger children. The business of a dance card? That was a term used only by the genteel.

The Sunday church and social was uneventful, on Monday Helen Langford took a trip to town. She said she needed a few things. Her first stop was at the telegraph office. She sent a telegraph to the office of the Pinkerton's in Chicago requesting information on Blaine. The telegraph included all information known since the killing of the three men.

The telegraph operator said, "Mrs. Langford. Usually I just do as I'm told. I just want you to know there was a shooting in Billings involving a Blaine. That is all the information I have at this time. The last name may be the same or it may be a different man, or may have been an alias. The timing does match with him."

Helen quietly asked, "And that last name?"

"McNaughton."

Helen added the information given to her in the telegraph to the Pinkerton's.

She was nearly out the door before she returned to request more information from the Pinkerton's. She requested knowledge of the background of the three men that killed Roland Williams.

Helen Langford thanked the telegraph operator and asked that her telegraph remain as discreet as possible. She knew every operator on the line would know of the request given to the Pinkerton's. Some of the operators may even volunteer information. When she arrived back home she noted four horses hitched to the front rail by the house, they had the Box B brand. Charlemagne came out to assist her mother, "Can I help you mother?"

Helen handed her a small box and asked, "I see we have visitors?"

Charlemagne smiled and answered the veiled question, "Colonel Bradbury wants to buy our ranch."

Helen pondered the thought for a moment, then said, "The Williams ranch is in between our two ranches. I wonder why he would want two ranches that far apart."

Charlemagne smiled as she said, "The Colonel has brought his foreman, Duke Bascom with him."

Helen looked at Charlemagne's playful smile, "He's a handsome devil. What do you think of him?"

Charlemagne smiled and nodded, "I agree."

Helen knew her daughter well, she had returned the teasing omitting an answer. Helen asked, "Charlemagne, tell me. The first time you met Duke Bascom, what effect did he have on you?"

Charlemagne shrugged, "I can't recall specifically."

Helen smiled, she didn't like Duke Bascom but he was perhaps the best looking and best connected of the eligible men in the area. That is until Blaine arrived, Charlemagne asked, "Why do you ask mother?"

Helen answered, "Sometimes our feminine intuition is important."

Helen took her daughter's hand and walked up the steps. Alton Langford happily made introductions, "Helen. You remember Colonel Bradbury?"

Helen smiled, "Yes of course. And I recall Mr. Bascom." The Colonel seemed more gracious than he had ever been before. He spoke for five minutes before Helen reined him in. She bluntly asked, "Charlemagne tells me you are interested in purchasing our ranch?"

The Colonel seemed a bit shocked she would bring up the sale of the ranch, he figured it was a subject that would be handled by the men. Colonel Bradbury nodded, "Why yes. I've been talking to Alton. I think I could offer you a fair price."

Helen smiled, she wanted a lot more information, "What sort of a price would you propose?"

The Colonel wanted to close Helen out of the conversation and deal with Alton. For some reason Helen Langford made him nervous. He smiled thinly and said, "I haven't given a specific dollar amount much thought. I'm sure Alton and I can arrive at a figure that we can both agree to."

Helen wasn't having anything to do with being dismissed. She laughed, "Oh, no Colonel. You rode all the way down here. You know the lay of our ranch, you surely have a fair idea what you would be willing to pay?"

Helen took a chair to signify she was going to remain a part of their talk, "I can't be calling you Colonel. What is your first name?"

He liked the Colonel title, he thought it gave him a presumption of authority. Begrudgingly he said, "Donald, Ma'am."

Inwardly Helen smiled. She wanted the price to see how honest he was, then she wanted one more piece of information afterwards. She smiled and asked again, "So Donald, what are you thinking of for a price?"

Donald Bradbury figured he wasn't going to get anywhere bluffing. He tendered his offer, "I thought twenty-five thousand for the ranch, another forty thousand for the cattle.

Helen stood up picked up her box of goods that she had purchased in town and said, "Very good Donald. We will discuss your offer and send a reply to you."

After she stood she asked sort of offhand, "By the way Donald, you would have to manage two ranches that are more than fifteen miles apart. That isn't very inefficient. How in the world would you do that?"

Helen observed a bit of shock on the face of the Colonel, he chose not to answer. Helen went into the kitchen with Charlemagne close behind.

When they were in the kitchen Charlemagne whispered, "When you mentioned the managing of two ranches fifteen miles apart Duke Bascom looked at you pretty close. What do you think that meant?"

Helen smiled, "It means you are pretty observant dear."

Shortly after the Col. and his riders left, Helen summoned the foreman. Helen met Bart on the veranda and gave orders, "Bart I would like you to take two men with you and make a social call on the Williams ranch. I would like you to tell them to be careful. Tell them I have reason to believe that there could be some danger from the riders to their north."

Bart asked, "From the Box B Ma'am?"

Helen smiled and answered, "Yes. But for now we'll call it from the riders north of their ranch."

Bart nodded, he knew the Box B was the only ranch north of the Williams place. He smiled and said, "I won't need any one to ride with me."

Helen said, "Nevertheless take two men with you. As a matter of fact. When the men go out to work on the range, have them go out with at least two men, preferably three."

Bart asked, "Are you expecting trouble ma'am?"

Helen did not commit, "Just being prepared."

Late in the afternoon the next day Aaron Folson rode up to the Langford ranch and asked for Helen. She met Folson on the porch along with Charlemagne. Aaron addressed Helen, "Got some news."

Helen offered Aaron a chair then said, "Go right ahead. I don't keep any secrets."

The threesome were joined by Alton. Helen introduced them, "Aaron Folson, this is my daughter Charlemagne. Charlemagne, this is Aaron... Aaron is the telegraph operator. I asked him to send a telegraph to the Pinkerton's early today looking into the background of Blaine and the three men that killed Roland Williams. What did you find out Aaron?"

Aaron quickly related what he had learned, "Blaine McNaughton was involved in a shootout over at Billings. Two men were killed. Blaine wasn't held, but the telegraph operator in Billings said that the sheriff told Blaine to get out of town. It seems Blaine was somehow connected with the Hash Knife outfit below miles city. I heard they had a mighty rough crew at the Hash Knife. The gunfight was somehow connected to the Hash Knife rustling."

Alton nodded, "I've heard. The Hash Knife crew were death on rustlers but some of the Hash Knife men took to rustling themselves. The owners didn't know who they could trust. This Blaine McNaughton may have been one of those rustlers?"

Aaron shrugged, "I don't know what his involvement was at the Hash Knife. I just got the information that he was somehow connected with the Hash Knife and all that rustling."

Helen asked, "Did you learn anything else?"

Aaron nodded, "The three men that killed Roland Williams? Two of them were part of the Box B crew. I don't have any information on the third man."

Helen asked, "Aaron. Can you stay and dine with us?"

Aaron shook his head, "No Ma'am. I have to be at the telegraph key in another hour."

Helen asked, "Aaron. I would like you to use my name and inquire into the background of Duke Bascom and Colonel Donald Bradbury. Of course I will reimburse you for your time and any costs you incur."

Helen looked to Alton, "Is there anything I missed dear?"

Alton smiled, he sensed his wife was trying to get to the bottom of a few more issues than just Blaine McNaughton, he knowingly chose not to interfere. He added, "Since Bradbury is using the Colonel title with his name, a telegraph of inquiry could be sent to the Department of the Army to see what military service he has seen. As for Blaine

McNaughton, if he's been in a shooting scrape, we will soon enough know how dirtied he is."

Helen smiled, "Yes dear. If he has been dirtied as you say."

As Aaron left, Alton said to Helen, "You know dear. Aaron or one of his cronies could be feeding your inquiry directly to Colonel Bradbury."

Helen stood, "Sometimes I have to trust my intuition dear." Helen looked at Charlemagne, "Don't you think intuition is important dear?"

Charlemagne merely smiled, after discussing her first meeting Blaine McNaughton with her mother she figured if she trusted her intuition during her first look into Blaine's beautiful blue eyes, she was in deep trouble. She smiled as she thought that her dear mother was coaching her to follow her intuition.

Blaine McNaughton, Molly and the two boys were just returning to the ranch as the three riders from the Langford ranch where leaving. Mary Jane met them in the stable. She gave orders to the boys and Molly, "You three get washed up for supper. I have to talk to Blaine for a minute."

As soon as they were alone Mary Jane explained, "Helen Langford sent her foreman over to warn us about a possible threat from riders north of us. Bart said Helen sent him with two men and gave orders to work in small groups and keep a lookout for trouble. That was about all he could say at this time. Helen told Bart the Box B wanted to buy their ranch. She also told Bradbury that our ranch is in between. To that Bradbury did not respond."

Mary Jane looked at Blaine, "What do you think?"

Blaine finished with his horse and turned it loose. Blaine explained, "I've only been on your ranch for a short time. The Box has a lot of land but not much for water. That's why the drift fence was necessary. If Bradbury was interested in expanding, your place would be in the way. Your ranch is smaller but it has two good streams, one that you share with the Langford's. If the Box B buys the Langford ranch they would have to get access to your two streams."

Mary Jane nodded, "I agree. I don't understand the Langford warning, they have never been overly friendly."

Blaine asked, "Have they ever been unfriendly in any way?"

Mary Jane shook her head, "No."

Blaine smiled, "Mary Jane. If I were to trust anyone it would be Helen Langford. She reminds me of my mother. I just don't see her doing anything but good. I'm wondering what Roland's attitude was toward the Box B and the Langford's?"

Mary Jane solved the mystery for Blaine, "Roland was always gruff with the Langfords and he ignored the Box riders to the point where their cattle were getting free range on our land."

Blaine considered that with Roland's standoffish attitude, Blaine better understood the family being so cautious around people. Blaine asked, "You have indicated that you own the stream between you and the Langford ranch but you and Roland told the Langford's they could have access to the stream. It seems to me there isn't any reason to distrust the Langfords. They have more to gain by maintaining friendship with you. I would say, don't look a gift horse in the mouth."

They neared the ranch porch, Mary Jane stopped, "Blaine. I have another question. As you say; I hate to look a gift horse in the mouth, but you've been here a month. You haven't asked for a penny?"

Blaine smiled and questioned, "Yes?"

Mary Jane smiled and tried to explain, "Don't get me wrong. I've been very thankful you are here. Everyone in the family is happy you are here, that includes me. I just don't know what is keeping you here. I know it isn't Rose or Molly, you to treat them like a big brother. Actually, you treat the whole family like a big brother. I think Faye, Catherine and little Johnny would cry for a week if you were to leave."

Blaine offered his arm to Mary Jane. He smiled and said, "For now Mary Jane, it's your cooking. Let's go eat. And don't worry, I'll give you at least two-week's notice before I leave. And, I don't expect a raise."

When they entered the house everyone seemed to be a bit fearful. Rose had spoken to her brothers and sisters, they thought Blaine may be leaving. Two-year-old Johnny took Blaine's hand and said, "Are you staying wiff us?"

Blaine took Johnny's hand and went to the wash basin, "Johnny. There is a dance tomorrow night. I want to watch you and Rose dance. I want to see if you are getting better at dancing."

They arrived at the dance early, Blaine sat on the porch steps and watched as all the little ones played tag in the yard while the women folk set up the tables inside. Johnny was soon worn out and joined Blaine on the steps, he plunked himself in Blaine's lap to take a rejuvenating much-needed rest. A little while later Catherine needed a rest also, she sat beside Blaine and leaned against him like he was a comfortable pillow. It wasn't long and both were up and running again. The music started and the dance Hall was soon filled. Aaron Folson got something to eat then spoke to Helen Langford and Charlemagne, "Nothing different. Blaine McNaughton definitely was at the Hash Knife during the rustling problem. I don't know what part Blaine played yet. He was involved in the shootings at Billings. He killed two Hash Knife men and wounded at least two others. He's mighty handy with a gun. So far nothing yet on the rest of your inquiries. Nothing else on Blaine McNaughton. Nobody knows a thing, or nobody is talking."

Charlemagne thought about the prospect of Blaine being a rustler, she scowled, she didn't like the idea. Charlemagne had watched Blaine sit on the porch, he was satisfied to watch the play of all the little children. She watched as Johnny sat in his lap taking a much-needed rest from play. She watched as Catherine treated him like a pillow. Both children chose to do their resting close to him. Then she felt some shock because for some time she had been actively seeking somebody to share her life. Someone at ease with

134

children. The shock came when she recognized the attributes she wanted in a man may exist in a purported rustler and a killer… with beautiful blue eyes.

Charlemagne watched as Blaine danced with the Williams family. He was not only at ease with them, he enjoyed dancing with them.

Later Blaine walked towards Charlemagne and her mother, when he arrived he surprised Charlemagne. He said, "Good evening ladies. Helen, this is a waltz, would you like to dance?"

As they danced, Blaine said, "Thank you for warning Mary Jane about the possibility of trouble."

Helen smiled and said, "Mary Jane spoke to me when we were setting up. She thanked me also. Mary Jane told me you were somewhat of an enigma. She said you were working for nothing, and she said you'd give her a two-week's notice if you decided to quit. Two-week's notice when you are working for nothing, that's pretty generous."

Blaine nodded, he recognized there was a question in there someplace. He said, "I came into a little money not too long ago. Right now I'm sort of hiding, laying low for a while."

Helen asked, "Is it the law or a woman you are hiding from?"

Blaine laughed and replied, "Neither one." Helen wondered what was causing him to hide. She informed him, "Did you know that two of the men that killed Roland Williams worked for the Box B?"

Blaine shook his head, it was more information than he was able to find. He smiled as he replied, "No. I suspected involvement. I still have two of the Box horses, I didn't know if they were stolen or not. Is that why you warned Mary Jane?"

Helen shook her head, "No. That was a woman's intuition. I just figured that Mary Jane has the access to water and that the good Colonel wants it. And, I figured he intends to get his hands on the MJ ranch any way he can. That is intuition speaking."

135

Blaine smiled at the information, "And here I am. I came to the MJ ranch just to hide."

Helen asked, "You didn't tell me what you are hiding from and what you are trying to do here?"

Blaine smiled as the dance ended, "Next dance we'll talk about it. Right now I'm going to see if your daughter will dance with me."

Blaine escorted Helen to where her daughter Charlemagne was standing. Helen smiled and said, "Blaine I believe you've spoken briefly to my daughter Charlemagne?"

Blaine slightly bowed then asked, "Charlemagne would you be so kind as to have this next dance with me?"

Charlemagne recognized an easy relaxed bond existed between Blaine and her mother. Charlemagne respected the insight of her mother. There was a lot about Blaine that was intriguing. She offered her hand, "Thank you. I would like that."

They danced about for a minute before Blaine was able to get his composure. He finally smiled and confided, "Charlemagne. Your mother told me that you wouldn't be impressed if I told you how pretty you are. I want you to know; the first time I saw you I had trouble speaking. Speaking usually isn't a problem with me. Whether or not you desire to be told you are pretty, I think you are a beautiful lady."

Charlemagne was disarmed by his honesty. She smiled and asked, "And a lady?"

Blaine was quick to respond, "I sense the lady part."

Blaine smiled, "There was no way I could miss the beautiful part. Now that I've had the privilege of dancing with your mother a couple of times I'm sure of the lady part."

Charlemagne asked, "Is this the way you talk to all the girls you meet?"

Blaine chuckled and responded, "I have to admit, when I looked up and saw you at the table serving, I cannot even remember what I said or if you replied. And, I guess I've been told I am sometimes a little too honest."

136

Charlemagne had always appreciated honesty, she didn't like discovering hidden agendas later on. She asked, "You can't recall what was said?"

Blaine smiled, "No. I'm sorry. I'm sure it wasn't too bright. My tongue seemed like it was a foot thick."

Charlemagne thought, since he couldn't recall, then she wouldn't have to apologize. She decided to be honest, "You asked if I had space on my dance card. I'm afraid I told you I was very busy."

Blaine chuckled, "Dance card? I think the last time I was exposed to a dance card, I was about sixteen-years-old in Chicago."

Charlemagne's halfhearted apology was graciously ignored as Blaine continued, "Charlemagne you have a regal name and a very grand lady for a mother. Your dad seems to be a little bit more reserved."

Charlemagne smiled, "Dad takes a little longer to form opinions than Mom does. Mom has a lot of faith in her intuition. Tell me. What brings you to our little Valley?"

Blaine explained, "Roland Williams. I brought his horse back for the Williams family."

Charlemagne nodded, "I've heard. Tell me, why do you stay?"

Blaine wanted to be a little evasive, "Mary Jane asked me to stay. So now, I've got a job."

Charlemagne smiled, "Blaine. You have a job but you haven't been paid. Mary Jane told my mother you haven't even talked about pay, and, you've told Mary Jane you'll give her two-week's notice before you leave. I'd say there are some other reasons you are here."

The dance ended and little Johnny was suddenly at his side. Blaine smiled and said to Charlemagne, "Yes. You have just added to the reasons I'm here. I would love to dance with you again. Maybe we can work on some more reasons for me to stay in the area."

Blaine escorted Charlemagne to her mother with Johnny skipping along. Blaine was then joined by six-year-old Catherine. The three of them danced away holding hands.

Helen asked Charlemagne, "Any insight?"

Charlemagne slowly shook her head, "It is hard to conceive of him shooting people and rustling cattle, he seems very nice."

Helen smiled, "There is a lot more happening with him than we know. But, he assured me that he wasn't hiding from the law or a woman."

Charlemagne was surprised, she smiled, "Mother! He told you that?"

Helen smiled and shrugged, "I asked. He didn't hesitate one bit to answer either."

Charlemagne asked, "And you believe him?"

Helen nodded, "A woman's intuition."

Helen smiled and asked, "When you first saw him at the serving table, what did your feminine intuition say to you?"

Charlemagne smiled and hesitated, Helen chuckled and said, "It's all right dear. I didn't mean to embarrass you. Remember, I was your age once."

Charlemagne laughed and said, "You've taken to reading my mind."

Helen smiled, "I'm your mother, and, I'm not that old yet. I'm going to dance with your father. Why don't you see if you can torment Blaine some more."

Charlemagne laughed and said, "I'm beginning to think I'm the one being tormented."

Helen smiled, "Oh no, no, dear. Try to stay in control."

Charlemagne looked in Blaine's direction, she thought of his deep blue eyes and smiled, "Easy for you to say mother dear."

Sometime later Colonel Donald Bradbury arrived at the dance, strangely without Duke Bascom. The Colonel went directly to Alton Lange to talk of the proposed purchase of his ranch. It wasn't long and Helen joined them.

Charlemagne danced a few more times with Blaine and decided she didn't like the idea of Blaine being a man wanted by the law. During the dances with Blaine, Charlemagne noted a quiet bond developing. His respect and feelings for her seemed obvious and she was drawn to his warmth. She decided she simply loved being in his arms. During the last dance, Blaine said, "Charlemagne. I'm going to ride out to visit with you sometime this week."

Charlene surprised herself. She smiled and replied, "Well, don't wait too long."

On their way to the door Helen asked, "Well Dear, how is everything going with Blaine?"

Charlemagne fanned her face with her hand and replied, "My intuition is working overtime I'm afraid."

Helen showed her approval with a chuckle.

The Williams family left early on Sunday to return to guard the ranch. On Monday at noon Blaine rode into town and stopped at the telegraph station. Blaine asked the telegraph operator, "Any messages for BMC 44?"

Now Aaron Folson was confused. He had sent an inquiry about the man in front of him. Now, Blaine McNaughton was the recipient of the coded telegraph from Miles City. Aaron handed the message to Blaine. Blaine stepped outside and interpreted the lengthy message using a small book. For some time Blaine wrote a message from the same book, finally he brought the message in and gave it to Aaron. Aaron couldn't understand either message. The return message went to miles city.

From the telegraph office Blaine rode out to the Langford ranch, he wanted to talk to Helen Langford and he wanted to see Charlemagne. Part way out to the ranch he noted a rider coming his direction, it was Charlemagne.

Charlemagne stopped her horse and waited for him, he stopped his horse facing her. Charlemagne said nothing, they were all alone; she smiled invitingly, almost a challenge. Finally Blaine asked, "Charlemagne. Have you ever been kissed while riding on a horse?"

139

Charlemagne smiled and replied, "Let me think."

Blaine slowly leaned toward her, Charlemagne had to lean forward to complete the distance. It was a long soft and loving kiss. As they parted Charlemagne thought the kiss was something she wanted… over and over... Charlemagne felt and saw the warmth in Blaine, she was certain he felt the same. Charlemagne turned her horse around as they headed back toward the ranch.

Blaine took her hand while they rode. Charlemagne asked, "To what do I owe the pleasure of your company?"

Blaine smiled, "I came out to see you and now with the welcome I received, I'll have to ride this way very, very, often. By the way the pleasure was all mine."

Charlemagne looked coyly at Blaine and admitted, "No Blaine. The pleasure definitely wasn't all yours."

In response, as they rode Blaine leaned over and kissed her again. Charlemagne smiled and said, "You are welcome to come riding any time. But, we better quit this kissing while riding or someone will get bruised."

As they approached the ranch they rode down a small Hill where they were temporary hidden from view of the buildings. Charlemagne stopped her horse and got off, she smiled and asked, "Blaine would you check my horse? Maybe he's picked up a stone."

Unsuspecting, Blaine stepped down, "What hoof is it?"

Charlemagne smiled and put her arms about his neck, "There is no stone. Just you and I."

Blaine returned the embrace, they kissed for a long time and their bodies seem to meld together, for the time, nothing else existed. Blaine started to release her, Charlemagne wasn't quite ready to part; she remained pressed against him.

Finally she put her head on his chest. She was breathing heavily as she said, "Blaine. You are going to have to visit quite often."

Charlemagne admitted, "I've never felt this way before." She hesitated, then against her wishes added, "We better be going."

140

They rode in silence back to the buildings where Charlemagne finally said, "Help me take care of my horse, then you can come up to the house to talk to Mom."

After they unsaddled and put Charlemagne's horse in the pen, Charlemagne stopped him in the confines of the horse stall. She pressed him against the stall and kissed him for some time. Finally she backed away, she smiled and said, "I just wanted to know if those kisses keep getting better."

Blaine nodded, "Wow. Yes. However, we can't rest on our laurels, we'll have to keep working on them."

As he started to lead his horse to the house Charlemagne stopped him. "Tie your horse in the stall for the time being."

Blaine was invited to the house, both Alton and Helen were there. They talked of horses and cattle for a time then Helen smiled and asked," I know this isn't the next dance but, maybe you can tell us why you are hiding and who you are hiding from?"

Blaine smiled as he pulled the telegraph from his pocket and handed it to Helen. She looked it over then admitted, "It doesn't make any sense."

Blaine laid the telegraph on the table and explained, "This is from a Pinkerton detective office in Miles city. Three years ago I was hired to look into losses at the Hash Knife holdings in Montana. The owners are friends of my father's. I hired on for a year, I worked as a rider. After the first year we ended up getting rid of most of the hands. They were rustling from the ranch while they were killing off rustlers that dared steal from the Hash Knife.

"Needless to say I made a lot of enemies. I caught up with a few of them in Billings. I followed three more out of Billings. I was told they were part of the rustling somehow connected to the Hash Knife. Unknowingly, after I found Roland Williams half buried with a bullet in his back, I had a run-in with the three of them. Once I got Roland's horse back and explained to his wife, I figured I was all done with the rustlers. But when I got to the MJ, I saw a few strange brands on cattle that matched the brands on the horses I got

141

from Roland's killers, the Box B. I decided then to stick around. Thanks to your telegraph, I found out there was a definite connection between the Box B and the Hash Knife rustling. You are quite the detective Helen."

Helen looked at Charlemagne and replied, "Just a woman's intuition. Does your telegraph say anything about the Colonel or Duke Bascom?"

Blaine shook his head, "False names. Oh, yes. Don't expect a reply to your telegram about the Colonel or Duke. If the information comes back, the telegram will be coded so they won't be able read it."

Alton asked, "We were told you were asked to leave Billings?"

Blaine nodded, "Yes Sir. I had a little run in with some men that were rustling Hash Knife cattle. The Sheriff agreed to ask me to leave to keep my cover. He set me on the trail of the three men I shot it out with in Columbus. They robbed Roland Williams, shot him in the back and left him buried barely alive half covered in a dry wash."

Blaine smiled, "So far I think my cover has worked. I don't think they know who I am. Of course I'm not sure who they are but I think they are on the Box B."

Helen smiled and asked, "So what do you do when this is all over?"

Blaine explained, "I know it's mighty sudden, but Mary Jane has been asked to move to town and marry the widower, Tollifson. I guess they've been friends for many years. Rose isn't far behind, there's a cowboy getting pretty serious with her. Molly has had two Cowboys come to visit her. I just might buy the MJ and become your permanent neighbor."

Alton asked, "Roland has always allowed my cattle to use the southern branch of the stream bordering our properties."

Blaine nodded, "Mary Jane told me about the agreement. The only difference, we would have to put it in writing for you so you won't have to worry about water use in the future."

Blaine smiled, "He leaned forward, looked at Alton and said there's one more thing I would like to ask?"

Alton seriously answered thinking there was going to be some condition placed on his access to the water. Alton asked, "Yes?"

Blaine took Charlemagne's hand, "I would like your permission to court this wonderful daughter of yours?"

Charlemagne placed her hand on his and said, "I thought you'd never ask."

Alton was somewhat surprised at Charlemagne's reaction, "That would be up to Charlemagne, so it looks like you have your wish."

Blaine looked at Charlemagne and said, "I'll see you soon then."

Charlemagne smiled and said, "I'll walk you out to your horse."

When they got to the stables Charlemagne again pinned him to the wall in the horse stall and kissed him. Again they seem to meld together in a hot bliss. After an immeasurable time Blaine came up for a breather. Charlemagne smiled and said, "Now do you understand why I had you leave your horse in the barn?"

Blaine kissed her briefly and replied, "Yes. I can see I am going to have to rely on your judgement in the future."

After another heated exchange Blaine rode off toward the MJ. Until he was nearly out of sight Charlemagne stood and watched. Finally she walked to the house, her mother met her on the porch. Her mother asked, "Well. Is he a pretty good kisser?"

Charlemagne was still flushed. She sounded indignant, "Mother!"

Charlemagne then answered, "I didn't want it to end."

Helen laughed, "That's a good sign. I figured when it took fifteen minutes for him to get into the saddle, something more than idle chat was occurring."

Helen asked, "When will you see him again?"

143

Charlemagne smiled, "Come to think of it, he said something about in three days it would be all over. Then we'd be seeing a lot of each other."

They talked for a half hour before the telegraph operator arrived. Aaron was invited onto the porch and given a cup of coffee. Helen then asked, "Aaron, what news do you have for us?"

And shook his head and started, "Today Blaine McNaughton himself showed up at the office to collect a telegraph message. It was a lengthy one. And it was in a code used by the Pinkerton's. Not only did he receive a message in code he sent a message in code."

Helen asked, "So Mr. McNaughton may be a Pinkerton?"

Aaron nodded his head, "Yes indeed. He's somehow connected with the law."

Helen asked, "Did you get anything about the Colonel or Duke Bascom?"

Erin shook his head, "Nothing. The Pinkerton's you hired usually are sending telegraph messages back and forth, there has been nothing."

Helen shook her head thoughtfully, "Well Aaron. No news is good news as they say.

"Are you able to stay and dine with us?"

Aaron stood, "I have to head back to the office, maybe another time."

After Aaron left, Helen sat quietly for some time, then she exclaimed, "Three days and it will be all over!?"

Charlemagne wondered what her mother was thinking, "That's what Blaine said; in three days it will be all over."

Helen suddenly stood, "I'll get your father; you go get Bart."

A short time later Helen gave orders, "I believe perhaps in three days men will arrive from Billings or Miles City to visit Colonel Bradbury. I need to keep a few people safe during the next three or four days. Bart I want you to take four men and bring the Williams family back here. Have the rest of the men report to Alton as soon as they come in from work. Alton will put our men to work guarding the Williams

144

family here. There will be no work for the next four days. Bart you will leave the four men at the Williams ranch as guards and you will bring back the Williams family.

"Charlemagne. I think the two Williams boys will remain there. Maybe Molly too. They may need a good cook. Do you want to go over there for the next three or four days?"

Charlemagne rose, "I'll go pack some things."

Helen spoke to Alton, "Alton. Talk to the men and make sure they keep an eye out. Make sure they know their job is to protect the ranch. I'm going to help Charlemagne pack some items in case somebody needs patching."

Alton asked, "If Bradbury does attack, will he hit the Williams ranch first?"

Helen shrugged, "Bradbury made it known he wants both places. When we told him we weren't selling he was mighty upset. We are the strongest, we have more men. It depends on how bad he wants both places. It won't hurt to be well prepared at both places. While Bart is gone you can get the rest of the men prepared."

Alton agreed, "Helen. For once I hope your intuition is all wrong."

Helen nodded, "If the Colonel waits four days his goose will be cooked. If he attacks in the next three days we'll be ready. I hope I'm wrong too dear but I don't think Bradbury is going to be any too patient."

When they arrived at the MJ they were greeted by a well-armed family. Charlemagne explained to Mary Jane her mother's fears and the hope that Mary Jane and the children would spend the next few days at the Langford ranch. Blaine returned to the house about that time after checking the approach from the north. He thought the idea was well thought out. Within an hour everyone except Molly and Pete were on their way to the Langford Ranch.

The four men from the Langford ranch were told to stay out of sight in the stable and remain watchful. Molly, Pete, Charlemagne and Blaine would stay in the house, the first day passed without incident. Late in the afternoon Blaine rode to the rock outcropping above the drift fence. There was no movement, late that evening he returned. Charlemagne was visibly anxious and happy to see him.

That evening everyone was in bed, Blaine took the first watch; Charlemagne was to relieve him. When it was time to wake Charlemagne, Blaine touched her shoulder, she was quick to awaken. She took his hand and smiled and said, "My mother always told me the best hugs are those when you first wake up."

Blaine sat on the bed and gathered her in his arms. After some time he murmured, "Your mom is right about so many things. You are so soft and warm."

Charlemagne moved her cheek along his and sought his lips. After a blissfully hot exchange she whispered, "That will give me something to think about during my watch."

The lights were out in the house, a partial moon lit the yard. It would not be possible for riders to approach unseen. Through the night Molly and Pete took their turns on watch, Blaine had the early morning watch. Faint light began to show outside.

As Blaine stood beside the window and watched the road leading to the ranch, he heard soft footsteps behind him. He turned to see Charlemagne in her nightgown, he smiled at her boldness. Charlemagne whispered, "During the entire time on my watch, I was thinking of those early morning warm and soft hugs. I decided I'd deliver one of those hugs for you."

Blaine pulled her to him, his hands stroked her back and she moved even closer. They quickly sought each other's lips. After what seemed like a bonfire Charlemagne put her hands on his chest. She said, "Wow! Mom asked if you were a good kisser. How do I explain that?"

Blaine kissed her briefly, pulled her to him and said, "I think you better get dressed before we have other things we have to explain."

Charlemagne returned the kiss, as she moved away she smiled and said, "I'll get dressed, but, reluctantly."

It was daylight, a fire was started and coffee was brewing when a rider trotted up the lane. Blaine quickly took the telescope and checked the trail behind the rider. He could make out three men partially hidden, perhaps waiting. Blaine quickly checked the other sides of the house then returned to greet the rider. He warned Charlemagne, "Wake Molly and Pete. There are three more men waiting down the lane. If they have a good rifle shot with them, they could hit the house. Tell everyone not to stand in the windows and get behind solid cover."

Blaine went to the door, "They sent a man I recognize by the name of Jay Brandon." Blaine told Charlemagne, "Jay fancies himself with a gun."

Charlemagne peeked out the window, "That man calls himself Duke Bascom now. He's Colonel Bradbury's foreman."

Blaine stepped onto the porch and quickly moved to the left keeping the gunman's horse between him and a potential shooter from down the lane. Blaine greeted him, "What do you want me to call you? Duke or Jay?"

The gunman smiled confidently and swung his leg over the horse to dismount. As he dismounted he spun and drew. Blaine's first bullet hit the gunman in the belt buckle the next bullet hit him in the chest.

Blaine stood above the gunman who was clutching his belly and ignoring the hole in his chest. Blaine asked, "Should I put Jay Brandon or Duke Bascom on your marker?"

In great pain the gunman laughed, "Neither one. The name is Lonnie Anderson. Are you McNaughton?"

Blaine nodded, the gunman chuckled as he squirmed in pain. He clutched his belly and said, "I heard you were pretty fast. How the hell did somebody from Chicago get to be so damn fast?"

Blaine explained, "My father deals in guns. I started handling guns when I was six."

Suddenly Blaine heard hoof-beats. He darted into the house amid gunfire and splinters of wood flying from the door jam.

He felt the pain in his neck as he slammed the door behind him.

Molly, Pete, and Charlemagne were behind barricades, Pete shot then there was a burst of gunfire from the stables.

Within a few moments all three men were down in the yard.

Blaine made a quick check to see if everyone was all right. Before going outside he commanded, "You three stay put."

The three riders were dead, Lonnie Anderson was still alive. Blaine asked, "Did your boss send men over to the Langford ranch?"

Lonnie was still clutching his stomach and squirming in agony. He answered, "How the hell did you know?"

Blaine explained, "Helen Langford guessed, Helen sent four men over here. They were hiding in the stable. All three of your men are dead."

Lonnie Anderson grimaced, "World will be a lot better off without them. They came to move the family out then do them in."

Blaine was shocked, "The whole family?"

The gunman nodded, "Yeah. All of them."

Blaine shook his head, "You are telling me that the world is a lot better off without your friends? You were leading them. You are getting a little holier-than-thou aren't you? I believe it's a little late for religion isn't it?"

Lonnie curled up a little tighter because of the pain in his stomach, "They say, better late than never."

Blaine asked, "Who bought the bulk of the cattle that were rustled from the Hash Knife?"

Lonnie Anderson's laugh seemed part of his pain as he answered, "The Colonel. He bought most all of them. He sold some, he kept a lot of the breeding stock. Most of the rustled stuff are blotted over and kept on the northern end of the Box B. He was going to take over the entire valley."

Blaine admitted, "The reason I stayed here was because of the blotted brands on the cattle and the Box brand on the horse. The bottom of the B covers part of the Hash Knife brand but it does a lousy job."

"Bradbury thought he was so far away from the Hash Knife spread that nobody would make the connection."

"Did Bradbury send those three after Roland Williams?"

"Yeah. The orders were to let him sell the cattle first, then rob him and kill him on the way back. Bradbury figured with Roland out of the way, he'd have no problem getting his hands on the MJ and the water he needed. Then you showed up."

Lonnie was in pain as he spoke, "How the hell did you find your way to the Hash Knife in the first place?"

Blaine quickly explained, "Family friends with the owner of the Hash Knife."

Lonnie again doubled up in pain, "Oh, Jesus."

Blaine wondered, "There you go again trying to get into the good graces. I don't think it's going to work for you."

Lonnie Anderson curled up in more pain and said, "Bout all there is left is religion..." his voice trailed off and he relaxed in death.

Blaine summoned the four men from the stables and quickly informed them that the bulk of the Box B men were on their way to the Langford ranch. He gave them leave to saddle up and returned to the Langford ranch and told them they could come back tomorrow and help with the burials.

Blaine went to the house to explain to Charlemagne Molly and Pete. When he entered the house Molly's eyes were wide with fright. Charlemagne ushered Blaine into a chair by the table. He had a gash in his neck from the ricochet and the splintered wood. His shirt was soaked in blood. As Charlemagne patched him up he explained that most of the Box B men were headed to the Langford ranch. He indicated the four Langford riders were heading back also.

Quickly he explained, "I'm thinking we should all mount up and head to the Langford ranch to lend a hand."

Charlemagne asked, "What if they burn the MJ?"

Blaine shrugged, "The house can be rebuilt. I don't think there'll be any way of replacing your mom or Mary Jane for that matter."

149

Alton Langford's stint in the Army was put to good use. He deployed his men so that any attack would come under a withering crossfire from the house, bunkhouse and mess hall. The early morning attack did not come, he figured the next best time would be noon. Just before noon he rang the dinner Bell then waited. This day the dinner Bell was a signal to be prepared. Ten minutes later fifteen men charged into the yard expecting to catch everyone eating their noon meal.

The four men had returned earlier from the MJ and explained the attack was imminent. Alton had everyone in position around the ranch buildings. It wasn't long afterward and Blaine, Charlemagne, Molly, and Pete arrived and added to the firepower in the house.

As they were waiting, Alton Langford noted the attention Charlemagne was giving to Blaine. He had listen to a lot of misinformation fed to him by the Colonel and Box riders regarding Blaine. He figured he would have to take a new look at the lad based on Charlemagne's attachment.

As the Box B riders entered the yard Blaine stepped to the front door. He said to Alton, "I'm going to have to try to avert a slaughter. I'm going to see if they will surrender their arms."

As Blaine spoke he pulled a badge out of his pocket and pinned it on his shirt. He shrugged and explained, "Deputy US Marshal looking into the rustling of Hash Knife cattle. I'll explain later."

Blaine stepped out onto the porch, he noted a large wooden rain barrel off to the left side of the porch. As the riders approached he was prepared to jump behind the barrel. Blaine held up his hand in an attempt to get them to hesitate. Most of the men had guns already drawn, from where they were they could see the badge. A shot was fired. Blaine didn't know the source, suddenly the air was filled with gunfire. Blaine dove behind the barrel, within seconds eight of the attackers were on the ground. The rest of them threw up their hands.

Blaine's neck was bleeding again as he limped out to make his arrests. Only two of the seven men still in the saddle were without wounds. The Colonel lay face down in the dirt, the man closest to Blaine fell out of the saddle from wounds he had received. Blaine was getting a little wobbly from the loss of blood. When Alton arrived Blaine took the badge off and handed it to him. Blaine smiled as he explained, "I'm afraid I'm about to cave in Sir. You'll have to take over."

Blaine woke up in Charlemagne's bed, his neck was bandaged and another wound to his thigh was bound. When he awoke Molly left the room to get Charlemagne. Soon Charlemagne was at his side. Charlemagne looked at him and noted his smile. She leaned over and kissed him gently. Then she said, "It takes a lot to get you into my bed."

Blaine smiled and beckoned her, she kissed him again, "I'm trying to help to hasten your recovery."

Blaine looked about and said, "I'm in heaven. I don't think I want to hurry this recovery business."

Charlemagne asked, "You mean you don't want me to help?"

Blaine smiled, "I'm going to want a lot of that kind of help night and day. I just don't want to do the hastening part."

Introduction; "The Orphan Train"

In about 2009 I learned that the Wisconsin Child Center was built at Sparta to take advantage of the railroad and the Orphan Train. Excess children from the same center where I spent nearly six years were placed on the train every Tuesday. (The center numbers were kept at a level that would make it less likely for diseases to spread. When children were housed in crowded conditions, diseases would spread rapidly among the population.) I've read many of the stories written by participants of the Orphan Train, the circumstances were more shocking to me since I was once at the Wisconsin Child Center.

I have scribbled two books of short stories about Orphan Train kids, "The Orphan Train Ruffian," and "The Orphan Train Twins and Their White Horse Dream." In other books I scribble, there are stories about the orphaned, rejected or disenfranchised. I guess my affinity for the subject matter has something to do with the way I was removed from my family as a child and my stay at the Wisconsin Child Center for nearly six years.

While I write about the struggles of orphaned, disenfranchised or rejected children, I have also developed a very warm regard for parents who adopt, those who take in foster children and of course good parents.

During the era of the orphan trains, up to a quarter of a million orphaned, neglected or abandoned children were removed mostly from larger cities out east and dispersed throughout the country. The lucky ones were adopted into well intentioned families, some were indentured, literally enslaved and many terribly abused.

(Given my personal experience I have always wondered, what is it about the human spirit that allows some of those subjected to such treatment to rise above and succeed in spite their condition.)

The Orphan Train ran from 1854 until 1929, according to records at the (MCLHR) Monroe County Local History

Room in Sparta, Wisconsin, the train stopped taking children from the Sparta facility in 1933. In 1878 Wisconsin built the 'State School for Orphan and Dependent Children' at Sparta Wisconsin. The facility was built near the railroad station to take advantage of the practice of shipping orphans to western states.

On Tuesdays, overflow children from the Sparta orphanage were added to others already on the train and sent west. The Orphan Train idea was born in New York which had about 30,000 street orphans in 1854. It is estimated up to 250,000 children were sent on trains all over the nation and Canada during the years the train was in existence.

In the late 1800's a parent or a guardian could merely drop an unwanted child off at the Sparta, Wisconsin center. The center would attempt to find a local home, if adoption, or indenture of those over thirteen-years-old, did not occur, the child was put on the orphan train. The train made stops from town to town, children would change into their 'good' or 'show' clothes and would be placed on display. People wanting a child would have them sing or say a poem; they would push, pull, turn, check their teeth, squeeze their arms to check for muscle and otherwise jostle the orphans about to inspect and make selections. At the end of the train run, if nobody chose the child, the child was put back on the train and returned to New York.

Some children over thirteen were old enough to be indentured, in that case the family receiving the indentured child was supposed to educate them, provide food, clothing and a place to sleep. At the conclusion of the indenture, at eighteen years old, the child could be brought back to Sparta, in which case the family would be charged a fifty-dollar fee. Lest you think that I escalate the bad conditions in my stories, consider the following. In a US Children's Bureau assessment; circa 1923, they described indentured homes to be; "deplorable-filthy, with little attention to medical, social, or educational needs, children were shifted from one home to another, they had no training outside of house or farm-work

153

and as a result drifted from one job to another after they completed their indenture."

I have written stories of orphans adopted into good families and stories of children literally used like slaves, there are many stories of orphan train riders. The following story is fictional, the basis for much of the writing was taken from actual occurrences. Unlike the lives of many of the orphans, in this story and most of the stories I write, everything turns out well in the end.

One of the most difficult things to do while trying to write about the orphans is relate their feelings. After spending nearly six years at the Sparta, Wisconsin Child Center, I think I have some insight into the thinking of orphaned or children separated from their families. However, it is still very difficult to communicate how the child would feel, in some instances it is heartbreaking just to attempt to, 'go there.'

Let me relate a brief story to point out the thinking of those institutionalized. A lad I knew at the center, went into the service upon graduation from high school, after the service he became a mailman, he retired from the mail service. A sister found him after all those years, she knocked on his door, told him who she was, he would not allow her in his house. Through the partially open door they arranged to meet later on. I have no idea why he did not allow his sister into his home, but then, through the same partially opened door, he asked her the question that plagued him all his life, "Was I bad?"

He wanted to understand why he was removed from the family as a child, why he was treated differently. His pain, his question, 'why' is probably on the minds of many of us kids who have been in some way rejected or who were chosen to be removed from the family. After many years, he is now communicating with the family again. Some normalcy has returned, some of his questions have been answered. When his sister described the situation to me, I could not respond I felt so bad for him, I guess I understood his question and his pain.

In the final analysis, as one writes stories of the orphaned or those taken out of the family; how does one portray the pain of separation? Even with a bit of experience, I'll probably fail miserably in regard to describing the child's joy when things work out well or their heartbreak during mistreatment or rejection.

Introduction to, "Orphan Train."

Ethan Gillette was taken from the woods of northern Wisconsin, placed on a train headed for Milwaukee where he could beg in order to live. After being set upon by gangs of other children he was forced to steal. Ethan was picked up by a mounted policeman, he was sent to Sparta and the Home for Wayward and Dependent Children. From there he was placed on the Orphan Train. On the many stops, Ethan wasn't getting picked, fearing being returned to New York, he decided to run away. He jumped off the train when a faint road led to where, he did not know.

Orphan Train

Part I

Ethan Gillette awoke wrapped in one of his mother's handmade quilts among the boxcar load of logs when the train jolted to a stop in Milwaukee; he was nearly twelve years old. Ethan was placed on the boxcar and told there would be plenty of handouts in the big city to keep him alive. Upon his arrival Ethan soon found that surviving on the streets was a lot different than living in the country. Unaware of the dangers, the first day a gang of kids waylaid him and took his bag containing what meager fare was sent with him. Along with enough food to keep him alive for a few days, his coat and quilt were stolen, he had nothing. He spent his first two nights hidden, shivering with fear and loneliness in the hay mow of a livery stable.

After two days hiding and watching others orphaned and living in the streets he was hungrier than he could ever recall. It was getting on in the afternoon, although he didn't have anything left to be stolen, Ethan was avoiding the same gang of kids by sneaking between two houses. The smell of fresh baked bread stopped him in his tracks. Not two steps from him cooling in the window just high enough so he could reach was a beautifully browned fresh baked loaf of bread. Ethan had never stolen a thing in his life and he was a half mile away from that window before he slowed down enough to rip a chunk off the loaf.

As he walked Ethan had put away a goodly part of that loaf when he started across the railroad tracks. The yardman espied him and his loaf of bread as he boasted, "I'm feeling mighty strong today! Hey young man! I see you have a loaf of bread there. I'm going to make you a bet. I'll bet you a silver dollar against that loaf of bread I can move this railroad car loaded with coal, with only one hand."

The prospect of making a dollar lit up the eyes of Ethan, besides, there was no way a man could move that monstrously huge loaded coal car with just one hand. Ethan looked the boxcar over, it was gigantic; he knew no living man could move that boxcar, especially using only one hand. The yardman wasn't a very big man, he sweetened the bet; "With a silver dollar you could buy a couple of meals and a pocket or two full of candy…"

Ethan nodded his acceptance, the yardman clarified the bet, "If I move this car using only one hand, I get the loaf of bread. If I can't move the car with one hand, I'll give you a dollar."

Again Ethan nodded signifying he understood the bet they were making; the yardman stepped to the side of the car and picked up a bar with an odd shaped piece of steel on the end. He put the piece of steel under the wheel and pried using only one hand, the car inched ahead, Ethan's heart sank when the boxcar loaded with coal moved. Without talking the yardman reached down and took the loaf of bread from Ethan.

Ethan lost his loaf of bread, he'd been tricked, he couldn't think of anything but having no food for the rest of the day or maybe for the next few days. Ethan's chin dropped to his chest at the loss. He had hated to steal in the first place, now he'd probably have to steal again.

The yardman watched the devastated young man, "Boy. Let this be a lesson to you. Never ever bet unless you have a sure thing."

The yardman handed Ethan back his loaf of bread, Ethan gladly took the loaf and mumbled, "Thank you Sir."

Not a hundred yards away, Patrick Reardon, a policeman on horseback watched the exchange with interest. One of Reardon's duties was to rid the streets of runaways and orphans; he figured this one was an orphan. Reardon watched as Ethan made his way into a small area of brush next to the track. Reardon made his way around to the other side, he would intercept Ethan there.

When Ethan came out from the trail through the brush Reardon was waiting; "How do you do young man. I see over at the railroad yard you almost lost your loaf of bread?"

Ethan looked up at the officer he was told to avoid but this one smiled at him as he spoke. The first thing that came to mind was his stolen loaf of bread, Ethan didn't see the policeman in time to hide his loaf, he stood his ground. Another thing Ethan never learned to do in his life was run away or talk back to adults or people of authority, "He won the bet, he could have taken the bread."

Reardon looked the boy over, his shoes were a working variety usually worn by country lads; Reardon laughed, "He has used that gimmick on a lot of kids. It is sort of a joke with him."

Reardon smiled as Ethan remained silent, "How long have you been in town?"

Ethan wanted to run, but he figured; Where am I going to run to, and, how can I get away from a man on horseback? Ethan decided to tell the truth, "Since day before yesterday."

Reardon continued to seek information, "Who dropped you off?"

"Neighbor."

Reardon nodded, "You're not from town."

"Live out in the country, the neighbor put me on a boxcar loaded with logs. He told me the train was going to stop here in Milwaukee."

"No bag of food? Blankets?"

Ethan shook his head, "Stolen the first day I was dropped off."

Reardon asked, "Kids or adults?"

Ethan quickly responded, embarrassed, "Bunch of kids."

Reardon saw the cuts and bruises on Ethan's face and recognized his embarrassment, "You put up a fight?"

Ethan shook his head, "No."

Reardon smiled, "If you put up a fight they may have done you more harm.

"No Mom or Dad?"

Ethan's head sort of jerked at his uncomfortable response, he choked out the word he hated, "Dead."

Reardon still had his mother and father and he started a family of his own. He noted the boy had trouble admitting his parents were gone; the street orphans were the heartbreaking part of his job, "What's your name?"

"Ethan Gillette."

Reardon reached down and held out his hand out to Ethan, "Ethan. I'm Patrick Reardon. C'mon up here. We'll go for a ride. I'll talk to you a little bit. I'd like to help you out or help you figure out what you should do.

"You can't be living on the streets in this town Ethan. Boy your age, without good food and water you'll be sick or dead when winter sets in if not before."

Ethan didn't hesitate, he surely didn't know what he was doing trying to live on the streets, maybe the officer could help him. Seated behind Reardon with his loaf of bread tucked under his arm they headed down the street while Reardon filled him in, "Ethan. Our good state of Wisconsin just opened a place for kids without a home. One of the things they do is find kids without family a home to live in. You are from the country, more than likely they will find you a place in the country."

Ethan nodded, "I'd like that."

Reardon took Ethan to a child pickup spot near the railroad station, "The people here will help you out. They will feed you and tell you what to do. Good luck to you Ethan."

Reardon looked at Ethan, his face was pretty crusted with the remnants of injuries, wicked colored bruises and a bunch of scabbed over wounds, "Ethan. One more thing. The kids that stole your pack, did they do that to your face?"

Ethan reached up and touched his face, he shook his head, "Day before I was put on the train, the logs I was skidding turned on me."

Reardon smiled, he was glad to hear that he didn't have to arrest someone for doing damage to the boy, "Ethan. I'm from the city. You'll have to explain what you were doing."

Ethan patiently explained, "I was standing on a bunch of logs I was skidding out of the woods for firewood. One of the logs must have hit a stump, the load turned and tangled up my feet, I ended up under all those logs I was skidding. When I fell I dropped the reins, the horse took off, so I was dragged pretty good under those logs."

Reardon shook his head, "You could have been killed."

Ethan nodded, "Yes sir. I'm mighty lucky I didn't break a few bones."

Reardon smiled, "You'll do alright Ethan, and in a couple of months you'll look like new again. Until then, you are a sight to look at, but those folks inside will take care of you."

Ethan was led into a building with numerous cots, he was given soap and a towel and told to clean up. Later he sat on the edge of his cot, a gentleman came to him and asked him questions about how he lost his parents. Ethan related that his father died in the war about six years earlier, his mother took sick and passed away just recently. A neighbor took him in for a month then decided he didn't want the responsibility. The information was all written down, the man asking the questions stopped, he looked carefully at Ethan and asked, "Did your neighbor beat you?"

Ethan reached up and felt the bruises on his face, "No. I was standing on a stack of logs, the logs turned, I fell in among them and was dragged a ways."

The man looked at Ethan and said, "Those welts and cuts will heal in a month or two."

Ethan nodded, "That's what Reardon the policeman said."

The interview was over, an hour later he ate in a sparse dining facility, the food was better than he had eaten since his mother passed away. After eating Ethan was asked to help wash dishes after which he returned to his cot. He closed his eyes; he was warm, he wasn't hungry, fearful of gangs, being beaten for no reason, or having to worry about where he would eat next. He pulled the covers up and tucked himself into that lonely fetal position of self-protection against a world too big, an unknown future and no family to lean on.

Ethan woke up in the morning to a lot of bustling about in the dormitory, one of the men on duty called his name, "Ethan Gillette."

Ethan raised his hand, "Yes sir."

Ethan was given an envelope, "Take this with you. When you get to Sparta, they will ask for it. You are taking a train today. You will go to a placement facility in Sparta. It will be their job to find you a home."

Ethan was happy with the prospect of belonging to a family once again; his recollections of his father before the war were good memories. Ethan was happy to board the train, a few of the other boys and a couple of girls were crying. Ethan didn't understand what the tears were about, he didn't know their story, he supposed after getting cast out they were going to get a chance to be a part of a family again, besides the city was a fearful place for Ethan.

The train ride to Sparta was uneventful; when they arrived they were led to the placement center about a half mile away. Not far from the railroad tracks Ethan was told to carry a three year old that couldn't keep up. The girl was very slight, like Ethan and most of the others in the group they probably hadn't been getting enough to eat. Ethan smiled, the girl was comfortable in his arms but seemed to stare at all the scabs and wounds on his face, by the time they got to the center the girl was sleeping and Ethan's arms were sore.

For the next three weeks Ethan's job was to sweep and clean out the main building where the offices were located. At night he and other children were housed in large cottages. As Ethan cleaned the floors he noted now and then people would come to pick up a child. Twice Ethan was looked at and passed over because of the many wounds on his face.

Ethan was happy the three year old he carried from the train station was adopted quite fast. He observed that several younger girls were adopted during the two weeks and one older boy was indentured. Ethan figured evidently people were more likely to take girls than they were boys.

While sweeping, Ethan noted there was a vent in the floor of the main office where he could hear the conversations of the men above. When he had spare time he would head there to see if he could hear about any prospects of his placement. Just two days earlier one of the men mentioned the date, the day before had been his birthday, he was now twelve years old. Ethan imagined that birthdays for everyone at Sparta probably went by with the same lack of fanfare.

Ethan was sitting in the room listening, the two men above were determining the fate of some of the children, "Bill, here's what you have to do. The orphan train gets here on Tuesday. We have to get our numbers down below two-hundred where we can manage them. We just do the math. We have room for two-hundred, that means we've got thirty-eight too many. Next week it may be ten or fifty. For now that means we have to send out thirty-eight kids. You have to make your decision and stick to it."

Bill responded, "Homer, what happens to the kids we put on the train?"

Homer's voice raised; "That isn't any of our concern. Don't get emotionally into this job or you won't be worth a damn. The kids are taken out west. The train stops in towns on the railroad right of way. The kids are cleaned up, put on a stage, the people check them over and if they decide they want them, they have a child."

Bill quietly spoke, "The people probe them like a roast in the butcher shop?"

Homer didn't answer, Bill's voice was subdued, "If nobody wants them?"

Homer's voice seemed more gruff, factual, "They are put back on the train and shipped back to New York. From there they may get a ride down south."

Bill obviously didn't like the idea of putting kids on a train and shipping them into the unknown, "Seems like we could make room here for a few more?"

Homer this time seemed more patient, "We've tried that. If we get a disease it travels through this place like a prairie fire on a windy day. We've already started a cemetery; we don't want to add to it unnecessarily. If we get them out of here as fast as we can, it is healthier and safer for the children."

Bill's voice now seemed more resigned to act but what knowledge he possessed made it difficult, "So we have Sue Flanders. Sue has no parents, she is skinny as a twig, not the best looking girl; she has been here for a month."

Homer snapped, "Put her on the damn train."

Bill wavered then described what Sue Flanders went through and why she was at the center. Homer again snapped, "Bill, that train leaves every Tuesday of the month, don't bury yourself in all the pain."

Bill was quiet for some time before he spoke up again, "But, take Johnny Bellman. Johnny has no parents, he's…"

162

Homer interrupted, "He's been here for three weeks, put him on the train."

Bill went through a list of another fifteen boys and half dozen girls, only one didn't get placed on the train, finally Bill noted, "That's pretty close. We've got twenty-six."

Homer again snapped, "You've got a long way to go. Twelve more."

Bill was mad when he next spoke, "The three Rowser boys are on the list of those available to be put on the train. Three brothers. Who's to say they won't be broken up?"

Homer's voice shown irritation, "No guarantees. Not our end of the deal. The agent who rides the train takes care of all that the best he can. If someone wants the threesome, fine. If not they will be broken up." There was silence for some time, then Bill continued until there was only one left, Homer directed, "Give me the list."

A short time later Homer asked; "What about Ethan Gillette? He's been here about two weeks."

Bill explained, "The kid is a good worker. He's the one that keeps the place clean, he's a hard worker and a polite kid. His face is healing pretty good, he'll get placed pretty soon."

The papers rustled as Homer handed them back, "Put Ethan on the damn train. We can get someone else to sweep up."

Bill was silent for some time, then he spoke, "Those kids on that train are at the mercy of people we don't know. Some of the girls are going to end up in trouble, some will never make it back. How many of them will be happy with their lives? We have no way to check up on them."

Homer was heard walking toward the door, "That's right. Even the ones we place right here at Sparta, we don't have the time or the people to check up on them. We will do our job at this end, someone else can worry about the details at the other end. We know we can't house them all here at Sparta. Legislators are the ones that have given us this job. Bill, make up your mind. If you don't want to do this job, get into some other line of work. I'm not going to go through the list with you every week."

163

The door shut as Homer left, Bill cussed, Ethan left the room and headed for his bed, he had some serious thinking to do. Ethan didn't know whether or not he wanted to be poked, pulled and pushed about like a chicken carcass in the meat market. He would be at mercy of people looking for help, some actually looking for children to be in their families. He heard Bill talk about the few choices for boys, the fact that many of them were worked to death or abused. Ethan wondered if he wanted to take a chance of being one of those abused. Ethan liked to work, but he figured he didn't want to work for room and board and then be brought back when he was eighteen years old. Ethan figured for all those years, all they would have to pay is fifty dollars? He spent many hours day-dreaming about what a new family would be ideally be like; he thought being placed with just about any family would be better than remaining here at Sparta.

Homer and Bill also wrote out indenture agreements on some of the older boys, the prospective home would agree to exchange work for room, board and the learning of a skill, schooling or a vocation. Ethan thought, with an indenture, at least he would know where he stood and he would feel better, if he decided he didn't like the arrangement he could run away.

Tuesday rolled around faster than Ethan wanted; he was given a bag with spare clothes, a small bar of soap and a towel. The directions given to the thirty-eight marched to the train was to put the clean clothes on only when told. Each time they arrived at a town where they were to be paraded before people interested in them, the children were directed to wash and change into their clean clothes. If they were not chosen, when they returned to the train they were directed to change into their 'regular' clothes.

At the first town only two children were taken, the rest changed back into their old clothes and were placed back on the train.

After the eighth town they were issued back onto the train, this time Ethan was directed to sit next to Sue Flanders, the

164

girl Bill indicated was skinny as a twig. Ethan glanced out the window, with his many facial wounds he was uncomfortable sitting next to a girl. Ethan noted her reflection in the window, he turned and whispered, "Sue? Why are you crying?"

Sue shook her head, then she looked at Ethan and quietly answered, "I don't think I'll be picked."

They were down to six kids, only two stops left, Sue asked, "I wonder what happens to us if we aren't picked?"

Ethan didn't know if he should tell her, he decided she would want to know, "I heard Bill and Homer at the administration building talking. If any orphans don't get picked they'll be put back on the train and shipped back to New York."

Sue looked at Ethan and shook her head sadly, "I don't want to live in New York or any city. I've always lived in the country."

Sue looked like she was going to cry again, "Sue. You can't cry. People don't want sad kids or mad ones."

Sue sniffed a bit, looked at Ethan and asked, "What about you?"

Ethan chuckled nervously, "One look at my face and they turn away quick. I'll heal up in another couple of weeks, but right now I'm a fright to look at."

Sue asked, "Did somebody beat you?"

Ethan smiled, "No. Did it to myself. Got dragged under a bunch of logs I was skidding out."

Ethan shrugged and smiled, "Not much to look at; am I?"

Sue smiled and shook her head, "I guess not, right now."

Ethan continued, "No matter what happens Sue, you have to keep smiling. You'll get picked. Do you remember when we first left Sparta? You led everyone singing to keep our spirits up. You are a good singer. I bet you can cook and sew too."

Sue nodded, "Of course. I like to do housework and I like to work outside in the garden or with animals."

Sue felt better, Ethan was glad, Sue seemed to be a very nice gal, and he recalled the story of how she became orphaned, Sue shook her head as she continued to whisper, "I don't know if I want to get picked, did you see what happened to the Rowser boys?"

Ethan nodded his head, "Doesn't seem fair to break up a family like that?"

Sue whispered, "The three brothers stayed together for several stops, all three clinging to one another, then a kindly gal selected five year old Roland and he went into her arms eagerly. The oldest of the boys had a painfully forced smile on his face as he waved goodbye to his littlest brother. As his littlest brother was carried out of the room he looked over the ladies' shoulder and screamed for his, 'brovers.' Another man soon stepped up and took Dennis' other brother, again Dennis was forced to wave goodbye."

Sue Flanders shook her head as she recalled, "Did you see the look on Dennis' face when he ended up all alone on the stage?"

Ethan nodded, "Dennis was picked at the next stop, he didn't look too happy."

Sue agreed, "I know. I hope everything turns out all right for him. He has every right to be angry. Did you see what the agent, Mr. Stapling did to him?"

Ethan shook his head, "No. I heard them talking but they were up at the other end of the car."

Sue shook her head, "Dennis had an envelope his father gave him with his father's address on it. Mr. Stapling took it out of his pocket. All three of those boys were on the floor looking for that envelope. Mr. Stapling told Dennis, it was best he made a clean break with the past. Then he just walked away and left Dennis and his two brothers hanging onto each other."

Ethan shook his head sadly, then he smiled as he related, "The happiest one was that little five year old we dropped off a couple of stops ago."

Sue smiled, "Katherine, she saw the lady waiting on the railroad platform holding up her number, she ran to her yelling, 'That's my new Momma!' I think everything will turn out all right for her, but we are older."

Again Ethan looked at Sue with his scabbed up face and tried to be reassuring, "Sue. You will be fine. Someone can't help but take you in and treat you as their own. You are a fine gal."

Sue looked down as she whispered, "I hate it when they grab my arms and pinch me to see how strong I am. One farmer with dirty hands stuck his fingers in a girl's mouth to check her teeth. That was after he asked her to sing and dance. The poor girl was left crying."

Ethan chuckled as he whispered, "It was funny when those two men both wanted the boy at the second stop. It looked like they were going to have a tug of war with him. Finally the boy told one of them he wouldn't go with him he was so mean, he ended up with the man that seemed nicer."

They talked quietly for some time while most kids slept, when they pulled into Rawlins, Ethan smiled and nudged Sue and whispered, "Remember, smile."

They lined up on the stage in Rawlins, Wyoming. Ethan was at the far end of the stage, Sue Flanders was the first one in the line. Ethan watched as a plump gal of about forty who seemed to be a happy sort was looking over the remaining two girls, she walked past Sue Flanders and looked another girl over about seven years old standing next to Ethan. She spoke quietly to her husband as she passed by Ethan, ".. and that one is too young."

The children were told to keep quiet and speak only when spoken to but Ethan whispered to the woman, "Ma'am. If you are looking for a girl. That one on the end can cook, sew and clean, and garden. She can sing as sweet as a whip-poor-will, she loves animals and she is smart and good natured too."

The woman looked at Sue, she smiled and whispered back, "She your sister?"

Ethan smiled and shook his head, the woman again whispered, "She's a pretty slight thing."

Ethan shrugged, "She been orphaned, she's gone through some mighty tough times, she'll fill out with your good cooking."

The woman whispered, "She's looking sort of sour?"

Ethan shook his head, "That's because you passed her by. Poor gal has a lot to be sour about, but you go talk to her for just one minute. She'll light up like a candle on a Christmas tree, you'll see. She's a great gal. Give her a chance. If you are looking for a girl, you can't do no better."

The comments brought a big smile from the woman; she walked to the opposite end of the stage to take another look at Sue. After a short discussion the woman put her arm around Sue and led her from the hall. Sue turned to look and smile at Ethan who was still on the stage. Ethan gave a smile and a weak wave as the agent Mr. Stapling ordered the remaining foursome back to the train.

Part 2

Mr. Stapling, the orphan's agent didn't waste much time, he led the remaining four back to the train. Ethan had already made up his mind; he wasn't going back to New York. He didn't like Milwaukee; he figured he surely wouldn't like New York. Ever since he found out he was going west he thought of being a cowboy, the idea appealed to him and the vast space observed out the window drew him. The train had one more stop and he made up his mind, he wasn't going to be jostled about any more.

After directing the children to their seats, Stapling fell fast asleep in the seat across from Ethan. Ethan figured the man was tired, that was why he was in such a hurry to get them back to the train. Ethan stepped out of the seat, with his bag under his arm he walked quickly down the aisle through the door and out onto the platform between the two cars. He

168

slung the bag over his shoulder, climbed to the top of the car and continued toward the rear of the train. When he got to the caboose he climbed quietly and slowly down the ladder. He peered into the rear window of the caboose, a man sat at a table playing solitaire.

Ethan stood on the edge of the rear of the caboose for several minutes, then up ahead he saw a seldom used road leading off to the north, a ranch or a small town, either would do. Ethan looked at the sandy landing he would end up in, as he passed the road, he looked ahead and jumped. When he hit the ground, the sand, a few rocks and some brush nearly ripped his clothes off, but when he quit bouncing he stood, harbored a bunch more bruises, a few scabs were torn off but he was not seriously hurt.

Ethan walked back, picked up his bag and started down the road. It was about four in the afternoon. Ethan had eaten at noon and squirreled away several pieces of bread for this occasion. When it turned dark he sat down in the middle of the road and ate.

Ethan was going to spend the night in the road rather than the brush, he decided to walk a while longer since he wasn't tired. Sometime during the middle of the night he lay down in the road and slept. When he awoke the sun was shining; it was still early morning. While lying there he looked around in front of him for snakes or scorpions, seeing none he slowly stood. Once on his feet he thought his caution wasn't needed, he turned about and saw a rattlesnake curled up by the side of the road.

Ethan ran down the road a mile or two before he slowed to eat some more of his stashed biscuits and bread. At noon he was beginning to wonder if the road had an end, then ahead of him he observed what looked like a small town. A half hour later he walked into the yard of a ranch, a cowboy rode up to him and smiled, "Howdy Pard-ner, you out looking for a job?"

Ethan nodded, "Yes sir."

169

The cowboy introduced himself. "The men call me Chick. Pard, what's your handle?"

Ethan shrugged, "My handle?"

Chick laughed, "What are we going to call you?"

Ethan smiled, "Oh. My name is Ethan. Ethan Gillette."

Chick remained on his horse, "C'mon Ethan Gillette. Follow me. I'll take you to the boss. We'll see if he has some work for you to do."

Chick led Ethan to the opposite side of the ranch yard, to a man leaning on the fence looking off to the north at someone as they rode away. Chick spoke to Ethan, "Wait here for a minute, while I talk to the boss."

Chick dismounted, strode up beside the man before he took his eyes off the rider, "Chick. Where the hell did I go wrong with that kid?"

Chick looked at the boss's son as he rode toward town, "Can't figure boss. He's about the luckiest kid in the world and yet he has to drink himself to oblivion every chance he can get. That and his mean streak."

Tal Forester shook his head, "I tried sweet-talking, yelling, taking a switch to him. I don't give him a penny, yet he's drunk all the time."

Tal Forester continued to look after his son, "I'll tell you Chick. The saddest thing is; I've about given up. I don't care anymore. Where Benton is concerned, I'm like a fresh broke horse. I feel pretty used up, I don't have any fight left in me."

Chick shook his head, "Wasn't going to comment, him being the boss's son and all. Many could get himself fired. But, boss, you've done everything you could. Your son hasn't met you half-way. Half-way hell, he hasn't made a move your direction. Most of us boys that have been around for some time, have told him to settle down, but he just ain't doin it. Some men can't ever get out of a bottle once they get in it. The meanness part… Hell boss, I don't know if there is a stick big enough to take that out of him."

170

Tal Forester patted Chick on the shoulder, the fact that all the men had tried to sway his son was welcomed news, "Thanks Chick. I believe I'll go in and read a bit."

Chick stopped him, "Sir. I believe we got one of those orphans off the train."

Tal Forster looked at Ethan standing with his bag, he whispered to Chick, "Who the hell is responsible for bringing him?"

Chick whispered, "He brung himself. I see him coming down the trail from the south. Not much down there besides the railroad."

Tal asked, "That's a mighty long walk. He say he's an orphan?"

Chick shook his head, "No. My idée."

Tal asked, "Jesus. Looks like someone beat the hell out of him."

Chick nodded, "Most of those are old wounds, a few look fresh. Do you figure maybe he jumped off the train?"

Tal winced at the thought, "That train is moving when it goes by here, I can't see a kid like that having the guts to jump off. But, there's not too many other ways he could have gotten here from that direction."

Tal Forster was both impressed by the idea of the boy jumping off the train and angered that the people charged with the care of the orphans could allow a child to get away with attempting such a feat, "Must have wanted to get away pretty bad if he jumped from the train. What does the boy want?"

Chick could see the old man soften, "You better get the short of it from him. His name is Ethan Gillette. If you don't want to deal with him, I can put him to work for a while and see if he can cut the mustard."

Tal shook his head and motioned to the boy to come to him, "He's just a boy. If he jumped from the train he's lucky he didn't get killed. He spent the entire night out there and half of the day, hell he's got to be hungry right now."

Ethan obediently came when beckoned, he held out his hand, "Hello sir. I'm Ethan Gillette, I'm looking for a job."

Tal Forester shook the hand and tested, "Are you sure you aren't looking for a handout?"

Ethan shook his head, "No sir. I'm willing to work at anything you want. I'm willing to indenture for room and board just to learn."

Tal asked, "You know anything about ranching?"

Ethan shook his head, "I was brought up in the country with animals, but farming in Wisconsin and ranching is a sight different."

Tal looked at Chick and then asked, "I don't like thieves about. You ever stole anything in your life?"

Ethan gritted his teeth, then nodded his head, "Yes sir."

Tal shook his head, somehow he figured the honest admission was painful, "How do I know you won't steal from me?"

Ethan didn't hesitate, "I only stole once in my life. At the time, I figured it was steal or starve."

Tal was taken aback, "What did you steal?"

Ethan was genuinely hurt by the need to tell of his time of weakness, "I was dropped off in Milwaukee to beg. I'm afraid I wasn't any good at begging. I wasn't getting anything to buy food with. After two days I stole a loaf of bread."

It was Tal Forester's turn to grit his teeth, "C'mon in the house. We better get you something to eat. Chick, I'll take care of the lad for now."

Ethan followed Tal into the house, "Throw your bag in the second room on the right down the hall, then come on into the kitchen."

Within minutes the cook had bacon, eggs, milk and buttered bread in front of him. While Tal watched, Ethan downed the meal hungrily, he wiped his lips and looked at Tal, "Thank you sir. That's the best meal I've ever eaten."

After Ethan was done eating Tal took him into the living room and sat him down, "Tell me about your family."

172

Ethan was hesitant, "My dad went to the war; he didn't make it back."

Tal asked, "How old were you then?"

"Six or seven. I lived with my Mom; she got sick and died a couple months ago."

Tal asked, "What happened to you then?"

"Lived with a neighbor for a month; then one day, he put me in a buggy and drove me to a railroad headed to Milwaukee. He hid me in a car filled with logs."

Tal nodded, "That's when he told you to beg for your food?"

Ethan nodded, "Yes sir. But I couldn't beg. Mom always said I should put in a good day's work if I expect to get fed. Which means I'm in debt for the fine meal."

Tal looked at the boy for a minute, "Ethan. I'm trying to find chinks in your armor. Do you know what I'm talking about?"

Ethan shook his head, "No sir."

Tal shrugged and stood, "It doesn't matter. I'm going to take you to the cook-shack. You will be cook's helper in the afternoon. In the morning I'll find some other things for you to do. What I will try to do is teach you everything there is to know about work on a ranch."

Ethan's face lit up, he smiled; "That will be swell sir."

A month later Tal was watching Ethan rope a calf from horseback, Chick approached Tal, "It was a good day when that kid came a waltzing in here."

Tal nodded, "Fine boy. His face is all cleared up of those scars. Works hard, catches on mighty fast."

After considerable hesitation on Tal's part he explained, "I've tried just about everything to test the lad and get him to the point where he balks. I've had no success. Takes to everything we throw at him like a duck to water. Works with the cook at whatever the cook asks, cleans out the stalls, gardens, makes his bed, washes dishes, rides, ropes, cuts wood, hauls,..."

173

Chick nodded, "All the men watch over him. He's a keeper boss. Nice boy. Doesn't get under the skin of any of the men. Even Dirk likes him; Dirk hates kids."

Tal recalled, "When Ethan first came here he said he would work for nothing, he would indenture for learning, room and board. So far he hasn't mentioned money."

Chick shrugged, "What does a twelve-year old need money for?"

Tal shook his head, "He doesn't even ask if he can go to town."

Tal spoke to Ethan, "Ethan, shake that loop out just a little bigger and take your time until you know what you are doing. Later on you can work on your speed."

They watched for a while longer, Chick mentioned, "Yes sir. Sure does take direction well. Not a bit of meanness in the lad. I think he could use a pair of boots though."

Tal smiled and nodded, "You going to town tonight?"

Chick nodded, "Yes Sir. There's a dance, and I'm the king of the fancy footwork."

Tal nodded, "Well King. Take a drawing of Ethan's feet and get a pair of boots. Get them a size too big so he can grow into them. I figure he's got a lot of growing to do."

Chick started for the bunkhouse, then he turned and asked, "Want a report on your son?"

Tal looked down at the ground for some time, then he said, "You know Chick, if you do talk to him, just tell him I love him. Tell him I'd like to have him back here working on the ranch with the rest of us. And remind that crowd he's with they'll get not a penny out of me. I'm not paying for his drinks."

Two days later Chick delivered the boots to the house in the morning, the fit, according to Ethan, was perfect. Ethan was overjoyed. Chick watched the happy response of Tal. As Chick was leaving the house, Tal stepped out behind him, "Chick. What did my son say?"

Chick's head swayed back and forth, Tal urged him on, "C'mon Chick, I've got broad shoulders. And I know my son."

Chick hung his head, "Damn boss. He just laughed. I'm thinking he just can't think anymore. Hell I'm wondering where he's getting his money."

Tal shook his head, "Did you remind those friends of his I'm not paying out a penny to any one of them for buying his drinking."

Chick quickly reported, "He's got some money. Somebody must think you are bluffing or he walked out with a sock full of money."

Tal shrugged, "If he did, he didn't take much, he should run out before long."

Chick returned to the bunkhouse, Ethan stepped out of the house with his new boots on, proud as can be he stepped beside Tal and looked down at he boots, "Sir. Now I really owe you big."

Tal looked down at the enthusiastic lad, he patted him on the back as he told him, "Don't worry about owing boy, you needed shoes."

Ethan was so overwhelmed he gave Tal a hug, "Thank you sir."

Tal wondered when the last time he got a hug, "C'mon. Let's go for a ride in those new boots. I'll teach you how to check the condition of the cattle."

Part 3

Six years passed at the ranch, Tal Forester stood with Chick and watched a fully grown Ethan snap a rope over a steer, toss the steer and put a pigging string on his feet in seconds. A minute later the steer was branded, on his feet and running off to rejoin the herd.

Chick commented, "That lad is greased lightning with a rope and a gun."

175

Tal nodded, "He's works hard at everything he does. The gun business I wish he wasn't so good at."

Chick shrugged, "You know the boys. Guns are like a part of their gear. We like to play with them."

"Yeah, I know. Chick. Do me a favor. Take Ethan to town to that dance you always speak so highly of. Chick, you realize the boy is eighteen? He's never had a girl in his arms or a beer in his hand. I'll tell him to leave his gun here. He's learned to get along with everyone on the ranch, let's see if he has any common sense when it comes to people he meets away from the ranch."

Chick wanted a little clarity in what he was going to try to accomplish, "Do you want me to get him drunked up a bit? Do you want me to fix him up with one of the town's bawdy ladies?"

Tal shrugged. "I don't want you to lead him astray. Let mother nature take its course. I just want him to interact with people away from the ranch. See what direction he takes. In the past six years he's been to town three times to pick up boots and clothes because he's outgrown his. Other than that, the boy hasn't been off the ranch."

Chick figured he had his orders pretty clear, "You going to give him a few dollars so he can spend it on the beer, food, or some lady?"

Tal shook his head, "Yeah, we'll see if there are any chinks in his armor."

Chick shook his head. "Damn boss, seems like you've been testing him for chinks a long time already."

Tal nodded, "So far he's been..."

Tal stopped saying what he had been thinking for the past six years, that Ethan was more like the son he wanted than his own son.

Tal handed Chick a five dollar bill, "Chick, I'll give you the five dollars. I haven't paid the boy a penny in the past six years."

Chick looked at the boss smiling, "That is something. He's a top hand. Worth forty to fifty a month at least, and he doesn't seem to care if he has a penny in his pocket."

Tal nodded, "Yup. He never has asked for a penny. Yet, I think he's happy."

Chick took the five dollars and started away, "I have to get cleaned up. This is going to be an interesting night. I'll give you the full report when I get back."

Chick started for the bunkhouse, he saw Ethan come out of the tack room, "Ethan. Go get the smell of that oil off you. You are going with me to the dance in town."

Ethan wrinkled his nose, "Naw. I was just about to toss a rope on that paint."

Chick smiled, "Wrestle with the paint later. Get going. Boss's orders. We are leaving in a half hour. Make sure you get washed behind the ears."

Ethan looked at Tal for corroboration, Tal smiled and pointed to the house, "You better hurry it up. Take that long legged black filly of mine."

The thought of going to the dance was a little unsettling to Ethan, but the prospect of riding Tal's favorite horse overbalanced the scale. In a half hour Ethan was cleaned up and had the tall black mare saddled and ready to go.

On the way into town Chick handed Ethan the five dollar bill, "Here's a loan. Spend it any way you'd like, beer, gals, whatever you'd like."

Ethan slipped the five dollar bill into his pant pocket, "I'll try to pay you back tonight after the dance."

They rode for some time before Ethan asked, "Wonder why Tal wanted me to go to a dance?"

Chick looked at Ethan, "That's right. I forgot. Give me your gun. Boss said no gun, reckon he don't want you to get frisky and shoot a hole in your leg or someone else's."

Without questioning Ethan unbuckled his belt and handed the .44 to Chick. Chick put the weapon in his saddle bag and they continued into town. Chick wanted to head to the saloon, Ethan wanted to get something to eat, Chick decided,

177

"Tell you what, we'll get a beer, then we'll go get something to eat, then we'll head to the dance."

Ethan shrugged, "Did you ever drink beer before?"

Ethan smiled and nodded, "Yes. Had a birthday party for my grandfather, he had a keg of beer. I tasted the foam off the top of a beer, decided I'd rather have milk and cookies."

Chick laughed, "How old were you then?"

Ethan smiled, "Five, maybe six."

They tied up at the saloon, Chick led Ethan into the bar, "Tal's son is here. He can be an ornery cuss, so we'll try to keep out of his way."

Chick moved to the opposite end of the bar as Tal's son. Chick ordered two beers, lifted his glass to Ethan, "Bottom's up Pard."

Ethan tasted his beer and sat it down, he figured he'd swap with Chick when Chick's glass was nearly empty, "What'd ya think?"

Ethan smiled good naturedly and quietly answered, "I'd still prefer milk and cookies."

Chick laughed heartily, then Tal's son was suddenly beside them, "What's so funny Chick?"

Chick laughed as he explained, "Ethan here was saying, he'd rather have milk and cookies than beer."

Ethan had never met Tal's son before, "My name's Benton Forester. Friends call me Ben."

Ethan offered his hand, "Nice to meet you Ben. Your dad has talked about you from time to time."

Ben snarled, "I can imagine what he's said about me."

Ethan replied without feeling, "Tal's always spoken well of you, I've never heard him say anything bad."

Ben laughed cynically, "I'll bet. I hear you moved into the house."

Ethan nodded, he continued to talk conversationally, "When I got there I was twelve, your dad had me bunk in the house instead of out with the men. I guess, since I wasn't asked to move out, I just hung around. Closer to the library. At night I read a lot, especially in the winter."

178

Ben polished off his beer and asked for another, "Cozy with my old man. I suppose you've got your hand out or in his wallet?"

Ethan felt a little icy inside, but he told himself that he was talking to Tal's son, he should tread easy and with respect, he smiled again as he replied, "Actually. Other than a few pairs of boots, some clothing, a roof over my head and something to eat, I haven't asked for or received a penny from your dad."

Ben's talk became a snarl, "Damn stray whelp. You are hard to rile. I ought to take you down a peg."

Chick scratched his chin and smiled, he didn't know if Tal wanted this exchange to take place and Chick didn't know whether to let it go on or not. Chick shrugged and remained silent while Ethan answered, "I came to town to go to a dance. I didn't come to argue or fight, especially with the son of the man who I have a lot of respect."

Ben stepped around Chick, "Can't get you riled huh? You are nothing but a damned yellow belly,.."

Ben took a swing at Ethan, the blow was slow in coming, Ethan blocked the blow then grabbed Ben by the collar and turned him about then pinned his arms at his sides. Ben Forester spent most all of the last six years hanging out in a saloon, he was weak, slow, and his judgment clouded with alcohol. Ethan quietly spoke to Ben as he removed his pistol and tossed it on the bar, "Ben. Chick and I are leaving. As I told you earlier. Your dad misses you. He would like for you to come home and work on the ranch. Your dad thinks the ranch is where you belong."

Ethan turned Ben loose, took the shells out of his gun and slid the gun down the bar toward the bartender. Ethan motioned to Chick that he was leaving, "Chick. Seems there's time to get us a piece of pie before the dance."

Ethan turned to Ben, "Welcome to come with us Ben."

Benton Forester again snarled, "Go plumb to hell."

179

Ben stepped back to the bar, pocketed the shells and picked up Ethan's still full glass of beer; Ethan turned and walked out of the saloon.

The dance hall was already crowded when they arrived, Chick hung up his gun as they entered. The atmosphere was to Ethan's liking with the music and the steady hum of conversation, "Well Chick. You got me here, what happens now?"

Chick nodded over to the corner of the room, "That crock over there has probably got a kick to it by now. Some of the boys pour a bottle or two into the water. The ladies made up some things to eat if you get hungry. The caller, the man with the fiddle, will get us all into some of the dances and tell us what to do. During the one on one dances, you are on your own. Most of the gals will help you to learn to dance if you tell them you are new to dancing."

Ethan looked across the room and espied the woman that adopted the orphan Sue Flanders off the train, "Chick, I see someone I'd like to talk to. See you in a while."

Chick couldn't figure out who Ethan would know at the dance, he watched as Ethan made his way to a corner and introduce himself to none other than Millie Baxter.

Ethan noted there was a seat beside the lady, he made himself at home, "Ma'am? You won't remember me. I was on the orphan train about six years ago. I talked to you about one of the girls, Sue?"

The woman's eyes opened in recognition, "Oh my goodness! Of course I remember."

The woman seemed overcome with emotion; tears appeared in her eyes, "My boy, I've thanked you many times in my thoughts and prayers. My name is Millie Baxter. The girl I adopted was Susan Flanders, Susan is getting me a cup of coffee; she'll be back shortly. Whatever happened to you?"

Ethan shrugged, "Well Ma'am, I didn't get picked. I jumped off the train just outside of Rawlins where you selected Sue. One more stop and I was going to be sent back to New York. I didn't want to take a chance, so I jumped near a road, walked the road to a ranch, I've been at the ranch ever since."

Millie smiled, "You've been right in this area? Sue wrote to Sparta trying to learn what happened to you, she didn't get a reply so I wrote to them. I learned that you were called a runaway, nobody knew anything about you."

Ethan nodded, "I wasn't going to write them and let them know where I was hiding in case they decided to bring me back and start all over again."

Millie laughed, her first question was appropriate, "Are they treating you well?"

Ethan smiled, he didn't have anything to compare with but he nodded, "I'm very happy."

Millie pushed, "Did they adopt you?"

Ethan shook his head, "No Ma'am."

Millie asked, "What's the name of the ranch?"

"Bar T."

Millie nodded her recognition, "Big ranch. Tal Forester's place."

Ethan nodded, "Yes Ma'am. I walked and ran more than a day before I got to the buildings."

Just then Sue returned with a cup of coffee and a couple of cookies, "Here Mom. Someone baked your favorite cookie."

Ethan admired a grown up Sue. Sue was a couple of inches taller, she put on some weight, she was still proud and in Ethan's eyes now quite a pretty gal. Millie Baxter smiled at Ethan's obvious admiration; she noted Sue did not recognize Ethan, "Dear, do you know who this young man is?"

Sue nodded without smiling, "Yes mother. He is the owner of that beautiful black mare we saw out in front of the saloon."

Millie smiled and opened her eyes in pretended shock, "Owwwuch."

Millie looked at Ethan and smiled, "I bet that hurt a little?"

Ethan laughed, "I'm not ashamed of my visit to the saloon, first time I've ever been there, besides coming from Sue. I fully understand and I'll accept the criticism."

Sue raised her eyebrows in disbelief, "Mom told you my name?"

Millie Baxter smiled, "Sue, you have to rein in your runaway team here. He already knew your name from a long time ago. He started this conversation asking about you. This gentleman is the one that helped me to adopt you, this is Ethan Gillette."

Sue looked again at Ethan as he stood to shake her hand, he was a head taller than her now, "Oh goodness. I'm sorry. I'm afraid my high ideals get me into trouble now and then."

Ethan nodded, "I'm the same way. I know where it comes from. But sometimes living in a world of dreaming about what should be; can be troublesome in the real world."

Sue nodded, Millie laughed, "Yes indeed. I'll move over a bit so you two can sit and talk."

For most of the evening they talked, Ethan learned to dance and decided he had to tell Sue as the night ended, "Sue. Thank you. I was scared coming to this dance. You turned this into a beautiful night. Your Mom is wonderful. I'm glad you are happy. I hope to see you again, you,.."

Sue recognized his hesitancy, she smiled and asked, "I what?"

Ethan smiled, "You are still real easy to talk to."

Sue also wanted to see Ethan again, "We are now your close neighbors, we live just outside of town. Stop by and we can talk some more."

Millie Baxter added, "Yes Ethan. Come and see us when you get a chance."

It was a little past three in the morning when Ethan and Chick unsaddled their horses back at the ranch. Chick was up early in the morning, Tal was out at the corral looking over his mare, Chick went out to give his report, "Looking for broken legs?"

Tal smiled and petted the mare affectionately, "Had to check. She's none the worse for wear. How did it go in town?"

Chick shrugged, "A little tame for me. Like a Sunday school picnic."

Tal wondered, "I see you two got back a couple hours past midnight. What happened?"

Chick smiled and continued, "Got to town, towed Ethan into the bar, he took one sip of his beer, your son Ben finished it for him."

Tal shook his head, "I didn't count on those two meeting up. What happened?"

Chick absently wiped a fleck off the mare's hip as he spoke, "Ben jumped Ethan, told Ethan he had his hand in your pocket and was taking all your money. Ethan didn't even raise his voice. He told Ben you worried about him. He told Ben you've never spoken ill of him. You loved him. Ben called him a liar and a yellow belly."

Tal winced, he shook his head, "No?"

Chick seriously nodded, "Yes sir'eee. Then Ben took a swing at Ethan."

Tal was astonished, "Unprovoked?"

Chick nodded, "Yes Sir. But you know how quick Ethan is. Ethan grabbed him by the shirt, spun him around and put him in a bear hug. Then Ethan took Ben's pistol away, let Ben go, took out the shells and slid the gun down the bar to the bartender. When we walked out of the saloon Ethen told Ben he should come home to the ranch where he belonged. Even invited him to the café for pie and to the dance. Ben told him to go to hell, then stumbled to the bar and drank Ethan's beer."

Chick went on, "Then we went to the café, had us a piece of pie and some cold milk, then rode over to the dance."

Tal wondered, "You boys were back early. He glue himself to one of the walls for the night?"

183

Chick shook his head, "Remember Millie Baxter? Well she moved back onto the home place when her dad died. She's been there for two years now. Anyway, Ethan saw her and went and sat down with her and talked at least a half hour. Millie adopted one of the orphan train kids, tall good looking gal. Ethan spent most of the night with them. He learned how to dance and told me he had a wonderful time. He wants to do it again."

Tal nodded, "So I needn't have worried about him."

Chick smiled, "I should say. The only worry I'd have would be if you were insulted or set upon. When Ben had words about you, Ethan got pretty serious. When he spoke to Millie Baxter, she said she couldn't get Ethan to say one bad thing about you or the ranch."

Tal thought for some time before he spoke, "Thank you Chick. Besides being a good hand, you are a good friend."

Chick started to walk away, then he turned, "One more thing, Ben told Ethan he heard Ethan was staying in the house instead of in the bunkhouse with the rest of the men. Ethan just passed it off, said it started that way when he was twelve, now he likes being in the house because it's close to the library."

Chick added with a smile, "Tell you what, boss. I figure both you and Ethan like things the way they are and both of you are afraid to admit it."

Chick smiled and touched his hat, "Goin to get me something to eat boss."

It was a month later that Tal Forester decided to take a trip to town, "Chick. I've got a question for you."

Chick smiled good naturedly, "Fire away boss, I'm rarin and ready."

Tal smiled, "Give this some thought. Who around here has enough money to keep my son housed and in beer for six years?"

Chick took some time before he responded, "Boss. Other than you, I couldn't tell you."

Tal nodded, "Exactly what I've been thinking."

184

Tal yelled, "Ethan. Why don't you saddle up and ride to town with me, we'll leave shortly. I want to visit with the Baxters and talk to the banker and my lawyer."

Chick smiled, "You got some idea about what's going on?"

Tal nodded, "I guess I'm sort of dense, but I think I do Chick."

On this occasion for some reason nothing was said about Ethan's .44, it was the first time Ethan accompanied Tal into town. On the ride to town they talked of cattle, the land, horses, winter feed and just about every aspect of the ranch, "Ethan, you've been doing a lot of reading. I see some of the things you are reading deal with the business of ranching. If you were running the ranch, what would you do different than we are doing right now?"

Ethan had considered a couple of things, "I'm thinking the ranch runs at good profit right now, but I've read where people are making small dams to hold more water for summer use and expanding range of the cattle. The far eastern part of your range is pretty useless because there is no water. It would be pretty simple to build a couple of dams in those gorges. When it does rain we lose a lot of water to runoff. We could put up a couple of windmills and add to the water supply on outlying parts of the ranch."

Tal smiled, "How do we take care of the windmills?"

Ethan shrugged, "Man on horseback could ride out a couple of hours, check up on the cattle. From what I gather the windmill is rigged to turn on and off with some kind of float in the water. The other thing is the area the men call the flats. The flats make for good grazing, but cattle go in there in the early spring and trample a lot of grass. When we cut grass for winter feed, we don't get a very good harvest. That area could be fenced off, we could cut hay a couple of times during the summer. On part of the fenced area we could grow our own grain instead of buying. We could build a barn of some type to hold all the hay, grain, wagons, and of course a pen for your mare."

185

Tal had to smile at Ethan's reference to the mare, "How did the old girl act for you?"

Ethan smiled, "Sweet. Like riding on a pillow."

Tal wondered, "If you had your choice of horses, which one would it be?"

Ethan didn't take long to think, "There's that gelded paint, a really tall horse that is the best cutting horse I've ever sat on. When you ride him you better be awake and stay over the center of the horse or he'll leave you behind. He's quick and he thinks about two steps ahead of the cows."

Tal wondered, "You'd take him over this mare?"

Ethan shrugged, "She's the best horse on the ranch. But that's your horse. I wouldn't take her from you."

Tal smiled at the response, in the past five years Ethan had always showed good judgment, always with kindness..

While Tal was in the bank and with the lawyer, Ethan sat outside and waited, after a while Tal stepped onto the boardwalk, "Ethan, step in here for a minute. You are going to join me in this meeting. I want you to be a witness, you don't have to say anything unless I ask you."

Tal sat down and motioned for Ethan to take a seat, "Ethan, this man is my lawyer, Stuart Bennington, this other gentleman is my banker, Ron Carsten. I've met with both men separately and now they've outlined financially where the ranch sits. At this point I want you to bear witness to the fact that I am no longer going to use Mr. Bennington as my lawyer."

Bennington's face turned crimson, Tal went on, "On my visit to the bank, I find money has been routinely withdrawn by Mr. Bennington. Mr. Bennington in turn sends me a different set of figures. I assume that Mr. Bennington is paying for my son's saloon expenses and a place for him to stay in town. I've a feeling that in the end, Mr. Bennington is expecting to end up with the entire ranch as repayment."

Bennington rose and picked up a large stack of papers, Tal quietly ordered, "Bennington. Sit down. I'm not done yet."

Bennington ignored the order and continued to gather his papers, Ethan stood, he towered over Bennington. Ethan calmly ordered; "Mr. Bennington. Sit down please."

For a moment Bennington looked at Ethan, then he put the papers down and took his seat, Tal continued, "Over the last six years, it seems that more than five thousand dollars have been taken from the ranch account. Before I get the sheriff in here, I would like to know how the five thousand dollars will be replaced. That is the reason both of you gentlemen are here. Who will repay the five thousand?"

Carsten looked at Bennington, Bennington looked to Carsten, Carsten broke the silence; "I've assumed all along that Mr. Bennington had authorization to withdraw the money?"

Tal waited for Bennington to defend himself, there wasn't anything forthcoming, Tal looked to Ethan and smiled, "Well what do we do Ethan? Beat the hell out of both of them?"

Tal's eye's rested on Ethan. Not really knowing if an answer was requested, Ethan decided to venture his opinion, "I would say the bank is responsible for the unauthorized withdrawals. I would say that Mr. Bennington will spend about five years in prison for doing the withdrawing. From what I've read I believe it is called embezzlement."

Ethan looked to Tal with a slight twinkle in his eye, "But sir, I can take Bennington out and beat the hell out of him if you'd like, before I take him to the sheriff."

Bennington looked with hate at Tal, his hand plunged into his bag, instantly Ethan drew his gun and jammed the butt on top of Bennington's wrist. Ethan spoke calmly as he pinned Bennington's wrist against the bag with the sharp point of the butt of his .44, "Bring your hand out slowly Mr. Bennington. And empty. You really don't want to get shot over five thousand dollars, do you?"

Tal took Bennington's gun and the stack of papers, "Ethan, go get the sheriff. Fill him in on the way here."

Ethan returned briefly with the sheriff and a set of manacles for Bennington. After securing Bennington's wrists, the sheriff asked, "Tal. Where the devil you been? You used to come into town quite often."

Tal nodded, "Ever since Polly died I guess I've been a little hollow."

They reported to the sheriff what had transpired, the sheriff took Bennington's gun then looked to Carsten, "I believe Ethan is right about the money being your responsibility Ron. I'd suggest putting a lien on all of Bennington's property right away. Lock up his office, his house, everything of value so he doesn't hide anything."

The sheriff nodded, "Ethan, I've heard good things about you. Nice to meet you finally. Don't be hiding out to that ranch like Tal here."

The sheriff started to lead Bennington out the door, then he asked, "Tal. How did you figure out Bennington was stealing money from your account?"

Tal grinned, "I finally asked myself who could afford to pay for my son's lifestyle. I figured I was the only one. So, I figured it was Bennington or Ron taking my money. I checked the bank's record of withdraws against the accounting of my lawyer. Bennington's figures at the bank and what he sent me weren't the same. He must have made some kind of deal with my son."

The sheriff grinned, "I think that place your son is staying belongs to Bennington. Ron. You better look into putting a lien on that place also."

The sheriff pushed Bennington out the door, Carsten apologized to Tal, "I wish you would have looked the account over sooner."

Tal stood, "Haven't been to town in the last seven years except to buy the boy a pair of boots. I'll try to get in more often. You can write me and let me know how the account will be repaid. Take your time Ron."

Tal shook hands with the banker then dismissed Ethan, "Ethan, there's one more thing I have to say to Carsten. Go over to the café, I'll be right over."

Alone with Carsten, Tal was about to put in a simple request, the banker shook his head, "Christ Tal. I've never seen anybody move as fast as Ethan. If Ethan would have been slower, he'd have to have shot Bennington. Ethan wasn't about to let him harm you."

Tal thought for a moment, "Is that what you read?"

Carsten nodded, "Without a doubt, Bennington looked at you with hate in his eyes and he went for that gun. Where the devil did Ethan get to be so fast?"

Tal shrugged, "You know the boys. They are constantly playing around. Ethan is a fine lad, at any other time I don't think he would hurt anyone."

Tal begun to describe the scene in the saloon, the banker nodded, "Heard from the bartender. Ethan did a good job of telling your son what you stood for. What is your son going to do now that his supply is cut off?"

Tal shrugged, "I hope he comes home."

Carsten wondered, "You would still welcome him?"

Tal nodded, "Keep the door open. Ron, there is something I want you to do for me now that I don't have a lawyer. I'm going to the café for a piece of pie, I'll be back to sign the paper in a half hour."

Tal explained what he wanted, the banker indicated the paper would be ready in fifteen minutes.

It was a little past noon when they stopped at the Baxter residence, Millie met them at the door, "Tal Forester and Ethan. This is a pleasant surprise. Two of the nicest people in the world on my doorstep at the same time. Come on in. Sue, put on the coffee pot."

Sue smiled warmly when she saw Ethan, Tal asked, "Where is Bart?"

Millie shrugged, "Working. You know that man, he works around the clock. Besides Sue's coffee, what brings you two out?"

Tal explained, "Millie. I need to talk to you in private for a minute."

Millie waved her hand, "Sue. We'll do the coffee later. Take Ethan and show him about. I'll call when it's safe to return."

When Ethan and Sue were gone Tal asked, "Millie. I have some things I'd like you to do for me. First of all, the next time you are at the bank, there is a paper there I want you to sign as witness. Another thing: I'd like you to tell me how you know Ethan."

Millie started out by saying Ethan was a Godsend, then related the incident at the orphan showing, "If it wasn't for that lad I would have left Sue behind. Every time I think about the possibility I may have missed her, I'm about in tears. Ethan whispered all about her in a short period of time. Sue said the kids weren't supposed to talk unless spoken to. Truth is, I wanted to take Ethan with me too, I went back to get him but they left the hall and the train left town so fast I didn't get there in time."

Tal asked, "How did Ethan end up at my ranch?"

Millie was puzzled, "Didn't you ask him?"

Tal hesitated, Millie explained, "The guard fell asleep, Ethan knew there was only one more town, after that he would be sent back to New York. He didn't want to go to New York, so he somehow got on top of the train, went back to the caboose, climbed down, waited for the man in the caboose to look the other direction. As Ethan waited on the platform of the caboose, he picked out a road not knowing if it went to a town or a ranch or nowhere; he told me he got lucky when he picked your road."

Millie smiled, "Tal, I bet you've never seen him in a card game with friends betting?"

Tal nodded, "I guess you are right. I know he's not a betting person."

Millie explained, "One time he stole a loaf of bread."

Tal again nodded, "I heard the story."

Millie asked, "Did he tell you about the bet?"

190

Tal shook his head, "No. What bet?"

Millie explained how he bet the loaf of bread a man couldn't move a railroad car filled with coal with one hand, Tal shook his head, "Can't be done."

Millie laughed, "The man went and got a pry bar, with one hand he moved the car. He took Ethan's loaf of bread, that's all Ethan had to eat in two days. The man gave the loaf of bread back and advised him not to bet. It's a lesson that's had a lifelong effect."

Tal smiled, then he asked, "Millie. I've never seen him cry. There has been a few times he's been hurt bad enough it almost made me cry, but he didn't cry."

Millie smiled, "I imagine the lad did all his crying early in life. Truth of the matter be told he probably learned quick enough that crying doesn't do a bit of good. I asked Sue one time why I've never seen her in tears. Sue said she cries when she is happy now and then. If I were you Tal, I'd just figure the lad is stronger than most. Be happy the way he is."

Tal nodded, "I've always been happy with the lad. Since my wife died and Benton left home, Ethan has made the entire ranch a better place to live."

Tal stood, "Millie, you'll see the reason I had you sign the paper as witness. I think you'll agree with me. I'm glad you are back as neighbors again."

Millie smiled, "Me too. We ought to get together for a shindig like we used to when Dad, Mom and your Polly were still alive. At least come in to the next dance. There's one in three weeks at the school house."

Tal nodded, "I'll give that some thought."

Millie walked him to the door, they watched Sue and Ethan as they came out of the stables, Millie remarked, "They make a fine couple."

Tal had been thinking the same thing.

They rode in relative silence back to the ranch, Tal had a couple of questions he wondered about, "Bennington was a damn fool reaching for his pistol that way."

Ethan nodded, "I'm mighty glad he was as slow as he was, I've never shot a man. Tell the truth, I think that'd be the kind of thing that would stick with you."

Tal figured the answer was another he wanted to hear, to not have guilt guiding a person was a thing Tal feared. His son seemed to be one that just did things that were wrong and couldn't figure out why they were wrong. His son had no guilt, "Got another question for you Ethan. You told Millie Baxter about Sue. Millie ended up adopting Sue. Did you know Sue before you two stood on that stage?"

Ethan was silent for a bit, usually he had a quick response, "Sort of. Sir, when I was at Sparta, my job was to keep the administration building clean. There was a room below the main office with an air vent. Through the air vent I could hear what was said by the men that sent us out on the train. One man by the name of Bill had a good conscience. He read the files of some of the kids. Sue's story is a sad one. Sue Flanders' father and mother were returning late from a church meeting, there was a storm. It was raining pitchforks and hammer-handles, the wind was blowing bad, they couldn't have seen... They had a two horse hitch and they were coming down the hill way too fast in the dark. They rounded a sharp curve, a tree came down in the road, they didn't have time to stop the horses. The horses tried to jump over the tree. Horses and rig got tangled up in the top of that downed tree. Sue's mother was thrown out, she died of a broken neck. A branch was driven through the carriage and into Sue's father's chest. The next day when Sue went to look for them, she found them. One of the horses was dead the other one couldn't get up. Sue went home, got a gun; put the horse down. Then she went to a neighbor for help.

"I want to tell you Tal. I had to put that flea bit down when it broke his leg last fall. I liked that horse, I didn't sleep right for a month. When I think of Sue's story I just can't imagine her pain.

"Afterward Sue was taken to Sparta, she probably hadn't been eating. Because she was so thin, nobody wanted to take a chance on her.

"I heard a lot of those stories during the time I was at Sparta. Every one of them hurts to tell.

"Me. I was so lucky. I just happen to pick the road to your ranch. And, I didn't get killed jumping from the train. When I hit the ground I skipped around like a flat rock on a pond, but I didn't get hurt bad."

Tal Forester had all of his questions answered but one, "I've wondered, when you turned eighteen the state of Wisconsin lost jurisdiction over you."

There was silence for some time, Ethan laughed, "I think they lost jurisdiction in my case when I jumped off that train."

Tal asked, "You ever think you may want to go back?"

Ethan didn't hesitate this time, "Sir. You've given me an education. A home I never tire of. I'll be honest with you. I think I've adopted you. If I was forced to leave the ranch, I'd have to try to find another one just like this one with a teacher and a friend like you. You took the place of the father I lost and I couldn't have hoped for better."

Those were the words Tal wanted to hear, he felt Ethan had established roots at the ranch and wanted to be there, but he didn't know for certain. Tal was quiet for some time, then he asked, "You've met my son Benton?"

Ethan nodded, "Yes sir."

Tal asked, "Now. If you were in my shoes, would you let him back on the ranch?"

Ethan didn't hesitate with his answer, "Yes sir. I think I already told you, a man gave me some good advice about people. He told me to keep the door open. You can set the rules, but keep the door open so they know they can get back in once they decide they want to obey your rules. If you slam that door, then there isn't room for bending. Compromise is what he called it."

Tal figured he'd have to take more rides with Ethan, he learned quite a bit from him, "Ethan. Since you came to the ranch, I've noted you read people pretty good. You know when they are happy, mad, sad, whatever. Seems you know then how to cheer them up. Where did you learn how to do that?"

Ethan shrugged, "You learn in a hurry living on the streets or in an orphanage. I read in one of your books about being humble, best way I can describe how you feel once you've been in an orphanage and at the mercy of others you don't even know. Humility."

Tal wondered, "Do you ever feel mad about being put on that train?"

Ethan smiled, "Doesn't do any good to look backward. If I wasn't placed on the train, if I was picked, if I wouldn't have jumped, then I wouldn't have made it to your ranch."

A few days later the sheriff opened a letter from Tal Forester, he mulled it over for some time before he decided to proceed. The sheriff went in to the cell occupied by Bennington, "Stuart! You sleeping again? Just had some news I thought you'd be interested in. Seems Tal Forester is considering making out a will and leaving everything to Ethan Gillette. If that happens, you'll lose your cash cow won't you?"

The sheriff laughed and walked away.

Part 4

A week passed by, Chick and Ethan spent the day on the southern edge of the ranch pushing cattle away from the railroad tracks. They decided that a fence would eventually have to be built to keep the cows from wandering near the tracks. Tired and hungry they rode into the ranch yard just after dark. The sheriff's horse and the doctor's buggy were at the hitch-rail. Ethan and Chick rode directly to the house, the sheriff met him on the steps, "What happened?"

The sheriff answered, "Tal's been shot. The doctor's with him."

Ethan was going to walk past the sheriff, "Wait just a minute. I want to talk to you and Chick.

"Where were you two today?"

Chick was now on the porch also, "By the railroad tracks pushing cattle this way. What happened?"

The sheriff shook his head, Ethan pushed his way into the house, the sheriff stopped Chick, "Was Ethan with you all day long?"

Chick nodded, "Yup. We got up before daybreak and headed south, it made for a long day. Why do you ask?"

The sheriff smiled, "I just wanted to make sure he had a good alibi."

Chick was fuming, "Alibi? Who did the shooting?"

The sheriff shook his head, "Got word in town that Ethan did the shooting."

Chick shook his head, "That damn Benton. Worthless no account, mean… Where is Benton?"

The sheriff shook his head, "Too early to tell where he was. I have to get back to town so I can ask some questions early in the morning. Do you have anyone here that is good at cutting sign?"

Chick shook his head, "Not that good. When you get to town, you send Bart Baxter out. He's like a bloodhound. I'll tell the boys to stay away from where Tal was shot."

The sheriff explained, "Tal was north of the buildings, about an hour out. He said he went to check out a piece of cloth hanging in a bush. When he got there someone shot from behind him. They hit him good but he got out of there, the horse ran a mile before he slowed down. Then Tal fell out of the saddle, the horse stopped, Tal got back up and made it to the ranch. Rolly about killed a horse getting to town to get the doc and me."

Ethan stepped into Tal's room, he noted the picture of Polly on the dresser along with a picture of his son Benton. Tal's eyes were closed, "Doc. How is he doing?"

195

Tal's eyes opened, he smiled weakly, "The sheriff tells he got word you may have shot me."

Ethan shook his head and took Tal's hand, his vision was clouded with moisture, "I heard. How are you feeling?"

Tal looked up at Ethan's tear filled eyes and smiled, "Feel like I've had a hot branding iron run through me."

Ethan asked, "You had a feeling something like this may happen."

Tal nodded, still he retained his smile, "Yes I did. And like a damn fool I made it happen and walked right into it."

Ethan was confused, "You made it happen? What did you do?"

Tal admitted, "I sent a note to the sheriff, I told the sheriff to tell Bennington I was making my will out and you Ethan, were the sole inheritor."

Ethan understood how the news may then get to Benton, "Why did you do that?"

Tal smiled, "Because, the truth is; I've already made that will out. I thought by telling Bennington it would bring things to a head."

Tal started to tire, "Ethan. I want you to know, if I don't make it. I'm really happy you stumbled on the road to this ranch. Really happy. Best day of my life."

Tal closed his eyes, the doctor motioned to the door, "That's enough. Let him get some sleep."

Ethan got himself something to eat then sat in a large chair in Tal's bedroom. Without any women on the ranch Ethan figured staying with Tal was the thing to do.

Morning came and Tal was still resting comfortably, the doc checked up on him then left for town. Half hour later Ethan got up from the chair when he heard a buggy and horses in the yard. Ethan stepped outside as Millie Baxter and Sue were walking up the steps, "How is he?"

Ethan had a look of fear on his face, "Still sleeping."

Millie Baxter threw her arms about Ethan, "I want you to know lad, he loved you like his own son. He was proud of you. You just continue to be yourself. Things will turn out.

196

I'm going in and see if there is something I should be doing with Tal."

Millie looked at Sue standing awkwardly, "Well Sue, give the man a hug, and a reason to smile again."

Sue put her arms around Ethan and held him gently without talking, then she reassured, "Tal will be all right."

Ethan weakly nodded, "Thank you Sue."

Sue put her hands on his shoulders and said, "On the way here, Mom explained, it is important that you don't get angry about this. Upset, sad, mad, but don't get angry. Be yourself. You are a good person.

"Ethan. I think you know, when one has had a background such as you and I have had, we feel very deeply about many things. Sometimes we seem to see or feel things others may ignore. When I made the comment about you being in that saloon? That came from ideals I think both of us share. It was inappropriate that I shared my ideals when I did. I have since heard all about your visit to the saloon, instead of setting upon you I should have been cheering for you. I did to you what I'm asking you not to do now. Don't react before you have all the facts. And then, don't react out of anger."

Ethan considered Sue's advice, she was a gal that been through the storms of life, one that had a background similar to his, one that knew the depth of his feeling, "Thank you Sue. Coming from you, that advice means a lot to me."

"Let's go check up on Tal and Mom."

When Ethan and Sue got back into the bedroom where Tal lay, Tal turned his head to look at the two of them. Tal seemed to meekly smile, then he reached out and took Ethan's hand, then he closed his eyes and slept. Ethan felt as though he was being summoned to remain, Millie Baxter smiled and related, "Ethan. You just stay right here with him. I'm thinking you are the best medicine for him right now."

Millie pushed the chair up to the bed so Ethan could remain where he was.

197

Bart Baxter looked over the area where Tal was shot, careful to take in all the information provided by the sign remaining. Bart found where the shooter laid. He knew the shooter spent a considerable amount of time there. Bart knew the shooter had a bottle with him, the imprint was still visible in the sand. He knew from the sign how the man rolled his cigarettes, how much of the cigarette the man smoked, he saw that he had a pair of binoculars with him and an over-worn boot heel on his left foot.

Bart slowly moved toward the piece of cloth hanging in the bush. Cloth didn't vary much, this cloth was red, he retrieved the cloth he looked down at the heel marks in the sand. Again the left boot heel was more heavily worn than the right. Bart raised his hand and motioned for Chick, Rolly and the sheriff to ride up.

Bart slowly showed the three of them the evidence he had gathered, in the event of a court hearing there would be corroboration. The sheriff shook his head, he seemed disgusted with himself; "I think I have a few more questions to ask in town."

Bart Baxter asked, "Something you seen or heard here help Sheriff?"

The sheriff nodded, "The down in the left heel and the bottle. That wasn't a canteen. Just a couple of men in town drink that early in the day, one of them is in jail.

"Chick. Rolly. Right now I know you are mad as hell. But I'm depending on you two to keep the lid on at the ranch. Especially Ethan. He's a nice lad. I want him to be around these parts for a long, long time, so keep him to home till I wrap this up."

Chick nodded, "Sheriff. I know you're thinking what I'm thinking. This is the work of Benton. I'll tell you the truth, I'd just as soon shoot that twisted fool myself, but I'm hearing you. Rolly and I will keep Ethan at the ranch and we'll sit tight. Anything else?"

The sheriff hung his head and admitted, "Got one more thing. When you boys are on that ranch, keep your eyes and ears open day and night. Tell Ethan to keep his gun handy and stay close to Tal. I hope Ethan doesn't have to shoot that fool Benton, but all of you boys protect yourself and Tal."

Chick and Rolly rode back to the ranch and relayed the sheriff's advice in the company of Millie and Sue Baxter. Millie Baxter lost all of her usually joy, "Does the sheriff really think that boy will steal in here and try to kill his father again?"

Chick was wringing his hat as he spoke, "Yes Ma'am. The man has lost any sense of right and wrong he did have."

Three days later Tal was able to get up, Millie decided she would go home and leave the nursing to Ethan and the cook. They were all sitting at the kitchen table when Millie announced, "Tal. I think you are able hands with Ethan and Cookie here. I believe I'll pack up and head back home. I'm going to ask Chick to ride with us; that would make us feel better."

Millie looked at Ethan and smiled, "Ethan, I'm going to take Sue with me if you don't mind?"

Ethan's face reddened as he replied, "You two have been a blessing. I've gotten used to you taking over. I don't know if I can get along without Sue. We'll have to give it a try, but, if Tal has a relapse, we'll come and get you in a big hurry."

Millie got up and patted Ethan on the hands, "You're doing good. Just stick by Tal.

"By the way. Any news from the sheriff?"

Ethan shook his head, "As of last night, he still hasn't seen hide nor hair of Benton. So we'll just hold up here until he's caught."

Tal got up, "Been up long enough, I'm going to take a nap. But you listen here. Next week is the dance. Ethan and Chick will be there. I'll have Rolly, Cookie and Dirk guard the house."

Tal embraced both of the gals then made his way to the bedroom.

The week passed quickly, on the day of the dance Tal gave parting orders to Chick and Ethan, "Boys. This is hard orders

I have for both of you. You are both wearing guns. Those guns are for your protection. I think my son Benton is no longer in control of himself, I think he'll try to kill Ethan, or maybe me. If need be, protect yourselves. Ethan. I know you are good with that side-gun of yours. Don't use it like you did with Bennington, and don't get fancy and try to wound Benton. Benton fancies himself with a gun and he'll use it. If you are forced to pull that thing out, then you use it."

Tal turned to go to his favorite reading chair, "Oh, yes. You boys have a good time. Next dance, I'm going with you."

The sheriff stood in front of Bennington's cell, "Stuart. I've been looking at the statutes. I think I can add accessory to attempted first degree murder after you got the word out to Benton. People around here really like Tal. A lot of people depend on his ranch for a livelihood. I think I can get a conviction, especially since Benton is a little touched."

Bennington scoffed, but the sheriff could see that he was thinking about the possibility of being convicted of murder. As the sheriff walked away he mentioned, "Let's see, that would be another thirty years in prison. Be sort of hard on you. A man like you carrying more weight than you ought and having to spend all day splitting all them rocks."

The sheriff looked out the window, he could see the school house was lit up, a thought suddenly struck him. The sheriff grabbed his hat, checked his pistol and hurried out the door.

The dance was well underway when Chick and Ethan arrived, Ethan rode the black mare into town and took Sue to the restaurant for an hour before the dance started. Soon after the dance started Sue asked Ethan why he was wearing his gun, "I promised Tal I would wear the gun. He also made me promise I would use it to protect myself."

Ethan shook his head slowly, "Sue, I think if I got my foot caught in the stirrup and was being dragged, I may be able to shoot the horse. Maybe. I don't know if I could draw this gun to protect myself if it was Tal's son."

They were dancing, Sue offered, "I'm afraid to tell you that I see the distinction. Your love and respect for Tal creates the question. And you are very important to Tal also. Benton is important to Tal, but Tal knows Benton is sick. I want you to know Ethan Gillette. You are important to me also. I guess that is why I see the distinction Tal is making. I don't want to see you laid out in a bed with a bullet in you. I felt bad enough when Tal was wounded."

Ethan smiled at Sue and said, "Sue, we will get through this. You are important to me also. I think you understand how I feel about you."

Sue edged a little closer as they danced, she smiled, looked up at him and said, "No, I want you to explain."

Ethan smiled, looked down into her eyes, recognized the mischief and the warmth, "Now I'll be tongue tied. How do I begin to explain how important you are to me? For one thing, when you and your Mom showed up and helped when Tal was shot, I realized I needed more in my life than cattle and ranching."

Just then Benton Forester ran into the room and pointed his gun at Ethan, immediately Ethan forced Sue away, "Sue please step aside."

Benton screamed his orders, "No! Everyone stand still!"

People still scrambled to get out from behind Ethan. Sue was only two steps away from Ethan, Ethan ordered, "Sue, step away please."

Benton again screamed, "No! Stand still! I'm going to kill you Ethan and I'll bet you don't know why?"

Ethan held his palms up above hip high, he slowly stepped away from Sue, "I don't know why you want to kill me Benton. I don't know why you tried to kill your father."

Benton gritted his teeth and snarled, "I shot him so I would get the ranch. Now Bennington told me you were going to inherit the ranch when the old man died."

Benton laughed, "Now I'm going to ruin my father's plans, I'm going to kill you, then I'm going to kill that Baxter girl you were dancing with."

201

At that moment the sheriff stepped into the room, he was behind Benton, he called, "Benton, this is the Sheriff. Drop the gun, I've got a gun aimed at the middle of your back."

Benton looked at Ethan then at Sue, Ethan watched Benton's eyes dart back and forth, Ethan sensed Benton was thinking about killing Sue then taking his chances with him. Benton focused on Ethan, Ethan sensed Benton was ready to pull the trigger, Benton's eyes and gun flashed toward Sue. Ethan dove to shield Sue as Benton swung his gun toward her. As Benton's gun fired the sheriff and Chick fired. Benton crumbled to the floor.

Ethan lay on top of Sue on the floor, blood stained the back of his shirt. Ethan's cheek lay on Sue's cheek, he looked at Sue and weakly asked, "Sue. Are you all right?"

Sue's hand on Ethan's back was stained with Ethan's blood, "He was going to shoot me. I'm all right. You've been shot."

Ethan nodded, before he passed out he smiled, "He knew hurting you would hurt me more, but… you… you are all right,.. love..."

Ethan woke up at the Baxter home, sitting at the bedside holding his hand was Sue, Ethan smiled, "This is getting to be a habit."

Sue stood, bent over and kissed him, "Let's make this the last time you get shot."

Ethan smiled, "Do I still get to see you real often and get more of those kisses without being shot?"

Sue kissed him again, "As often as you'd like. I'd prefer without being shot."

Ethan nodded, "You've got a deal."

About the author: (E-book print 7/2015)

Parts of the story stem from real life occurrences. The bet with the loaf of bread happened when I was about eight years old, except at the time I purchased the loaf I didn't steal it. In the 1940's we were a very poor northern Wisconsin family and I was entrusted to bring the loaf home with me. When that yardman took the loaf of bread from me, I felt simply crushed, he too returned the loaf of bread and sent me on my way, lesson learned, don't bet.

"The State Has No Conscience," was written before I knew about the existence of the 'Orphan Train.'

While at the WCC I didn't have to sweep the administration building, on occasion I worked in the dining hall and the kitchen located on the east end of the administration building. In the 1950's some of the workers had apartments in the old building and I did deliver newspapers there and every once in a while at night a broom was jammed into my hands so I could do mortal combat with bats inhabiting the old wooden building.

While a resident at the WCC, a boy is much like Ethan. In my case I was nearly eighteen before I held or kissed a girl. I was eighteen before I tasted a beer, except when I was about six years old and sipped some foam off a beer at my grandfather's seventieth birthday party. In my case, while at the center, on six occasions my birthdays passed and I didn't know I had a birthday until I recalled days afterward.

Being at the Wisconsin Child Center for nearly six years wasn't fun, but my stay there was minor compared to what many of the children on the Orphan Train must have been exposed to. The part of the story dealing with the ability to 'read' people, and being humbled by the experience, is also true. There is also a feeling of guilt for those of us that were at the WCC; many may not want others to know it was necessary for them to be there. Personally, very infrequently I do share some of the occurrences with family and close friends. Prior to this writing I used a pen name to avoid 'going there' with friends.

As for the idealizing, when one spends a lot of time wishing and hoping instead of experiencing family, parents, brothers or sisters, love; one of course hopes for the ideal, not something less. Of course the actuality isn't ever perfect and in many cases there is disappointment when for instance, during the fostering process, the ideal isn't met. The end result is a situation that cannot be reached by either side, the foster parent can't live up to the child's ideal; the child in most cases will not be accepted unequivocally as a birth child. Of course in a fictional story, the ideals can more easily be attained. In reality, currently, I would hope that an education by open discussion would be given to both foster parent and foster child preceding the fostering process.

Introduction to, "Sometimes I Cry in the Night' and Orphan Train stories.

Author's note. [In the following story, the title came first. I woke up with tears in my eyes, I cannot recall why; bad dream, maybe allergies… I had been thinking about orphan train children, the title, 'Sometimes I Cry in the Night' came to me. I wrote the title down then, during a forced down time due to an operation and knowing something of the orphan train, I wrote the story to mesh with the title.]
"Sometimes I Cry in the Night," relates the tale of an Orphan Train rider that turns his rejection into independence and reclusiveness until years later he sees a mirror image of himself in a runaway lad from the Orphan Train.

"Sometimes I Cry in the Night"

The orphan train pulled away from its stop at Sparta, Wisconsin after picking up another thirty-eight orphans from the State School for Dependent, Orphaned and Neglected Children, now two-hundred-twenty-five in all; they were destined for the unknown. Many of the newcomers broke into song, they had hopeful thoughts of being part of a family. Marissa Lamont, a passenger since the stop in Milwaukee, still had tears running down her cheeks. Tears at the recollection of the tragic loss of her family and now bewildered at why and where the train would take her. Through tears, Marissa's eyes chanced another glance across the aisle at the boy referred to as Rory, his expression hadn't changed in over two hundred miles.

Like Marissa, Rory didn't join in singing, he sat bolt upright, on this trip he held no hope for the eventual outcome, nor did he share in the newcomer's happiness, for he had insight into what the rest of the orphans would be going through. This was Rory's second trip on the orphan train. Although Rory appeared remote, aloof and indifferent, he was constantly watchful, his eyes missed nothing; such was the defensive, self-protective makeup of many orphans. The girl across from him had been crying since she was put on the train in Milwaukee, Rory remained aloof but, on the inside, her tears bothered him.

The orphan train made many stops in Wisconsin and Minnesota, by the time they got through Minnesota many of the orphans had been picked. Among the remaining was Rory and Marissa along with about thirty others. It was early evening, Marissa moved across the aisle and sat down beside Rory. Tears stained her cheeks as she continued to cry. Rory didn't understand why she sat beside him but he gently advised. "You will have to try to stop crying or nobody will pick you."

Something had drawn Marissa across the aisle, it seemed to Marissa there was a strength about the aloof boy; and, she didn't want to sit by herself. Now she appreciated that someone chose to talk to her. She was numb, drained of emotion, she shrugged, "I don't care."

Without feeling Rory replied, "You must care. Do you know what happens to you if nobody takes you?"

Marissa shook her head, "No."

Rory explained, "At the end of the run they put you back on the train and take you back to New York."

Marissa asked, "New York? How do you know?"

Without feeling, Rory answered, "This is my second trip. I was sent back the first time."

As Marissa looked at Rory, she marveled at how steadfast he was. Marissa asked, "A lot of kids cry. I've never seen you cry."

Without emotion, Rory quietly responded, "Everyone cries."

Marissa pushed, "Even you?"

Rory dodged the question, "I don't want people to see me cry. I don't want them to know that I'm weak or afraid."

Again, Marissa asked, "Do you ever cry?"

Rory had the slightest smile at her persistence. Quietly, secretly, seeming apologetic, he replied, "Sometimes I cry in the night."

Rory's admission helped her to explain; as Marissa choked back tears, she told of the deaths of her entire family. "Mom, daddy, my brother, and sister Ellen died. Our house burned down. I was away at the neighbors taking care of their children."

Rory realized that her luck at being away from home now became guilt. It seemed Rory understood too much for one his age. Rory asked, "What's your name?"

"Marissa Lamont."

Again, Rory showed that he understood way too much for one so young. He said, "Marissa. You must consider yourself lucky."

Marissa exclaimed, "Lucky!?"

Gently, Rory explained, "Yes Marissa. Always remember your family. Always remember what your family was like, that way you can someday... someday start over with a family of your own."

"What is your name?"

"Rory."

"What is your last name?"

Rory shook his head, "I'm not lucky."

"What you mean you're not lucky?"

Without smiling Rory replied, "I don't have a last name. I don't know who my mother or father was. I don't know if I have had brothers or sisters."

Marissa continued to poke at his hardened exterior, "Is that why you are so quiet?"

Rory shrugged, indifferent to the question. Marissa asked, "Are you mean?"

Rory shook his head, "No. I just like to be alone. That way I get into less trouble."

Marissa had stopped crying for the first time in the past day. She asked, "Is it alright if I sit with you. I'm scared. I feel better talking to you."

Rory shrugged, "It's alright, I don't mind."

Marissa asked, "Are you afraid?"

Rory shook his head, "No. Whoever takes us, they will have to feed us and protect us. My job will be, to do the best I can at what I'm told to do. I'm thinking it will be a little bit like having a mother and father."

Marissa started to whimper again. Rory said, "I'm sorry. Don't cry. If you do your best, if you do what you are told, you will be all right."

Rory asked, "Tell me about your father. Was he good to you? Did he hit you?"

"No. My dad was a good father."

Rory explained, "Some kids at the orphanage said their fathers would beat them. Some kids were taken away from their families because their dad or their mom didn't treat them right."

After some consideration, Marissa said, "I think you are right Rory. I was lucky. My mom and dad were good to us. They loved us, they loved each other. I'm going to take your advice Rory. I'll always remember what a family should be like."

The statement was meant to be thankful but Rory was saddened because he had never experienced a family. What would he pattern a family after? Would he ever have a family? He thought not. Someday he thought he wanted to be far away from people, but now, what was it about Marissa's reliance on him it gave him pause? Marissa made him feel better, more complete, almost a part.

The train parked on a sidetrack for the night, bagged lunches were provided, soon most of the children were fast asleep. Marissa again crossed the aisle to be with Rory. She seemed to be more at peace in his presence. Mr. Zimms announced there would be no more talking, soon Marissa fell asleep and ended up leaning on Rory. Rory again had a good feeling, as if he was her protector. Puzzled by this strange new emotion, he reached over to touch her hair, then more at ease than usual, he too soon fell fast asleep.

At daybreak Delbert Zimms yelled orders from the back of the railcar. "Listen carefully. Sit up straight and listen. If you have to go, do it as soon as I get done talking."

Delbert carried his paddle with him as he walked down the aisle. "Our next stop will be in about two hours. Get dressed in your good clothes, make sure you are clean and your hair is combed."

Marissa was back across the aisle from Rory, she motioned that his shoe was untied. Rory bent over to tie his shoe. At that time Delbert Zimms appeared behind Rory, Delbert delivered a mean, stinging blow across Rory's shoulders. Surprised and pained by the blow, Rory sat up and rubbed his back. Delbert snapped, "I told you to set up straight."

Rory politely explained, "I was tying my shoe, Sir."

Without remorse Delbert snapped again, "Do as you are told."

Rory looked straight ahead, stoic, remote, aloof, unknowingly retreating into his shell of self-protection. The warmth, sharing and caring from the night before, suddenly forgotten by Delbert's unwarranted blow.

Two stops later Marissa spoke quietly to Rory, "I'm sorry."

Rory shrugged and replied, "You weren't the one that hit me."

Marissa shook her head, "He hit you so hard. I don't understand."

Rory nodded, "I think some people feel like they have to hit. I don't know why."

Marissa asked, "Can I sit with you?"

Rory moved over, Marissa crossed the aisle, they sat in silence for some time. Finally, Rory said, "You stopped crying. That's good."

Marissa had a slight smile, "I don't feel so good, I wish I would get picked so I can be done with the shows. I hate the shows. One man asked me to dance; I don't know how to dance."

Rory explained, "Some can be unreasonable. First, they take the real young girls and bigger girls that can work. You are

209

in between. But you'll get picked. You won't have to go back to New York."

Marissa replied, "I hope so."

Marissa looked up at her aloof friend. She asked, "Are you angry with the mister?"

Mister was the name given to their male keepers, Miss or Mrs. to the women in charge. Most orphan train riders would not be with their keepers long enough to learn their names. Slowly Rory shook his head, "It doesn't pay to be angry. It just leads to more beatings. I think we're better off if we try to do our best. If we try to get along."

Marissa asked, "Do you just bite your tongue?"

The saying was common among the orphans and those somehow squelched from saying what was on their mind. Rory smiled and nodded agreement. Marissa offered, "I am eight-years old."

Rory glanced her way and responded, "I am twelve."

"I hope you get picked, Rory."

"This trip I am bigger than I was during the first trip. At the orphanage, Mr. Paul said I should grow to be good sized because I had big feet."

Marissa smiled, she looked up at Rory hoping for approval, "Maybe someone will look at your feet and pick you."

Rory recognized her joke, he smiled thus giving her the approval she sought. Marissa added, "Maybe I should steal the big pair of shoes."

From the back of the railcar Delbert Zimms addressed the group, "Get into your good clothes, comb your hair and make sure your shoes are clean. Remember to smile, be at your best, we are running out of stops."

Marissa touched Rory's arm and said, "I hope you get picked by someone real nice."

The seven remaining orphan train riders were lined up in front of the church. Three kids were taken right away, sometime later a tall well-dressed woman selected Marissa. Marissa walked away with a smile; just before leaving she turned and waved at Rory.

Rory had seen or heard hundreds of orphan stories, the saddest among them was the splitting up of families. Brothers and sisters torn apart and led out screaming after being picked, some never to hear from each other again. Such was Rory's thinking as his new friend Marissa was led out of the church.

An hour later a man entered the church, he looked the children over for some time before talking to Delbert Zimms. After a lengthy discussion with Delbert, the man signed some papers. Delbert motioned to Rory to come forward. Rory stood in front of Delbert who simply said, "Rory. This is Wilbert Becker. He has agreed to take you on as an indenture. You listen to him and do as you are told."

Such was Rory's introduction to Wilbert Becker, for almost two years, Rory was Becker's shadow and helper as Becker built his house from the ground up. Rory learned much of the many facets of building and later on of cabinetry. The house was large, the Becker family would soon arrive by rail from Chicago. Rory wondered what the family would be like, he wondered which of the rooms he would occupy. He wondered again what it would be like to be part of a family.

Within a very few days the Becker family was due to arrive. While Rory was sawing up firewood for cooking and winter heat, a man entered the yard and spoke to Becker. Rory watched, it was evident that money exchanged hands. After some time, Becker yelled, "Rory! Come here."

As Rory approached, he heard the stranger say, "You sure he knows what he's doing?"

Becker nodded, "He's a smart lad. Good with figures and writing. Knows all about building from the ground up. I've never had to take a stick to him. He knows what he doing. He can guide you from start to finish."

"Even the cabinets and doors?"

Becker nodded, "Yes. Even the cabinets. He's good with doors."

211

Becker introduced Rory, "This here is John Goodman. John is building a house, he can use some help. You go get your things together and go with him."

Rory asked, "Will I be coming back?"

Becker responded, "Just do as you are told."

Rory figured he just got bought by John Goodman. Without emotion he turned about and went to gather his meager belongings. He was fourteen years old, he had learned much in the past two years and had nearly forgotten he was but an orphan. He would have to stay alert, learn from those around him, he recalled anew his goal of independence, living alone away from people thus insulated from the world's pain and rejection.

Rory had learned much of building in the past years from Becker, but he still lacked strength enough to take on the entire job of building a house by himself. Becker explained that Rory would need good help.

John Goodman's expectations for Rory were high, meanwhile Goodman, his wife Martha and his son Luke were sorely lacking in ambition. To make matters more unworkable, Goodman's wife and son seemed to run roughshod over Goodman. Rory thought that all three were lazy.

When Rory arrived at Goodman's, he was disheartened. The family lived temporarily in a Conestoga wagon. The ground was haphazardly cleared and a layer of logs were set for the new house. At a glance, Rory recognized the logs were out of square and were not level. Since it was early evening, they ate, then Goodman took Rory out to look over the building. Goodman said, "Well, what do you think?"

Rory pointed to the corner of the building that was nearly a foot higher; he pointed out how out of square the logs were as set. Goodman asked, "How can you tell?"

Rory was placed again in a precarious position. He wanted to say, you would have to be blind not to see the problem, but he had learned long ago not to intentionally insult. Rory kneeled so that his eyes were at the level of the top of the

212

logs. Rory replied, "From here you can see how high that corner is compared to the rest of the logs. As to the square, if we measure from corner to corner, we will know exactly how far off the foundation is."

"Does it matter?"

Rory politely responded, "Yes sir. If the bottom is off, the entire house will be off. It will be impossible to correct later on."

Rory thought he would give a simple example to keep from making Goodman angry. "As Mr. Becker would say, it would be all right if we were building a chicken coop or an outhouse."

Goodman scowled at the innocent insult, "Tomorrow me and the woman are taking a trip to town. Luke will stay here to help you. You make it right, just so we can get the house up before winter sets in."

Rory was up early working to make corrections in the foundation, late in the morning Goodman and his wife left for town, Luke left shortly afterwards to go hunting. Rory was left on his own to work on the building. Begrudgingly, Rory spent most of the day leveling the foundation, later in the afternoon he dug in the Conestoga to find something to eat. Later that day as he worked at squaring the foundation logs, many uncomfortable questions ran through his mind. Who was responsible for him now that he was with Goodman? When this house was built, would there be a place for him? Already he felt as though the son, Luke, and Goodman's wife Martha wanted nothing to do with him. What if he was on his own for the winter? He decided that he had to have a man to man talk with Goodman when he returned.

It was noon the next day when Goodman and his wife returned. Goodman's wife went immediately to bed in the Conestoga, Goodman walked up to observe progress on the house. A scowl etched the face of Goodman as he spoke, "Doesn't look like you've done a damn thing."

Rory decided to merely tell the truth, "Luke went hunting. I haven't had any help. I leveled the base, squared up the foundation and notched four logs. I'll need help to get them in place."

Goodman shook his head, obviously displeased, "Why didn't Luke lend a hand?"

There was a lot that Rory wanted to say but he decided to be a bit snide, "I don't know. He's your son, maybe you should ask him."

Goodman turned to go, angrily he said, "Get back to work. I'll talk to Luke."

Rory stopped him, "Sir. It is past time I got something to eat."

Begrudgingly Goodman replied, "Come on. I'll get the woman to fix something."

Rory was thinking how unlucky he had been. On the first orphan train trip he didn't get chosen to be a part of the family because he was too small to be a good worker. This time around, he was chosen to help build a house. Once the house was built, he was sold like a tool no longer in use.

Goodman shook the wagon canvas and said, "Martha. We need something to eat."

Martha's angry voice snapped back from inside the wagon, "You just ate in town."

"The boy didn't."

Martha was obviously angry at being disturbed, "Where's Luke?"

Goodman looked at Rory, Rory shrugged he had no idea where Luke was, "Luke didn't tell me where it was going."

Martha's angry voice growled out again, "I'm not getting out just to feed some stray."

Rory shrugged, "I guess I'll pack my things and be on my way then."

Goodman yelled, "You can't leave. I paid good money for you."

Rory stood up for himself, "I can't build your house without help. And, I have to eat or I can't work."

214

Martha angrily emerged from the wagon, "I want my house built!"

Rory thought the problem seemed to be too big for Goodman, Rory wished he was away. At least with Becker he didn't have to barter for sleep or food. Rory repeated, "I'm mighty hungry. If I am to work, I need to eat."

For the next two weeks food was provided regularly, Luke and Goodman worked, they were poor workers but they did help. The walls were nearly in place, the dangerous part, hoisting the rafters into position was next. Goodman had no idea what he was doing.

In the presence of Luke, Martha and John Goodman, Rory decided it was time to ask another important question. While they were taking a lunch break Rory asked, "What happens with me when your house is built?"

Goodman looked to his wife, his wife looked to her plate, Luke laughed. Rory smiled, he figured he had to get shed of the Goodman family. As he worked that afternoon, he considered that he was fourteen years old, he had skills that perhaps he could sell, rather than being sold himself.

A day later Rory was preparing rafters to be hoisted into place. He had the first pattern set of beams nearly ready to go, he was finishing the notch on the peak. Goodman had left for the day with Martha on another trip to town. Rory knew the task of raising the rafters would have to wait until Goodman's return. Suddenly just over his shoulder he heard a loud crack. Rory looked behind him, Luke had a bullwhip, he had attempted strike Rory and had just barely missed. Luke laughed giddily as he pulled back the bullwhip to take another try. Instead of pulling away, Rory darted toward Luke, on the inside the bullwhip was useless.

Rory grabbed the middle of the whip and jerked it out of Luke's hands. Rory walked past Luke tossing the whip to the ground. "Thanks. You just helped me make up my mind." Rory picked up his gear and walked down the road. Luke yelled after him, "You can't leave! My father paid good money for you!"

Rory had no idea what he was going to do, but if Goodman was willing to pay for him, surely, he could sell his services. Denver was a fast-growing town, there were many opportunities to work. Rory stayed on the outskirts where a lot of new building was occurring. After being turned away at two sites where they were building, on the third he met Lars Peterson. With his little bundle of clothing under his arm he humbly asked, "Sir. My name is Rory. I've helped with home building and some cabinetmaking. I'm looking for a job."

Lars Peterson was blunt, "How old are you boy?"

Rory had just turned fourteen, "Going on 15."

"Let me see your hands."

Rory showed Lars the palms of his hands. The calluses showed Lars that Rory was used to hard work. Lars said, "You are a little runt."

Rory answered, "Give me a chance."

"What do you expect as pay?"

Rory didn't hesitate, "Food, clothing, a warm place to sleep for the winter."

Lars slowly nodded, the kid didn't go off halfcocked, even when he called him a runt. Lars thought, he had nothing to lose giving him a try and he needed a helping hand. If the kid worked out, he would be pretty cheap help. Lars pointed, "Put your things on the porch. I'll try you out for a week, if you hold up your end of the stick, I will have work for you throughout the winter."

Lars Peterson was true to his word. He kept Rory busy through the winter. In the spring Lars took a job at a sawmill and let Rory go along with many tools that Rory would need as a builder.

Working with Lars and Becker, Rory learned much of building, for the next four years he worked hard on his own. After a day of working from sunup to sundown, Rory thought, now at least he was his own slave. At nineteen-years old Rory was a foot taller, he was respected as a builder, and he was taking on jobs on the outskirts of

Denver. Now he was well paid for his skills, but the last seven years had done nothing to erase his distrust for his fellow man. His goal remained independence and isolation. Rory claimed eighty acres just outside of Denver and built his own home. Modeled after some of the homes he built for others, working in his spare time, it took nearly two years to complete. One day, when entirely finished, he sat on the front porch and smiled. He said out loud, "My lifelong dream. Now that it's completed; I wonder why." He had no idea why he took so much time to build such a large and fine house.

Some weeks later Rory was constructing a house just adjacent to the railroad station. As he looked out the upstairs window at the railcar, he noted a dozen children looking out the windows. The sight gave him a chill, it was the orphan train. Rory stopped what he was doing and watched. Looking at the orphans made him very uncomfortable. Chills swept over him as he recalled his experiences on the trains, the rejection and the tears of many orphans.

Mesmerized by the recollections, he continued to stare. As he watched he saw a boy, about ten-years-old dart away from the train, he was heading directly for the house that Rory was building. Rory looked down from the second floor through the open joists into the eventual kitchen where the boy was crouched, hiding amongst some of the lumber stored there. A minute or so later none other than Delbert Zimms carrying his stick came looking for the boy. Zimms started toward the house, Rory stopped him, "Can I help you?"

Zimms looked up to the second story window where Rory was standing. Zimms asked, "Did you see a young boy. He came out this direction."

Rory shook his head, "Sorry. I've been really busy."

The boy looked up at Rory and wondered why he wasn't reported. Rory looked down at the boy and grinned. Zimms went back to the railcar, Rory wondered what he was doing, but when he saw the boy hiding, he was reminded of his own abuse as an orphan. It was like he was looking into a mirror.

217

Many things went through Rory's mind. Would his life had been different if he chose to run away from that first orphan train when he was ten? Rory gave the boy credit, it may not be the smartest thing, but the boy had the strength of character to make the decision to run away.

Rory climbed down the ladder and went into the kitchen where the boy was hiding. Rory picked up his lunchbox and sat on the lumber pile where the boy was crouched. Rory said, "Do you know why you're running away?"

The boy looked like he was about to run. Rory smiled and asked, "I'm going to eat a bit. Would you like some bread-and-butter?"

It seemed to Rory that the boy relaxed a little. Rory asked, "Do you know where you are running to, or do you just want to get away from the orphan train?"

Rory tried again, "I'm guessing you just want to get away. You didn't get picked?"

The boy nodded, Rory handed him a piece of the buttered bread. The boy took the bread and ate hungrily. Rory then asked, "Did you go to school?"

The boy nodded, Rory asked, "At the orphanage?"

The boy nodded then very quietly answered, "Some. Not much."

"What's your name?"

"Blake."

"The train is pulling out Blake. Are you sure you want to be left here alone?"

The boy nodded as he ate the bread. Rory asked, "Do you have any idea what you're going to do?"

The boy shook his head, Rory said, "You can get up now the train has left."

The boy did not move, Rory figured he really wanted to be away from that train badly. Rory suggested, "Blake. There is a school not too far from my home. I live alone, do you want to go to school?"

Blake nodded, Rory offered, "Since you don't know what you want to do yet, you can go home with me. In the morning on my way to work I can take you to school. I'll pick you up after school on my way home. If you want to leave, I'll try to help you get to wherever you want to go. How does that sound?"

Blake responded, "Good."

After they got done eating Rory explained, "I build houses for a living. For the next couple of hours, I will be putting on floorboards, upstairs. Do you want to help me nail for a while?"

This time Blake eagerly nodded his head.

When they got to Rory's home Blake explored the house then remained close to Rory. That night sometime after Blake went to bed, Rory heard sniffling coming from Blake's room, it was evident Blake was crying.

Rory sat at the dining room table with his head in his hands, he asked himself, "What have I done? I know nothing about what it takes to keep an orphan comfortable much less happy." As Rory thought back, he remembered his nights at the orphanage. Bedtime was the worst. Without activity or something to focus on to keep one's mind busy, the time before sleep was a time to think about one's condition.

Rory got up and went to Blake's bedroom door, Blake was still sniffling. With some trepidation Rory knocked and entered Blake's room. "Blake, I heard you crying. Is there anything I can do?"

Blake stopped crying, "I've been thinking about my mom."

Rory asked, "Did your mom pass away?"

Blake nodded and answered, "Yes."

"Blake. When I was your age, I put myself to sleep thinking about my favorite games or things to do, or, I would make up happy stories. What things did you enjoy doing?"

Blake offered, "When mom was alive, my job was to take care of the chickens. I liked taking care of the chickens."

"Chickens?"

Blake nodded, "Yes. I like chickens."

Rory shrugged, "Should we get some chickens?"

Blake smiled, "But you don't have a chicken coop."

Rory shrugged, "I've built a chicken coop. I think I could build another. Do you want to help me?"

Blake seemed excited, "That would be swell."

Rory smiled, "OK. We will build a coop. Now you think about the chickens and what we need for feed and get some sleep. We will have a long day ahead of us. In the morning we'll draw up a plan. We'll start building when we come home after school."

Five minutes later Rory stopped outside of Blake's bedroom door. Not hearing any more crying, Rory felt a sense of accomplishment. Still he figured that the welfare of Blake perhaps entailed more than he understood. He thought maybe he could use some help. Considering the idea of getting help, didn't sit well with Rory, somehow, he wanted to succeed, somehow the idea of being alone and independent was still with him.

On the way to school, Rory asked, "Did Mr. Zimms hit you with his stick?"

Blake was surprised, "How did you know his name?"

Rory explained, "I rode the orphan train a couple of times myself. Mr. Zimms hit me across the back for tying my shoe."

"Tying your shoe?"

Rory smiled and nodded, Blake explained, "He whacked me for turning around in line."

"Well Blake, there will be no more of Mr. Zimms."

For the next month things went well, Blake's chicken coop was built, chickens were purchased and most important to Rory, there was no more crying in the night. Blake seemed to be opening up. On the way to school Blake asked, "Rory. How come you don't look for a wife?"

Rory explained, "I don't know. During my life, it seemed every occasion where I've dealt with people, I was either beaten, cheated, or in some way mistreated. So, I thought maybe I should live alone."

Blake replied, "Now I'm living with you, and, all those people that treated you bad, they were men. Most women aren't like that."

Rory asked, "What about your teacher? You said she was a little bit mean."

Blake nodded, "Teachers have to be mean. Besides she's too old for you."

Rory asked, "Why do you want me to find a wife? You want a mother?"

Blake thought for a bit then answered, "That would be a good idea. You're not a bad cook, but, if you had a wife, she could help with the housework."

Rory considered Goodman's wife, "What if she was lazy and ornery?"

Blake thought a bit, then he grinned broadly and replied, "In that case we would both have to run away again."

Rory laughed, laughter was something Rory had not experienced much of until Blake came to live with him. Rory was pleasantly surprised at Blake's easy-going and every-ready sense of humor.

One day toward fall, Blake came home from school with a bruise on his cheek. Rory asked, "Do you want to tell me about the bruise?"

Blake shrugged like it was no big deal, "Some kid teased me for being on the orphan train and not having a family. I smacked him. We wrestled for a bit. The teacher broke it up and made us write sentences; we will not fight. Fifty times. Did you ever have to fight?"

Rory nodded, "That's one of the reasons I live alone, I don't like to fight. When I was your age, it seemed I got smacked pretty often. Sometimes I had to fight. It seemed there was never a good ending, even if I won the fight. I really didn't like fighting."

Blake laughed, then replied, "After writing, we will not fight, fifty times, I think I would rather fight than write."

Rory laughed, "If you don't like to write, then you better not fight. But if you fight, you could improve your handwriting."

Blake laughed, Rory said, "Blake, I have to thank you for making me laugh. Before you came, I didn't find too many reasons to laugh. I worked almost round-the-clock."

Blake explained, "Marissa Lamont needs a reason to laugh, she never looks happy when she picks up the Wilson kids from school."

"What's her name?"

"Marissa Lamont, I think she's the housekeeper for the Wilson kids."

Rory asked, "Wilson? I think I've heard of him. Is he the preacher?"

Blake nodded, "I think so. Marissa picks up the kids every day."

"Marissa Lamont. Does she have real dark hair?"

Blake nodded, "Yeah. It's pretty dark."

Rory recalled the ride on the orphan train and Marissa sitting next to him. He recalled it was the first time he ever considered companionship. Rory asked Blake, "Today when you are in school, I think I'll go talk to Marissa."

Blake smiled, "Are you going to try to make her laugh?"

Rory shook his head, "No. That would be your job."

The next day before his lunch hour, Rory went directly to the Wilson house, Marissa answered the door; at first, she did not recognize Rory. "Yes. Can I help you?"

"Marissa Lamont. You are much taller than you were when I saw you last on the Orphan Train. I am Rory."

Marissa's face lit up, "Rory. I always wondered what happened to you."

A shrill woman's voice sounded from within the house, Marissa looked suddenly afraid, "Who is at the door?"

Marissa responded, she was suddenly different, unsure of herself, afraid. Marissa answered, "A friend."

The shrill voice now held anger and demand, "Don't be lolly-gagging! You have a lot of work to do young lady."

After observing a distinct change in Marissa's demeanor, Rory quietly suggested, "I'll talk to you when you pick the kids up from school."

222

Marissa, obviously relieved, smiled and whispered, "I will leave here about three thirty."

For the rest of the day Rory had a problem working, he looked forward to seeing Marissa again. He felt good yet puzzled at her obvious fear of the owner of that shrill voice. From a distance Rory watched the Wilson house for Marissa to emerge. Rory intercepted her on the way to school, she suddenly seemed very happy. Marissa inquired about his life since the orphan train and was surprised that they lived so close all that time. Rory told Marissa about Blake and the fact Blake made him laugh.

Rory asked, "Marissa, it seemed you were afraid when I talked to you at the house. Is everything all right with you?"

Marissa suddenly got quite serious, "Mrs. Wilson can be very mean. She has beaten me. She sometimes does not allow me to eat. The worst punishment is locking me in the root cellar. She tells me that the papers she signed keeps me indentured until I am twenty-one. I don't know if I can make it that long."

Rory responded, "Marissa. You were too young to be indentured. Indentures can't start until the person is at least twelve, most of the time, thirteen-years-old. Indentures can only last until you are eighteen-years old. Besides being mean, Mrs. Wilson is a liar. A very mean liar."

The school bell rung, kids were coming out of the school. Rory asked, "Marissa, do you want me to talk to Mr. and Mrs. Wilson?"

Marissa smiled, his desire to protect her made her feel good, Marissa smiled, "Tomorrow, we'll meet here after school. We will make a decision together."

Blake ran up to Rory and Marissa, he smiled and said, "You made Marissa smile! Did you say something funny?"

Rory pointed to Blake, "This is Blake. Here we are, three orphan train riders. What is there to laugh at?"

All three laughed, as the Wilson kids approached, Marissa smiled and said, "I have to go. I will see you tomorrow."

The next day Rory waited at school, Marissa did not show up. Blake met Rory and announced, "Billy Wilson said Marissa is being punished. I don't know what that means." Rory directed, "Go home. I'll be home soon as I can." Rory ran to the Wilson home, he knocked on the door, Mrs. Wilson opened the door, when she saw Rory, she quickly tried to shut the door. Rory stuck his foot in the door and pushed it open. Rory walked in and asked, "Where is Marissa?"

The shrill voice of Helen Wilson was even more shrill now that she was threatened and angry. She screamed, "Get out of my house or I'll call the sheriff!"

Rory snapped right back at her, "Good. Maybe he'll throw you in jail for kidnapping. Where is Marissa?"

Being familiar with construction, Rory went first to the kitchen, sure enough there in the floor was a trap door. Rory threw open the trap door, he was relieved when Marissa emerged unscathed. Rory directed her, "Do you have any other clothing or possessions? If so, get them. We are leaving. You're coming with me."

Rory turned on Helen Wilson, "I should throw you down into that cellar and lock the door. You had a faithful person that you treated like a dog. I can't believe that your husband is a minister. What in the world does he preach? Hate, slavery, privilege, superiority…"

Rory had to turn away from her, he felt like bodily throwing her down into the cellar. Thankfully, Marissa arrived with a small bundle of clothing. She took Rory's arm and led him to the door.

They were halfway to Rory's home before he was able to admit, "Marissa. I wanted to pick her up and fling her right down into that the root cellar."

Marissa smiled, she took his arm, "I saw your anger."

When Marissa took his arm, it was as though the problem was shared, divided, his anger seemed to melt away, Rory immediately felt better. Marissa asked, "What are we going to do now?"

Rory admitted, "I have no idea. All I could think about was getting you out of there. Nobody should ever be treated the way they treated you."

"I thought of running away. Where would I have run to? It got so, all I wanted to do was to make it through the day."

Rory was a bit more relaxed, "I don't know what we'll do, but you are not going back there."

When Marissa saw Rory's house she was surprised, "You said you were a builder. You really built your own house?"

Rory explained, "Yes. I took ideas I liked from other houses that I built or helped to build. Blake said it is too big. He said maybe we should start an orphanage."

Blake came out of the chicken coop with a basket of eggs. When he saw Marissa he exclaimed, "Marissa. Did you come to visit or are you staying?"

Marissa could see Blake's playful nature, "I think I will be here for a while."

Blake replied, "Good. I was getting tired of picking on Rory."

Two hours later the sheriff and a deputy arrived. Rory quickly gave orders to Blake, "Take Marissa upstairs, hide in the secret closet."

In the back of an upstairs closet, the wall was built to slide aside revealing an additional space. It was an idea taken from another house Rory had constructed. Downstairs Rory opened the door and met the sheriff on the steps, "Good afternoon."

The Sheriff announced, "We came to arrest you for breaking into preacher Wilson's home and threatening Mrs. Wilson."

Rory admitted, "She opened the door when I knocked. I went in. I told her I would like to throw her down into the root cellar. I did not touch her."

"You threatened her?"

"Yes sir."

The sheriff asked, "What is your name?'

"Rory."

"Your last name?"

"I never had a last name."

"Where are you from?"

"East. New York. I got out here about ten years ago on the Orphan Train. I was twelve-years-old when I got here, I was indentured to Wilbert Becker."

"Oh. You are the builder? You built for Art Remington?"

"Yes sir."

"You did a good job. I have heard good things about you. How did you learn to build?"

"From Becker. Then Lars Peterson, then I was on my own when Lars took the job at the sawmill. Lars gave me some tools to help me get started on my own."

The sheriff said, "Rory. You're going to have to come with me. I have a complaint I have to act on."

Rory was puzzled, why didn't the sheriff mention Marissa. The sheriff asked, "Do you have a horse?"

"No sir. I have my lumber delivered, I take jobs within a mile or two of home so that I can walk. I can walk to jail, I know where it is."

Sheriff shook his head, he never had such a cooperative person he had to arrest. Once at the jail, the sheriff sent his deputy to get the preacher. The sheriff explained, "Rory. I'm going to put you in a jail cell while we talk to the preacher. That's for everyone's protection."

The Preacher entered the Sheriff's office loudly threatening, "You lock him up and throw away the key. He broke into our house, he threatened my good wife and walked out with an arm load of stolen goods."

Rory wondered why he hadn't mentioned Marissa. The sheriff asked, "Mr. Wilson. Will you fill out a complaint in detail, listing what Rory ran off with?"

The Preacher exploded, "Of course."

For some time, Wilson scribbled out a formal complaint. Among the items he listed as stolen were mainly clothing. Rory grinned, so far there is still no mention of Marissa. To confuse things, Rory noted he was two sizes bigger than the preacher. When the preacher left, the sheriff came to Rory's cell, "Did you hear all of that?"

"Yes sir. I don't know what to say. He's a liar. But what he said has nothing to do with why I was at his house."

The sheriff unlocked the cell door and had Rory come out into the office. The sheriff admitted, "I know there is more to this than meets the eye. You're going to have to let me in on what has happened here. So far all I have to go on is the preacher's written complaint that doesn't make a bit of sense."

Obviously pained by the situation, Rory told the sheriff everything. The sheriff was amazed, "And you say the girl is now eighteen-years old?"

"Yes sir. Marissa was eight-years old when the Wilson's selected her. At eight, she was too young to be indentured, she was supposed to be part of the family. All this time Marissa has been a servant or a slave in that house."

The Sheriff shook his head, "Rory. You've given me your life story. Effectively you put your head in my hangman's noose. How do you know I won't tighten the knot around your neck?"

Sheepishly Rory replied, "Sir. Marissa told me sooner or later I have to have trust in people. I guess, hangman's noose or not, for some reason you will be the first."

The sheriff smiled, "Well now, what in the world are we going to do?"

Rory shrugged, he had just put his life, Marissa's and Blake's lives in the hands of the sheriff. Deep in thought, the sheriff rose from his desk, he walked over and looked out the window. He stood and stared for some time, thinking. He looked to his left, down the street a block was the steeple of preacher Wilson's church. As he looked at the church, an idea came to mind.

The sheriff turned to Rory and asked, "Rory. Have you ever been to church?"

Rory shook his head, "No sir."

Sheriff smiled and asked, "Then, you've never had to go to confession?"

It was Friday, late in the day when Rory returned home. He sat with Marissa and Blake to explain what the sheriff directed him to do. Rory smiled and said, "I want you both to know, I am scared."

Marissa took his hand and said, "You are afraid for the two of us, aren't you?"

Rory nodded, "Yes. I'm also afraid for the three of us."

Marissa continued to hold his hand as she spoke, "Do you recall our talk when we were on that orphan train? We spoke of family. You said you wanted to be alone because you had no family experience. You told me to hold onto my memories of family so I would know how to start a family on my own. Rory, family is all about looking out for one another. Protecting the weaker, that's what bonds a family together. You are already doing those very things with Blake and I. Blake told you that you would make a good father, I agree. You have taken on a lot pain in your life and somehow turned it into just behavior. Justice, honesty, and now your trust in the sheriff; you have nothing to be scared of."

It was Sunday morning, the church service was edging closer to the time for Wilson's sermon, the sheriff sitting in the front pew smiled, he was somewhat relieved as the church door opened. Rory sheepishly entered, briefly looked about the gathering until he espied the sheriff sitting in the front of the congregation where he said he would be. As Rory walked down the aisle, preacher Wilson stared in disbelief. The preacher finally spoke, "What are you doing here?"

The preacher announced to the congregation, "This man is the one I spoke of that threatened my good wife, Helen. He stole from me. What are you doing here? Sheriff what is this man doing here?"

The Sheriff asked, "Rory. What did you come here for?"

Rory quietly explained, "I came to confess."

The sheriff looked to the preacher who wanted none of Rory's confession. The preacher directed his response to the sheriff, "Sheriff! What is this man doing here? He's supposed to be in jail."

In the sheriff's usual quiet manner, he replied, "Rev. Wilson. You have always welcomed people to the pulpit to confess of their sins. This man wants to confess. I would say, let Rory bare his soul. I'm sure the congregation would love to hear his confession. Rory. Since you don't go to church here, why don't you start out by telling us who you are, where you came from and what you do for work."

As directed, Rory turned about and faced the congregation, he spoke quietly, the entire congregation strained to hear. Rory started, just as the sheriff had coached him a few days earlier, "Thank you. My name is Rory, I don't have a last name. I was raised in three different orphanages in New York. When I was ten, I was sent on the orphan train. The first time I didn't get picked, so I was sent back to New York to another orphanage. When I was twelve, I was put on the orphan train again. This time I made it as far as Denver."

The congregation was very interested, they remained quiet, the only one fidgeting was the preacher. Rory continued, "When I got to Denver I was picked by Wilbert Becker. I guess I was indentured. With Mr. Becker I learned to be a builder, we built his house, when it was completed, he sold me to John Goodman so I could help Mr. Goodman build his house. I ran away from Mr. Goodman, because his son took a whip to me."

The sheriff asked, "Why did Luke take a whip to you?" Rory shook his head, "I don't know. He thought it would be funny. He was laughing."

Sheriff asked, "How long have you been here in the Denver area?"

"Ten years."

The sheriff smiled to himself, "Do you recognize anyone in the congregation that you worked for?"

Rory answered, "Yes sir. I see Mr. Becker. I see John and Susan Beckman, Arthur Remington…"

The sheriff asked, "Could you tell us exactly what occurred at the Wilson house? You have been accused of stealing, breaking in, and threatening Mrs. Wilson."

Rory nodded, he looked at Helen Wilson directly and said, "I'm sorry. I knocked on your door looking for Marissa Lamont. Marissa told me she was going to meet me, when she didn't show up, I thought you may have locked her in the root cellar again. When you opened the door, I went into your house looking for Marissa. I found her locked in the root cellar. I told Marissa to get her belongings, I was taking her with me. Mrs. Wilson, I was afraid. I thought, if you could lock her in a root cellar without food, I was afraid of what else you would do to her."

The preacher stammered, he wanted to shut Rory up and repair any damages that Rory had already made. He yelled, "Sheriff! You instigated this fiasco. Exactly what are you trying to do with all these lies?"

The sheriff held up his hands, "Preacher. You and the good people of this congregation and community all elected me to get to the bottom of lies. You said Rory was lying. I see a couple of newcomers in the back of the church. Marissa Lamont and Blake, would you come up here please?"

Marissa and Blake made their way to the front of the church and stood beside Rory. The sheriff smiled as he saw the obvious comfort within the threesome. The sheriff asked, "Marissa, is there any part of what Rory said that is a lie?"

Marissa answered simply, "No."

The sheriff asked, "Has Rory ever lied to you?"

"No."

The sheriff then concluded, "Then, Helen Wilson has locked you in the root cellar a few times?"

"Yes. Many times. Sometimes when she was leaving for church or to shop."

"How old are you Marissa?"

"Eighteen, nearly nineteen."

The sheriff smiled and said, "Well, Rev. Wilson, Helen Wilson, I have to admit, this has been the most interesting confession I have ever heard in any church. Now, I'll tell you and the congregation about the quandary I am in as sheriff of your community. I need to act on behalf of Rory and arrest Mr. Becker, and Mr. Goodman for a variety of broken laws. Slavery, battery, breaking a signed agreement on the part of Mr. Becker, and I don't know where to start with Mr. Goodman. Then, on the behalf of Marissa Lamont, I have to file charges of kidnapping, imprisonment, child slavery, starvation, maybe even torture... That will not look good on your record Rev. when you go looking for another church."

The sheriff looked at Marissa standing by Rory's side, he grinned mischievously and asked, "Blake. You ran away from the orphan train, and you are staying with Rory. For your protection, should I take you away from Rory and find you a different home, perhaps with the preacher here?"

Blake's eyes were big as he pleaded, "No. Thank you sir."

The sheriff asked, "Blake, are you telling me you are happy with Rory? He doesn't mistreat you?"

Blake responded, "No sir. He's mighty good to me."

Facing the congregation, the sheriff shook his head and explained, "It seems, as a community we've ignored a few things that we shouldn't have. I'm walking these fine folks' home. Seems like this congregation has some things to deal with today. I will be having some discussion with a few of you in the near future."

By the time they got to the church door, the congregation was already talking about the ouster of Wilson. Once outside the church, the sheriff shook Rory's hand, "Rory. You are an honest man. You have been put through a ringer and you still hold your head high. I congratulate you. Marissa, I'm going to try to get some recompense out of the Wilson's for all your years of service to that family. I'm going to have to hurry, I have a feeling they'll be leaving town shortly."

Marissa said, "Sheriff. Rory told me and Blake about your plan at the church. We have all wondered... why... You

231

seem to have such insight… It was as if you could read us like a book."

The sheriff grinned, "That's a Sheriff's job."

Marissa shook her head to note her disbelief, the sheriff admitted, "When Rory told me all about you two, I was already convinced Rory was a good man. Rory talked openly about his fears and what he perceived were his shortcomings. Those battles are what sometimes makes some of us strong while some people weaken. When Rory told me the story about his shortcomings, and admitted, sometimes he cries in the night, then I knew how open and honest Rory was. You see, I recalled; sometimes I cried in the night."

It was the sheriff's baring of his soul, the recollection of memories that caused his anguish, such that the sheriff visibly had trouble relating. The sheriff explained, "In 1855, I was on one of the first orphan trains. I was fourteen, I had grown up mostly on the streets. I was selected in Iowa, I ended up at the home of a Nebraska farmer. He was mean, I ran away from him when I was sixteen. I got to Denver during the early days of the gold rush, I worked my way up from deputy to Sheriff; I didn't like digging for gold. Now, I don't want you telling folks that tale, they may get the idea that I'm a little soft."

Blake, in the way of a child, threw his arms around the sheriff to show his empathy and his appreciation.

The sheriff patted Blake on the back and then said, "I'll give you a little advice, you'll be living in the same house. I would suggest you to go see the justice of the peace pretty quick so that you stop the people from talking."

Rory didn't know what the sheriff was referring to; to Rory's puzzled look the sheriff explained, "Go to the courthouse and get married. And, any questions you have in the future, don't be afraid to ask."

Blake smiled and enthusiastically asked, "Can they do adoptions at the courthouse?"

232

The Sheriff nodded, "Same place. I want to thank the three of you. And, I want you to know, today has been one of the most satisfying days of my sheriff's career."

Introduction to, "The Boy with No Name"

At the graveyard of the Wisconsin Child Center in Sparta, Wisconsin there are unmarked graves. An elderly relative of my wife that had taken in foster children from a much earlier time heard about the unmarked graves; she was greatly upset. Her response was; "Just throw them aside. Forget about them. It is easier to forget them if they don't record the name." Whether bad bookkeeping or a desire to forget, giving dignity to each and every child by referring to them by name should be a goal of a society such as ours; even in America, that wasn't always the case.

In the article I wrote for the Monroe County Local History Room, 'The State has no Conscience,' I spoke of a boy who died in an accident involving a bolt swing. I recall a couple days after he died a few black hearses made their way to the Center's graveyard. Many years later I met the family of that boy at the Center, they had no record of where their brother was buried. I feel he lies in one of those unmarked graves. One route of the orphan trains ran through Sparta, the first train left New York in 1854. Whether the orphan train was a kindness or a blemish on our history will perhaps be determined by the stories we hear. My experience would suggest that most of the participants of the orphan train that had bad experiences were unwilling to step forward to have their stories told. There was much abuse, many children were used like slaves, given away or sold when they no longer had a use for them. In part, what I attempted to do with this particular story, was show the insular nature of the orphan. Orphans, like most children, are very adaptable, whether it be into a street gang, orphanage or home. As the orphan complies with those charged with their care, they find ways to insulate themselves from additional emotional scars. Without normal social interplay, they find ways to occupy

234

their minds, in this short story the indentured orphan, who has orders not to talk, busies himself by studying people. One can only imagine the emotional vulnerability of an orphan; imagine being placed on a train with great trepidation, bound for... hope. Imagine then being subjected to lineup after lineup, the hope; win the lottery, an orphan's dream, the hope, to be a part of a family. Instead, as an eleven-year-old, imagine being picked in order to be silenced, isolated and enslaved until you are eighteen years old, the end of your indenture. I no doubt make a feeble attempt to "go there," to tell the story emotionally from the standpoint of the orphan. The last orphan train left Sparta in about 1933. I was at the center for nearly six years, my experience did not compare with those of the orphan train children.

(For a setting, I picked as the end of the line for this orphan train rider, a far western and short-lived gold rush community, around the 1880's. In an attempt to 'feel' what the lad was thinking, I wrote the story in, first person.)

"The Boy with No Name"

Everyone figured Paddy O'Brien was a clumsy drunk, except me. I knew Paddy wasn't clumsy, and, I knew he wasn't a drunk. My boss, Jason Sanborn, the man I was indentured to, told me to keep my mouth shut and not tell secrets. So, that's what I've been doing. I think I just turned thirteen sometime this spring, I've been working at Jason Sanborn's livery barn for nearly two years now.

I'm not supposed to talk, but I see and hear a lot. I hear everyone in South Pass thought Sanborn was nuts when he built this big of a barn. He built it next to the old one, then he tore down the old barn and put in a few pens for horses where the old barn was. The barn Sanborn built is a big thing, it towers over Maggie's "house." Maggie Maguire didn't like a huge barn next to her "house," but, from what I heard, a gal being in her line of work, she couldn't put up too much of a fuss.

The town seemed to build down the street away from Maggie's, but after dark, Maggie still gets plenty of traffic. My boss, Jason Sanborn, also built a blacksmith shop beside the jail across the street from the barn and Maggie's. The blacksmith has a room in back of his shop, but I don't know why he didn't just take up permanent nighttime residence at Maggie's.

Heading west down the street was Maggie's, the barn where I worked, the horse pens, the gunsmith shop, Lottie's Notions shop, the café then a few houses. Across the street from Maggie's and the barn heading west was the blacksmith, the jail, the bank, saloon, mercantile, the preacher's house, church, then a few homes including my boss, Jason Sanborn's house.

As I said, the barn is a mighty tall thing, from the upper window of the barn on the street side I can see down into the blacksmith shop, the jail, the bank, the saloon, the mercantile, and a few more places down the line. I spend a lot of time up in that haymow, the breeze comes through that upper window of the barn during the summer and it makes the heat bearable. Some nights I even sleep in the hay by that window.

As a part of my indenture to Jason Sanborn, he has to feed, clothe, house me, and provide an education. Regarding the education part, I'd say Sanborn was upholding his end of the bargain only if peeking through that knothole down into the enclosed backyard at Maggie's counted as my education. Nobody ever came to check up on Sanborn to see if he was fulfilling any part of his obligation, so in Jason Sanborn's mind everything was fine, and, I didn't have anybody to complain to. Besides, I was no longer in an orphanage, so, I thought I was a little bit better off, although during the winter I had misgivings.

Jason Sanborn didn't want me eating or sleeping at his home, so I had three meals a day at the café. That part of the deal was all right by me, because I didn't like to be in Sanborn's company either. The café was on the same side of the street as the barn and Maggie's house.

While eating at the café, I was always stuck by myself in the corner at a small table. At first, I didn't like being cast off by myself, but I soon learned to like it there. It seems the sounds carried well into the corner and I could see everything going on in the café.

Like I said, Jason Sanborn told me to keep my mouth shut. So, when everyone in town talks of Paddy O'Brien being a clumsy drunk, I just smile because I know better. I was up in haymow in the barn when Paddy first arrived. I watched as he put his horse in the stall, took off the saddle, curried, fed, and cared for his big sorrel. Paddy marked his name on the tally sheet for the oats, hay and stall, then walked to the front of the barn. He stood in the shadow just inside the door for a moment then suddenly put on his drunk act. I thought there were just the two of us that knew he wasn't a drunk, later on I learned there were three of us.

After Paddy left the barn he stumbled across the Street and headed right to the saloon. At the café later on that night I learned Paddy had paid for his two bottles of liquor in gold. I was still up in the hay mow when Paddy returned. He looked about, dumped those two bottles into the horse droppings, put the empty bottles in his saddlebags and rode out the back way. It was curious behavior, so when people talked of Paddy O'Brien, I was a better listener but I still wasn't talking.

That same evening when I was sitting in the corner of the café there was a lot of talk about how big a strike Paddy O'Brien had made. He had enough gold for a couple bottles, but an ounce of gold could get a man armload of liquor.

Two days later I was cleaning stalls when Paddy arrived. Paddy took care of his horse and paid me for the items on the tally sheet from his earlier visit. He was honest and he treated me kindly, then he stumbled over to the bank to make a deposit before heading to the saloon. At the saloon he again picked up two bottles of booze and stumbled back to the barn for his horse. By this time, I was hiding up in the haymow. Again, Paddy quickly dumped the two bottles of booze into the horse droppings, he put the empty bottles in his saddlebags and rode out the back way. I watched as Paddy headed out the same route, then I got distracted by that knothole overlooking Maggie's enclosed backyard. That Billie Sue sure had a mighty complete suntan.

Like clockwork, Paddy came into the barn two days later. He paid me for the care of his horse then headed to the bank. After he got done in the bank he crossed over toward the café. I quick flipped the 'out to lunch' sign over and hustled to my table at the cafe for my noon meal. As I sat in the corner, I could see Paddy at the counter, I thought it was strange, usually Paddy was in a hurry to leave town.

It wasn't long when Irwin Northrup came in and plopped himself down right next to Paddy. I almost never see Northrup come in the place so I watched carefully. They didn't seem to talk to one another which was strange, people even said things to me now and then just to be polite even though I didn't talk back. When Paddy was at the barn he talked easily, so I knew he wasn't the quiet type. I figured them not talking at the café was part of a previous agreement, part of the act. I watched as Paddy put a folded piece of paper under his elbow and then slid his elbow over to the waiting hand of Irwin Northrup the telegraph operator. I sure wish I knew what was in that note.

Irwin Northrup had a cup of coffee and left, soon afterward Paddy stumbled toward the saloon. I headed back to the hay mow. From the front of the hay mow I could see the street, the buildings across the street and the alleys between the buildings. Paddy came out of the front of the saloon at the same time two men came out the back. The two men were Wick and Lonnie Carlson, two hired guns who I knew worked for Jason Sanborn.

I already mentioned that knothole in the East of the barn overlooking Maggie's enclosed backyard where Billie Sue picked up her tan. From the front of the barn overlooking the street I didn't see any tanning going on but I learned a lot. I learned that my boss Jason Sanborn owned the Mercantile and he also owned the saloon. I learned that Sanborn also owned a big share of the Sheriff. In the alleyway behind the bank the Sheriff and Sanborn met quite often. I noted that when Sanborn talked, the sheriff listened.

In the little town of South Pass, Wyoming, there had been plenty of robberies and killings over what little gold was found. If I were a betting man, I'd put every red cent I had on Jason Sanborn being at the bottom of it all. That bet would come to $19.21. As a part of my indenture, Jason Sanborn didn't have to pay me a penny. All he had to do was clothe, feed me, provide a roof, and educate me. I think Sanborn figured if he kept my mouth shut, he had a slave until I reached eighteen years old.

I watched as Paddy O'Brien emptied the bottles into the manure, he rode out the back as usual, this time I ignored the knothole so I could keep tabs on Paddy. I watched him for nearly half a mile before I saw Wick and Lonnie Carlson get onto his trail. When they were out of sight, I took a quick peek at Billie Sue before a couple loads of hay came in. The reason I knew Wick and Carlson were hired by Sanborn is because of a little cheating with the hay loads. When they brought in the hay, they were supposed to write down their name and mark each load on the tally sheet. Since I was working up in the loft and never talked, Wilbur Wells figured I didn't keep track of the hay loads. Wilbur scribbled down a few extra loads onto the tally sheet. If I let it go, Sanborn would have to pay for loads of hay he didn't get. I didn't like Sanborn, but I didn't like cheating either, so I told Sanborn. Soon afterwards Wick and Carlson visited with Wilbur Wells and showed him the error of his ways. After that he never added to his hay load tally.

When Sanborn built the barn, he put two hay tracks into the ceiling. The barn could hold a lot of hay. When the hay loads were brought in, by cables they would haul huge fork-loads of hay up to the track then pull the load down the track to where I wanted the hay dropped inside the barn. I would then have to spread the hay out so that I could walk on top without falling into a hole. There were six hay-shoots in the barn where I could climb up a ladder or toss the hay down. When the barn was full there was more than a twenty-foot drop from the top of the hay to the floor. One had to know what he was doing up there in that hay mow. Also, when the barn was filled to the top, I couldn't see out the knotholes to the East or to the West, so I made sure that didn't happen.

I forgot to tell about the view to the West. Billie Sue did her tanning during the day to the east of the barn. To the west, the cook did his waltz to Lottie's Notion Shop after work. The cook and Lottie Wainwright of the Notion Shop had something in common but I doubt if it was sewing.

Since Jason Sanborn never gave me a penny, where would I get money for a $19.21 bet? My savings for almost two years... most every penny came from Mrs. Cecilia Ardell. Cecilia Ardell was the bright spot in my week. I always looked forward to seeing her. When Mrs. Ardell came into town for Sunday church or to go shopping, she would stop at the livery. Before church she picked me up, drove the buggy to the churchyard, I dropped her off then drove her rig back to the barn. I fed, watered and curried her horses. Then I cleaned the leather on her rig so that it shined. When the church bell rang, I went to pick her up. She paid me for the services, then each time she gave me fifty cents extra and told me, "The fifty cents is yours. Not Mr. Sanborn's!"

I guess I would have done just about anything for Cecilia Ardell. Mrs. Ardell was pretty much the sole source of my income. In the last few months Cecilia and her husband Delbert even ate with me a couple of times at the café. When that happened, it made me feel good for a week or two afterwards. In the company of Delbert and Cecilia Ardell, it seemed that I gave up more information than I got. Sometimes I figured they knew more about me than I knew about myself.

Just last Sunday as we arrived at church someone made a comment about Paddy O'Brian being a bungling drunk. I quietly hinted to Cecilia, "My mom said you can't judge a book by its cover."

Mrs. Cecilia Ardell looked at me very carefully, I would say with interest and concern. She ignored my reference to Paddy O'Brian, the book, judge and cover business, she put her hand on mine and said, "Do you have memories of your mother?"

Judging a book by its cover was just a saying, adding a fictional mother into the mix was a mistake because I had absolutely no recollection of a mother. Of course, I felt like I lied to my favorite person in the world. At the same time, right then and there, with all those people around, emotionally, I couldn't discuss my mother or becoming an orphan. I wanted to melt into the seat or disappear, I couldn't answer. I just hung my head. It seemed Cecilia understood my predicament, she patted the back of my hand, I glimpsed up at her, from her looks I thought maybe she felt some of my pain.

Cecilia stepped down out of the carriage and I was somewhat relieved that I didn't have to talk, I didn't know if I could. On the way back to the barn I felt good and bad at the same time. I kept feeling my hand, recalling Cecilia's reassuring touch. I worked harder than ever cleaning and polishing her rig that day.

In some ways I thought I was better off because of my orders by Jason Sanborn to keep my mouth shut. I didn't want to talk to people and explain where I came from. I was uncomfortable and embarrassed because I didn't really know. I wanted to be like everyone else, but I knew that wasn't to be. I didn't want people to know I was picked out of a lineup fresh off that orphan train just because I could read, write, and was good at figures. Because I'm an orphan

241

with no one to turn to, in some respects I felt safe hiding in the hay mow of that big barn.

Cecilia and Delbert, her husband, owned the Slant A, a ranch a few miles out of town. They were ranching, raising cattle and horses long before gold was found in the area. They didn't come to town often, but they supplied meat for the town and did some horse trading. They raised three girls and a boy, they were all married and out of the house. Neither Cecilia or Delbert looked very old, they were both warm, strong and active people.

It was warm that day, I was up by the window in the barn enjoying the breeze. It was early evening when Wick and Lonnie Carlson rode back into town, I would have bet they would head straight for the saloon and they did. They rode them horses all day and left them standing saddled in back of the saloon till well past my bedtime. It wasn't too long after they arrived and Jason Sanborn met them both in the alleyway between the saloon and the mercantile.

I kept a watch the next day, Jason Sanborn visited the Sheriff, seems they argued a bit out back of the bank but Sanborn got in the last word. I wondered what the Sheriff's orders were; what Sanborn told him to do. I didn't learn much the rest of the day, I was busy putting more hay in the mow.

When Paddy O'Brien came into town he usually arrived in the morning. He took care of his horse, paid me for the oats and hay then went out the front of the barn. Every time he got to the front door he would stop, as though he was either looking the town over or getting ready for his clumsy drunken act.

I had wondered what the Sheriff's orders were from Sanborn. It wasn't long after Paddy arrived that morning when I found out. The sheriff stopped Paddy in the middle of the street and questioned him. I sneaked up to the front door to see if I could hear what was being said. All Paddy admitted to was, that he was prospecting and, that he had indeed picked up a few nuggets. Information Paddy hoped the Sheriff would keep under his hat. The sheriff said he wanted to protect Paddy but he didn't have any idea where his mine was. Paddy wasn't telling. The Sheriff told Paddy that he couldn't help Paddy if he didn't know where to find him. Paddy still wouldn't tell the sheriff where his mine was. The sheriff told Paddy to be careful, there had been a few miners that were killed, he suspected over gold. Then Paddy went straight to the bank with another sack of gold.

While staring out that window in a cool breeze I thought a lot about Paddy, I thought if he was mining for gold, he was getting plenty of it. Depositing gold every other day meant a mighty fine strike. I also knew Paddy wasn't a drunk or clumsy, that was an act. As I sat up in the hay mow watching the back of the saloon, I gave it some thought. I figured the mining was an act too. I figured everything about Paddy, including his name was more than likely an act. Then I saw Wick and Lonnie Carlson head out of town. I figured they were going to either waylay Paddy or get into a position where they could discover where his diggings were, in any case the outcome wouldn't be good for Paddy.

I was supposed to keep my mouth shut. I thought about Sanborn's express orders to me not to talk to people. Paddy usually stayed in the saloon for a while, then returned to the barn. Today he headed to the café. I swung down on the rope, turned over my "out to lunch" sign and ran out the back of the barn. I was able to step into the café a few seconds after Paddy. I took my seat in the corner.

It wasn't long and the telegraph operator, Erwin Northrup, took a seat beside Paddy. Sure enough, another note was passed to the telegraph operator. No words were exchanged, the telegraph operator left and the Sheriff came in and sat down next to Paddy. Usually when people talk at the counter, I can't hear all of what they are saying, but the Sheriff made a point to speak loud enough so everybody in the place heard him. He got up and repeated, "Remember O'Brian, I warned you, you're all by yourself. Someone could easily waylay you. So, you be careful."

Being in an orphanage and living with a bunch of different kind of people, you learn how to read people. The Sheriff was smug, like he accomplished what he came for. I had a feeling since the sheriff couldn't get the location of the mine, Wick and Carlson would either find the mine or kill Paddy while trying. I ate quickly and went out the back of the café so I would be at the barn when Paddy showed up. Today I figured I had to break Sanborn's rule and talk to Paddy.

When I got to the barn, Mrs. Cecilia Ardell was there waiting with her rig. In the two years I've been indentured, I talked with her more than Jason Sanborn and the entire town put together. Somehow the no talk rule never worked with Mrs. Cecilia Ardell.

I don't know how long Cecilia had been waiting, but she wasn't cross. Come to think of it, I had never seen her upset. Today she had a bunch of questions for me. She asked, "Does Mr. Sanborn pay you for your work?"

I was told by Sanborn not to tell any secrets, but I couldn't lie to her; for some reason or other I was always compelled to answer her honestly, "No ma'am. I'm indentured to Mr. Sanborn till I'm 18."

"Mr. Sanborn feeds you at the café."

"Yes ma'am."

"You sleep in the tack room?"

"Yes ma'am. Some nights I sleep in the hay."

"What happens during the winter?"

"It gets mighty chilly sometimes."

"He doesn't allow you to sleep at his home on cold nights?"

I shook my head, "No Ma'am. I do have horse blankets."

Mrs. Ardell was now within arm's length of me. She softly asked, "As an indenture he is also supposed to educate you. Does he allow you to go to school?"

"No ma'am. He told me, learning how to take care of the stables and the horses was all the education I would get."

Mrs. Ardell got closer to me and I got more uncomfortable, "And there is no one for you to complain to?"

I nodded, I could see that information upset Cecilia. Her look was kind, it made me nervous, I was even more nervous when she said, "We have a well-stocked library at the ranch."

I thought she was going to offer me books to read, I was very surprised when she frankly stated, "I have watched you for more than a year, almost two years now. I think you deserve more. Would you like to come to our ranch to live? You'll be a member of the family. Not an indenture. I have a lot of faith in you." Cecilia told me all of this when she was less than an arm's length away, there was no doubt in her intent.

I looked at her, I thought; I was about thirteen years old and I've been in an orphanage all the life I can recall. I can't remember my mother or my father, the only adult that looked at me was Jason Sanborn and that was only because I was strong enough and smart enough to take care of the stables. Jason Sanborn showed up now and then to collect the money and to remind me to keep my mouth shut.

I am thirteen years old, I can't recall ever being spoken kindly to. I can't recall being held, my tongue was tied with the dream, now the hope of being part of a family. I choked away the tears. Cecelia Ardell read me like one of those books in her library. She gathered me in her arms while I cried like a baby. This kindly lady was inviting me to belong, to experience real self-worth. I couldn't recall the last time I cried, but I let it go and I held onto Cecilia for dear life. If the promise didn't come to fruition, it didn't matter, the dream-like idea was something wonderful to cling to.

After some time, I wiped my nose and dried my eyes. Cecilia smiled and said, "I take it you like the idea?"

I just nodded, the emotion was so powerful; I was so thankful, I couldn't put my feelings into words without blubbering again like a baby.

Cecilia explained, "I am expecting a telegram soon which will allow Dell and me to adopt you. As soon as we get the word, we can take you to the ranch. I'm not going to tell Mr. Sanborn until the adoption is final. I would suggest you shouldn't tell him either. Dell said I shouldn't talk to you until everything was settled, but I couldn't wait."

Cecilia stood back, I was reticent to let go, she kept her hands on my shoulders and said, "Right now I'm going to check again at the telegraph office. I promise you all the hugs you need. I imagine you've got some catching up to do."

With more tears I nodded, she held me again for a bit, I did consider what I had missed in my life. I didn't feel saddened for what I had missed, I felt joy because a future outside the confines of Sanborn's hay mow was promised. My tears now were tears of joy.

As Cecilia released me, Paddy O'Brien made his way to his horse. I could see he was at bit confused, he said, "Cecelia Ardell of the Slant A?"

When Paddy spoke, it seemed he wasn't using his usual clumsy act. Cecilia nodded, "Yes. And you are Paddy O'Brien. Much has been said of you."

Paddy smiled and got on his horse, I couldn't let him go. I said, "Wait Paddy... or whatever your name is."

He didn't seem to pay much attention to me, I told Cecilia, "I've got to talk to him."

Cecilia took my hand and said, "Mr. O'Brian. Wait one moment. The boy has something to say."

Paddy looked down at me as if to say, hurry it up. I said, "I have to tell you. Wick and Lonnie Carlson will be waiting for you out there someplace."

Paddy O'Brien grinned broadly and said, "That's the first time you said more than two words to me boy."

I looked at Cecilia Ardell, she held my hand. Confidently I smiled, "Things have changed."

He got down off from his horse, then said, "Maybe you should explain."

So, I explained all I knew while my new potential mother stood and watched, "Did you want me to explain why I'm talking?"

Paddy's questions weren't threatening, he softly asked, "First of all, what about Wick and Carlson?"

I wiped my eyes again and said, "Wick and Carlson have been following you."

Paddy nodded, "I knew I was being followed. I just didn't know who it was."

"This time they left as soon as you got to town. I think they'll ambush you or meet you further up the trail to find out where you go."

Paddy smiled and asked, "You also said; whatever my name is?"

I nodded, "Yes sir. I know the drunk part and the clumsy part is an act. You've been emptying the bottles into the manure and faking the clumsy stuff. I figure the gold deposits at the bank to be part of the act too, you are trying to get someone to come after you. I figure the name maybe is an act too. I decided to warn you about Wick and Carlson."

Paddy grinned, he shook his head and said, "If you saw through me, I wonder who else did?"

Cecelia Ardell shrugged, "The word is all over town, you're a clumsy tenderfoot who likes to drink, and, you hit a very well-paying gold strike."

Paddy looked at me and smiled, so I decided to give him the entire picture as I saw it. I took a breath and then went in deeper, "I think Wick and Carlson get their orders from Jason Sanborn. I think Sanborn tells the Sheriff what to do. Sanborn talks with the Sheriff a lot out behind the bank. He talked to the sheriff, then the very next time you came to town the sheriff questioned you out in the street trying to find the location of your mine. Sanborn talked to the Sheriff before you came into town. I think at the café the Sheriff warned you so it would look like he was trying to help."

Paddy O'Brien was smiling as I continued, "I also know you've been sending telegraph messages secretly."

Paddy O'Brien laughed heartily, then he said, "Since you two seem to be in cahoots, I'll have to explain. There has been too much killing going on in South Pass. I am US

247

Marshall, Brandon Dougherty. I was sent here to unravel the mystery. The mystery you have unscrambled for me. The next time I take on a job like this, I'm taking you with me. Now that you told me about everything I want to know, are you going to be safe from Jason Sanborn?"

Cecilia answered for me, "He's going with me to the ranch. He'll be safe."

Cecilia looked at me, she smiled and explained, "I was going to wait until I got the telegraph, but things have changed."

Cecilia looked at the Marshall and said, "Mr. Dougherty. I'm expecting a telegraph with a message that my adoption of the boy has been completed. In light of what I've heard here. Papers or not, the boy will be in my care."

Marshall Dougherty smiled, "I'll make it legal. In light of the potential for harm. I'm putting the boy in your charge."

I couldn't believe my good luck, I was going to be part of a family right then and there. My new mother smiled warmly at me as she replied to the Marshall, "Meanwhile Mr. Dougherty, if you'd like, you can accompany us to the ranch and deputize half a dozen of my riders to help you finish your job here."

Introduction; "There Were Eight"

The title came first; which was somewhat weird because at the outset I only considered an indentured runaway lad who wanted to be alone. He wanted to experience no more abuse, no more pain and he thought to be alone would the way he could assure peace, quiet and happiness. His goal was no involvement with anybody. When I started I had no idea where the number eight came from but I wanted the story to be about companionship, brotherhood, mankind's desire for community. Yes, I know, from an indenture, lonesome to eight...

I started this story with Reed getting a beating prior to him running away. In this story, Reed Maddock, runaway indenture had his fill of people, his quest was to get away, to live alone so that no one would ever be able to hurt him again. For a couple of months as he traveled westward shadowing the Oregon Trail, he successfully avoided contact, then he demonstrates who he is when at his own peril he saves a drowning Crow warrior.

Reed's goal of being alone is not to be. The Crow joke about whether he is crazy or has great medicine. To test his medicine he is given a gift of his freedom and a captive Blackfoot sworn to kill her captors until she is killed. Reed is sent away with winter looming on a horse with a bound captive slave. The Crow believe he won't survive the coming winter or the captive who has sworn to kill her captors or be killed.

In the midst of the very cold winter an ancient Cheyenne on a long winter's walk is saved by Reed. Next, even the laws of marriage will be challenged when Reed rescues three survivors from an attack on pilgrim wagons. Although the laws, customs and morays governing marriage were understood, sometimes the lives of early settlers made it necessary to reject conformity. There was much common law marriages and Mormon's of course established their own religious ideas regarding plural marriage.

Set upon by thieves, their relationship with the mighty Crow helps but Reed's plan for isolation is dashed, now his plans must consider the lives of those around him.

There Were Eight

"Life is hard!" Elmer Nordstrom screamed as he swung his belt in a drunken rage. Elmer seemed to enjoy the beatings most when he was drunk. Elmer felt a sadistic controlling joy as he lay his belt across the shoulders of his indenture. Again, Elmer screamed, "You think you can wriggle out of your job and I won't notice!"

Reed Maddock stood with his hands on the fence as ordered while Elmer whipped him across the shoulders with his belt. Indentured, Reed knew it was useless to try to plead his case when Elmer was drunk. Usually when Elmer was in his usual drunken condition, the blows had little sting. Tonight, things were different, Reed tired of the ordeal.

Elmer hit Reed three more good licks before Reed turned around and caught Elmer's belt before it landed another blow. Under threat of beatings and starvation, Reed had worked hard all his life, he had a grip of steel and his back had toughened under the belt of Elmer. Reed's blue eyes held no emotion, curiously he smiled as he calmly striped the belt from Elmer's grip. Reed held Elmer's belt and his wrist, Elmer was helpless.

Red-faced, Elmer yelled, "Turn me loose, you damn slave!" Reed slowly shook his head, "I'm indentured; I'm not a slave. I'll accept no more beatings. You are drunk. You don't know what you are doing. I did my job and then some." Elmer stopped struggling, fuming, he stepped away as Reed let go of his wrist. Reed smiled and handed Elmer his belt. Elmer was helpless and livid, it was the first time his indenture ever spoke up, frustrated, Elmer turned to go, then

250

stopped. Elmer pointed his belt at Reed, he shook with drunkenness, anger and exasperation. Elmer angrily said, "When I got you off that damned orphan train, they told me your fanny was mine until you reach eighteen. They said if I bring you back it will cost me fifty dollars. I don't intend to pay no damn fifty dollars. I'll see you dead first."

Reed grinned and said, "I figured that was in the back of your mind."

Elmer shook his belt at Reed, "I'll wipe that damned smile off your kisser. You'll be behind the damned walking plow all day tomorrow. Have the cows milked and the team hitched to the breaking plow at sun up or you'll get no breakfast."

Elmer stumbled off toward the house, Reed rubbed his back; he smiled at his own plans for the next day. Reed had been indentured to Elmer for the past five years, Elmer had indeed treated him like a slave. Reed always knew he had nowhere to turn, he had been orphaned at two years old, he couldn't remember his parents or how he became orphaned. He spent two years in an orphanage, then two years with a family before the family decided to go West without him. Reed spent another six years back in the orphanage before he was big enough to be of benefit to Elmer Nordstrom. For the past five years from sun up to sun down he may just as well have been a slave.

Reed Maddock had read much of the adventures of Kit Carson, Lewis and Clark and the explorer, Fremont. Reed had made up his mind, he would be on a boat heading up the Missouri River when the sun came up in the morning. He would miss breakfast, Elmer had perhaps figured since Reed was still short of his eighteenth birthday by a few months, that Elmer retained control over Reed. Reed had always been very predictable during his indenture to Elmer. Tomorrow Elmer would be surprised; Elmer would have to get up and milk his own cows and plow his own field. As darkness set in, experience told Reed that Elmer would be fast asleep, the lights in the house were already out. Reed picked up his pack and walked away.

It was about two o'clock in the morning when Reed weaved his arm through the straps of his pack and fell asleep on the deck of the riverboat, Far West. As day was breaking he was nudged awake with the boot of a tall well-dressed man. Without expression, he spoke, "You look like you need a job."

Reed stood and slipped his backpack over his shoulder, "Yes sir I don't have quite enough money to get to Fort Pierre. I was hoping I could earn a bit."

"If you look on the dock you'll see about forty boxes down there. Load them all on the deck and I'll get you as far as Fort Pierre."

Reed smiled and replied, "Thank you sir." This was a novel thing for Reed, it was the first time he had ever been paid for working. He quickly scurried back and forth and placed the boxes on the deck of the Far West, not long afterwards the boat pulled away from the dock. The tall Gent asked, "It is getting pretty late in the fall, what will you do in Pierre?"

Reed didn't really want to answer, since he wasn't eighteen, his indenture was still in effect. Reed shrugged, "I thought I would maybe catch up with a wagon train, maybe go to Oregon."

"Your parents know you are out here?"

"I have no mother or father." Reed didn't mention he was also indentured.

"Getting late in the year for wagon trains and it won't be too long and it will be freezing cold and more snow then you have ever seen. Man walking alone out on that Prairie, it's mighty dangerous. Do you have a gun?"

"No Sir. I know how to use one, I had to do some hunting, but I've never been able to afford a gun."

"How are you going to eat?"

Reed shrugged, "I figured maybe I would snare some rabbits."

"No gun and you are going to snare rabbits? You are anxious to get away. If I were a betting man, I'd be betting that you wouldn't be alive in the spring. I figure if the Indians don't get you, winter or starvation will. The further you go north the colder it gets in the winter."

When they arrived at Fort Pierre, the tall Gent that he had worked for stopped him as he was about to disembark. He handed Reed a carbine, a box of shells, and a telescope. He smiled and said, "Son, I don't know what you're running away from. If you step out onto that prairie, you are going to need this rifle; and, the telescope might keep you out of mischief with the Indians. The rifle is accurate, but don't shoot it unless you have to. The sound travels a long way. If you change your mind, my name is Philip La Fleur. The people who run steamboats on the Missouri know me, they'll I'll get in touch with me. If I don't see you again, I wish you well."

From Fort Pierre, without a horse, Reed started walking in a westerly direction. He wondered why La Fleur had given him the gun and telescope. It was strange meeting someone that kind, something that he had never experienced before. Reed's hopes were to meet up with the Bozeman Trail and a wagon train; in the meantime, stay out of harm's way of any Indians in the area. Reed understood that the Sioux had recently moved the Arikara Indians out of the area around Fort Pierre. From what Reed was able to learn, if he maintained travel westward he may avoid contact with Indians for some time. With the use of his telescope and very cautious travel he was able to avoid contact until after he crossed the Bozeman trail.

The walk gave Reed much time to consider what he wanted to do in the future. After being tossed about all his life he decided he wanted a place to call home. A place of his own. As an indenture he was forced to build, work with animals and do all kinds of farm labor. He was confident in his background and ability… He wanted to be completely independent-self-sufficient, far away from anyone.

Reed thought about Elmer Nordstrom; what made the man so mean? One of the things Reed noted as he interacted with others; the meanness didn't get them anywhere. There didn't seem to be any satisfaction in those he had observed to be ornery. There surely wasn't any appreciation seen by those affected or observing the meanness.

Reed recalled being sent to the neighbors to help out for three weeks. He worked hard for them. Reed had always worked hard, at first under the threat of a beating, later working hard became a habit. After three weeks working with the neighbors he was surprised. They thanked him profusely and even gave him money for his services. He was given orders not to give the money to Nordstrom. The experience for Reed was very gratifying. Reed also recalled returning to his indentured home and having the money taken from him while he slept. He smiled at the memories, recalling the generosity of La Fleur, it would be easy for him to figure out who to pattern his behavior after.

Reed had never had a brother, the closest he had come was talking about brothers and family while he was at the orphanage. Reed felt strongly there would be nothing better than having a brother to rely on; one to share joy, laughter and pain. He thought perhaps not ever having been able to share with someone close, either the pain, joy or trials in his life; made him think kindly about what it would be like to have a brother.

While on the boat the Far West, Reed heard that the Bighorn River was a rugged and beautiful sight to see. He understood if he passed the Bozeman Trail, then followed the Bighorn River he would eventually come back to the Bozeman Trail. The canyons of the Bighorn River were beautiful and very difficult to maneuver. With the River on his right and a tall bank and mountains on his left he made his way down the Bighorn River. He had spent more time than he wanted exploring the Bighorn Canyons, it was getting quite cold at night and snow was accumulating on the tops of the Pryor Mountains.

Ten Crow warriors and their captive Blackfoot woman sat mounted on the Cliff above Reed Maddock. They debated whether they should go down and kill him. Running Elk smiled, "He is all alone. We will let winter kill him."

Laughing Bear said to their leader Running Elk, "He must have been cast out. He has no horse. He has a gun, we could use another gun."

The leader, Running Elk shook his head, "We must hunt. If one of us does not return, women and children will suffer through the winter."

Running Elk smiled at Laughing Bear, "You go down and get the gun, if you don't return, I'll keep your wife warm this winter."

The warriors laughed, just then Laughing Bear rose in the saddle and pointed upstream from where Reed Maddock was walking, "Look, it is your brother, Little Elk."

Little Elk entered the stream above Reed Maddock, Little Elk's horse suddenly spun and threw Little Elk into the frigid water. Little Elk's horse turned about and came back to shore. Little Elk could not swim, from high above on the cliff they were helpless to render aid. They watched as the freezing water carried Little Elk downstream toward Reed Maddock. They watched in awe as the white man ran toward the drowning Little Elk while shedding his rifle, his knife, his shirt and then his pants. They continued to watch as the white man dove into the water and started to pull little elk toward shore.

Running Elk gave orders, "Laughing Bear, take two warriors; gather Little Elk's horse and the white man's belongings. White Buffalo, start a big fire where the white man has pulled Little Elk to the shore. They will need to get warm soon or they will die."

Running Elk kneed his horse up River to where the bluff sloped down to the water. Running Elk did not believe he would be able to talk to his brother again, he feared both his brother and the white man both would be dead.

Reed Maddock landed in the icy water, the shock of the frigid water rifled through his muscles like a giant vise, he forced his muscles to react; he knew he had to get out of the water fast. Quickly he grabbed the Indian by the scruff of his leather Buffalo Cape and dragged him as fast as he could to shore. The icy water already took its toll, when his hand came in contact with the sandy shore he clawed and scratched his way up the bank, finally he got his feet dug into the sand enough where he could apply leverage to pull the Indian out of the water. He was freezing, he thought he would surely die, with one more pull he managed to get the Indian entirely out of the water. Reed Maddock had turned blue, the Indian didn't fare much better; he was nearly white. The next thing Reed Maddock knew, he was being dragged toward a fire, he was convulsively shivering, he couldn't believe his eyes. In a cold induced stupor, he thought he was in heaven, he thought Indian angels were attending to him, drying him, rubbing his arms and legs. The Indian he had just pulled out of the water was also by the fire, the flames of the fire grew; Reed Maddock could feel the heat entering his body. A dry buffalo cape was draped around him to hold in the heat.

To Reed Maddock, things finally started to make sense, he wasn't in heaven. It was actually Indians that had saved his life and the life of the person he pulled out of the water. After some time, the convulsive shivering stopped, Reed Maddock looked across the fire at the Indian he had pulled out of the water, he was smiling; he too would live.

One of the Indians handed Reed Maddock his clothing which he quickly donned. After he was fully dressed, Reed Maddock sat down and extended his hands toward the fire to drink in more of the heat. In his present company he knew he wasn't going anyplace unless the Indians allowed him to leave. Resolved that his fate was in someone else's hands, he smiled, he was still alive. Reed Maddock didn't know a word of any Indian language, he didn't even know what kind of Indians were in charge of his fate. Reed Maddock's rifle, his knife and his bag lay at his side, he waited, enjoying the heat of the fire.

Laughing Bear said to Running Elk, "What are we going to do with him?"

Running Elk held up his hands, "I don't know if he's crazy or if he has great medicine. I'm not going to kill him since he saved my brother's life. I like my brother… there's no way I would get in that water to save his life. The white man did not hesitate. He went in the water to save an Indian. Someone he didn't know. I don't think he is crazy. I think he has great medicine."

Laughing Bear chuckled, "We don't have to worry about killing him, if he goes swimming this time of the year, he'll kill himself. Winter will kill him even if he doesn't go swimming." They laughed at the joke and Reed grinned right along with them.

Running Elk shook his head, "Red Buffalo. Where is the captive?"

Red Buffalo grinned, "She is tied, on the ridge. I left her there, I was in a hurry."

Running Elk motioned, "Go get her. Bring her to the fire."

Red Buffalo smiled, "Maybe I should take somebody along to make sure I make it back alive."

Running Elk laughed and waved him away, Laughing Bear foresaw the humor, he laughed heartily, "Are you going to give her to the white man?"

Running Elk smiled, "I'm going to see how good his medicine is. If he can live with both the winter and that woman trying to kill him, I will say that he has great medicine." Running Elk laughed, "We will leave one horse for them."

Laughing Bear chuckled, "They will both have to ride the same horse? The white man will be dead before the sun goes down."

Before long, Red Buffalo returned, an Indian woman sat astride an Indian pony, her hands were tied behind her.

Running Elk asked, "Red Buffalo, did you make her ride down that steep hill with her hands tied behind her back?" Red Buffalo laughed, "Yes, I want to live out the day." Running Elk ordered, "Make sure her hands are tied well. Put the white man on the horse in front of the woman. Give him his rifle and his bag and let them go. We must go also, we need to be hunting."

Red Buffalo motioned to Reed Maddock to get upon the horse, with the captive up on the back, two warriors helped him mount. They handed him his bag and rifle. Reed Maddock looked to Running Elk, he smiled and raised his hand. The warriors watched with interest as Reed Maddock and the captive woman road off to the North. They watched until the twosome was out of sight. Red Buffalo shrugged, "They are out of sight and she has not killed him yet." Running Elk nodded, "I think he has great medicine. We must go. We have to hunt, more has to be done to prepare for winter."

Reed Maddock didn't know what to think of being set free with a horse and an Indian woman with her hands tied. For some time, the Indians had laughed a lot, Reed couldn't conceive of them laughing and doing him harm. When they turned him loose, he didn't know what to think. He wasn't about to look back and give the Indians an idea that he may be the least bit fearful. Quietly he asked, "Do you speak English?"

There was silence. He asked again in broken Norwegian, "Cond du snuck Norse?"

He was met by silence once again, he laughed, then he began speaking just to break the silence, "My new friend. My name is Reed Maddock. You are the first person I've talked to in two months. I've had a lot of bad luck in my life. I don't' know why you are with me, but now, you are going to share some of my bad luck. When I was born I must have been so ugly that my mother gave me away. No, she didn't give me away; I guess my mother threw me away. I was adopted; then, when I was five years old, my adoptive parents left for

258

Oregon. I was put back in the orphanage. I'm now eighteen-years-old, it is getting close to Christmas. I want you to know, you are the very first Christmas present I've ever had in my life."

Reed Maddock laughed at his joke, then he continued, "I know you don't understand a word I'm telling you, but I want you to know, you are the first person I've ever told those secrets to. I want you to keep our secret."

Reed laughed, he glanced behind them and noted that they could still be seen by the Indians. He continued to talk to pass the uncomfortable time, "I suppose you're wondering how long I stayed in the orphanage the second time? Well my talkative friend, I was there until I reached eleven, then I was given to a farm couple for slave labor. Afterwards I was given to an old man. I got tired of being beaten. The last time he tried to take a strap to me, I took his strap away and told him I was all through being beaten. That night I walked away with a bag of tools; a knife and a big smile on my face. I've been walking and hiding and smiling for nearly three months. Now my good friend, I'm sorry but you will share my bad luck."

Reed rounded a small creek bank, he knew he was now out of sight of the warriors. Reed dismounted and tied the horse to a Bush. He said, "We are out of sight of the warriors. I'll take a look and see if they're following us."

Reed climbed up the bank and looked back with a telescope, "Our Indian friends are moving off to the east. I would say, they are going to leave us alone."

Reed laid his rifle on his bag, he withdrew his knife as he explained, "I'm going to cut you loose. You can have the horse and you can go. You may know where you are going, I don't. I'm lost. Hold still while I cut the leather."

She looked down at him as he cut her bonds, Reed looked into her eyes and smiled, "You are a pretty woman. When you look at me like that, it almost seems that you understand what I'm talking about."

The captive rubbed her sore wrists, then she said in broken English, "Since you have told me secrets; I was born Shoshone. I too was a captive. I was raised by Blackfeet. The warriors that just left were Crow, they were going to take me to their village as a slave. I told them I would kill them one by one until they killed me. They let me go with you to be funny. They think, either I will kill you, or winter will kill us both."

Reed was smiling broadly, "I'll be darned. You can talk!"

"Yes," she nodded, "My Blackfoot mother's sister was a white captive. She taught me well."

"What's your name?"

"I am Hurit."

Reed held out his hand, "Hurit; I'm Reed Maddock."

Hurit pulled back away from his hand not understanding his intent. Reed explained, "I'm sorry. I was going to shake hands. It is the way we greet."

Hurit didn't seem to understand, she asked "What will you do for winter?"

Reed shrugged, "I don't know."

Hurit explained, "It is as the Crow warrior said. Soon we will die. Soon the snows will be upon us. The mountains above us are already snow covered."

Reed asked, "If you ride hard, can you find your way back to your village?"

"No. Too far and over the mountain."

Reed looked up toward the mountain tops, they did look foreboding, he smiled and asked, "Well Hurit, what are we going to do?"

Hurit looked at the boyish smile, he seemed undaunted by the forecast of certain death. She made a decision, "Come. I know of a place where we have a chance."

Reed picked up his bag and gun and followed. They left the lowlands and headed more westerly staying closer to the base of the mountains near a stream. After ten miles, Hurit stopped the horse and got off. She ordered, "You ride now. We have far to go."

Reed was used to walking days on end but he rode for an hour before he got off and allowed Hurit to ride. Surprisingly Hurit continued on well after dark. Reed figured it was nearing midnight when they came upon a small cabin. Hurit stopped the horse, pointed at the cabin and said, "You look!" Reed knocked on the door, the cabin was abandoned. Reed entered, found some tinder; using his striker and flint he soon had a fire going in the fireplace. He heard a tentative voice, "Reed?"

Reed stepped to the door and explained, "The cabin is empty. I have a fire started. I'll tie the horse, you can come in."

Hurit shook her head, "I'll wait for you."

Hurit was visibly afraid of entering what she considered a cave-like structure. Reed tied the horse on a long rope he found in the cabin then went back into the cabin with Hurit in tow. Reed asked, "Have you ever been in the white man's home?"

"No. It is like cave. Will it fall on me?"

Reed assured, "It is well built. There will be no danger."

Reed opened his bag, "I roasted rabbit this morning. Are you hungry? Would you like some rabbit?"

Hurit took a leg of the rabbit then asked, "Where will we sleep?"

There was a small bed on one wall of the cabin, a small table, one chair, a few utensils, a couple of pots, a couple of plates and a frying pan. Reed motioned to the cot, "You can sleep on the bed I'll sleep on the floor by the fireplace."

Reed had a slicker and a blanket, he spread the slicker on the dirt floor and gave Hurit the blanket. Reed was very tired, he lay down on the slicker and was soon fast asleep. When Reed awoke in the morning, Hurit was sleeping beside him on the slicker, the blanket covered them both.

Wounded Bear was a very old Cheyenne warrior, his shoulders were no longer strong enough to pull a bow string or throw a lance any great distance with killing power.

Wounded Bear had trapped all the rabbits within walking distance of the winter camp, now at night the cries of hungry children haunted him. It was late in January, in the way of the Cheyenne, during a hard winter starving time the old and unable would take a long winter's walk, there would be less mouths to feed.

Wounded Bear was saddened at what he considered to be his duty but he felt guilty when the little ones were hungry. He made up his mind; this night he would leave, he would take a long winter's walk.

Wounded Bear would take a minimum of his possessions hidden in his Buffalo Cape so no one would suspect his intent. He would tell his daughter, Crying Eagle, he was going out to gather more wood and check his rabbit traps. He would not return.

Wounded Bear climbed the mountain walking in the tree line beside a steep slide area. It was a cold moonlit night, he thought, a good time to die. After a long and tedious climb, Wounded Bear started to cross where the slide area started, the snow was deep; he stopped, stooped down deep into the snow and waited. A large elk with a broken front leg was coming his way. He waited. The elk was huge–it struggled in the deep snow. Wounded Bear took out his knife and with rawhide strings tied the knife to the end of his walking shaft. Excited about the prospects of making a kill, his old fingers worked well. Within minutes he had a usable spear. He crouched lower in the snow and waited.

The Elk was struggling in the deep snow above the slide close to the edge. If Wounded Bear could use his spear, wound or kill the elk, he could then push it over the edge. The elk would be found by the villagers in the light of day. The elk came closer, if Wounded Bear allowed the elk to get much farther it would have good footing and Wounded Bear would then lose the advantage. Wounded Bear rose from his hiding place in the snow, quickly stepped closer to the struggling elk, when the elk floundered he found an opening, Wounded Bear buried the knife to the hilt. It was a good stroke, the elk quickly weakened with a wound to the neck. Blood spurted into the moonlit snow.

The old Indian squatted and waited, it did not take long for the elk to succumb to the wound. Wounded Bear cut the tongue out of the elk for his own use, he then proceeded to drag and roll the carcass closer to the edge of the slide area. After a while, Wounded Bear managed to push the elk over the edge. The result was better than he expected, the elk ended up more than half way down the steep slide area. In the morning the elk would appear as a dark blotch on the slope. The villagers would investigate at the same time they would be out tracking him.

He looked at the village below and the elk carcass, he smiled as he sang his song of death. Then he chewed on the still warm elk tongue as he continued up the mountain. The meal of elk tongue gave him strength, he slowly climbed well into the night.

When the sun came up in the morning he sat at the base of a tree in dense pine boughs drinking in the sun's warmth. Wounded bear tucked his feet beneath him onto his Buffalo robe to keep them warm, as he fell asleep he smiled, the peace of sleep, then freezing to death; it is what he had come up the mountain for.

Wounded Bear woke up late in the morning, he looked up at the mountain; it would be colder up higher; he would then complete his task. On the slow climb up the mountain he finished the elk tongue, it gave him the energy to climb even higher.

Late in the afternoon he found a well-used rabbit trail and set a snare. Confident of a catch, he stroked the back of his knife on a Flint and coaxed a fire. He walked about the area to stir movement, before long a rabbit was caught in his snare. Wounded Bear smiled, this night he would die with a belly full of warm meat.

An hour later, his stomach full, he continued up the mountain. He was able to make good progress on a trail blown nearly free of snow. At the end of the windblown area he came to a steep slope, one that would be very difficult to ascend. He looked up and considered; if he slipped, he may end up in the valley on the opposite side of the mountain. Wounded Bear looked down the steep slope, he could barely make out a small trail of smoke coming from a white man's house. He was getting colder, the warmth of the fire down below pleased him. He stood looking at the cabin for some time before he made his decision. Wounded Bear smiled, he would slide down the mountain, he would be warmed by the fire of the white eyes or he would be killed. He arranged his buffalo cape beneath him, he sat down and slid down the slope. It had taken him more than a day to climb the mountain, it took him a few minutes to get to the bottom, the last few hundred yards he skidded out of control just missing boulders and grazing a couple of trees.

Reed Maddock just happened to be looking up at the mountain, he watched as a dark speck got closer, it looked like a bear falling down the mountain, then the form of a man took shape. The last few hundred yards the shape fairly flew. Reed quickly ran to where the form ended the slide; buried. Reed dug him out of the snow, retrieved the Buffalo Cape and carried the old Indian to the cabin.

Hurit wiped the snow off Wounded Bear's head, she removed his shirt and dried him off. She removed his pants, dried him and covered him near the fire. Hurit explained, "He was hit on the head. I think he will live, but I think he was out for a long winter's walk."

Reed asked, "He was out taking a walk on the mountain this time of year?"

Hurit smiled and shook her head, "Many old Indians go for a final walk at this time of the year so that the rest of the tribe doesn't have to feed them."

Reed asked, "He was committing suicide?"

Hurit asked; "What is that?"

"It means, was he trying to kill himself?"

"Yes. So that he doesn't take food from children and those younger."

Reed thought for some time, "My! That would take bravery. That would be the height of giving."

Hurit smiled, "You mean giving, like jumping in a freezing river to save someone you don't even know? Or giving, like allowing a stranger to have your horse; probably your last hope to survive?" Hurit smiled knowing that Reed gave no selfish thought to his own needs.

Wounded Bear moaned, they moved to his side. Wounded Bear looked at the twosome, he looked again, smiled and said, "Which one of you thieves stole my pants?"

Hurit laughed, then explained the joke to Reed. Reed laughed and then pointed to Hurit.

Hurit asked, "Do you know English?"

Wounded Bear nodded "Some. Not good. What are you named?"

Hurit pointed and answered, "Hurit. Reed."

Wounded Bear nodded that he understood, "Yes. Very amoh'en ah. You are Blackfoot? You are too amoh'en ah to be Blackfoot."

Hurit explained, "I was raised by the Blackfoot. I was born Shoshone."

Wounded Bear smiled, "I see. I have heard the Shoshone have beautiful women. I know the Blackfeet, they are not so amoh'en ah."

The conversation was explained to Reed. Reed asked, "Hurit means pretty?"

Hurit nodded, then she asked, "What is your name?"

"Mah ha'his. I went for a long winter's walk. I saw your fire."

Reed asked what he said, Hurit interpreted, "His name is Mah ha'his, Wounded Bear. He says he is an old man, he went for a long winter's walk; then he saw the smoke from our fire."

Wounded Bear chuckled and rubbed the knob on his head. He added, "When I saw the smoke from your fire, I decided to drop in on you."

They laughed heartily, Reed said, "Wounded Bear. Since you like to laugh, we are glad you dropped in. We have plenty of meat. You won't have to do any more walking this winter. Are you hungry?"

Wounded Bear rubbed his stomach, "Plenty Volk oh."

Reed again looked to Hurit. She responded, "Rabbit."

Reed offered, "I have plenty elk if you want more to eat."

Wounded Bear looked to Hurit as she interpreted, "Reed has said he has moh eth, elk."

Wounded Bear smiled, "I think I came to a good place."

The remainder of the winter went by faster with the ever-present banter of Wounded Bear in the cabin. When spring came, Reed offered Wounded Bear the horse so he could return home. Wounded Bear's answer was surprising and in broken English. He pretended a scowl and said, "Are you trying to cast me out?"

Reed laughed, "No, no. Stay as long as you want. You are free to come and go as you like. We enjoy your company."

Wounded Bear's laugh came easy, "I'm a Cheyenne. I am living with a white man and a Shoshone-Blackfoot woman in the land of the Crow. Funny! I like it! Someday-maybe-so, I'll go back over the mountain… Maybe."

Reed had considered heading to Oregon, with Hurit and Wounded Bear, he kept delaying his departure. Neither Hurit nor Wounded Bear mentioned leaving.

Later that spring there were four wagons that observed the stream heading off into the Pryor Mountains. The wagon train of 45 wagons were heading westerly on the Bozeman Trail. The mountains were awash with greenery, the scenery looked enticing, the four wagons elected to follow the stream. The captain informed them that the Pryor Mountains were rugged terrain in the heart of Crow territory with occasional raids occurring from Sioux. They were told their only safe decision was remaining with the wagon train. Oregon would be a much better and safer place to live.

Before the day was over, three of the four wagons were burning when the war party left.

Suzanne wells had listened well to her father's directions. She was told not to let out as much as a peep until dark. 'Do not come out until after dark.'

Sixteen-year-old Suzanne wells whispered to her two little brothers, "Shush, close your eyes. Remember what dad said. It will be dark soon, then we'll get away."

Suzanne could see seven-year-old Billy and eight-year-old Ned's eyes just barely visible in the dark enclosure built into the wagon bed. The boys obediently closed their eyes to await nightfall.

Reed and Hurit observed the smoke from the burning wagons and rode down to check for survivors. They rode double, a look with Reed's telescope showed the raiding Indian war party had left. Reed spoke, "Do you smell that?" Hurit's hands tightened on his waist, "Burning flesh. The smell of death."

"It is strange, one wagon didn't catch fire."

They dismounted and walked among the dead oxen and people. Reed said, "Nobody is alive. I'm wondering why the one wagon didn't burn?"

Reed walked over and examined the wagon, he seemed to be thinking out loud, "I've never seen a wagon built like this. Part of it is covered with very thin sheets of metal."

Hurit was motioning with her hands to Reed, Reed followed her actions; he kneeled down to look under the wagon. Fluid was dripping from between the boards, Hurit whispered, "There is somebody hiding in the wagon."

Astounded there were survivors, Reed looked to the center of the wagon at a large box like structure. Reed spoke loudly, "I know there is somebody hiding in the wagon. You can come out now, the Indians have gone."

There was no response, Reed tried again, "The Indians have gone. It is safe to come out now."

Still there was no response, Reed took Hurit aside and explained, "Someone or something is inside a built-in box. If

I open the box, will they have a gun inside and will they start shooting?"

Reed went back over to the wagon and examined it more closely. He knew how they got inside but he didn't see how to open it. He tapped lightly on the metal that encased the box and said again, "My name is Reed Maddock. I'm a white man, I saw the wagons burning, I came to help. I know you are in there, now open the door or I will get and axe and chop it open."

Reed was ready to duck if he saw a gun barrel stick out, he waited. Ingeniously the container was opened from the inside. The first thing Reed saw was a feminine hand clutching a large .45. To be safe Reed grabbed the barrel and kept it pointing toward the sky. Suzanne Wells saw Reed and cried tears of relief.

Reed stuck the gun in his belt and said, "You'll be all right. I'm sorry to say, everybody else has been killed. I think we should leave here as quickly as we can."

Suzanne slid out of the container, Reed continued to hold her hand gently after he took her .45; she felt relief. She looked into Reed's eyes, they were good eyes and he smiled reassuringly as he took the gun. Again, he reassured her, "You will be all right. But, we should leave soon. The Crow may return."

Susanne heard a female's voice come from the opposite side of the wagon, Susanne could not see who was talking. Hurit said, "They were not Crow, they were Sioux."

Suzanne emerged from the enclosure with Billy and Ned right behind her. Reed stopped them from getting up and seeing the carnage. He said, "I don't think you should see what happened here. What is your name?"

"Suzanne. This is Billy and Ned."

"Suzanne, I don't think you should see what happened here. Suzanne, blindfold the boys and I'll take them out away from the wagons."

Suzanne answered, "I'll have them shut their eyes."

Reed shook his head, "No Suzanne. You should blindfold them for their own good."

Suzanne reluctantly agreed, she realized she was in no position to negotiate. The two boys were blindfolded, Reed scooped them up and carried them away from the remains of the wagons. Reed set them down facing the mountains just out of sight of the carnage. He removed the blindfolds and said, "I'm going to get your sister. You boys stay here, I'll be back soon."

The boys seemed comforted by Reed and the proximity of each other. Reed ran back to the wagon. Hurit was talking to Suzanne, reassuring her when he returned.

Reed asked," Suzanne. What do you want to do? Close your eyes-be blindfolded-or-..."

Suzanne interrupted, "I would like to face the problem."

Suzanne started to sit up, Reed put his hand gently on her shoulder and stopped her. Reed kindly explained, "Suzanne. Whatever you can imagine in your worst dreams has happened here. If you feel you must face this; be prepared for the worst."

Reed took her hand, Suzanne sat up, she started to step out onto the wagon wheel, one look at the remains scattered about caused her to faint into Reed's arms. Suzanne was in Reed's arms, she retched then cried at the sight. She forced herself to take some of it in. She saw evidence of murder, rape, torture, dismemberment and mutilation all around her. Reed turned her face into his shoulder, he then picked her up and carried her to where her brothers were.

Reed gave orders to Suzanne before depositing her with her brothers, "Suzanne. Be strong now. Hold on to your brothers."

For some time, Suzanne remained in his arms for consolation as she wept trying to drive the memory of the carnage out of her mind. Reed and Hurit made four trips to the wagons retrieving the items Susan spoke of and a few other items and supplies they would need for the three-extra people at the cabin. After the blankets were packed onto the horse and other items were safely hidden, Reed spoke again with Suzanne. "Suzanne. Do you have relatives on the wagon train?"

Suzanne shook her head. Reed asked, "Nobody? "

Suzanne mumbled, "Mom and dad came from Holland. We have no other relatives in the country."

Reed offered, "For now we'll get you away from here, we'll take you to our cabin. You can decide later what you want to do. You walk with Hurit. I'll take the boys with me on the horse."

Ned's eyes were looking back at Hurit. Finally, Ned asked, "Isn't she an Indian?"

Reed chuckled, "Yes indeed. Her name is Hurit. Hurit in Blackfoot means pretty girl. Ned, do you think she's pretty?"

Both Bill and Ned had to check Hurit out again, Billy exclaimed, "Boy! Is she ever!"

Reed laughed and added, "Hurit is also a fine person."

Billy looked again and nodded, "Hurit hugged Suzanne. Suz is crying."

Reed glanced back, Hurit was consoling Suzanne. Reed explained, "Your sister Suzanne is a strong girl. You have lost a lot, both of your parents and most all of your possessions. I think your sister Suzanne is worried about you two boys. You two boys will have to be strong, you'll have to do as she tells you. She's your mother and your sister now."

Reed got off the horse and walked beside the two boys as he continued to talk to them, "You can see the cabin up ahead. Before we get there, I want to tell you boys this. You've lost a lot but always remember, you have each other. There is no word in the world better than brother. Sister, mother and wife come close. If you don't remember a thing I tell you, make sure you brothers remember to stick together and protect each other."

The boys were pretty solemn for a minute or so, then Billy exclaimed, "There is someone sitting on the steps of the cabin!"

Reed laughed and said, "That is your new grandfather. His name is Wounded Bear. Wounded Bear is a Cheyenne Indian, he lives with us. Wounded Bear is a funny man; you boys will like him."

In the short three-mile walk to the cabin Suzanne learned to trust and lean on Hurit. At first Suzanne was skeptical, Hurit quickly took away all of Suzanne's fears. The waves of terrible memories, the resultant nausea was overridden by a warm and consistent Hurit.

Suzanne noted that Reed doted over her brothers and they in turn were attentive to his every word.

Reed took three trips to the wagons to retrieve needed items. Their larder of meat was also now stocked with flour, salt, sugar, coffee, pots, pans, knives, and utensils of all sorts. Wounded Bear rigged a travois to retrieve a small cook stove and a couple of links of tin stovepipe.

The summer passed rapidly, the boys were taught by Reed and Wounded Bear. They had a surrogate grandfather, father and two mothers.

On a day late in the fall, Reed was up on the mountain hunting, Running Elk and a band of his Crow warriors surrounded the cabin. Wounded Bear informed everyone, "They have no paint. They are hunting, getting meat for winter. There are too many for us to fight."

Hurit recognized Running Elk, she walked boldly out the door and challenged, "What are you doing here?"

Laughing Bear recognized Hurit, "It's the Blackfoot woman I traded for. It was the worst trade I ever made."

Running Elk asked, "What did you do with the white man? Did you kill him?"

Hurt snapped, "He is hunting to provide food for winter. It is what you should be doing!"

Running Elk smiled, he saw a pair of eyes staring out of the window at him, he ordered, "Tell everyone to come out. They will not be harmed."

Hurit snapped again, "Why do you want them out?"

Running Elk smiled, "I don't want to get shot."

Wounded Bear heard the conversation, he came out with the two boys in hand; Suzanne followed. Running Elk asked, "Is the old man your father?"

"He is Wounded Bear. A Cheyenne that Reed dug out of the snow after his long winter walk."

Running Elk laughed, "The white man has good medicine. Now he has saved a Cheyenne."

Running Elk said to Hurit, "I want the white man's medicine. When will he return?"

Hurit angrily snapped back, "How would you take his medicine?"

Running Elk shrugged, "Maybe I will kill him. His medicine will be mine."

Hurit shook her head, she answered like she was talking to a child, "You cannot take his medicine. His medicine comes from giving of himself. He nearly gave his life to save your brother."

Running Elk asked, "Why are you still here?"

Hurit answered factually, "Reed, cut my bonds. Reed gave me my life and the horse. He allowed me to go. I chose to stay."

Running Elk asked, "What of the old man?"

Hurit explained, "After Reed dug him from the snow and brought him back to life. Reed offered him the horse so he could return to his village. Wounded Bear chooses to remain with us."

Running Elk asked, "What of the others?"

Hurit quickly explained the Sioux attack on small wagon train. Running Elk answered, "They are brothers and sister?"

"Yes."

Running Elk shrugged, "Maybe we will take the woman with us."

Hurit didn't know if she was being tested are not. Hurit said, "You will lose all of Reed's medicine if you steal his woman."

Running Elk asked, "She is Reed's woman?"

Hurit snapped in reply, "Of course. You say you want Reed's medicine? You can gain his medicine by giving. The more you give, the greater the medicine of Running Elk. Only after much giving will you have Reed's medicine. Then you will be his brother. Then you will truly have his medicine."

Running Elk looked to his brother, Little Elk. Running Elk smiled and said, "It is a great honor to be called brother." Hurit explained, "The white man's word is, brother." Hurt turned about and called, "Billy-Ned. Come here."

Hand-in-hand the twosome strode forward seemingly unafraid. Hurit said to Running Elk, "Reed has taught them well. I will ask them in the white man's tongue, what is the greatest word they know. They will answer true."

Hurit said, "Billy. Ned. Reed has taught you. What is the greatest word you have learned?"

Billy answered, he was echoed by Ned, "Brother." "Brother."

Running Elk smiled, he respected Hurit's loyalty to Reed. He said, "Now Reed is uncle; he has two women and an old Indian in his tepee."

Hurit answered, "Yes. Sometimes the boys call Reed brother, sometimes father. They have learned much from Reed."

Running Elk smiled warmly," We will come again. Maybe I can gain Reed's medicine." Running Elk and his braves rode away to continue their hunt.

That night in the cabin, Hurit related to everyone what happened during the conversation with Running Elk. First of all, she explained about the medicine gained by giving and the end goal of brotherhood. She explained the importance of brotherhood in the teaching of Billy and Ned and its effect on Running Elk. Hurit went on to explain the threat of Running Elk regarding Suzanne. Suzanne exclaimed, "He was going to take me?"

Hurit nodded, "I told him you were Reed's wife. I told Running Elk he would lose all Reed's medicine if he took you."

Weeks later as Suzanne and Hurit were gathering berries, Suzanne asked, "Are you and Reed married?"

Hurit laughed, "We sleep and play together like we are married, but we are not. Someday, I may want to return to the Shoshone village where I was born. I have told Reed of my thoughts. I go to him of my own desire. He has not asked or forced me in any way."

Suzanne smiled, "I notice he doesn't fight or wrestle to keep you away."

Hurit laughed, "No, you are right, our wrestling has never been to fight the other away."

Suzanne asked, "What made you decide to stay?"

Hurit related the beginning of her meeting Reed, then she spoke of the arrival at the cabin, "Reed would have let me have the horse to go back home. He would have died. The winter would have killed him. When I was captured I saw the cabin. I thought, Reed had a gun and maybe he would know how to live in the cabin and stay alive. When we got to the cabin, Reed went in and started a fire, I was very cold. Reed took me into the cabin, I think he saw the fear in me. He smiled. He put his arm about my shoulder and said, "We will get through this together." He was like a brother. Indians, in the cold of winter, we share our body's heat beneath the buffalo robes. It is the way we stay alive. On the first night at the cabin, I took my blanket and lay with him by the fire. He treated me like a sister. All winter we worked together to live, we shared our warmth. I went to him, he did not force me. It became like we were married."

After a short time Hurit asked, "Suzanne, why haven't you played with Reed?"

Suzanne had a puzzled and embarrassed look, Hurit laughed, "Don't tell me you have no desire. I have seen it in your eyes for some time. How old are you Suzanne?"

"Seventeen."

Hurit exclaimed, "Oh my. I remember what it is like to be sixteen and seventeen years old. I took many walks into the woods to be alone."

Suzanne asked, "Weren't there any men you liked?"
Hurit shook her head, "I wanted to get back to my Shoshone
village. I didn't want to stay and become part of a Blackfoot
family. I was running away when I was caught by a white
man and traded to a Crow."
Hurit smiled and said, "Suzanne. You have been here all
summer long, do you spend some time in private?"
Suzanne chose not to talk about her desire and didn't try to
defend herself. Again, Hurit laughed and said, "Suzanne.
You have chosen to stay with us for the winter rather than go
back to join a wagon train. It gets to be a very long time
during the winter. You are mother to your brothers. You
share in all the work, you are like a sister to me. You can go
to Reed if you like. It is our way."
"It is the Indian way to have two wives?"
"Yes. Many times. Sometimes more than two wives. A wife
may invite her sisters into her lodge to help. They become
wives. They share the work, just like we share the work."
Suzanne smiled at the idea, still she did not answer; she
continued to pick berries.
That evening when the boys were sleeping behind a tarp with
wounded bear, Hurit got up from the blankets by the fire and
took Suzanne's hand. Hurit led Suzanne the few steps to the
blankets, Suzanne went willingly. Hurit lay down behind
Reed, she drew Suzanne down so that Suzanne was laying in
front of Reed. Hurit pulled the blanket over them then
reached across Reed and tugged Suzanne closer.
With their noses nearly touching Reed gently pulled Suzanne
closer, he whispered in her ear as he stroked her back,
"Suzanne. Are you sure this is your wish?"
Suzanne had been considering what went on beneath the
blankets next to the fire ever since she arrived. Her feelings
for Reed as a person were great, her desire had been building
for some time. Suzanne eagerly pulled him to her as her lips
met his.

The two fugitives made their way up the slopes of the Pryor Mountains with the posse not far behind. Billy Sunderland figured the money in their saddle bags wouldn't be worth much if the posse or the Indians caught up with them. Billy asked, "Hoss, do you know where we're going? They are getting mighty close."

Hoss shrugged, "Took a wrong turn back there, allowed them to catch up. If they get too close I'm going to pick a few off." Horace Shattuck laughed at their dilemma, "I thought we lost that posse in the Bighorn Badlands but now we will lose them in the mountains. They won't follow us much longer."

Billy asked, "Why is that?"

Hoss laughed, "Because these mountains belong to the Crow Indians. Nobody likes to tangle with the Crow."

Billy had always felt confident traveling with Hoss. Billy figured there was no meaner SOB in the world than Horace Shattuck. Horace told Billy about his growing up; Hoss laughed but after listening, Billy recognized just how mean Hoss could be. Growing up, the kids abbreviated Horace's name, they called him horse apples, horse shad or worse. Finally, when Horace reached eighteen he grew eight inches. He was big enough then to bend an oak board over some guys head for calling him worse than horse shad. The oak board didn't bend, the man died and Horace had been running ever since. Hoss killed a farmer in Missouri because he needed a rifle. As he made his way north he killed two more men before Billy met up with him.

Billy was talked into robbing a bank with Hoss, when they galloped out of town one more man was killed by Hoss. The last one was carrying a water pail-he didn't even have a gun. The killing didn't seem to bother Billy, he felt a little safer in the company of Hoss.

They stopped well up on the slope of the mountain where they were hidden but had a good view of the pass below. Hoss dismounted and took out a telescope and braced it on a rock. Hoss exclaimed, "Damn! They aren't turning back. They are setting up camp."

Billy asked, "What does that mean?

Hoss laughed, "It means that they figure we will have to come back out the same way we went in. They think we'll turn back. They don't want anything to do with the Crow and they are betting we'll be the same. They'll wait till we empty our saddlebags of grub figuring we'd rather hang than starve."

Hoss laughed at his joke then looked about for a way out where the posse couldn't see them. Hoss ordered, gather a couple of good sized armloads of wood. We'll make a fire that will produced a little smoke. Then we are heading down into that gully and sneaking out of here."

Billy quickly gathered the wood and built a fire among the rocks adding a little green wood so there would be a little smoke.

As soon as the fire was started Hoss and Billy left, they stayed in the foothills of the Pryor Mountains until they came to the four burnt out wagons. Hoss looked over the wagons and made his report. "Indians did a lot of killing. Didn't find anything in the pilgrim's pockets. It looks like a travois pulled a load off in that direction up the Creek. That was a mighty long time ago."

Hoss looked the wagons over again and said, "Didn't find anything much of value, I figure the Indians took whatever they found in that direction."

Hoss pointed off toward the mountains, then got out his telescope. "Damned if there isn't a cabin up there a few miles. Someone is there. I can see smoke. Never heard of Indians living in a cabin. Must be pilgrims. Wonder how the hell they stay alive in this territory? Way I heard, nothing stays alive in this country besides Crow and sometimes other raiding Indians."

Hoss checked his guns then said, "Let's go. Where there's pilgrims and smoke, there's home cooking."

An hour later Hoss and Billy cautiously approached the cabin. Hoss again took out his scope, then handed it to Billy. Billy exclaimed, "Damn. Is she a pretty one or am I seeing a mirage?"

Billy continued to look through the scope, "Oh my! There are two of them! One for each of us."

Hoss took the scope back and looked again, "They are both lookers! What are we waiting for? Our horses will need to rest because they won't be able to go much farther. What a stroke of luck." Hoss laughed, "I wonder how long that posse is going to wait there for us?"

When they approached the cabin the two boys and Suzanne were in the house, Hurit met them in the yard. Wounded bear knelt down behind the water trough and rested the gun on the edge. Hoss shifted in the saddle to better be able to draw his 44. Hoss growled, "Mighty unfriendly! I thought I saw a white woman?"

Hurt answered, "You did. She's in the house with a rifle aimed at you right now. So is her husband and a boy."

Hoss figured it was a bluff, "Missy. I figure I'm going to shoot that old buck, then you and I will have to tussle a bit."

Hurit crossed her arms, "I think unless you can climb that mountain fast and hide in the rocks, you'll be dead and scalped within the hour."

Hurit pointed down the slope to the northeast, "Our good friend Running Elk and a band of Crow warriors are headed this way."

Hurit pointed toward a valley not too far away in the mountains, "On the other side of that rock you can make it over the mountain. You don't have any time to waste."

Hoss took one look at Running Elk's band of warriors, he decided with his tired horse, he had no time to wait. As he turned the horse away he said, "We'll be back."

When Billy and Hoss made it to the spot Hurit directed, he found it impossible to climb with horses. They were sent into a trap. Unless they dismounted and climbed into the rocks the Indians would catch up with them. They abandoned their

278

horses, they took their money, guns bedrolls and a few supplies and quickly climbed up into the rocks. Before too long the band of Crow arrived, looked up into the rocks, took their horses and left.

Hoss and Billy didn't waste any time to see if they were being pursued, three days later they were back down the opposite side of the mountain. Billy Sunderland was getting worried about his traveling companion. They hadn't been eating the best and Hoss seemed meaner than ever. Billy got to wondering if he would end up on the menu. They were walking in the general direction of Red Lodge, Montana but they had at least a two-day journey ahead of them on foot. Thankfully, Billy spotted three Buffalo off to the north. Hoss made a simple plan, "You circle ahead of them and I'll go the other way. First one gets a good shot, takes it."

Billy was lucky, there was a knoll with some brush on top for a natural blind, the Buffalo walked below him less than fifty feet away. Billy dropped a small bull with a well-aimed shot.

Hoss was so hungry he didn't worry that the sound may bring Indians; Hoss began gathering sticks for a fire. Hoss growled, "Hurry up and cut out a chunk of that hump, I'm hungry enough to eat the whole damn carcass raw."

They skewered a large piece of the hump and rigged a support over the fire. In about fifteen minutes they were eating partially roasted Buffalo.

Preacher Sam Reardon had six followers, they were surprised when they heard the gunshot. Preacher said, "Harley. Take Lindsay, sneak over there and find out what kind of company we have. I don't want an audience when we rob that stage."

Harley motioned for Lindsay to follow, in ten minutes they were watching from hiding while Billy and Hoss gorged themselves on partially roasted buffalo. Harley sent Lindsay back to report to Preacher, meanwhile Harley drew his side arm and walked his horse out toward the twosome at the fire.

Harley calmly asked, "You men have enough so you can share with company?"

Hoss spun around as he grabbed for his gun. Harley had his gun out and ready, "Just go back to eating. I'm not going to do you any damage. Matter of fact, I could do with a taste of that hump myself."

Harley put his gun in the holster and drew his knife. Not getting a very friendly response from Hoss, Harley mentioned, "I sent a man back to the boss to tell him what's going on. Where are your horses?"

Billy shrugged, "Other side of the mountain. Indians got them."

After introductions were made and more of the hump consumed, Harley asked, "This is mighty lonesome country to be without a horse. Won't be long and you'll have to think about winter."

Billy laughed, "We know, not much of a mountain but it was dang cold coming over the top." Harley asked, "Where are you boys going to hold out for the winter?"

Hoss explained, "Maybe Red Lodge."

Harley nodded, "You men don't look like pilgrims."

Billy smiled, Hoss growled, "We manage to get by."

Harley nodded, "The money you got out of that bank help any?"

Hoss smiled, "So far we haven't been able to spend a penny."

Harley laughed and admitted, "We are in the same line of work. Red Lodge won't be a good fit for you boys, they already have your description. Stage two days ago let everyone know all about you."

Hoss nodded, "Thanks. Guess we'll have to find someplace else to spend the winter."

Harley informed, "We got a job coming up. Afterward we are heading south toward Denver or beyond. Here comes the boss. I have to forewarn you two boys, he likes to be called Preacher but don't talk to him about religion. He's also the boss and he doesn't want anybody questioning him. Around him, it's like my sainted mother once said, keep your eyes and ears open and your mouth shut."

Billy smiled and asked, "If he is a preacher why doesn't he want to talk about religion?"

Harley laughed, "The boss is everything opposite of a preacher. Get on the wrong side of him and he just may kill you for the fun of it."

Preacher Sam Reardon and four men soon arrived, Harley introduced everyone. They put more of the Buffalo on the fire to roast while Lindsay was sent to keep tabs on the trail. To Billy, Preacher seemed a man of few words, he quietly explained, "There is a stage coach due through here in two or three hours. We're going to relieve them of their money, steal their horses and set them afoot back to Fort Bridger. Maybe we can get you boys back onto a horse or two."

Hoss asked, "How much will the stage be carrying?"

Preacher's look at Hoss seem to scare Billy. There was something ominous about the man. Preacher gave Hoss a rather hostile look as he cut off a piece of the roasting Buffalo hump. Preacher growled a brief answer, "Rumor has it one or two thousand."

Hoss did the math quickly, "From one to two-hundred-fifty apiece."

Billy noted that Hoss got another rather deadly look from preacher. Preacher looked to Billy as if he didn't want to talk to Hoss. The preacher asked, "How'd you lose a posse without horses?"

Billy explained their escape into the Pryor Mountains and the posse stopping to wait for their return. Billy explained the stop at the cabin, the Indian woman and the loss of their horses. Preacher asked, "There is a cabin over there?"

Billy explained, "Yes. It's a sixteen by sixteen-foot affair. They had a fire going in their cook stove, there was a white woman and an Indian woman. Both lookers. They built another little shed off the ground, looked like it was filled with meat."

Harley announced, "Stage coming boss."

281

Hoss and Billy rode double as far as the trail, Preacher gave orders, "You two get off the horse and walk out onto the trail. The stage will stop for you. Rest of us will be waiting. Don't do any shooting. Just pretend you are lost pilgrims." After Hoss and Billy dismounted Harley quietly warned, "Do exactly as you were told and you'll have a horse under you shortly."

The plan seemed simple to Billy, he wondered how Hoss would react to taking orders. Billy was leery, he figured Hoss wasn't too good at following directions. Before long the stage approached, Billy and Hoss stood in the trail as directed. When the stage came to a stop, Hoss drew and killed the man riding shotgun. Preacher and his men soon surrounded stagecoach. Preacher called out to those inside, "Everyone out of the stage. Keep your hands empty and where we can see them."

There were three men on the stage, they all followed directions, soon Preacher's men were rifling through the stage. The horses were taken out of the harness and were tied together. Preacher gave more orders, "You men start walking back to Fort Bridger."

When everything of value was removed from the stagecoach, Preacher led them back to the Buffalo carcass. He ordered his men to roast and dry as much of the meat as possible. Hoss wondered out loud, "I think we should get away from here as far as we can."

Preacher didn't respond other than give Hoss and unkind look. Soon, Buffalo was being roasted on three small fires. Hoss snarled again, "Let's divide up the money and get the hell out of here."

Harley calmly spoke, "I'm almost done counting the money. It's a mighty long walk back to Fort Bridger. Keep your shirt on Hoss."

Hoss snapped, "Don't be telling me what to do!"

Billy saw another scary return look coming from Preacher, Billy also saw something else in Preacher he could only characterize as a cold resolve.

Harley went back to counting the money, when he was done he handed it to Preacher. Preacher had removed his pistol and laid it in front of him. Lindsay gave his accounting, "There's seven hundred there."

The men all gathered around Preacher, nobody stood behind Hoss. The money was doled out into seven stacks. Hoss quickly corrected him, "There are eight of us!

Preacher's left hand picked up a stack the money, Hoss quickly reached for it. As Hoss reached for the money Preacher's right hand picked up his pistol. The bullet from Preacher's gun hit Hoss just under his chin. Preacher replied to Hoss's dead body, "Seven of us. I told you not to do any shooting."

Preacher handed Billy his share and said, "Now Billy, tell me some more about that cabin on the other side of the mountain and how to get there. We will be in need of a place to hold up for the winter."

Billy asked, "Aint it a little early to be holding up for the winter? If a posse gets on our trail they'll have time to catch up to us before the snow flies."

It was suddenly obvious to Billy that Preacher didn't like being questioned, he explained as he held his .45 about two inches from Billy's eye, "We have to get some place where we don't make any tracks for a while. It sounds like that cabin would be a good spot. You've said we've even got a couple women there that will do the cooking for us too. Now Billy. I know these mountains and I know there isn't much time left before winter sets in. I don't want to have to explain myself ever again. When I have questions you just provide answers."

Billy could tell by the look in preacher's eyes that he wouldn't hesitate to pull the trigger. Billy decided he would answer questions from that time on. Billy also decided that the first chance he got he would get as far away from the preacher as he could.

Hurit, Suzanne and Reed lay beneath the blankets in front of the fire, everyone else in the cabin was fast asleep. Reed said, "On the way out here I asked myself, where do I want to go? What do I want to do? I decided then, I wanted to be alone, by myself and independent. I wanted to build a home of my own. Hurit, Suzanne, you have shown me… I've learned how important a friend can be. Companionship. Thanks to Hurit, Wounded Bear, Suzanne, your brothers, and the Crow, I have found out how wonderful people can be. Now, I cannot think of a home by myself. It seems I have to ask both of you: where do we go? What do we do?"

Hurit replied, "It is good that our talk is of we; all of us. Where do we go? That is the question of life. All of us that give thought to life ask the same questions. Depending on others and having them depend on me has caused me to ask those questions. What I want of life. It is the reason I have not left. I planned to go. After the first winter here, I was going to leave. I was going to go to the Shoshone, back to where I thought I belonged. I was thinking of seeking a new beginning, a life with the Shoshone. In the spring I did not leave. I continued to think about leaving, but, after spending the winter with Reed, I was confused, I wasn't so anxious to leave. Suzanne, when you and the boys showed up. I soon decided, this is my family, I will go wherever everyone else goes; that is where I belong."

Hurit reached across Reed and stroked Suzanne's hair, "Now, it seems that I never think about leaving."

Suzanne agreed, "We were called pioneers. We were going to Oregon and the promises of Oregon that we all looked forward to. Land, good soil… now, if I go, where do I go? Whatever I do, I must think of my brothers, and Reed, and you Hurit and Wounded Bear."

Suzanne smiled, with her hands under the blanket she grinned and said, "Now, if I go to Oregon or some other place, will I have something greater than what I hold now?"

Reed laughed and drew Suzanne closer, then said, "It is too late in the year to travel now. But we have to talk about this

284

or another year will go by. We have to think about the two boys. I have thought of how important you two are to me, I think the boys should be part of a larger community so they can find companions. I too wonder about Wounded Bear, if we decide to leave, what will Wounded Bear do?"

Hurit answered, "Tomorrow I will talk with Wounded Bear. I will see, what is in his heart."

Mid-morning a few days later, Running Elk and his band of warriors rode up to the cabin in plain sight. Upon their arrival they were greeted by Reed and Hurit. Reed looked at Hurit, she had a blanket wrapped about her; her black hair was blowing in the wind. She was naturally as beautiful as the sun rising in the morning. Reed smiled and said, "Hurit. You have great beauty. I fear Running Elk will want to steal you away."

Hurit did not speak, she smiled, the blanket parted and the blade of her knife was seen. Reed smiled, when Running Elk rode up, Reed surprised him when he called him brother in a Siouan dialect. Running Elk smiled and repeated, "Chin YEH. It is good to be called chin YEH."

Hurit interpreted for Reed, then saw the faces of two white girls peeking out from behind two of Running Elk's warriors. Running Elk explained, "We came to hunt. On the way we found two white-eye children. They were captives of a Sioux raiding party. You were close, they are small and afraid."

The two girls were lowered to the ground, Reed could see they didn't know where to go, or what to do. He spoke softly, "Girls. You're safe now. These Indians are your friends. Walk over to me."

Hurit could see the two girls were afraid of her. They were shivering from fear and the morning cold. Hurit removed her blanket and softly said, "Come. Take the blanket. It will keep you warm, walk slowly to the house. You are safe now."

The girls wanted to stay close to Reed, Hurit smiled at the immediate relief shown by the girls being in Reed's presence.

Reed spoke to Running Elk, "The hunting has been good. You have had a long ride. We will eat."

Hurit interpreted and explained that Wounded Bear, Suzanne and the two boys were gathering berries. Running Elk laughed as he watched the two girls cling to Reed, he said to everybody, "Now, there are eight. Soon, Brother Reed will have his own tribe."

For the next two hours they ate meat roasted over two open fires, Suzanne and the two boys returned. Suzanne helped with the cooking of the meat. Running elk looked up at the sun, "Our bellies are full. We must hunt. Soon the day will be gone."

Just then one of Running Elk's Braves rode up to him and informed, "Seven white men come."

Hurit interpreted, then Running Elk asked, "Are they friends?"

Hurit explained that she did not know. Running Elk quickly formed a plan. He ordered his Braves to hide and related to Hurit, "You put the blanket back on. If you drop the blanket to the ground they are enemies. If you keep the blanket on, they are friends."

Very quickly all the braves were hidden, Reed and Hurit stayed outside close to the house, everyone else went inside."

Billy Sunderland wanted to get away someplace in the mountains but he was watched constantly. He patiently waited his opportunity, once he directed them to the cabin he figured they would be less vigilant, then he would get away. He thought he would get away or they would kill him and take his money. At this point Billy figured he would be glad to give them the money just to get away.

As preacher and his riders rode up through the Valley they noted the smoke from the small fires. Harley wondered out loud, "Why the two outside fires?"

Preacher stopped his horse, he saw Hurit and Reed standing in the yard, as if they were waiting. Preacher started his horse and speculated, "Smoking meat. Setting up food stores for the winter. Come on, I'm hungry."

Billy was summoned up to the front, Preacher asked, "There's a white man down there. How many do you figure now?"

As Billy answered he was feeling pretty good about still being alive, "Just the old Indian, the white woman and a couple of kids."

As they approached, Preacher was mesmerized by Hurit's beauty, he noted she was covered by a blanket. He smiled, she appeared vulnerable. He announced to his followers, "Boys. I think I'm going to like wintering here."

Hurit stood on one side of the water barrel, Reed stood on the other side. Reed was noncommittal, "They don't look unfriendly."

Hurt waited until she recognized Billy, then she said, "Get ready to jump behind the water barrel. One of them was here before. They said they were going to kill Wounded Bear, then take me. Stop them before they get too close."

Reed raise the rifle barrel then yelled, "That's far enough! What can we do for you?"

Preacher couldn't take his eyes off from Hurit, it was his undoing. Preacher smiled wickedly, "Been a long time since I've been with a woman."

Reed's rifle barrel was aimed at Preacher, Reed calmly replied, "Hurit. Give him your blanket!"

As Hurt tossed the blanket to the ground, Hurit took refuge behind the barrel as Reed pulled the trigger. There was a shot quickly followed by another shot both coming from the cabin. Two men dropped from their saddles, at the same time the brush erupted with shots from the Crow warriors. Reed emptied his rifle into the surprised and tightly grouped band. Within seconds all seven men were on the ground, only Harley remained alive. Reed spoke with Harley, he learned of the holdup and the killing of Hoss. Running Elk was at his side, Reed related what Harley had said. Running Elk shrugged and asked, "Do you want this one to die?"

Wounded Bear interpreted, Reed was about to answer when a brave galloped up to them pointing and speaking to

Running Elk. Running Elk quickly mounted and gave orders. Within seconds all the Indians were gone. Reed asked, "Wounded Bear. What happened?"

Wounded Bear pointed up toward the mountain, "Men with stars come." Wounded Bear tapped his chest, Hurit explained, "Lawmen come."

Reed asked, "A posse?"

Hurit shrugged, she didn't know what a posse was. The posse came from the same direction as the Preacher and his gang. The sheriff looked at the dead men and said, "Harley. You are still alive. We figured the stage may be robbed, and we heard that Horace Shattuck could be around. With eight horses, you guys left a trail a child could follow."

Harley explained, "The Preacher never thought you'd follow over the mountain this late in the year."

"You figured wrong Harley. Seems that I told you to put some distance between you and the Preacher. Can you walk?"

"Can't move at all."

The sheriff got down and gave orders, "Search them all. The money should still be on them. Jamison. Write down all their names. When you know who they are, bury them."

The sheriff spoke with Harley for some time before Harley died. The sheriff turned to Reed, "You must have had some help here."

Reed nodded, "We were prepared. They came to do us and the women harm. Running Elk was visiting, he lent us a hand."

The sheriff looked at Hurit and Wounded Bear with rifles in their hands and smiled, "Running Elk helped you? I guess then you've got a chance of making it through the winter since the Crow are friendly. We aren't going to be any help to you. We are heading back over that mountain very shortly. We don't have enough provisions to make it back around the mountain if we get snowed in. Reed. In the spring you come to Red Lodge and pick up the reward money. Jamison. What do you have?"

288

Jamison read his information, "There are known rewards on the Preacher, Harley, Johnny Bain, Lew Driscoll and Len Sharp. I have the names of all the others. We can check the wanted posters when we get back into town. So far, the reward will be sizeable. The Preacher and Harley alone will be over fifteen-hundred."

The sheriff ordered, "Might as well add Horace Shattuck to the list. That was the one we found on the other side of the mountain. Preacher did us a favor and shot him. Harley said that Shattuck is the one that shot the guard on the stagecoach. His partner Billy is here. Harley didn't know Billy's last name."

Jamison nodded, "I'll add them to the list."

The sheriff looked around at Reed's gathering and said, "By the looks of the size of your clan here, you'll be able to use that reward. I'll see you in the spring. What's your full name?"

"Reed Maddock."

"Jamison. Write down Reed's name so we know who to give the reward money to."

Jamison got the correct spelling of Reed's last name. After the sheriff mounted, he reached down and shook Reed's hand, "I don't know what kind of magic you've brought with you Reed; since you have survived, and you are all doing well, I'd say keep doing whatever you've been doing. I wish you well and I hope to see you healthy in the spring."

As the posse left, Hurit listened to their conversation.

Soon all eight of Reed's 'tribe' were outside, the two newly arrived girls were more comfortable now. Suzanne smiled and said, "Running Elk said when he came, now, there are eight of us."

Hurit smiled, "When the posse was leaving, one said there are six of us. Another said, 'there were two more kids that stayed in the house; there were eight.'" Hurit grinned, rubbed her stomach and said, "I think maybe by spring there may be nine of us."

Suzanne laughed and admitted, "Maybe ten."

That night as they lay by the fire Reed related, "I talked to Wounded Bear. Wounded Bear laughed, he wants to stay with us whatever we decide. He said we have given him a new life, part of his new life is; he enjoys being uncertain. He said, he took a long winter's walk for his family. Now, he didn't lose his family, he has gained another family. He tried to give me a word."

Reed described the word Wounded Bear used. Hurit translated, "He tried to tell you, we have become his friends, family, your word is companion. He has given us a great compliment."

Reed further described his talk with Wounded Bear, "Then, when Wounded Bear finished, he laughed and said he liked the way he was being fed. He said without us he would be eating a lot of volk' oh."

Again, Hurit translated, "Rabbit. He would have to catch a lot of rabbits to eat."

"Suzanne, what did you learn about the girls?"

"Sue and Ellen. They said their father saw a wagon track and followed it. They made it half way through the day before they were attacked by Indians. When Running Elk came along, he chased the other Indians away and found the girls hiding. They don't know of any other relatives. None that they can seek out. I think they like the boys and Wounded Bear."

Reed smiled and repeated what Running Elk and one of the posse had said, "There were eight. You girls please tell me, do you know when our numbers will increase?"

Hurit moved closer to Reed and answered, "I think maybe in March or April."

Suzanne guessed, "Perhaps in May."

Reed admitted his lack of knowledge, "I don't know anything about giving birth."

Hurit laughed, "Most times it is the woman that has that kind of experience."

After much light-hearted banter, they spoke of where they would go and what they would do. Reed wanted to farm, they needed a place where good soil existed. Suzanne added, "Farming would be a good way to feed our tribe. We farmed in Illinois. We have something else to consider. The children are not related, and we will have a man with two wives, and a man with two children by two different women." Suzanne chuckled and added, "That means we will have to seek good soil."

Hurit laughed, "You did not say that two of us are Indians. We will have to find very forgiving neighbors."

Reed pulled Hurit a little closer and replied, "Girls. You are right. Good soil and good neighbors. I don't mind living far from other people, but I think community is good for the children."

Suzanne chuckled and added, "If we keep adopting, we'll have plenty of company, we'll have our own community. Wounded Bear is right. There is great power in companionship."

Reed laughed and added, "I started out in an orphanage. I came out here thinking I'd be alone, now I can't conceive of how I'd live without any of our family. In the spring, we can look back and say; there were eight, and that was just the beginning."

Introduction to "The Connection"

I've strayed from the western theme into Amish romance in the novella, "Two World's Ridge," in the case of, "The Connection," I stray into science fiction. In perhaps 1995 I had a rather detailed, sharply focused dream. Such dreams seemed to occur mostly when I had too many onions, or too much pizza late at night. "The Connection," dream was very vivid, in this instance, in the morning I wrote down a lot of the details. The following story came from the dream. I've had several similar dreams, in some cases I write down the details in the morning before I forget. I have a small file I call the 'Onion Chronicles', the following effort is one of the stories in the 'onion chronicles' file.

"The Connection"

The Paris office of Winthrop Computer International (WCI)

Carleton Winthrop stepped out of the private elevator into his office on the tenth floor of the French division of World Computer International, Carleton tossed his briefcase onto a leather couch and made a quick call on the private intercom, "Caught you in your office."

The company's CEO of the French office answered the private phone, "Got here an hour ago."

"Are you trying to impress your boss?"

The CEO, John Dewitt laughed, "Nah. I must have already impressed him."

Carleton asked, "Can you come to my office?"

John Dewitt smiled, he recognized some urgency in his boss' tone, "Be right there."

A minute later the CEO stepped into Carleton's office, "So CW? What did you decide?"

Carlton Winthrop shook his head, he appeared uncharacteristically down, "I guess I'm going back home."

Dewitt held up his hands in resignation, "If you don't want to go; hire a lawyer. Get your wife out of your hair."

Carleton slowly shook his head, "This isn't about my wife."

Dewitt held up his hands, exasperated, "So don't tell me you are missing your wife?"

Carleton didn't hesitate, "No. It's the child I'm thinking about."

Dewitt grinned, "The child? Hell, you're the one who didn't want children. Hire a good lawyer and have her wet-nurse the kid."

The joke didn't seem funny to Carleton. Carleton merely shook his head, he sat on the couch and looked out in the direction of the Eiffel Tower, "John. Every day it gets worse. It's like I'm being summoned."

Dewitt shook his head in disbelief, "You mean your frigging wife is calling you?"

Carlton shook his head, "No. Thankfully my wife hasn't even made an attempt to contact me since I left. After she somehow got pregnant, I made my feelings known; since she hasn't bothered to contact me, I figure she's glad to have me away."

Dewitt tried to put things in perspective for Carlton, "You are the richest man in the world. Hire a damn lawyer. Give your wife the ten million agreed upon in the pre-nuptial and get her out of your frigging hair. Then we'll go to the nearest pub and get drunk celebrating."

Carleton shook his head, "The pre-nuptial didn't include a child. My wife said she couldn't have children. She showed me a copy of the doctor's report, and, on top of that she said she didn't want children. Seven months into our marriage she told me she was five months pregnant."

Dewitt chuckled, "So you've been hiding here in France ever since. It's been what? Two years? Is it a boy or a girl?"

Carleton shrugged, "A girl. She is a little over a year and a half old."

Dewitt smiled, Carleton never wanted children, he figured Carleton wanted to invent. His life was seeing progress. Dewitt asked with sarcasm, "So now you want to go home because you missed her birthday party?"

Dewitt couldn't summon any humor in his boss; meanwhile Carleton stood and stared out the window, "I'm told the child is mute."

Dewitt suddenly became serious, "Christ! Mute?"

Carleton nodded, "Evidently. She hasn't mumbled a peep, she doesn't make a sound, even when she cries."

Dewitt shook his head, "If your wife hasn't contacted you, who the hell told you?"

CW mumbled, "One of the maids at the house sent me a letter. She tried to get me up to date. I haven't heard from the maid for two months."

Dewitt shook his head, "No text or e-mail?"

CW shook his head, he didn't want any electronic messages, "I didn't want any way for anyone to be able to trace my correspondence. I don't want the entire world meddling in my personal business. Letters only."

Dewitt nodded, "I see. So, the maid hasn't replied, because you haven't replied."

CW shrugged, he smiled, then continued to stare at the Eiffel Tower, "I called her about six months ago."

Dewitt scowled, "And now you feel like you are being summoned?"

CW nodded then shook his head in exasperation, "Yes I can't explain it."

Dewitt again tried to hand out some free advice, "Is this because she's mute and you feel sorry for her?"

CW shook his head, Dewitt continued, "I'll have to start over. You made it clear you never wanted children. Put the child up for adoption, pay off your wife and get back to doing what you do best."

294

Carleton nodded, "All the possibilities I've considered. Doctors, operations, professional homes for the child. As for my wife? I'm imagining she'll want the child."

Dewitt growled, "Damn. Good move on her part. The prenuptial gave her ten million, with the child, she can eventually own the entire company and everything you have."

The revelation didn't have any effect on Carlton, "I'm not even sure why, but I'm leaving late this afternoon."

Dewitt knew his boss fairly well, "Well. If I can't talk you out of staying-how about if you leave your keys to your Jaguar for me?"

Carleton laughed, dug in his pocket and tossed a set of keys to Dewitt. The Jaguar was a brand new $145,000 XJ, "Don't wreck it and get yourself hurt. I need you in good health. You can drive me to the airport. My traveling bag is in the back seat."

Dewitt raised his hands in resignation, "Why don't you take one of your private jets?"

Carleton went to his desk to finalize items needing attention before his departure, "I'll take the passenger airline. I could use a little time to think. Our jets are heavily booked making me money. Besides; I'm not too anxious to get home. I've got a few puzzles to solve."

Dewitt shrugged, "I'll get ready to drive you to the airport, did you want me to alert the LA office you are coming back home?"

CW shook his head, "No. I'm going home and getting settled. I'll see what's pulling me. Afterward, I'll look in on the business."

Home for Carleton Winthrop was a mansion on four hundred acres overlooking the ocean just an hour north of Los Angeles. The home was occupied by his wife Kim and his daughter Angelica. Jolene Gomez, the nanny was a friend of Kim's. The maids, the cook and the gardener had apartments in the rear of the home.

Jolene Gomez finished dressing Angelica when Kim entered and took a chair. Kim didn't bother to look at the child, "Let's go shopping. I need a couple pairs of shoes."

Jolene laughed, "What about Angelica?"

Kim shrugged, "Doesn't matter. Same as yesterday. We can have the maid check up on her."

Kim laughed, "She's pretty easy to take care of, she doesn't complain."

Jolene shook her head as the baby stared at Kim, then Jolene, Kim exclaimed, "Damn. Sometimes I figure she understands us. She's a spooky kid."

Kim didn't smile this time, "That spooky kid is my ticket to a fortune and a mighty big yacht."

Jolene put the rails of the crib up, stepped back and reminded, "That fortune will only happen when Carleton is out of the picture."

Kim nodded, "He's not in the picture right now. I have no idea when or if he ever will be back in the picture. When he discovered I was pregnant, he left for France."

Jolene shrugged, "And you were glad to see him go. Why don't you go shopping for a substitute?"

Kim stood to go, "I told you. I can't. I don't want to provide any reason for grounds for divorce. I'm where I intended to be well before I got him to marry me. Now, if he comes back, we'll have to talk about how to do him in so I can have it all."

Kim walked to the door ignoring the child, "Let's get out of here."

An hour after Kim and Jolene left the mansion Carleton Winthrop walked up the steps. He stood in the grand ballroom inside the front entrance of the home; it was about eleven o'clock in the morning. Not much had changed in the house, he smiled when he considered his key still worked. He thought he would talk to the cook and alert her of his presence. Instead, as if magnetically drawn, he looked to the staircase leading to the household bedrooms. He moved to the stair and slowly made his way to the top, he was about to turn left toward his suite but he was again somehow drawn down the hall to one of the bedrooms on his right.

Carleton thought about turning around and going to his bedroom but he was somehow compelled to continue down the hall. He stopped in the doorway to one of the bedrooms. There sitting in a crib looking at him inquisitively was his daughter, something seemed to pull him to her. Slowly, seemingly involuntarily he approached. He feared scaring her but the child smiled, grabbed the railing to help herself to stand; she stood facing him.

As Carleton stood in front of the crib Angelica looked up at him, she clung to the rail and stood facing him. Then while continuing to smile she leaned against the rail and held her hands up to him, she opened and closed her hands beckoning him to pick her up. The impulse to do so was overpowering, Carleton picked her up then absently he took a blanket from the crib and carried her from the room.

For reasons he felt rather than understood, Carleton took Angelica out of the room, down the stairs and outside. They walked about the grounds for nearly an hour before he returned her to her crib. As he put her down, he somehow felt she was hungry.

He touched the intercom and summoned a maid, "Who is in charge of feeding Angelica?"

A rather timid voice returned, "This is Sharon Bronson. I just came on duty. I was about to check in on her. Who is calling?"

CW responded, "This is Carleton Winthrop."

Sharon quickly responded, "I'll be right up."

When Sharon arrived, Carleton inquired, "How long ago did Kim leave?"

Sharon seemed nervous, "I'm told they left some time ago."

Carleton nodded to Angelica, "Please. Feed her, she is hungry."

Sharon's eyebrows raised but she didn't ask how he knew Angelica was hungry, "How long has it been since her last feeding?"

Sharon responded, "I relieved the part-time maid at noon; she indicated she fed her about ten."

Carleton continued with his questions, "You indicated 'they' were gone for about three hours. It is noon now. I've been here for an hour. What did you say your name was?"

"Sharon Bronson."

Carleton smiled, "Sharon. Thank you for the letters keeping me up to date on the child. Now, I sense your reticence. I want you to know, ultimately, I pay the bills. That means ultimately, you answer to me. How long ago did Kim leave?"

Sharon looked directly at him and responded, "I was told they left about nine this morning."

Carleton shook his head, "They have been gone over three hours, when do you expect they will return?"

This time Sharon didn't hesitate, "They may not be back till late."

Carleton smiled, "Who are they?"

Sharon answered honestly, "Your wife takes the woman she hired as nanny with her when she goes."

Carleton's brow furrowed, in disbelief he asked, "This woman is hired as a nanny and she left with Kim?"

Sharon nodded, "Yes sir. Usually that's the way it goes."

Carleton was about to leave the room, he wanted to go to his suite, as he started to leave, he turned about to look at Angelica, she had a sad look on her face. A question without sound reached him, "Are you going away?"

Carleton stepped back to the crib and looked at Angelica, "Sharon. After you are done feeding Angelica, bring her to my suite."

Sharon responded, "Kim has taken over your suite."

Carleton didn't hesitate, "Sharon. When you are done here, remove all of Kim's belongings from my room. Hire any help you need to complete the job within the hour."

Sharon nodded, "Where shall we put Kim's things?"

Carleton shrugged, "For the time being, in the nanny's room."

Carleton looked down at Angelica, she again communicated without a sound, "I have to go."

Carleton shrugged, "Sharon. Would you take Angelica to the bathroom? She has to go potty."

Sharon looked at Carleton and questioned, "She has a diaper."

Angelica was holding onto Carleton's shirt, he nodded, "I know. I don't think she likes the diaper. Please. Take her to the bathroom."

Sharon shrugged, "But Sir, she isn't trained yet."

Carleton shrugged, "Call me Carleton or Mr. Winthrop. Please humor me and take her to the bathroom."

Sharon politely took Angelica into the bathroom, in a few minutes she emerged with Angelica, "She went!"

Sharon continued with the feeding, Carleton absently asked. "Do you want me to stay?"

Sharon answered, "That won't be necessary."

Angelica communicated silently, "I don't like the green."

Carleton asked, "Sharon. What is the green stuff you are feeding her?"

Sharon lifted the bottle and answered, "Peas."

Carleton spoke to Sharon, "Angelica doesn't like the peas. Angelica. The peas are good for you. Eat one spoonful. Sharon, next feeding substitute something else in place of the peas."

Sharon nodded, she was baffled by what seemed like silent communication between the baby and Carleton. Carleton explained, "Sharon. I'm going to look at my room. Bring Angelica when you are finished."

Carleton went to his suite, he looked in the closet, the anteroom and his recreation room. The pool table, his cues and cabinets were all missing, in place there was a small family theater. Carleton made another call and he was soon joined by the gardener with his two sons, "Ed. Your two boys are growing up. Are they making you proud?"

Ed nodded, "Both of the boys are on the dean's list. They are good boys."

Carleton nodded, "They have grown in the past couple of years. Ed, I have a problem here which I'd like you to clear up within the next three hours. I'd like the closet emptied and put in the nanny's room. Do you know where my clothes are?"

Ed nodded, "Just down the hall."

Carleton scribbled a list of things to do and briefly explained, "Where is my pool table?"

Ed shrugged, "Sold I think."

As Carleton wrote he explained, "Put everything back the way it was. Buy a pool table, a dozen cues, all the necessary equipment and have it all delivered here within an hour or so."

Ed nodded agreement, "Limits of money?"

Carleton shrugged, "Whatever. Tell them I want the room done over within the next three hours, bring a painter to get rid of that color. Get a decorator to pick out some appropriate paintings and cabinetry. Meanwhile I want Angelica's crib and clothing moved to my suite. I think I'll have Sharon move into the next bedroom while she is on duty."

Carleton ordered, "Move all my things back into this room. Take that thing out of here."

Ed nodded, "That thing sir, is a shoe closet."

Carleton smiled and shrugged, "Hire whatever help you need to get the job done. You are the straw boss. Don't do any lifting yourself."

Soon the cook and another maid arrived to assist, Sharon entered the room with Angelica. Angelica silently communicated to Carleton, "I have to go potty."

Carleton immediately spoke to Sharon, "Sharon. If you would be so kind? Angelica has to go to the bathroom again."

Sharon looked at Carleton like he was crazy but this time obediently took Angelica out of the room. Five minutes later they reappeared, Angelica reached for her father, "You were right again Mr. Winthrop."

Angelica gave her father a hug and communicated, "I'm afraid of falling in the potty."

Carleton smiled, "Sharon. Would you please get a child's potty for Angelica? You may take care of the matter yourself or you may delegate the task or call and have one delivered."

Sharon nodded, "I'll make a call."

Angelica clung to Carleton and communicated, "Sharon is nice."

Carleton stopped Sharon, "Sharon, before you go, I want you to spend some of your time with Angelica. She likes you. She trusts you."

Sharon nodded her head somewhat skeptical, "Yes sir. I'll make the call and be right back."

Carleton whispered to Angelica, "What about your nanny, Jolene?"

Angelica shook her head and clung a little closer, Carleton smiled and asked, "What do you want to do now?"

Angelica silently communicated, "Read to me."

Carleton inquired, "Does anyone read to you?"

Angelica shook her head and communicated, "I watched them read on TV."

Carleton smiled, "Television? You watched people reading on television?"

Angelica nodded as Ed walked in the room, "Pool table will be here shortly. Your bathroom has been returned to your liking. The painter will redo the color in the bathroom also. The bed has been changed. The painter is on his way. How about going back to the light green you had in here before?"

Carleton nodded, "Good. Are my cars still in the garage?"

Ed nodded, "I run the Cadillac a couple of times a month, I just changed the oil a week ago. The Jaguar hasn't been run for a week."

301

Carleton nodded, "Put a child's seat in the back of the Cadillac, and make sure the seat is properly fitted for Angelica. Also, order a good-sized matching walnut bookcase and stock it with children's books."

"Children's books?"

"Make a call or two, hire the filling of the bookcase to an expert. There should be a child psychologist available or a reading specialist."

When Ed left the room, Carleton smiled and whispered to Angelica, "Is there anything else?"

Angelica looked at her father for some time before she communicated, "Kim doesn't' like you."

Carleton smiled reassuringly and nodded, "I know."

Angelica continued, "Why doesn't' Kim like you?"

Unsure if he wanted to answer, Carleton said, "I really don't know."

Sharon returned with a couple of books, the suite was filled with activity for the next two hours while the pool table was set up and the room was restored to its previous state. While Sharon was reading to Angelica, Carleton sent the cook back to the kitchen to fix him something to eat. When the cook returned, Carleton sat at a table in the pool room and asked the cook to sit with him, "Rachel. You've been with me for some time. I need some advice on getting reacquainted with my home. I could always count on you for an honest answer. How were things in my absence?"

The cook seemed reticent, Carleton smiled and spoke, "Rachel. Just tell me everything. I can deal with the truth. I cannot deal with hidden issues."

Rachel seemed relieved. She began, "When you left, we were all given pay cuts."

Carleton was in disbelief, "Pay cuts?"

Rachel nodded, "Ed's salary and hiring budget was more than cut in half. My kitchen budget was cut by over fifty percent. Three maids were let go and the rest were cut in pay by nearly half. Jolene has hired a couple of part time maids."

Carleton shook his head, his food suddenly lost its flavor, "Assure the staff they will be reinstated and paid back pay."

For some time, Rachel related the cuts in the staff and household operation, it added up to nearly a million dollars a year, Carleton smiled, "I thought Ed seemed a little short with me. Rachel. How would you like to take care of the household finances?"

Rachel smiled, "No thanks. Why don't you ask Sharon? Sharon just completed an accounting degree."

Carleton grinned at Rachel's forthright manner, "Thank you Rachel. I've always been able to rely on you."

Carleton took another nibble from his sandwich, Rachel was about to go back to work when Carleton stopped her, "Rachel. Does Kim leave the baby alone very often?"

Rachel winced, "Yes sir. I'm afraid so. Sharon tries to spend time with Angelica, but she has a lot of work to do since she lost her assistant."

Carleton shook his head, "I'll talk to Sharon. She can hire whoever she needs so she can spend more time with the baby."

Carleton entered the room, Sharon was just finishing reading a book to Angelica. Carleton sat down and waited for the book to be finished. Carleton looked at Angelica, her eyes seemed droopy, Carleton stood and asked, "Are you tired?"

Sharon answered, "No. But I have a lot of work to do."

Angelica smiled and communicated silently, "I'm tired and I want to go to bed."

Carleton smiled, "I was asking Angelica. Would you please ready her for bed?"

Carleton watched as Sharon bathed and dressed Angelica for bed. Once in bed Angelica stood and silently pleaded for Carleton. Carleton stepped to the crib, Angelica climbed into his arms and silently communicated, "Daddy. I'm glad you are here. When I wake up will you be here?"

Carleton whispered, "Yes. I'll be here."

Sharon watched the exchange intently and saw what appeared to be a non-verbal communication between the two."

Sharon began to excuse herself, "Sir. I have a ton of work to do."

Carleton kissed Angelica on the forehead and laid her down, "Wait Sharon."

Carleton pulled two chairs up next to the crib, "Sharon. Sit down for a moment."

Sharon sat down, Carleton began to explain; "I spoke with Rachel. She told me about the firing of your help and Ed's help and the cook's relief. It seems the household budget has been cut by more than half. All the staff's back pay will be restored. Sharon, what I want to do is place the entire budget for the house in your hands. Your job will also be, Angelica. First Angelica, then the household budget.

"Now I have a question about Jolene. I'm given to understand you take orders from her?"

Sharon nodded, "Right after you left, Kim hired Jolene and indicated the entire staff were to answer to Jolene."

Carleton shook his head, "Sharon. Angelica doesn't like Jolene. From now on Jolene will have nothing to do with my daughter. And you will answer to me only. You are to direct the rest of the staff in that regard. None of the staff will take orders from Jolene. If Kim thinks of her as a guest, Kim can take care of her. Do you have any questions?"

Sharon smiled, "Not at the moment."

Carleton nodded, "I'll talk to a lawyer in the morning. The lawyer will provide you with all the tools you need to pay for staff and maintenance. Your pay will be raised commensurate with a trusted nanny and a household accountant."

Sharon was still a little unsure, "What prompted you to do this?"

Carleton looked at the sleeping child, "Angelica and Rachel. I've always trusted Rachel's word, I offered her the job; Rachel recommended you. And, like I said, Angelica likes you."

Sharon smiled, "I've been looking for other jobs. I've had a couple of tentative offers."

Carleton stood, "Good. To be happy with this job it is important to know where you stand. Before you accept any other offer, let me know what I need to do to keep you here."

They walked quietly to the door, Sharon stopped, "Thank you Mr. Winthrop."

Carleton shook his head, "No Sharon. Thank you for not abandoning ship. Under the circumstances I fear I would have left some time ago. I hope to rectify what you all have been put through."

Sharon started to leave then added, "I have a class at eight in the morning. I usually show up here from ten to noon."

Carleton shrugged, "I'll get Rachel to help me in the morning. You come in as soon as you get done with class so I can go see the lawyer. Let me have your cell phone number in case I need you."

Jolene sat across the table from Kim, she lifted her glass. "One more for the road?"

Kim shook her head, "No. The damn bartender is looking good to me and I have to behave myself. Part of the pre-nupt."

Jolene grinned, "We still haven't decided how to do in your husband."

Kim chuckled and nodded, "Yes. We wasted another day shopping. I'll have to figure something out."

Jolene shrugged, "When he gets back, we'll figure something out."

Kim laughed, "He just may choose to live out his life in France."

Jolene shrugged, "That wouldn't be bad."

Kim smiled wickedly, "We have to get rid of him or I'll never be able to buy that yacht."

Jolene picked up her purse, "We better get back and make sure the baby gets fed."

Kim again laughed cruelly, "It isn't as though the kid is going to complain."

Jolene chuckled, "Ideal child for you. When we finish off her father you can put her in an institution and be done with her."

Kim smiled and went back to her oft repeated theme, "Then I can buy that yacht I've been looking at."

Kim opened her cell phone, made a call then picked up her purse, "Cab will be at the curb."

Jolene took Kim's arm, "You are a financial whiz. Chopping the salaries of all the household workers so you have a bigger bank account of your own, that was a good move."

Kim giggled, "That way we can have our limo service and make money to put in the safe. I've put over one million in the safe in salary cuts and household changes over the last two years. If he stays away another year or two, I'll try to find a way to turn it into three million and make a down payment on a yacht."

The cab pulled away from the curb, the conversation became a whisper, Kim whispered, "If he comes home, I figure he has to accidentally poison himself-take the wrong pills-something like that. I'll have to work on it."

Jolene patted her hand and whispered, "Don't work too hard on it. I have been working on something also."

Jolene smiled, tonight she learned Kim was keeping an awful lot of cash in her hotel room safe. Jolene figured she had to keep all of her options open.

The cab pulled up in front of the steps, the twosome unsteadily made their way up to the door. When the door opened, Jolene informed Kim, "I'm going to the kitchen and have the cook make me a sandwich. Do you want one?"

Kim nodded, "Sure. Something light."

Sharon Bronson had been living under an oppressive stress-filled cloud for the past year. Since Carleton suddenly left for France, she hated her job. After having two of her assistants fired, her pay cut, and her hours tossed about at the whim of either Kim or Jolene she would have loved to quit but she had to pay for her schooling. She suddenly felt like Cinderella, the oppression was lifted, she was in glass slippers and being treated like a human being again.

Sharon invited Ed into the kitchen for a brief meeting where she talked about the changes Carleton made including the restoration of back pay. She thanked Rachel for recommending her and filled the staff in on the fact Jolene was to have nothing to do with giving any of the staff orders. Jolene was a guest of Kim and as such Kim was expected to take care of any of Jolene's requests.

The threesome was sitting in the kitchen drinking coffee and having a snack when Jolene stepped into the kitchen and announced, "Looks like I'll have to recommend another cut in salary for the three of you. You seem to have extra time on your hands."

Sharon smiled, she felt she was going to enjoy this pronouncement way too much, "Actually Jolene. I was about to tell Rachel and Ed to leave for the night. We have all had too long and busy a day."

Jolene scowled and snapped, "Leave!? What are you talking about? Before you do anything, I want two Denver sandwiches and two Manhattans delivered to Kim's suite."

Sharon smiled sweetly as she explained, "Not tonight. You are through giving orders to any of the staff. In your absence, I've been hired to head the household's staff, the budget, hiring, and the accounting. There will be a position open for a part time cleaning lady; that is if you are interested."

Jolene's face was red with hate, "You can't fire me. I'm the nanny."

Sharon smiled as she reported, "That's another thing. As a Nanny, you've been released, as I said, I'm the new boss of the household and I am the nanny."

Jolene was very angry. She challenged, "Who hired you?"

Sharon's smile was fixed in place, "Mr. Winthrop of course. Oh, I suppose I should tell you. Kim's belongings and yours has been moved out of Mr. Winthrop's suite to your room at the end of the hall."

Rachel and Ed watched with undisguised glee. Jolene wasn't about to make her own sandwich, she rushed up the stairs to find Kim.

Kim walked by Angelica's room without looking in on her, she went to Carleton's suite, found the door closed and discovered the door was locked! Kim turned about, she figured she would have to go down and find Sharon and the key. She took about four steps before she heard the sound of pool balls clacking together in the suite. Just then Jolene appeared, red faced and angry. She hissed, "He's back!"

Kim stood shocked to silence, finally she spoke, "He's in there playing pool."

Jolene continued to fume, "You sold the damn table and bought a set of earrings with the money!"

Kim shook her head in disbelief, "He's a damned billionaire, he can have anything he wants, when he wants it."

Jolene was beside herself, she thought she had progressed to the point where she practically owned the house. Now she was an unwelcome guest, "I was just in the kitchen to put in an order for a Manhattan and a Denver sandwich. It seems our maid Sharon sent the cook home early. Sharon said she was hired to take care of the household budget and the hiring. She offered me a job as a cleaning lady. Part time!"

Kim was seething with hate, "Where the hell did they put our clothes?"

Jolene started to walk down the hall, "In my room, the last guest bedroom."

Still the twosome did not check up on Angelica, they stepped into the guest bedroom, the beds were covered with clothing that once was in dressers and closets neatly arranged by staff. Kim shook her head, "Let's be calm about this. That son of bitch is as smart as they come, we are going to have to be just as smart. Christ. If he tosses me out now, I'll have to settle for just ten million."

Jolene shook her head and gritted her teeth, "Right now we are going to have to put our stuff away ourselves. We don't have access to a maid."

For the next half hour, they put their clothes away, finally Jolene asked, "I suppose I should go check up on the kid."

Kim thought for a moment, "The hell with the kid. He left us a job to do right here. We'll let the kid be his responsibility tonight."

Kim tossed an armload of sweaters into a drawer and snapped at Jolene, "Go down and mix us a couple of stiff drinks."

Jolene's walk down the hallway and then the stairs made her think anew about her position. Jolene had worked her way into the confidence of Kim while sharing Kim's desire to end up with Carleton's money. With Carleton back, she realized the task would be more difficult. She considered Carleton's billions and thought perhaps she may have to settle for Kim's hotel room million.

The next morning Carleton woke up suddenly to what appeared to be a dream. Angelica wanted to visit the potty. Carleton got up and went to the crib, Angelica was standing, she reached her arms up and wrapped them around his neck, Carleton asked, "Did you sleep happy Angelica?"

Angelica nodded, then looked up smiled and again wrapped her arms around his neck. She silently communicated, "Daddy. I'm happy you are here."

After taking Angelica to the potty Carleton went to the intercom, it was a little after seven in the morning, Rachel would be busy in the kitchen, "Rachel. Would you come up to my suite for a brief time?"

In a couple of minutes Rachel was at the door, "Rachel. I know you are a mom. I'd like a quick lesson in giving my daughter a bath."

Rachel laughed and quickly poured water into the sink. She talked about the water temperature, the washing, what problems to look for in girls, drying and dressing."

Carleton smiled, his background in computers didn't prepare him for this, "Rachel. You are good at this."

Rachel smiled, "I think you will be good at it also. Tonight, you will perhaps have to give her another bath. If they are making a mess in their diapers all day, you have to make sure they are clean at night."

Carleton smiled, "Angelica doesn't like a messy diaper, so all I have to do is get her to the potty when she needs to go."

Rachel shook her head, "But sir. The child can't speak."

Carleton nodded as Angelica communicated, "I like her. I'm hungry."

Carleton picked up Angelica and replied, "Rachel. Angelica likes you."

Rachel laughed thinking it was part of a joke. Carleton added, "We will be right down for something to eat. Angelica said she is hungry."

After dressing, Carleton took Angelica downstairs to the kitchen, "Rachel. Is there a chair for Angelica?"

Rachel nodded, "Yes sir. I believe they had it upstairs."

Angelica didn't protest when she was thrust into Rachel's arms, "I'll go find her chair. You hold Angelica."

Jolene rose about seven thirty, at first she was startled by the strange surroundings then she recalled, "Damn, Kim. Remember, you have a hair appointment at nine this morning."

Kim rose and went into the shower, she would be there for fifteen minutes.

Silence reigned in the bedroom while Kim and Jolene dressed, finally Jolene announced, "I suppose I should look in on the kid."

Kim shrugged, "The maid won't be here until about ten today. Go check up on her, then we should get going. We have a lot to talk about today."

Within minutes Jolene returned, "The room is empty. The kid isn't there!"

Kim was deep in thought. Jolene asked, "Do you suppose he got rid of the kid?"

Kim smiled, "I hope so. I'll sue his ass for everything he has and then I'll be able to buy that yacht."

Kim looked at her watch, "Time for us to leave. We are going to drive ourselves today. We have a lot to talk about."

The twosome walked down the stairway, they glanced into the dining room where Angelica was seated in a high chair; Carleton was feeding her. As Kim and Jolene walked by Angelica's eyes opened wide at what Kim was thinking. Without a word Kim and Jolene walked past to the doorway leading to the garage.

When the door to the garage closed Angelica's, lip quivered as though she was about to cry, she communicated silently, "Kim wants to hurt you."

Carleton could feel the pain of Angelica, he put his arm around her, "Everything will be good. I promise. I have so many things I must do. I have to go away to the office today."

Angelica's lip began to quiver again; she was too scared to be left behind. Carleton read her thoughts, he kissed her forehead, "OK. You can go with me to the office. What the heck, I own the place."

Immediately Angelica smiled; watching all this from the doorway of the kitchen, Rachel was amazed at what she was seeing. The two seemed to communicate with only her father doing the speaking.

An hour later Carleton pulled his Cadillac into the executive parking lot of Winthrop Computer International in the space reserved for an engineer Carleton knew was stationed in France. Carleton got out of his car and retrieved the stroller from the trunk. He dragged it in front of the car, he couldn't figure out how to open the stroller.

Collette Stevenson was new to her job at WCI; she had been caught in traffic and was close to being late for her first board meeting. As she entered the executive parking lot someone pulled into her designated parking space, she didn't have time to argue, she parked in a visitor parking space. She grabbed her laptop and brief and hurried for the entrance as she dialed her secretary to explain she was occupying the visitor parking space. As she passed her parking spot the one who stole her space was attempting to open a stroller while holding a child.

Carleton asked for assistance from the first passerby, "Could you give me a hand?"

The young lady was practically at a run when she sailed on by emitting something which sounded like a growl. Carleton looked at Angelica and smiled, "I guess we'll have to ask someone else."

Then, inquisitive, Carleton asked, "What was she thinking about?"

Angelica silently communicated, "She was in a hurry. She doesn't want to be late."

Carleton continued to examine the stroller for a hint on how to open it, a few moments later another young lady passed by, "Could you help me open this stroller? I can't seem to figure it out."

The young lady smiled, quickly unsnapped a Velcro band, lifted the handle, snapped it into place then opened the seat portion, "That's all there is to it."

Carleton shook his head and smiled, "Thank you. What's your name?"

She smiled warily and asked, "Why do you want to know my name?"

Carleton shrugged, "So I can properly reward your kindness."

The young lady smiled, "That won't be necessary."

Carleton didn't press her, "I'm very grateful. Thank you."

Angelica communicated, "Her name is Cheryl."

Cheryl turned to leave, "You are welcome."

Carleton smiled as he put Angelica into the stroller he replied, "Cheryl is a pretty name."

Cheryl stopped, turned around and asked, "How did you know my name?"

Carleton grabbed everything he needed and locked the doors to his car. He smiled and replied, "You wouldn't believe me if I told you."

Carleton pushed the stroller up to the entrance, "Would you hold the door for me. I'm new at this stroller business, I wouldn't want to hurt anyone."

Cheryl shook her head, "You are going to need a pass to get in here. And, I don't believe they allow strollers."

Carleton wondered, "Why is that?"

Cheryl responded, "Safety reasons."

Carleton nodded, "Oh yes. Homeland security and all that. Well, I'll have to wrestle with the security people. Thanks again Cheryl."

Inside the door Cheryl showed her ID, then stopped for a moment while Carleton talked to one of the security guards, she figured he wouldn't make it past them.

The first security guard was a young man, not on the job long. "Sir? You can't come in here with a stroller and you'll have to have an ID card.

Carleton smiled at the young man, looked at his name tag and replied, "Pat. I don't have an ID, and, I'm taking the stroller and its contents to my office. To save yourself some embarrassment, you better call Mr. Tamblin for directions. Tell him Carleton Winthrop would like to take his daughter up to his office, now!"

The guard gulped, grabbed his phone and spoke with Bill Tamblin, head of security, within seconds Bill Tamblin burst from his office with red face, "Pat. Damn it, look at the picture in the office. Get to know people; especially your boss."

Bill Tamblin escorted Carleton to the elevator, "It's nice to have you back in town. Is there anything else I can do for you?"

Carleton nodded, "There was a young lady, Cheryl; she just went up this elevator to the seventh floor. Cheryl was dressed mostly in yellow, brunette, call me and let me know her last name. I want to give her a little bonus for being so helpful."

Carleton took the elevator to the tenth floor, this time the receptionist recognized him, "It is good to see you sir. It has been some time."

Carleton nodded, "Thank you Donna. I'll need to see the CEO this morning and the lawyer I use for household affairs. Check to see if the lawyer can make himself available early this morning."

The receptionist glanced at the calendar, "The CEO is about to start a meeting of all the department heads in the executive board room in about two minutes. I'll call your lawyer."

As the receptionist reached for the phone, it rang, Bill Tamblin was on the line, "Cheryl Timmerman. I'll let him know."

Carleton gave orders as he turned toward the executive boardroom, "Have a personal check made out for one thousand dollars. Give the check to her with the message; Carleton Winthrop is grateful for your assistance."

Donna smiled and asked, "Do you want me to notify the CEO you will be dropping in on the meeting?"

Carleton smiled, "No. Thanks Donna."

Carleton wheeled Angelica down the hall toward the executive board room; he figured he would put in a brief appearance and then return to his office. Carleton slowly pushed open the door, there were twelve department heads present, his CEO in charge of American operations sat at the far end of the table. The CEO rose with a large smile and nearly a shout, "Carleton! What a pleasant surprise!"

The department heads one by one shook hands and exchanged pleasantries until all but one was greeted. The CEO, Orville Finch, introduced Carleton to Collette Stevenson whose face became a bright red, "Carleton. This is the newest member of our team. Collette Stevenson. Collette-your boss, Carleton Winthrop."

Angela communicated to Carleton, "Daddy. She really feels bad."

Carleton picked up Angelica as Collette stammered, "I'm dreadfully sorry…"

Carleton stopped her, "Miss Stevenson. You were in a hurry to get to this your first meeting, don't give it a thought. A young lady was gracious enough to help me out; I sent her a check for a thousand dollars. She was perhaps the most expensive mechanic in town but worth every penny." Carlton addressed her and the entire board, "Now, Miss Stevenson, you've been hired because of your background in brain-computer-interfacing. Within the next few days I want to meet with you. I'll want a complete update on your success and failures. You will get help from some pretty brilliant computer minds here at WCI."

Carleton turned to the group, "Everyone, please have a seat and go back to your meeting. I just want you all to know of the importance of the promise of brain-computer-interfacing. I recognize both the hope and the potential of BCI. I want Winthrop to be in on the ground floor. I'd like to congratulate Miss Stevenson on her accomplishments in BCI and related research. We made the decision some time ago to invest in brain-computer-interfacing. It took us a little longer to find someone of Miss Stevenson's caliber."

Carlton smiled and spoke to Collette, "Miss Stevenson, I hope you enjoy your time here at WCI. I'll let you all get back to your meeting."

As Carleton looked toward Collette, her relief was evident, she smiled, "Thank you."

Angelica communicated, "She's nice."

When Carleton wheeled Angelica into his office suite the lawyer was waiting, "Come right in Bill, I'd like to get on this as fast as possible."

Carleton sat at his desk with Angelica on his lap. The lawyer was an acquaintance of his wife, he took care of his household business. The lawyer had nothing to do with the company. The CEO and several other lawyers took care of all legal matters dealing with the company.

Carleton outlined the responsibilities of Sharon Bronson, he described the verbal agreement with her and requested the lawyer draw up a contract to reflect his verbal offer. Next Carleton changed the focus to his wife, "Tell me Bill. If I decided to divorce my wife, legally, in your opinion how would I fare?"

The lawyer, Bill Pongrazzi, smiled, he seemed hesitant, out of his element. Carlton thought usually a lawyer would have something to say, even if he knew nothing. After some strangely uncomfortable stammering he said, "Your wife would become the child's guardian. At a minimum, she would receive a healthy sum beyond the ten million prenuptial agreement, to care for the child."

Carleton shook his head, "That should have been the first question. Angelica will stay with me. There is no option where Kim will even visit Angelica unsupervised."

Angelica leaned into her father and held onto his shirt a little tighter, the lawyer whistled and shook his head, "She would have to come at you with a knife to be denied visiting rights."

Carleton smiled, "Kim doesn't like the baby at all. I have household witnesses to the fact Kim regularly abandons the child unattended on a daily basis. She has nothing to do with the baby. With good witnesses, I'm sure I can build a case for neglect, and, perhaps abuse. I think she had Angelica so she could make more money."

The lawyer looked shocked, then forced a seemingly uncomfortable smile, he slowly nodded and carefully measured his response, "If Kim wanted money, and if she doesn't like the child, it may still be expensive to buy her off. Double or triple what you agreed upon, agreeing she leave town and do not return."

Carleton nodded, "And, if she wants it all?"

The lawyer shrugged, "If you die, she'll be guardian of Angelica. Indirectly Kim may control your fortune. We

316

could set up your will so Kim can't touch the company. Since you two had Angelica and your daughter is somewhat handicapped, separating Kim from Angelica would be nearly impossible and costly if Kim decided to fight for joint guardianship."

Carleton nodded, "That is about what I thought. Right now, set up a trust so Angelica will have control at age eighteen with the assumption she will be capable. Have the document ready to sign ASAP. I'll keep you apprised. I may let you negotiate with Kim. I'll let you know. First we'll protect Angelica with the trust."

Pongrazzi smiled, "I'm a bit confused. You left here because you wanted no involvement with children. Now, it seems to be all about the child?"

Carleton nodded but didn't respond. The lawyer shrugged, trying to seem indifferent, "I'll have this document by tomorrow morning."

When the lawyer left, Angelica communicated, "He knows Kim."

Carleton nodded as he put Angelica in the stroller, then he stopped, bent down and spoke quietly to Angelica, "Was he hiding anything?"

Angelica nodded, "Yes. He knows Kim."

Carleton didn't know how to get the information he wanted from Angelica, "Does he like Kim?"

Angelica nodded, "Yes."

Carleton thought for a moment, "Do they talk to each other?"

Angelica nodded, this was alarming to Carleton.

Jolene and Kim drove in silence until they were outside the gate, then Kim turned up the volume on the radio, "Jolene. I hate that son-of-a-bitch."

Jolene smiled, "I know you do. Now we'll have to act fast."

Kim angrily shook her head, "What's the hurry?"

Jolene fumed as she calmly related, "You said he's smart as hell and he has an army of lawyers in his pocket. If we don't

317

hurry, he'll find some way to cut you out of the picture entirely."

Kim shook her head, "I want all his damn money. I'm going to buy the biggest damn yacht in the world."

Jolene again suggested, "If you want it all you better get rid of him tonight."

Kim shook her head in exasperation, "How the hell am I going to get rid of him tonight and stay in the clear?"

Jolene quietly suggested, "If you can't get the job done right away, you could just take the ten million and what you have in the safe and leave."

Kim snarled her answer, "Don't mention that option again. I want it all! Now he's back, I'm sure of it. I hate that nerdy SOB."

Jolene spoke cautiously, "I know these people that could help us get rid of him. They can help with anything from a fall in the bathroom to accidental poisoning or a robbery attempt gone bad."

Kim's face was red with hate and fury, she snapped, "Damn it Jolene. We can't involve any of your friends. If they know who they are dealing with, they will blackmail us for the rest of our lives. This is up to you and I. Come up with something we can accomplish ourselves without leaving a shred of evidence which leads to us."

Jolene persisted, "If we kill him before tomorrow, you'll get it all. He won't have time to change his will that fast."

The frustration in Kim was obvious, "Then come up with something foolproof in a hurry that involves just the two of us."

Carleton wondered at his next step. Angelica seemed to sense his lawyer and Kim may be in league. If that is the case, the lawyer now knows Angelica is his priority.

Carleton pushed the stroller to the receptionist desk, "Is the exec meeting over yet?"

Donna nodded, "Just breaking up."

Carleton started the stroller out the door as he ordered, "Call Orville. Tell him I'll meet him in his office, now."

Donna quickly checked the posted schedule on the computer, "Orville has a meeting scheduled with…"

Carleton smiled, raised his hand and interrupted her, "I don't care if he has a meeting with the President. Tell him I'm coming."

Carleton pushed the stroller down the hall into Orville's office, Orville met him at the secretary's desk, "Carleton. You look a little stressed. Come on into the exec board room. We can talk there. I have the assembly team in my office."

As they walked down the aisle, Carleton softy spoke, "I have a request. I'm giving you a copy of my pre-nuptial agreement; I want you to read it over-see if there are any obvious flaws, particularly intentional flaws will jeopardize my position in case of a divorce. Then, I want you to draw up a will. Actually, a trust placing my daughter Angelica as sole heir. Tomorrow at about ten in the morning, I would like you to look over another trust document and give me an opinion. The trust you write will give my wife Kim nothing more than the ten million agreed upon in the pre-nupt."

Carleton didn't stop, "Then, there is one more thing. Say nothing to anybody about any of this. Don't even divulge the fact we created a document."

Orville gazed into the exec board room, a few department heads were still there, they turned about and headed back toward Orville's office. Orville asked the obvious question, "What the hell is going on?"

Carleton shook his head, not wanting to divulge all his fears. He ordered, "I want to protect Angelica, myself, and the company; in that order."

No mention was made about any change in the company. Orville felt reassured, "When do you want this ready?"

Carleton patted Orville on the back, "About nine in the morning. I'll be in my office."

Carleton looked about then said, "But, in the meantime, before tonight, if I'm, ah, taken out of the picture, I'd like a simple will written which keeps you in control of the company and Angelica as sole heir when she turns eighteen."

Orville stopped, "Christ Carleton. Are you thinking your life is in danger?"

Carleton nodded, "No details, but there is a lot going on. Hopefully I'll fill you in tomorrow. In short, I suspect my personal lawyer to be in league with my wife, and there may be a plot in the offing. So, Orville, this is your number one priority."

Orville nodded, "I'll have the overnight document ready in fifteen minutes. I'll be ready in the morning with the revisions, but we'll need at least two unrelated witnesses."

Carleton nodded, "I'll give the witness thing some thought; probably someone in the company who can be trusted with my privacy. I'll be in my office. And Orville, for the next couple of days, this will take priority over everything."

Back at his office something was bothering him about Angelica's ability to communicate with him. Carleton picked up Angelica and gave her a reassuring hug. Then he said, "Angelica. When I was far, far, away, I felt you calling me to come home. You can talk to me; can you talk to your Mom?"

Angelica sadly lay her head on his chest as she communicated, "I talk to my mom but she doesn't answer, she doesn't come."

Carleton thought perhaps Kim wasn't able to get the communication, "Kim can't hear you like I can?"

Angelica shook her head, "No. Not Kim. My mom."

Carleton sat down, he didn't understand, he was silent, Angelica answered his puzzled thoughts, "Kim is not my mom."

Carleton was stunned to silence, for most of the past year and a half he wondered how Kim got pregnant. She told him she didn't want children, she told him she couldn't have children, he saw a doctor's evaluation indicating Kim could not have children, yet he saw she was pregnant. Now, this revelation coming from a child who was not two years old. Carleton recognized Angelica to be a very precocious child but… it was difficult to consider Angelica's bond with Kim was conceivably only physical in nature…. He thought, how could a child divine the connection between herself and a biological mother? As he considered the situation, he was drawn to Angelica and there was an obvious connection, and he knew he was her father.

As he thought, he came up with more questions, he pressed on, "Do you know what Kim is thinking right now?"

Angelica shook her head, "Too far."

Carleton was almost afraid to go home, he feared Kim may indeed want to harm him. His fear was for Angelica, what in the world would happen to Angelica if he was out of the picture?

Carleton thought, perhaps Angelica may be able to warn him ahead of time of any plot or danger. Evidently Kim or the danger had to be fairly close for Angelica to be able to get a reading on the thoughts.

Carleton discovered Angelica became tense when he struggled with thoughts about potential danger, he smiled, gave her a hug and said, "Let's go down to a play area. There will be other children there to play with."

Angelica held on to his shirt, "Will you be with me?"

Carleton put her in the stroller, "Yes. I'll be very close."

Carleton figured by distracting Angelica, he would get some time to think without worrying her. He told his secretary where he was going and took the elevator to the second floor. As he wheeled the stroller into the play portion of the nursery he was stopped abruptly at the door, "Where is your badge?"

Carleton smiled and looked at the woman's name tag, "Actually Penny. I perhaps don't need a badge; I pay the bills. I'm Carleton Winthrop."

Penny's bad day was about to get worse, Angelica raised her hands to be lifted from the stroller. Carleton quickly picked her up as Penny snarled, "Yes. And I'm the frigging Wizard of Oz. Follow the rules! How the hell did you get a stroller into the building in the first place?"

Carleton looked at Penny and smiled again, "Penny. You are obviously having a bad day. Perhaps we should start over?"

Penny shook her head, she was disgusted, "Sure. You go get a pass to be in here and let me continue having a bad day."

Angelica clung tight as she communicated, "She's mean."

Carleton smiled once more, "Penny. I don't know who is in charge…"

Penny interrupted, "Hell yes you do. You own the place, remember?"

Carleton smiled, "I was about to say. Get whoever is in charge of the nursery before you lose your job."

Penny took out her phone and punched in security, "Hell, you'd be the second one today that wanted to fire me, and I'm still here."

Almost before Penny got done talking Pat ran up to their side, he looked at Carleton and said, "Yes sir. How can I help?"

Carleton smiled and replied, "Pat. I want you to escort this young lady to personnel. She has no business working with children. Tell them to fire her. Give her a two-month severance. Afterward, find out who vouched for her when she was hired. Try to find out who else she insulted today, I'll have to apologize to them. Tell personnel to get someone up here to take her place immediately."

As Pat led Penny away, Carleton wheeled the stroller into the room filled with toys and playing children. When Angelica was put down, she headed for the nearest toy. Carleton would be able to sit and think without worrying Angelica until Orville finished the temporary will.

While he was waiting, he considered his home, the layout and possible ways of being set upon. As he considered he made a call and had an electric golf car and night vision goggles delivered to his garage. He thought again for some time about the security system in the house and made another call to an acquaintance at the police department. He then made one more call to an electronics engineer that worked in the building.

The temporary will was signed, after an hour in the play room and an apology from the head of the nursery he went to Angelica's side, "Are you ready to go home?"

Angelica wrinkled her nose, hesitated then reached for Carleton to pick her up. Carleton thought she recognized his desire to leave, "We'll see Sharon when we get back, she'll read to you."

When they got home, Carleton picked Angelica up and asked, "Do you know what Kim is saying?"

Angelica shook her head, "Too far."

Carleton asked again, "Are Kim and Jolene good friends?"

Angelica nodded, "Good friends. They both want to hurt you."

Carleton smiled, trying to make light of the news so Angelica wouldn't get upset, "I wonder why they would want to hurt me?"

Angelica's answer seemed simple, "Kim wants everything you have. She wants to buy a big boat."

Carleton smiled and asked, "She wants a boat?"

Angelica shook her head and communicated, "The biggest damn yacht there is."

"Is that what Kim said?"

"All the time."

As they stepped into the house Sharon greeted them, "Sharon. Can you bring a couple of children's books and something to for us to eat up to my suite?"

Sharon nodded, "The books and the bookcase are in your room. I'll talk to Rachel and have her bring you something to eat."

Sharon started to walk away, "Sharon. How did your final test go?"

Sharon smiled, she didn't think he would recall, "The test went well. I felt good. I'll be able to get the results tomorrow on the internet."

Carleton nodded, "You'll do well. We'll see you upstairs."

When Sharon arrived, Carleton was setting up a recording device, "Sharon. Would you feed Angelica then read to her for a while? I'm going make some phone calls and play pool for an hour and I'll be making a recording of the noise I make. When I finish making the recording, you and the rest of the staff will leave the compound for the remainder of the day. You can all start tomorrow late in the morning. Don't arrive before ten. If anything changes, I'll call you. Tell the staff I'll pay for any accommodations they make for the evening. If Kim comes home, or if Angelica becomes agitated, bring Angelica into the pool room with me right away."

Carleton smiled, "Sharon. I know you think this is all strange, but do you mind if I wait until tomorrow to explain."

Sharon shrugged, "Whatever you say Mr. Winthrop."

Carleton was relieved; he didn't want to explain to Sharon he was getting key information from his mute daughter, "Thank you. I've given the information to the lawyer about you managing the household. He'll have the contract for you to consider tomorrow morning."

Carleton touched Angelica's head and went back to the pool room; he started the recorder, broke the rack and then shot balls making more noise than knocking balls in the pockets. Feverishly for the next half hour he made as much noise as possible while recording the session. At the end of his recording session Carleton hooked up the recorder to a telephone, he dialed the phone to try it out, the sound of pool balls breaking soon echoed over the television speakers in the room.

He reset the battery-operated recorder, made several phone calls then went in to see Sharon. Angelica was taking a nap, "Sharon. You can go now. Tell all the staff I want them off the grounds."

Carleton roughly counted out a wad of hundred-dollar bills, "Here's a thousand dollars to take care of everyone's stay for the evening."

Sharon shook her head, "Mr. Winthrop. This is a little frightening."

Carleton smiled and sat down in a recliner next to Angelica's crib, "Sharon. I hope by tomorrow I can tell you all about it."

Sharon started to walk away when the phone rang, she looked at the caller identification, "It's Kim."

Carleton waved his hand as if to tell her to answer, Sharon picked up the phone, "Hello. Yes. He is here with Angelica. Did you want to talk to him? Oh? I'll let Mr. Winthrop know."

Sharon relayed the information, "That was Jolene, she asked if you were here. I told her you were here with Angelica, Jolene quickly added, Kim would be staying with a friend for the night."

Carleton smiled slightly and nodded, it was just as he thought, he answered, "I suspected. You may go now Sharon."

Sharon was reticent, "I'll leave something on the kitchen counter for Angelica to eat tonight."

Carleton nodded, "Again. Thank you."

When Sharon walked out the door, Carleton breathed a sigh of relief, now nobody would be in harm's way except him and Angelica. Carleton opened a panel in the wall, eight small security televisions showed various parts of the outside of the house. Fifteen minutes later the last of the employees left and the front gate closed.

Carleton watched the television sets until Angelica awoke, he walked to the crib and smiled. Angelica frowned, he asked, "What is it?"

Angelica's lip quivered a little, "They want to hurt me."

Carleton picked her up, "Does Kim want to hurt both of us?"

Angelica nodded, Carleton asked, "Is she close enough for you to know what she is saying?"

Angelica shook her head. Carleton reassured her, "We will be all right because we are smarter than she is."

325

Carleton put Angelica into the stroller with a couple of favored toys. He figured she was too sensitive; most of her attention would be focused on him instead of the toys. Carleton asked, "When someone comes to the house, do you know who is coming?"

Angelica's answer didn't give him reason for confidence but he trusted her ability. She communicated, "Sometimes."

Carleton smiled, he didn't want Angelica upset; he wanted her relaxed, "I think tonight someone will come."

Angelica nodded agreement. Carleton figured she maybe was focused on him more than at any other time, he decided to run a little experiment. He carried her into the security center and pointed at the eight television pictures of the grounds. He explained, "This is a picture of the front gate. This is a picture of the back gate. This is a picture of the west hill. This is a picture of the east woods."

Slowly he pointed out the other areas covered by cameras, afterward he asked, "Which one is the front gate?"

Angelica pointed out the front gate, then the back, the west hill and east woods, after they went through the names a couple of times Carleton took Angelica to the kitchen. After feeding her he asked, "What would you like to do?"

Angelica didn't hesitate, "Read."

After several books had been read, darkness enveloped the mansion, suddenly Angelica looked up at her father and communicated, "Bad men's are coming."

Carleton rose and picked up a bag he had filled, "Where are they coming from? Front, back, east or west?"

Angelica didn't respond, she looked like she was trying to concentrate, Carleton didn't push. Angelica moved a little closer into Carleton's arms, then the lights went out. Carleton patted Angelica on the back to reassure her, "We'll go out the safest way. First, we have to know, where they are coming from."

Angelica was calm as she responded, "From the hill."

Carleton figured there was more than one. Someone had to be cutting off the electricity at the front gate while the others came in from over the east fence. Carleton wondered at Angelica's answer but he was already into the garage on the back side of the house. Carleton quickly put Angelica into a car seat then put the car seat on the floor of the electric golf car he had purchased earlier in the day. He donned the night vision goggles. The garage door was already open in anticipation, within seconds they were silently moving down the lane toward the back gate guided by the night vision goggles. Carleton asked Angelica, "Are they in the house yet?"

Angelica didn't answer right away. After a minute went by, she communicated, "Bad men in the house."

Carleton pushed the button on the phone that called the phone in his suite and would automatically start the battery-operated recording of the pool balls striking one another in the bedroom suite. The noise would be heard all the way down the stairway. Carleton looked back to the house, the shimmering of a flashlight could be seen through the rear windows.

Angelica communicated, "They are going up the steps."

Carleton pulled the cart off the path and waited as he punched send, on a text message on his cell phone. He waited for five minutes, a return message read, "House surrounded. Lights should be back on within a few minutes."

Carleton glanced toward the house and waited, soon Angelica communicated, "Daddy. Can you hold me?"

The intensity of his concentration must have bothered Angelica; Carleton scooped her up and quietly said, "Everything will be all right. The bad men will be removed from the house."

Lights came on in the house and grounds, Carleton received a text message, "Safe to return. Two men in custody."

Carleton started the electric cart and headed back to the house, he drove to the front where six squad cars were parked. Carleton carried Angelica as he approached the captain, "Captain Meriwether."

327

The captain nodded and reported, "Carleton. Seems you had the right idea. We surrounded the house and placed two men in custody. So far, they aren't talking. But, my experience tells me they'll be talking soon. Both men were carrying a garrote. I told them we had them on breaking and entering and attempted murder. We'll give them some time to think about it, they aren't going to want to take the rap for whoever hired them, "Are you going to be all right here tonight?"

Carleton nodded, "Sure."

Carleton looked to Angelica, "Are you happy Angelica?"

Angelica clung tightly as she communicated, "Bad man in our room."

Carleton smiled, "They took the bad men out of the house."

Angelica shook her head and communicated again, "Bad man in the room waiting for you, and me."

The captain smiled at the curious communication seemed to reach only an attempt on the part of Carleton, then Carleton spoke, "Captain. Do you have a K9 unit?"

Meriwether shook his head, "Not here. Do you want me to call one in?"

Carleton nodded, "I have reason to feel there may still be one man hiding in the master bedroom suite."

Meriwether looked at Carleton and smiled, "In the master bedroom suite? Do you mind telling me how you came to that conclusion?"

Carleton shook his head, "Would you check please? And Captain, they came to kill both of us."

The captain looked quizzically at Carleton then made a call; ten minutes later a K9 unit drove into the yard, the captain gave his orders, "I'm sending one man in with you. Walk through the house, we suspect there is someone hiding in there we didn't find. We suspect him to be upstairs, but you walk through the entire house."

Five minutes later they came out of the house with a third intruder, handcuffed, the captain inquired, "Did you search him?"

One of the officers handed the captain a garrote, "This is all he had on him."

The captain took the wire and held it in front of the man, "Attempted murder. You three will spend your lives in prison. Now tell me. How much were you going to get paid if you killed the two of them?"

The would-be assassin looked sharply at the captain; the captain smiled and continued, "You are surprised we knew you were going to kill the baby also?"

The assassin remained quiet, the captain went on, "The quicker you tell us who hired you, the more points you get for cooperating. We've got this sewed up without your help. Do yourself a favor and come clean."

The captain's cell phone buzzed, he smiled and looked at the would-be assassin, "Last chance."

The assassin's chin lifted, "It was Jolene."

The captain looked at Carleton while he put his call on hold, "Just Jolene? Where was she going to get the money to pay you?"

The assassin shrugged, he knew it was all over, "We were to be paid one hundred thousand each, with a promise of a share in what Jolene could get out of Kim when they were both dead."

The captain shook his head, "You would have killed a baby for one hundred thousand dollars?"

The assassin shrugged as the captain's phone rang, "I've got to take this call."

For nearly five minutes the captain spoke on the phone, he looked at Carleton and slowly shook his head, "I have Mr. Winthrop right here with me. I'll talk to him. Put a guard on the place and don't let anyone other than forensics in. Nothing to the news."

Angelica held on tight to Carleton, she communicated. "Kim."

While the captain continued to talk on the phone Carleton asked, "What about Kim?"

Angelica continued to hold on tight, Carleton patted her gently on the back, the captain closed his phone and shook his head as he stepped close to Carleton, "That was about your wife. She was found dead in her hotel room."

Carleton asked, "How?"

The captain shook his head, "Knife in the back. The door was locked, the safe was open. The officer said the blood was pretty much dry; she was dead for at least an hour, maybe two."

The captain gave orders to a sergeant to have an all points put out for Jolene, particularly the roads leading to the border. The Captain turned back to Carleton, "If Jolene was going to pay those boys one hundred grand, she must have gotten it out of the safe. Did your wife keep that much money in her safe?"

Carleton nodded, "According to my accountant, Kim has been diverting monies from the household account. She may have had close to a million in that safe."

The captain shook his head, "I'm willing to bet Jolene wasn't going to pay these boys at all. It's a shame; Angelica is without a mother."

Carleton thought about the statement for a moment then asked, "Captain. I'll need something for a DNA test on Kim."

The captain was obviously puzzled, "You haven't been away that long."

Carleton smiled, "I need to test the link between Angelica and Kim. I've already tested Angelica's DNA, I know she is my daughter. This may surprise you, but I don't know if Kim is the mother."

The captain shook his head, "Carleton. She was pregnant. I saw her."

Carleton nodded, "When I married Kim, I saw a doctor's report stating she could not have children. I've just got a feeling Angelica was part of a plan. I must know. Angelica should know."

330

The captain nodded, "Whatever you say Carleton. This should be interesting. I've never known you to be wrong, although this time I figure would be a good time to bet against you."

Carleton smiled, "Just bet what you can afford."

The captain smiled, then having a thought about the whereabouts of Jolene, he stopped at the car with the three would-be murderers. Meriwether opened the rear door and spoke, "One more question boys. Where were you supposed to meet Jolene to get the rest of your share? Gomez. Cooperate."

The one closest to Meriwether shook his head, "There is an all-night truck stop twenty miles south of Monterey; we were to meet there at midnight. Then we would take our cut, head to the border or go our own way."

The captain didn't seem surprised, "Jolene is quite the black widow spider."

Gomez nodded, "You got that right."

Meriwether thought he had a talker, he continued, "Why did she kill Kim?"

Gomez shook his head, "She said if she couldn't get Kim to go along with her plan, she'd kill her and take what she had in the safe. Kim had some screwy idea about poisoning the baby and the old man. Jolene knew it wouldn't work. Those two fought about how they were going to kill them."

Meriwether made another call about where and how-to pick-up Jolene, then he turned to Carleton, "You going to be able to stay here tonight? You and Angelica can come to my place."

Carleton shook his head, "Thanks. I appreciate your help. It's early. I put in a call to my maid, she, the gardener and the cook will all be able to come back yet tonight to stay. We'll be alright."

Meriwether patted Carleton on the back, "We are pulling out, but we'll patrol the area all night long. Meanwhile I'll get the DNA tests for you. If there is anything else, call me."

The next day Angelica wouldn't let Carleton go to the office without her, he tucked her into the child's seat after he made provisions for Sharon to meet them in two hours to feed and spend some time with Angelica. The ride to the office would take about twenty minutes, for the first ten minutes Angelica remained silent, then, she communicated, "Mommy!"

Carleton pulled over into the emergency stop lane, turned around and looked at Angelica. Angelica was trying to look out the rear window, Carleton asked, "Kim is gone."

Angelica pointed behind them, "Mommy."

Carleton looked at his watch, it was a little before nine, he pulled out into the traffic.

At the office, he met with his CEO, "Carleton, sorry to hear about your wife."

Carleton nodded, "Looks like my fears were well founded. I figured Kim was going to kill me. Kim had a friend, Jolene; Jolene worried things weren't going to go right, so she decided to kill Kim and steal her money."

Orville Finch shook his head, "What are friends for?"

Carleton shook his head, "They caught Kim's friend Jolene trying to cross the border with a little over a million in her car. She decided she wasn't going to share with the threesome she sent to the house to take care of Angelica and me."

Orville shook his head, "Why didn't Jolene stop the threesome from coming after you?"

Carlton shrugged, "Captain Meriwether told me one of those that broke into my place figured Jolene just wanted more time to get away with the money."

Finch held up his hands, "She sounds like a sweetheart."

Carleton nodded, "Now we don't have to panic writing up a will."

Orville Finch smiled, "I spent half the night on this, but, since Kim is out of the picture, I'll have to edit it a bit anyway. This time I'll have a few experts look it over. What else do you have going on?"

Carleton spoke of the DNA test and the belief Kim may not be the mother of Angelica, the CEO smiled and asked, "How in the world did you come up with that idea?"

Carleton leaned back in his chair, he decided to relate Angelica's ability to communicate with him, Finch's response was natural, "She told you Kim wasn't her mother? ESP? You are kidding?"

Carleton shook his head, "No. You know better."

Carleton spoke for some time from the beginning in France, being summoned to return home. Then Carleton explained Angelica's communication on their way to work thinking her mother went by the opposite direction.

Finch shook his head, "That's the most amazing story I've ever heard. What are you going to do?"

Carleton shrugged, "I've got Captain Meriwether looking into places where Kim may have stolen an egg and where she could have had it fertilized and implanted. He's got the lawyer in for questioning also. Tomorrow morning, just before nine, Angelica and I are going to be in the opposite lane waiting to see if her mom goes by again. If she does, we are going to attempt to follow her."

Finch shook his head in disbelief, "I'd love to watch that."

Carleton picked up Angelica, "I'll tell you all about it."

Orville Finch inquired, "What else do you have going here today?"

Carleton shrugged, "Just getting an idea of where the company is at, waiting for a call from Meriwether."

Finch held up his hand, "Wait a minute. This business with Angelica is intriguing, does Angelica know how to count?"

Carleton shrugged, "I don't know. She knows her colors very well. She learned colors from watching television."

Finch smiled, "I'd like to give Angelica a little test. Turn your back and let Angelica look over your shoulder at me. I'm going to hold up a red pen, a blue pen, or a green pen. Have Angelica tell you which one I pick up."

"She heard you. Just show her the pen."

Finch picked up the green pen, Angelica figured out the game, she communicated, 'Green one."

Carleton made his way to the door, "She said, green one. How'd she do?"

Finch shook his head, "That is the most amazing thing I've ever seen."

Carleton smiled, "No. That's not amazing. Put the colored pens in the drawer where Angelica can't see them. When you get them in the drawer, look at and touch one of the pens."

Carleton waited, Angelica smiled and communicated, "Red."

Carleton related, "You touched the red pen."

Finch shook his head, "Carleton. She read my mind. That's the first time I've ever witnessed ESP and mind reading."

Carleton turned about, with the door open he asked, "Remember, keep it under your hat."

Finch nodded, "I will. But you come in or call me tomorrow and let me know how it goes with the finding Mommy thing."

Just as Carleton was getting ready for bed that evening, the phone rang, "Meriwether. What did you learn?"

Meriwether could be heard chuckling on the phone, "I can't believe what news I'm going to give you."

Carleton shook his head in disbelief himself, "Kim was not the biological mother?"

Meriwether's answer was brief, "I'll send you the lab report, but in short, Kim had zero percent chance of being Angelica's mother. And, just to relieve your mind, Jolene wasn't the mother either. By the way, Jolene made the mistake of pulling a gun when she was confronted. She was one mean lady. Jolene is dead. We are trying to keep all of this out of the papers."

Carleton considered but a moment before answering, "I'll have someone contact you about the release of all the information. I figure the quicker the entire story gets into the papers the sooner I'll be left alone."

Meriwether was grateful, "Thanks Carleton. The quicker I get this out to the papers, the better off my job will be also. If your people want to put a given spin on the story, they can talk to me. I think I've plenty of fodder, the evidence says you'll come out well."

Carleton slowly shook his head, "Thanks Meriwether."

Carleton figured he could not benefit from giving the circumstance any spin. Carleton then smiled and shook his head, he didn't consider his computer company, he was thinking only about Angelica.

Carleton made the call to his personnel staff, after a brief talk they decided to give everything to the newspapers. The company would issue a statement giving full trust in Merriweather and the police investigation team; the company would not attempt to answer any questions.

The next morning after feeding Angelica, Carleton strapped her in the car seat, "We are going out the back way, and we are going to try to find your Mommy this morning."

Angelica was happy, she smiled and nodded her head as if she already understood what was going to happen. Sometime before nine Carleton parked his car in the lane going the opposite direction they took the previous day. A little before nine a city bus sped by, Angelica pointed and communicated, "Mommy."

Carleton shook his head in disbelief, he pulled out into the traffic, sped up then passed the bus, again Angelica communicated, "Mommy!"

Carleton slowed down and allowed the bus to pass, again Angelica pointed, "Mommy!"

Carleton followed the bus stopping wherever the bus stopped, after a half dozen stops Carleton asked, "Where is Mommy?"

Angelica pointed to the bus, "Mommy."

Three stops later a dozen women got off the bus and entered a gate to a large complex, Angelica pointed toward the gate, "Mommy."

The bus blocked Carleton's vision of the women, they entered the factory before he could see them. An hour later Carleton was sitting in the owner's office, after introducing himself, Carleton smiled, "I know this is a little strange bringing my daughter with me, but we are close. Angelica doesn't like to be too far away from her father."

Arthur Talbot was a busy man; he didn't quite know what to think. His secretary told him the richest man in the world was in his office, conceivably interested in purchasing the company, "Mr. Winthrop. I'm sorry for your very recent loss."

Carleton waved his hand as if to dismiss any discussion about his wife, "I'm afraid the entire marriage was a mistake. Later today questions will be answered by a company, spokesperson."

Talbot nodded and got down to business, "My secretary said you may be interested in purchasing our company. Are you familiar with our line of biological experimentation?"

Carleton nodded, "Viral engineering. Someday I figure your work will answer our addiction to antibacterial medication and hopefully repair the damage we've already done to our natural immunology. What I would like to do is talk to a few of your people about the company before I have my people do an in-depth search of where you are at financially."

Talbot smiled, "The Company is worth pretty close to three hundred million. Give us a look. Let me know what you think. I should preface the price and answer with; if you were anyone else, I'd ask you not to take up my time. But I figure you wouldn't be wasting your time here if you weren't serious and I figure you can afford to back any offer you'd give."

Talbot touched the intercom button, "Sylvia. Get a day pass for Mr. Winthrop. Carleton. You are in luck, many of the staff will be on break in about fifteen minutes. Sylvia will tell you how to get to the break room. Let me know if or when you would like to talk to me again."

336

Carleton made his way to the break room, he took a position near a wall and waited for the personnel to show up. At about ten-thirty a steady stream of women and a few young men arrived in the break room. They purchased coffee or opened snacks, Carleton had Angelica stand on his lap. He asked, "Angelica? Is your Mom here yet?"

Angelica didn't answer, five minutes into the break Angelica jumped up and down and communicated, "Mommy is here."

Carleton stood Angelica on the table, "Angelica. I want you to tell your mother to come to you."

Angelica reached her hand toward a table across the room and silently communicated, "Mommy. Come."

Several times Angelica repeated and she reached in the direction she perceived her mother to be. Carleton watched the reaction of the women in that direction Angelica pointed. One woman actually stood, then turned in their direction. Angelica repeated her call, the same woman looked puzzled and uncomfortable. Carleton picked up Angelica and made his way across the room.

Carleton moved to the table and sat down across from a woman in her late twenties, she had on a smock, prescription lab glasses. Her dark hair, much like Angelica's was covered with a lab hat. Carleton smiled and said, "Hello. My name is Carleton Winthrop, this is Angelica."

She was puzzled but she introduced herself, "My name is Angel Hartwig. What can I do for you Mr. Winthrop?"

Carleton was uneasy, how would he start and keep her from running away? Again, he smiled to show no threat, "Angel. I have a rather unsettling question. Whatever you do, please don't run away from us."

Angel looked puzzled, "Why would I run away?"

Carleton smiled, "This is going to sound bazaar, Angel. When we were sitting across the room, you looked about, you even stood. Did you think you heard something?"

Angel begun to feel uncomfortable, but she smiled, "How did you know?"

337

Carleton smiled and shook his head, "Angel. That was Angelica calling you. I don't know why, but there are over forty gals in this room, you are the only one which heard Angelica. This is the bazaar part. This is going to shock you, but Angelica so far has been mute, she has not spoken a word. She communicates telepathically, and Angelica seems to think you are her mother."

Angel smiled and shook her head in disbelief, "What?"

Angelica was sitting in Carleton's lap facing Angel, Carleton smiled, "Angel. You are taking this very well. Angelica, would you tell Angel your favorite color?"

Angelica quickly communicated, "Blue."

Angel didn't think before she spoke, "Blue is my favorite color also, but..., Angelica didn't say anything."

Carleton nodded, "Angel. You are taking this very well. Thank you. I have a long story to tell you. Did you hear about my wife?"

Angel nodded, "We've all talked about it. You two must be very sad."

Carleton explained the circumstances under which his wife was killed, then explained the reason why they attempted to kill him and Angelica, "Now, I am going to explain the conditions under which my wife set herself up to take over Winthrop International. When we got married, she indicated she could not have a child. We were married seven months when she indicated she was five months pregnant. Now Angel. This is the part which includes you. My wife, I think with the help of our lawyer, somehow got a doctor to steal an egg, fertilize it with my sperm and implant the egg in my wife. I checked the DNA, I am the father. Angel. My wife Kim evidently extended your name to Angelica. Angelica thinks you are her mother. Angel. Did you have eggs stored at an institute named, 'Medical Future'?"

Angel's eyes widened, the answer was obvious; Angelica communicated, "Mommy is mad."

Angelica's lower lip quivered, Carleton gave her a hug and replied, "Angel. Did you get the communication?"

Angel sadly nodded, "Yes. I did."

Empathy shown on the face of Angel as she stared at Angelica; Carleton smiled and asked, "Angel. Would you like to hold your daughter?"

Angel reached for Angelica, "This is all unbelievable."

Angelica wrapped her arms about the neck of her mother as she communicated, "Mommy. I tried to call you lots and lots of times."

Carleton explained, "Evidently when you were close by, Angelica felt your presence. Please, Angel; did you ever sense she was calling out to you?"

Now tears flowed freely down the face of Angel, "Yes. A couple of times I heard her call out to me. I thought I was going crazy."

For quite some time Angelica clung to her mother, finally Angel turned Angelica to a sitting position in her lap, "I'd better get back to work, before I get fired."

Carleton shook his head, "You are going to somehow have to help me raise our daughter. Don't worry about losing your job. I'll buy the company. What you have sitting in your lap is more important than anything in the world right now. Somehow, we have a beautiful connection that shouldn't be broken."

Carleton did some text messaging then sat back and watched, he smiled as Angelica communicated with her mother; two minutes later Carleton received a text message. Carleton dialed his cell phone, "Mr. Talbot. Carleton here. My offer will be three hundred twenty million; the offer will be good for one week. As a part of the agreement, you will stay on as CEO for two years, no biological patents can be sold between now and ownership transfer. You indicated your company to be worth nearly three-hundred million, the excess in the offer is for your continued leadership."

After closing a verbal deal with the company, Carleton put his phone away; looked at Angel and smiled, "Your job is safe. Now you are going to have to get used to being a mother. Where do we go from here? I'd like you to be with

Angelica as much as possible. Our home has several suites; you can take your pick."

Angelica looked up at her mother and smiled, "Mommy? Will you read to me?"

Carleton smiled as Angel responded, "I'd love to read to you. Let's go home."

Published E-book listings as of January 2020

"Five Star Ranch" short stories of the frontier
"Hangman" short stories of the frontier
"Lonesome Valley" short stories of the frontier
"Walking Mountain, Shadow Spirit"
"Eyes Like Sky"
"Long Road Home"
"Spirit Mountain"
"Rock"
"The Fated Winchester"
"Two Worlds Ridge" Amish love story
"The Orphan Train Twins and Their White Horse Dream" short stories of orphan train children.
"The Orphan Train Ruffian" four novellas of orphan train children